To Val

BEYOND BETA'S REJECTION

BOOK 1 OF THE DIVINE ORDER SERIES

AISLING ELIZABETH

Thank you for your support!

Aisling Elizabeth x

Copyright ©2021 by Aisling Elizabeth

All rights reserved.

No portion of this book may be reproduced in any form without written permission from the publisher or author, except as permitted by U.S. copyright law.

The story, all names, characters, and incidents portrayed in this production are fictitious. No identification with actual persons (living or deceased), places, buildings, and products is intended or should be inferred.

ISBN – 9798801134109

Cover Design by Get Covers (www.getcovers.com)

For Lacey and Finley, my two beautiful werewolf obsessed children. This book and everything is for you and because of you.

But please stop howling, the neighbours already think we are weird.

CONTENTS

Acknowledgments	X
Content Warning	XII
Chapter 1	1
Chapter 2	6
Chapter 3	11
Chapter 4	17
Chapter 5	24
Chapter 6	31
Chapter 7	36
Chapter 8	42
Chapter 9	48
Chapter 10	54
Chapter 11	60
Chapter 12	66
Chapter 13	71
Chapter 14	77

Chapter 15	83
Chapter 16	88
Chapter 17	93
Chapter 18	98
Chapter 19	103
Chapter 20	108
Chapter 21	113
Chapter 22	118
Chapter 23	124
Chapter 24	130
Chapter 25	137
Chapter 26	142
Chapter 27	147
Chapter 28	152
Chapter 29	160
Chapter 30	166
Chapter 31	172
Chapter 32	176
Chapter 33	180
Chapter 34	187
Chapter 35	192
Chapter 36	197

Chapter 37	203
Chapter 38	208
Chapter 39	214
Chapter 40	220
Chapter 41	226
Chapter 42	231
Chapter 43	237
Chapter 44	242
Chapter 45	247
Chapter 46	252
Chapter 47	257
Chapter 48	261
Chapter 49	265
Chapter 50	270
Chapter 51	278
Chapter 52	283
Chapter 53	289
Chapter 54	295
Chapter 55	300
Chapter 56	306
Chapter 57	311
Chapter 58	318

Chapter 59	323
Chapter 60	328
Chapter 61	333
Chapter 62	338
Chapter 63	343
Chapter 64	349
Chapter 65	355
Chapter 66	362
Chapter 67	368
Chapter 68	375
Chapter 69	381
Chapter 70	387
Chapter 71	392
Chapter 72	397
Chapter 73	404
Chapter 74	411
Chapter 75	417
Chapter 76	422
Chapter 77	427
Chapter 78	434
Chapter 79	440
Chapter 80	447

Chapter 81	453
Chapter 82	459
Chapter 83	466
About Aisling Elizabeth	473
Also By Aisling Elizabeth	475

Acknowledgments

I want to thank my best friend Bre. Even though we are miles apart, I couldn't have done this without your support while I ranted and told you every aspect of the story, and enjoyed your reactions to when I decided to kill you know who, and for constantly telling me that I am a good writer. Also, my other bestie Fay, for listening to my read through of chapters, making sure I ate and that I had the important real-life information, while I lived in my fantasy world.

To my fellow weavers Sydney and Tiffany, Emma and Steph in Concussion Recovery (all those slamming into walls really will do our characters damage someday) and all the support from my Puzzle Pieces in my group. Thank you for your amazing support and encouragement. Lastly, and more importantly, to my readers. Because without you and your continued support this would just be a pile of unfinished papers.

CONTENT WARNING

This book contains the potentially triggering elements listed below. If any of these elements are triggers for you please be cautious when reading. I try to be sensitive with the content and nothing is included for gratuitous reasons.

- Sexual, physical and emotional violence.

- Kidnapping.

- Death of character.

- Manipulation

An extra less conventional content warning. This book is based on a character that goes through a "weak to strong" transition. Character development is super important here and the main character could be perceived as "extremely weak" in the first part of the book. I assure you that if you continue to read though this you will see her come out of this "weak" phase and into a much stronger person. Yes, this part had to be involved so that you saw the weight of her development.

The book is set in the UK and is written and edited in UK English.

CHAPTER 1

Harper

"There, you are done," Katie, my best friend, declared and turned me around to look in my full-length mirror. I gasped at the sight of myself. I looked amazing, like really amazing. My normally boring straight brown hair cascaded in curls, framing my face and gracing my bare shoulders. My makeup, which was all silver and white, accentuated my features, from my prominent cheekbones with iridescent sparkles on them to my blue-grey eyes that looked bigger with the silver shadow. And all this was complete with my white lace dress that was fitted to my top and flared out at the waist and fell to just above my knee.

"Oh, Katie, I love it!" I squealed and hugged her.

"Anything for the birthday girl." She winked as she admired herself in the mirror. "You never know. The entire pack is going to be there tonight. Your mate could be one of them." I squealed again at her words.

The thought that my fated mate could live here in town right under my nose was enough to send goosebumps fluttering down my skin. And tonight was the night of the midsummer ball. It was a big deal and the Alpha and Luna of the Midnight Moon pack went all out. And it just so happened to fall on my eighteenth birthday.

When a werewolf turned eighteen, they could detect the mate that the moon goddess Diana decided was their perfect mate. It was called a fated bond, and there was nothing that compared to it in power.

"Oh, I hope my mate likes me." I was suddenly worried. I mean, I was no one special. My family didn't hold any sort of special rank in the pack, and I wasn't beautiful like Katie, with her mass of blond waves, piercing blue eyes, and ample chest size. Or even smart like my other best friend Louise, who was currently laid on my bed, refusing to get ready for the ball.

"Why would he not love you?" Katie exclaimed. "You are stunning and loyal. He would be lucky to have you."

Louise scoffed over on the bed but remained silent.

Katie stalked over to her. "And you, missy, need to get your sweet behind ready. We leave in an hour." Louise gave her a sideways glance.

"Told you I'm not going," she stated. "I don't see why I have to dress myself up for the lecherous dogs of this town to paw over, hoping they will get into my panties." Katie rolled her eyes, and I giggled. Louise was a firm believer in equality and hated pack life and pretty much anything werewolf. She thought the pack ranks favoured patriarchy, and the concept of the fated mates was supernatural mind control. She often declared that she planned on rejecting her mate if, and when she met him. She made her opinions very clear, loudly and often. I suspected she might have been kicked out of the pack if her father wasn't the pack Gamma.

"Louise, it's my birthday," I put on my best whiny voice. "Please come and spend it with me." Louise glanced at me and scowled.

"Fine," she gave in with a sigh. "But do not expect me to enjoy myself."

"Oh, we wouldn't dream of it," Katies said sarcastically. "Now up and ready, lady."

Forty-five minutes later, we were all downstairs in my small living room, with my mum taking pictures of us and my dad telling me how beautiful I looked. The pack colours were black, white, and silver, so all the balls and events had that colour code, and we were expected to comply. My father had a simple black suit with a black tie that held the pack seal in silver. He also had a silver seal on the collar of his jacket, which signalled him as a pack employee. My dad was the bookkeeper for the pack, and whilst there were no rank privileges, it gave the family enough money so that my mum and I were comfortable. My mum wore an elegant black evening gown that hugged her figure and ended just above her silver stiletto heels. Katie wore a silver-grey dress that left nothing to the imagination, and Louise had on a black fitted knee-length dress that showed her long legs.

We were all ready apart from one other person. I looked around
"Where's Tommy?" I asked. My mum rolled her eyes, and my dad scowled.
"Probably getting in trouble," he scoffed.
"Oh dear brother, you injure me with your words." My uncle Tommy walked in wearing a black tux and white shirt. He was my dad's much younger brother. In fact, he was only a year older than my sister Susie, who no longer lived with us. She had found her mate in the Star Dawn pack and moved there almost a year ago. Tommy looked at us and whistled.
"Damn ladies, you are looking good tonight." I rolled my eyes. Tommy had that James Dean bad-boy-type vibe going on, and the girls in our pack went crazy for it. I couldn't count the number of times girls tried to friend me because they wanted to get close to my uncle. I heard giggling and looked round at Katie, who had the biggest crush on him, which I found totally gross. I mean, he was twenty-five. That age gap was just creepy. But Katie had declared that she and Tommy were mates, and she was eagerly anticipating her eighteenth birthday to confirm it.

Tommy winked at Katie, which just made her blush, and then grinned at Louise, who just rolled her eyes. He then turned to me.

"Happy birthday, kid," he said as he pulled me into a hug.

"Not a kid Tommy. I'm eighteen now," I scoffed.

"Sure you are," he agreed. "But you'll always be a kid in my eyes, sprinkle." I glared at him, which earned me a laugh.

"Ok, let's get this show on the road," he declared. Tommy was our designated driver, while my parents would take their own car to the pack house. We all filed out into the warm midsummer night with Katie calling shotgun.

The drive was only about five minutes, and before long, we entered the grand hall in the pack house. It was decorated stunningly with silver and black cloth draping from the ceiling and white tea lights and lanterns leading out into the back gardens where the dancefloor was set up. Tommy held his arms out.

"Ladies, may I escort you to the ball?" he said in a mock chivalrous tone. Katie giggled and latched herself onto one arm, and he looked expectantly at Louise, who just glared at him and stormed on ahead. I noticed the brief look of hurt flash across Tommy's face before the smooth charm replaced it.

"Come on, my lovely niece, let's see if we can find your prince charming." I smiled and looped my arm around his, and we walked into the party.

The room and gardens filled up within the next half hour. After dragging Louise away from arguing with her dad once again, we managed to get a couple of dances before Alpha Daniel Chambers made a speech about the time of the year. He also said that even though the moon governed us, it was important that we must also give thanks to the sun. He talked about the balance of duality, which earned a loud, sarcastic comment from Louise, who was promptly pulled out of the room by the Gamma. Everyone, including the Alpha, laughed. They were used to Louise by now.

As the Alpha was coming to the end of his speech, I heard a noise from behind and saw the Alpha's son Damien sauntering in with his usual group. Of course, they were late because they could get away with being late. I rolled my eyes and turned my attention to the stage when something stopped me.

There it was, the most beautiful scent I had ever smelled. I sniffed again, and my senses were slammed with that rich pine leaves and rustic fire smell, and I knew there and then that my fated mate was in the room somewhere. The smell seemed to get stronger every time I smelt it, and my wolf was going mental in my head, begging me to go find my mate. But I couldn't leave while the Alpha was talking. It was disrespectful and grounds for punishment.

The scent was so strong that I was struggling to concentrate on the words the Alpha was saying, and I was feeling like I was going to pass out. Then I felt people pushing in from behind. I turned and almost growled as they pushed right in between me and Katie. When I saw it was Damien, the Alpha heir, I lowered my head in submission and hoped he didn't notice my almost feral glare.

I tried to breathe through the scent. I wasn't sure I was going to be able to get through this when I felt someone's hand on my arm. The touch sent electricity running through me, enough to make me gasp, and something came alive in me. I closed my eyes as I felt the hand trail down my arm. Whoever it was slid his hand into mine, entwining our fingers and gently squeezing.
"Breathe, Strawberries," a husky voice whispered in my ear, and I took a deep breath. I could feel his breath on my ear. "Open your eyes, let me see you, mate."

Shakingly, I opened my eyes and looked at the owner of the hand that was stroking his thumb along mine to calm me. Standing next to me was Colton Stokes. Best friend to Damien Chambers and the future Beta of our pack.

CHAPTER 2

Harper

Oh my Goddess, oh my goddess. I was currently holding hands with Colton Stokes, and he was my fated mate. I shyly looked up into his eyes through my lashes and saw that he was watching me intensely, and I immediately blushed at the look in his eyes and looked away again. I heard him chuckle, and I blushed even more.

Alpha Daniel finished talking, and everyone clapped, and I had to break contact with Colton's hand so I could clap, too. Not that I remembered anything the Alpha had just said. The clapping died down, and I felt sparks on my back as Colton placed his hand on me and guided me through the crowd quickly. I attempted to look back to see Katie, but noticed that she was preoccupied with talking to Damien.

We left the room. Colton grabbed my hand and pulled me into the gardens and around the side of the building. Once we were around the corner, he spun me around to face him and backed me up against a wall. He buried his face into my hair, his nose grazing my neck, and took a deep breath, sending shivers down my spine.

He growled in appreciation and whispered, "MINE!" and began kissing down my neck. I gasped and held on to his arm. I felt a heat in my stomach when his teeth grazed the spot on the crook of my neck, and my breathing became shallow. Colton lifted his head, and he had a lazy smile on his face.

"Wow, Strawberries, you smell amazing." He hooked his finger under my chin and lifted my head to meet his eyes. From this close, I could see that his eyes were hazel, and there were flecks of gold in them. I took the time to really look at him. I mean, I had seen him from afar, but never this close before. He had a soft face that didn't have any sharp features, apart from the slight point to his chin. He had a heavy stubble, and his medium brown hair was shaved short at the sides but then longer on top, and it was slicked back. From what I could see, his body was basically that of a Greek god, but then he was a future Beta, so it was in his genes to be beautiful.

I trailed my hand down his clothed chest over his black shirt, and I felt his hard toned muscles, and my hand continued down as I felt his eight pack under my fingers. My hands ended up at the line where his shirt disappeared into his tailored black trousers, and I hovered there. Suddenly I felt very hot, and that heat in my stomach was getting warmer. I involuntarily bit my lip as I noticed a bulge in his trousers.

"See something you like, Strawberries?" His voice sounded husky as he watched me. I looked into his eyes, which seemed to have more gold in them from a few minutes before.

I tried to compose myself. "Erm...."
Shit. Think, Harper.
"Erm..."
Oh crap, I was struggling to think of, well... words at all.
"What's on your mind, Strawberries?" he teased. He knew what was on my mind. It was written all over my face.
"Why do you call me Strawberries?" I asked, and he grinned and buried his head in my neck again and took a deep breath again, and then nibbled my ear before whispering, "It's what you smell like to me. Strawberries." It felt like electric currents were running down my body, and I gasped.

"You smell like beautiful juicy ripe red strawberries." And then he was in front of me, and his lips were so close to mine, his voice was a low husky tone again.

"I wonder if you taste like them." He closed the gap and pushed his mouth against mine. His lips felt as soft as they looked as they pushed against mine. His hands glided to my hips, and he pulled me towards him, so I was flush against him. I gasped into his mouth, and he took the invitation and plunged his tongue into my mouth, and the kiss deepened. I put my arms around his neck, and he pushed me against the wall, not breaking contact with my mouth or body.

The heat in my stomach dropped, and something lower down awoke in me. He finally broke apart from me just as I started to wonder if you could die from kissing and if it was a worthy way to go. We were both breathing heavily and just looking at each other.

He looked at me with a heated expression. "As much as you match the name strawberries, I would like to know the name of my little mate," he breathed.

"Oh!" I gasped, "it's Harper."

"Well, nice to meet you, Harper. My name is Colton."

"I know." I nodded. Then blushed because I wondered if I sounded like a stalker. "I mean, that you are our future Beta, so everyone knows who you are." I felt very hot again. "But me, I'm not Beta, or any rank really, so I'm not known, really." He watched me with an amused look while I rambled on before he placed a rough finger on my lips to shush me.

"Calm down, sweetheart," he chuckled. "No need to be so nervous." I focused on getting my breathing back in control while he rubbed circles on my hand with his thumb again.

When I felt a little more composed, I smiled at him.

"Thank you," I said, and he smiled in return and placed a soft kiss on my forehead.

"Should we go back to the party?" I asked.

"I'd rather not," he said, with a low growl in his throat. "I've just found my fated mate after three years of looking, and the last thing I want to do is to take her back into a room full of sex-starved unmated werewolves." He looked me up and down with a look that made me want to clench my legs closed. "Especially when she looks this good." Then he leaned in closer. "And when I can smell the amazing scent of her arousal." I blushed again, and he chuckled.

"I'm a Beta love," he said, and I quirked my eyebrows. "Alphas and Betas tend to run on heightened senses and urges, including the possessive nature of a newly acquired mate, and I suspect if we went back in there, I would rip some guy's head off for just glancing at what is Mine." That last word rumbled into a growl, and I nodded, trying to avoid thinking about the powerful urges that my own body was expressing down below.

"We... erm, we could take a walk," I suggested, and he smiled.

"Could we head towards somewhere more private so we can get to know each other?" he asked with a glint in his eye. "I mean, I would take you to my room, but there is a big party downstairs, so not ideal for talking."

"Oh, yeah," I beamed. "My house is about twenty minutes away on foot."

"Perfect, lead the way, Strawberries." He linked his fingers in mine, and we started walking to the front of the house and down the drive.

We talked about so many things as we walked. I told him about my family. He knew of my dad and knew Tommy. We talked about his family, which was basically him and his parents. We also talked about hobbies, music, and TV. By the time we reached my house, I felt like I had learned a lot about him and knew he had learned a lot about me.

I let us in through the front door and switched on the light. Colton stood by the door, looking nervous. I looked at him, puzzled.

"What's wrong?" I asked, taking his hand. He smiled and looked down at my hand, and then when he looked back up at me, his eyes were pure gold, and there was a look of pure raw heat.

He growled before saying, "I am trying to be a gentleman here." He walked me into the wall behind me and both his arms on either side of me, trapping me between his hard body and the wall. "I don't know if I can control myself around you," I gulped and tried to suppress a moan.

"Then don't control yourself," I whispered. "We are mates, aren't we? It's only natural, so -" His breathing became more ragged the more I talked, and he crashed his lips down onto mine, interrupting what I was saying.

"Bedroom," he gasped as he broke contact. I pointed up the stairs, and he growled and smashed his lips to mine once more, claiming them as his, and lifted me easily as I wrapped my legs around his waist, and he carried me up the stairs to claim my body too.

CHAPTER 3

Harper

Colton crashed into my bedroom door, pressing me against it. His mouth descended on my neck and sucked on the spot where he would soon leave his mark, right in the crook where my neck met my shoulder. The feel of it sent tingles through my body and turned some heat on inside my lower regions. I let go of him enough to reach around and grab my door handle.

It flew open as I turned the handle, and we fell into the bedroom. We landed on the floor, with him on top of me and my legs still around him.
"Ow!" I exclaimed as pain laced through my back from the impact, and Colton looked up, shocked.
"Shit, Strawberries, sorry." He pulled himself off me and stood up. He held a hand out for me, and when I grabbed it, he pulled me up, so I crashed into his hard chest.

He spun me around and ran his hands slowly along my back. He pulled my hair to one side and started kissing my neck and shoulder. I closed my eyes and allowed the feel of his lips on my skin to take over all my other senses. His hand found the buttons on my dress, and one by one, they popped open, revealing my back.

My breathing became heavy as he slid his hands along my shoulders, pushing the straps of my dress down my arms. At the same time, he places light feathery kisses on my back, sending shivers down my spine. I stood in my bra and panties as my dress slipped to the floor. I heard the rustling of clothes before his shirt came into view on the floor next to me. I went to turn around, but Colton caught me.

"Not yet, Strawberries," he whispered in my ear as he pulled my back against his front. "Soon." I felt my bra come loose, and as it was strapless, it just fell to the floor, exposing my breasts to the room. Colton ran his hands up my sides and grazed the side of my breast with his thumbs, and I gasped at the feel, the sparks sending an electric current right to my sensitive parts where I felt my panties beginning to get damp.

Slowly, his hands moved until he cupped both of my breasts, and he pulled me harshly against him.

"See what you do to me," he whispered as he rubbed the unmistakable bulge in his pants against my ass. He centred on my now very erect nipples and rolled both in his fingers, and I couldn't help but moan and rub my ass against him.

"Oh, baby girl," he groaned, sending even more shivers down my spine.

"Colton, please." I felt so much need in my body as one of his hands trailed down my abdomen and along the edge of my panties. He chuckled as he slipped a finger into the edge of them. And I gasped.

He spun me around to face him again and looked down at me with a heated look in his eyes. He dropped to his knees in front of me and captured my left breast in his mouth, running his tongue around my nipple. I moaned as his hand slipped into my panties and expertly found my pleasure point and began rubbing slow circles, each round increasing the heat inside me until my legs began to shake from the excitement coursing through me. I have obviously pleasured myself before, but felt nothing like this. Colton looked up at me as I gripped his shoulders to stop myself from falling and smiled slowly.

"Am I assuming this is your first time, Strawberries?" he asked as he ran his finger against my folds, leaving my nub pulsing for more. I gulped and tried to catch my breath to answer him, but settled for nodding. He smiled again.

"Don't worry, baby girl. I'll take good care of you." He pushed a finger into my entrance. It slid in easily. I cried out, and my legs gave way as heat rushed over me. I was vaguely aware of Colton catching me and lowering me to the floor as his finger moved in and out of me at increasing speed. I called out again as another rush of heat hit my body, arching my back briefly before I collapsed to the floor, panting.

Colton laid next to me, peppering light kisses on my body, each one sending shivers through me. He leaned over and captured my lips and took my bottom lip into his teeth. He let go again and grinned at me before moving down my body. I watched him, still trying to catch my breath as he lifted my legs onto his shoulders and settled between them, his breath playing along my core and his eyes never leaving mine.

"I wanna taste you, Strawberries," he said before running his tongue up my outer folds and finding my nub. I moaned, falling back onto the floor as he swirled his tongue around in circles before grazing his teeth against my sensitive parts and sucking deeply. I couldn't contain myself as I writhed under his expert tongue and cried out once more. He held firm as he pushed his tongue into my entrance briefly before switching back to my nub and back again. I thought it couldn't be more amazing until his figures found their way to my entrance, and he thrust two inside me, pumping them in and out, bringing me to the edge and pushing me over as I felt another wave of intense heat crashing over me.

"Oh, my Goddess!" I screamed, and he continued to pump his fingers in and out of me, and his tongue alternated between swirling and sucking on my nub and kept me riding wave after wave of orgasm that rocked through my body.

"Baby girl, I want you so much," he groaned, moving up my body and kissing me deeply, pushing his tongue into my mouth. I moaned against him, and he chuckled into my mouth. He lifted up from the floor and picked me up, pulling me into his chest, and I breathed in his scent of pine leaves and rustic fire, feeling at home in his arms. He carried me to my bed and laid me down. I watched as he unbuttoned his trousers and slid them and his boxers down, his manhood springing free. I gasped at the size, and he grinned proudly at my reaction. He slipped completely out of his pants and crawled on the bed between my legs so that his member rubbed against the outside of my suddenly very-much-throbbing-again core.

I gulped, suddenly feeling nervous. This was my first time, and I knew it wasn't his. I had seen him with various girls draped on his arm several times. Part of me, the wolf-part, growled at that, but the girl part, the inexperienced-me-part, was so afraid that I would be awful. Colton looked down at me and frowned.

"What's wrong, baby girl?" he asked, and I shook my head. He smiled. "Aw, Strawberries, you're nervous," he chuckled. "That's okay, baby. It's expected." He leaned down and kissed me lightly.

"Don't worry, you are going to be perfect, okay?" He searched my face again, and I smiled and nodded. He was my mate, fated to me by the moon goddess, and I trusted him completely. He smiled as I relaxed against his touch. He moved, lining his head against my entrance.

"Now, baby, it's gonna hurt at first," he said soothingly. "But I promise it will feel better real quick." I nodded again, nervously.

"I love you, Colton," I said, and he smiled down at me again and slowly pushed himself inside me, watching me as he did. I felt him hit up against my virgin barrier and winced. I knew it was going to hurt, but I was ready and so happy that I was losing my virginity to my mate. Colton smiled one last time and broke through with one quick thrust. I screamed as the pain hit me hard and grabbed his shoulders as tears escaped my eyes. He stayed still inside me and leaned down against my neck.

"Breathe, baby," he whispered, and I focused on his kisses against my neck rather than the full painful feeling below. I began to relax again and felt him smile against my neck. "There we go, good girl." He slowly pulled out partially before pushing himself back in. I gasped each time, and each time, the pain was less and less, and I started to feel the heat rising again as he increased his speed in and out of me. Soon, I was gasping for a different reason; the pain was long gone. I rocked against Colton as he drove his member deeper inside me.

"Oh goddess, baby, you are so tight!" he panted. "Fuck me, this is amazing." He continued to pound into me. I felt myself on the edge once more.

"Colton, please," I called, and he sped up at the sound of my voice.

"That's it, baby girl, cum for me, baby, scream my name." And I flew over the edge once more into an oblivion of pleasure and screamed his name as the orgasm ripped through me. I gripped onto him as he rode me hard and fast and dug my nails into his back. His movements became erratic seconds before he thrust himself into me one more time with a roar, and I felt his seed shoot deep into me before he collapsed on top of me, panting.

"Fuck me, Strawberries," he panted against my neck. "That was mind-blowing!" I giggled. "I knew sex with my mate would be different, but... wow!" I felt so happy that he had enjoyed it as much as I had and giggled again. I didn't even mind the ache between my legs or that he didn't mark me yet. He pulled himself off me and picked me up, pulled my covers down, and put me inside, which was fine because my legs were still shaking from the experience. He climbed in beside me and pulled me against his naked body, wrapping his arms around me. I relaxed into him as he nuzzled into my neck, sending shivers down my spine.

I felt my eyelids droop as I was enveloped by the beautiful scent and warmth of my fated mate, when I felt him kissing my neck. His hand lowers down my stomach and over my core. I wriggle under his touch, giggling.

"Oh my goddess, I'm not sure I can do that again." I breathe as I feel his fingers once again on my pleasure place as he rubbed circles once more. I instantly felt the heat building inside me as I moaned against his touch, and he chuckled again.

"You can do it as many times as I choose," he growled against my ear. "You are mine, Strawberries, to do what I want with." I felt a shiver run down my spine and let out a moan. He built up speed quicker this time, and I was already panting while gyrating against him. I was on the edge again, and I cried out as I got closer and closer to yet another amazing climax. He leaned in and grazed his teeth against my marking spot, and I called out.

"Colton, please claim me."

He chuckled and moved against my ear. "I, Colton Stokes, the future beta of the Midnight Moon pack, reject you, Harper Kirby, as my mate."

I screamed as simultaneously the pleasure of the orgasm and the pain of the rejection ripped through me.

CHAPTER 4

Harper

I screamed again, the pain too much to bear as tears streamed down my face. I tried to pull away, but Colton held me tight as he continued to rub circles on my nub while rubbing his hard member against my back. Another wave of pleasure chased the pain around my body. Both sensations seemed to run on endless cycles as I cried out and gripped the sheets that covered us.

"That's it, baby girl," Colton grunted against my ear. "Ride it through," he grunted again, and I felt warm liquid shoot up my back as he came again. He slowed to a stop as he leaned against me, panting.

I cried as I felt his lips graze my neck once more, and he wrapped his arms around me, whispering shushing sounds in my ear.

"Why?" I cried, "Why would you do that?"

"Shhh, it's okay," he said. "The worst is over." He relaxed his arms and pulled out from under me, and I curled up into a ball in my bed as I heard him rustling about behind me. I saw him as he came round the other side of the bed. He sat down and stroked my face.

"Sorry Strawberries, but I'm not the settling down type." He chuckled. "But I just had to know what it would be like with my fated mate. I heard it was the best sex ever." He looked at me and grinned. "Gotta admit, they were right."

He stood again and grabbed his jacket. "I'm sure I don't have to tell you that no one knows about this, about us being fated. I mean, I really don't need that getting out."

"Leave me alone," I growled, the anger seeping out. My wolf was pacing inside me. How dare he do this to me, to us? Colton turned and looked at me, his eyes shining gold, which meant his own wolf was close to the surface.

Suddenly, he was back on the bed. He pulled the covers off and grabbed me and flipped me onto my back, and captured my hand above my head with one hand. His other hand roamed down my body as I tried to struggle away.

"Listen to me now, Strawberries," he growled at me. "You will respect my rank above yours and do what I say, and don't you dare to think otherwise." He leaned down and licked the nipple of my left breast, causing me to gasp. I couldn't help the shiver of pleasure that ran through me at his touch.

"This can work out real good for both of us." He sucked my nipple into his mouth, running his tongue around it before letting go. "Or it could be very painful for at least one of us." He repeated, only after he ran his tongue around this time, he bit down hard, causing me to cry out before letting go again. Fresh tears welled up in my eyes as he grinned at me.

"I'm glad we have an understanding."

Colton leaned down. "Don't worry, Strawberries, I'll make sure all my buddies know how good you are, and I'm sure we can set something up again." I whimpered as he licked my neck, and he chuckled. He let go of me and jumped up as headlights shone from outside, and I heard a car pull up. Colton glanced out of the window and growled.

"That's my cue to leave." He winked as he rushed to the door. "See you around, Strawberries." And with that, he was gone.

I heard the door downstairs bang shut as I pulled my covers back on me and curled back into a ball. I couldn't believe this had happened on my birthday, of all days. Meeting your fated mate was meant to be the happiest day of your life, the day you are complete. But here I was, alone, crying and exposed in bed after the one person who was meant to love and care for me had taken my innocence and ripped my heart out.

The front door opened and closed again.

"Harper," I heard a shout. Crap, Tommy was home. "Harper, where are you?"

I heard him run up the stairs, and he burst into my room.

"Harper, what the hell!" he shouted. "Why did I just see Colton fucking Stokes slipping out of the door?" I pulled the covers over my head as he turned on my light.

"Leave me alone, Tommy," I whispered. I really didn't want him seeing me crying.

"Fuck, Harps, please tell me you didn't sleep with that jerk." He sounded angry. "He's bad news. You do not want to get messed up with that."

"Tommy, leave me alone!" I said louder, but he just ignored me.

"I thought you had more sense than that, really? I mean, I thought you were waiting for your fated mate." I had enough. I didn't need his judgement on top of everything, even if it was right.

I pulled the covers off my head and screamed, "TOMMY, GET THE FUCK OUT OF MY ROOM!"

He stopped ranting and looked at me in shock. "What the...?" Then a look crossed his face as he registered my tear-stained face. "Oh fuck, kid. Shit. Are you okay?" I burst into tears again.

Tommy moved nearer, probably to hug me or something, but I couldn't take it. I couldn't take his anger, and I certainly couldn't take his sympathy.

"Please," I pleaded, "Tommy, just go," I said, holding out my hand to stop him. He looked at me again and nodded sadly.

"I'll be downstairs," he said before leaving my room, quietly closing the door behind him. I listened as I heard him descend the stairs and take a breath.

I moved to cover myself again, but then felt something wet behind me and remembered that Colton had expelled his stuff up my back. Now my bed and I were covered in it. It was everywhere, in my hair, down my back, and all over my sheets. I felt sick at the thought of it and knew I had to get it off. I got out of bed, wincing at the pain between my legs, and glanced at the bed, which was covered with the stuff. I pulled the bedding off and dumped it in the hamper on the landing. I went into my private bathroom, turned on the shower, and set it to hot. I stepped in and spent the next half an hour scrubbing my body and my hair clean. I knew I had successfully cleaned myself within the first ten minutes, but I still felt dirty, so I continued to scrub until my skin turned pink.

I finally got out of the shower and dried myself. Finding some fresh pyjamas, I dressed quickly. I went into the hallway cupboard and pulled out some fresh bedding, and started to re-make my bed. The whole time, I was vaguely aware of the ache in my body and the empty feeling in my heart. I felt like emotions were out of reach as I moved through the tasks almost automatically.

It wasn't until I finished the bed that a scent caught my attention. Sniffing the air, I smiled despite everything and turned and followed the beautiful smell of chocolate downstairs into the living room just as Tommy walked in from the kitchen with two mugs of hot chocolate. I curled up in one of the armchairs, and he passed me one of the mugs with a weak smile.

"I, erm...." he hesitated, and I looked at him, knowing that my face was blank. "The bedding, in the hamper," he signalled upstairs. "I thought it best to wash before the parents came home," he shrugged. He was right. Living in a house of werewolves basically meant that they would have smelt Colton as soon as they walked in. I nodded to him in thanks. I didn't need my parents knowing how much of a failure I was.

"Harp," Tommy hesitated again. "I'm sorry, but I have to ask...." I shook my head as fresh tears threatened to appear again.

"Please, Tommy. Leave it," I said. "I was just stupid, that's all." I would rather he think I was a stupid slut than my own fated mate used me and then rejected me. He nodded again, and we lapsed into silence.

"Why did you come home?" I asked all of a sudden. I looked at the clock on the wall, and it was only 10 pm. Tommy was a big party guy. There was no way he should be home already.

He shook his head. "I noticed you were missing, and Katie said she hadn't seen you for a while. Then I heard how Colton had bagged a girl." He looked uncomfortable at that last bit. "I suddenly got a bad feeling, and well, I hoped I was wrong, but...." he trailed off again, and I closed my eyes in shame. How could I have been so stupid?

"I swear, though," he started again. "If he tells any-"

Just then, a searing pain shot through my heart and ripped through my body. I dropped my mug of chocolate to the floor and screamed as I clutched my chest. It felt so much like the rejection had felt.

"Fuck, Harper!" I felt Tommy's hands on me. I looked at him through the tears as the pain ripped through me once more.

"Tommy!" I cried. "What's happening to me?" I fell to the floor and started rolling around. I wanted to claw my heart out of my body. I vaguely felt Tommy pulling me onto his knees and heard him swear before. "Shit, Harp, you're burning up!" Then everything stopped, and only the echo of pain ran through my body.

"Harper?" Tommy's voice sounded clipped and careful. I glanced up at his face and winced at the furious look that was etched into it. "Harper?" he asked again. "Is Colton your fated mate?" Crap. How did he figure it out? "Harper, answer me." Tommy wasn't an Alpha or named rank by any means, but the authority in his command caused me to whimper before I nodded in confirmation.

He growled, and I tried to pull away. "Then why were you crying after he left?" I shook my head. No, no, no! I didn't want him to know how worthless I was. "Harper?" he growled. "Did he reject you?" I burst out crying again, and his face turned red.

"Please, Tommy, don't tell anyone," I cried, but he wasn't listening.

"That fucking bastard!" he snarled. "I am going to rip him apart!"

"Tommy, please." I knew if Tommy tried to go up against Colton, well, Colton was Beta blood, it would be bad for Tommy. Betas were faster, stronger, and more savage than regular werewolves. "It was my fault. I should have been smarter."

Tommy looked at me, shocked. "Harper," he said. "You are not to blame. The bastard used the sacred mate bond to manipulate you." He pulled me into a hug. "It's not your fault, kid."

Just then, another wave of pain hit me, and I screamed again. Tommy tried to hold me tighter, but I scratched at him to let me go as the pain seared through my body.

"I don't understand," I cried. "What's happening? Am I dying?" Why did the pain keep coming back, and it was so much worse this time?

"I know what's happened," Tommy said as he held onto me. "I'm sorry, kid, I can't do anything to stop it." He started rocking me in his arms as wave after wave of pain ripped through me before it became too much, and I finally dropped into blessed darkness.

I woke up in my bed. My light was off, but my door was open, and I could hear Tommy just outside, talking. It sounded like he was on the phone.

"This isn't about you and me. For fuck's sake, Harper needs you. Please, just get here." Silence as I guessed the other person he was talking to was speaking. "Fine, then I will see you soon."

Then I heard footsteps, and Tommy appeared in my room, holding a glass of water.

"Hey, kid," he said with a sad smile on his face. "You need to drink" he sat on the edge of my bed and handed me the glass. I sat up and winced. My whole body hurt like I had gone ten rounds with a gorilla.

"Yeah, you are gonna be feeling pretty sore, and you'll need more sleep," Tommy said.

"What was that, do you know?" I asked, and he nodded sadly.

"When Colton rejected you, did you accept it?" I shook my head. I was in too much shock to even think of it.

He nodded. "If you don't accept the rejection, then you are still bonded for three full moons," he said, and then looked uncomfortable. "What you felt last night..." I glanced at the clock as he said that and saw that it was 3 am. "What you felt was Colton with another woman." Tears welled up in my eyes again. He had dropped me and gone and found another woman. I felt sick.

"The thing is, kid, you aren't at full strength, and you can't just accept right now," he said. "You need to build your body back up to withstand the bond breaking completely. Otherwise, it could kill your wolf." I gasped, suddenly realising I had not heard from my wolf since after Colton had left. I tried searching for her but could only find the smallest of sparks.

"Is she gone?" I cried, and Tommy looked at me with sympathy.

"No kid, but you are gonna need rest until you can hear her again, and definitely no trying to shift, you understand?" I nodded in response.

The door opened downstairs, and I heard people running up the stairs seconds before Katie and Louise burst into my bedroom. Seeing them there looking concerned brought a fresh wave of sadness, and once again, I burst into tears.

"Oh my gosh," Katie cried, throwing herself onto the bed and hugging me. "It's ok, Harps, we are here." I felt Louise at my back as she joined in the hug, and before long, I was laid between them in my bed as I cried, and they both whispered soothing words.

Tommy stood at the end of the bed and smiled.

"Take care of her, girls. I got something to do." He started heading out of the door when Louise called him.

"Tommy?"

He turned back. "Yeah?"

"Don't do anything stupid." Tommy grinned, but even I could see the feral look in his eyes.

"Sorry darling, can't promise that." At that, he was gone.

CHAPTER 5

Tommy

My car screeched into the parking lot of the pack house, and I jumped out. I was furious; I wanted to find that little shit and rip him apart. I could hear the music of the party still going. These things normally lasted till past daylight. I was normally one of the last ones left standing, or if I was in bed, certainly wasn't sleeping.

But not this time. Katie had come looking for me, telling me she couldn't find Harper, and she was worried. I played it down and told her I would look for Harper and to go have fun. That was when she pouted and mentioned something about Damien. She said he was flirting with her until one of his friends came over and mentioned Colton had bagged that girl, and then he suddenly wasn't interested. She was very upset about it, but I told her she had a lucky escape.

It was niggling me, though, Damien showing Katie attention, and then Colton and some girl. My wolf Brun was grunting at me to find Harper. I trusted his judgment. I had found Darren, my brother, and asked if they had seen her, but nothing. In the end, I had gone home to see if Harper was there. And the first thing I saw was Colton fucking Stokes, leaving my house.

And now, knowing what he did to my poor sweet niece. To humiliate her in such a way was bad enough, but to take her innocence under the cover of the fated bond was beyond words. I stormed into the hall, looking for Colton, when Darren saw me.
"Tommy," he called. I could tell both he and Linda, my sister-in-law, had drunk a fair amount. I guess the deal went well, and he had got his raise.
"Tommy, my little brother." He clapped me on the back. "Where have you been? Did you find Harper?"
"Yeah, she's at home with a headache," I lied. It wouldn't do to have them worry, and I knew Harper didn't want people knowing what had happened.
"Oh, no!" Linda said sadly. "And on her birthday, well, we'll make it up to her tomorrow with cake."
"Erm... yeah, sure," I grimaced. "Anyway, I have something to do. I'll see you at home." I needed to find that snake and smash his face in.

I left my brother and sister-in-law and went searching. It wasn't long before I heard the voices of the ranked elite. The jumped up little shits thought they were the kings in this town. I didn't care if Damien was meant to be the Alpha. The boy was as corrupt as his own father. I didn't care what they got up to, but bringing my family into their dealings was over the line.

I had gone out into the back gardens where it was mostly the younger crowd when I saw the usual gaggle of girls, and of course, at the centre were Damien and Colton, along with some other jock douches that hung off them hoping for praise. Seeing Colton's smirking face as he laughed and joked was enough for me to see red, and with a growl, I headed straight for him.

I had got close when I heard snippets of the conversation.

"Yeah, man, it was fucking amazing. The way she wriggled against me as I made her cum against the pain was one of the best-" I'd had enough knowing he was talking about my niece.

"You fucking bastard!" I snarled as I lunged at him, knocking him to the floor. I had surprised him and started pummelling into his grinning face over and over. I was dragged off by two of the guys, and they held me as I tried to get back to the smarmy little shit. He jumped to his feet, his face a mass of blood and his eyes shining gold.

"Tommy, Tommy, Tommy," he gloated before delivering a punch to my stomach, sending me gasping to the floor. "It's all very chivalrous of you to stand up for the little slut niece of yours." I felt a kick to my stomach, and pain radiated. "But she really wasn't complaining when she screamed my name as I fucked her tight little pussy." He bent down and whispered, "And if I want to do it again." Colton grabbed my hair, yanking back, and punched me in the face as someone else kicked my side. I grunted against the pain, knowing I was not only outnumbered but outranked. "If I want to fuck her again, I know I will make the slut scream again."

All the fury hit me at once, and I could feel Brun forcing his way out. I felt the shift before they had noticed, and within seconds, I had shifted into my snarling and very pissed-off wolf. I saw everyone take a step back as I narrowed my sight in on the little shit's throat and pounced. He shifted in time, and his dirty brown wolf rolled away from my attack before counter-attacking. I knew his wolf was bigger, faster, and stronger than mine, and he had me by the scruff before I could get out of the way. I rolled, knocking him off me, and launched at him again. I knocked him to the floor and was about to set my teeth around his throat when I felt the unmistakable power of the Alpha.

"WHAT THE HELL IS GOING ON?" Everyone froze at the power radiating through the gardens.

"Colton, Thomas, STOP!"

We stopped at the Alpha command, unable to move. "Now shift." Pain ripped through me at the forced shift, and I was left panting, naked, and in pain.

Colton smirked at me as I heard the sound of his father on the approach. He knew very well that attacking a ranked member was punishable by exile or death and that I didn't stand a chance against the son of the pack Beta.

"Now, does someone want to tell me why my son is naked in the gardens?" he bellowed in his always too loud voice. Damien leaned over and said something to his father, who then turned his glare on me.

"Do you want to explain why you attacked the future Beta of this pack?" I glared over at Colton, who had sat up and was comfortable in all his naked glory.

"Might want to ask him what he did to my niece," I snarled. I remembered then that Harper had said that she didn't want anyone knowing they were fated mates. I had the feeling that it was more Colton that didn't want people to know. I grinned at him before I added, "Or should I say what he did to his fated mate?" Colton growled at me as a collective gasp went through the crowd.

There was a growl from Beta Eric, and I looked up and saw him glowering at his son. I looked at Colton and grinned again as he glared back at me.

"Party is over," the Alpha called. "Everyone, go home." The people immediately started moving to the exits like the compliant sheep they were. He then looked down at me. "Tommy, you can go home too." I looked at him in shock, but I wasn't the only one shocked.

"Wait! What the fuck?" Colton exclaimed. "He attacked me!"

"Colton, shut up," the Beta reprimanded him. "And get into the office now."

"But I haven't done anything wrong!" Colton snapped.

"Are you arguing with me, boy?" the Beta growled, and Colton shrunk back

"No, sir," he said quietly, and he pulled himself to his feet and stormed into the pack house. The Beta turned and stormed in after him, and the Alpha glanced at me.

"I trust you will say nothing of this, Tommy?" He phrased it as a question, but I knew the man enough to know it was a threat.

"Yes, Alpha," I responded.

"Good, give my regards to your brother." He nodded and turned and followed his Beta into the pack house. Damien was the only one left and went to say something, a sly smirk on his face.

"Damien, you too," the Alpha called back without turning, and Damien rolled his eyes but followed his father into the house.

I picked myself up and limped through the house to my car, stopping briefly when I heard muffled shouting coming from the Alpha's office. I grinned at the thought of the little shit getting his ass handed to him as I got into my car. I knew as well that I wasn't done with him either, as I started the car up and headed home.

Harper

We pulled back up to the house in Louise's car, giggling about the movie. I sat in front, and Katie was in the back with our obscene amount of shopping. It was the day after my birthday and the worst night of my life, and Louise and Katie had declared it pamper Harper day. We went into town and had lunch, and then some shopping, followed by a chick flick.

I looked up out of the window and was shocked to see the driveway full of cars, and despite knowing nothing about cars, I could tell that these were the luxury sort. I knew my mum had planned a cake this evening since we couldn't celebrate my birthday yesterday. My parents had no idea about what had happened last night, and quite frankly, I was happy for it to stay that way.

I glanced at Louise, and she looked concerned.
"That's the Alpha's car," she said, pointing to a gold-coloured monstrosity. "And that's the Beta's?" She pointed to a black sleek type one.
"What are the Alpha and Beta doing here?" Katie asked from the back seat.

I shrugged. "Maybe they are having a meeting," I said. My dad's office was here, so if they had to talk about finances, then maybe they called in.

I jumped out of the car and leaned against it as the girls grabbed the shopping. Since last night, I felt weak, and they were doing their best to make things easy for me. We headed into the house, and I walked into the living room to see my mum and Caroline Stokes, the Beta's wife, sitting drinking tea. My mum saw me and squealed.

"Oh, Harper, you are home." I glanced at the girls, and they shrugged. "Caroline, please meet Harper." Mrs Stokes stood up and took my hand.

"It's very nice to meet you, Harper," she smiled. "And happy belated birthday, dear."

"Oh Harper, why didn't you tell us!" my mum exclaimed, and I looked at her, confused.

"Tell you what?" I asked. I could tell she was about to answer when I heard my dad's voice.

"Harper?" he called. "Is that you?"

"Yes, daddy," I called back.

"Can you come to my office for a moment, please?" he called back, and I headed down to his office, where he was standing in the doorway smiling.

"Hi pumpkin," he said as I reached him. He then guided me into his office, which I was surprised to see was full.

The Alpha was sitting behind my dad's desk in my dad's chair, and the Beta was sitting in one of the other chairs, while Tommy was standing in the corner. He threw me a pained expression and then glared at something at the wall behind me. I suddenly had a bad feeling as I turned my head in the direction he was looking.

My heart dropped to my stomach, and my eyes fell on him. He was here, in my home. Colton leaned against the back wall, and I watched as he looked me up and down slowly, like he was undressing me with his eyes. His eyes met mine, and I couldn't help my breathing become shallow as he slowly licked his lips and smirked at me. What the hell was he doing here now?

"Ah, Harper darling, please come in," the Alpha's voice pulled my attention to him, and I turned back to the room. "Please take a seat." My dad guided me to the only empty chair across from the Alpha and next to the Beta, who was smiling at me, too.

"As I was saying, Darren..." The Alpha turned to my dad. "I am sure you're beyond happy about the new development, and such a merge will be very beneficial to the pack operations,"

"Yes, absolutely, Alpha," my dad said, and he smiled at me, too.

"And you agree, Eric?" the Alpha asked the Beta, who nodded.

"Who am I to argue with fate?" he said, chuckling.

"Well, then it is settled," the Alpha said. "And let me be the first to congratulate the new couple!"

Wait! What? I looked around. Well, everywhere apart from the direction of the eyes that feel like they are drilling into my back. Everyone was smiling at me apart from Tommy, who had his eyes closed and looked really upset.

"Daddy?" I asked. "I don't understand. What's going on?" My dad smiled at me, but it was the Alpha who answered.

"Why, yours and Colton's engagement, my dear," he said with a big grin.

I suddenly felt like I was going to be sick, and I felt the sparks before I knew he was there. Colton took my left hand and slipped a gold diamond ring onto my finger, and he smirked at me as he lifted my hand and kissed it. I shuddered as sparks ran through my body. Colton leaned into me and kissed my cheek and then whispered.

"You're all mine now, Strawberries."

CHAPTER 6

Harper

I looked at the ring on my finger and then back around the room. Tommy had the look of fury on his face. Everyone else was smiling and chatting. Colton ran his hand up and down my arm, and the sparks made it hard to think straight.

I was engaged! To Colton Stokes! At any other time, this might have been one of those dream-come-true moments. Hell, this time yesterday, I might have thought that this was my dream come true. But now circumstances were different, very different. I took a step away from Colton and shook my head.

"But he rejected me," I whispered. The Alpha stopped talking and looked directly at me. Then, I realised my father, and the Beta had stopped talking too and were also looking at me.

"What did you say, Harper?" the Alpha asked, his tone oozing with authority. I couldn't help but bite the side of my lip. The Alpha was an intimidating man.

"I said, he rejected me," I said a little louder and then looked at the floor, although I could still feel the Alpha's eyes on me. Then I heard him chuckle, and I looked up in shock.

"Oh, don't you worry, my dear," the Alpha said with a big smile. "Young Colton here was a little rash in his actions, but he regrets that now, don't you, young man?"

"Yes, Alpha sir, I do," Colton replied before grabbing my hand in his. "And Harper, I am truly sorry, and I would like this opportunity to make it up to you and show you how much of a loving husband and mate I can be." His tone was sincere, but I knew it was just for show.

"But you rejected me," I said again, more insistently. "So the bond... it's broken, isn't it?" I looked around at the men in the room.

"My dear child..." the Beta smiled at me. "I was under the impression that while my son was somewhat foolhardy, you didn't actually accept the rejection."

I nodded. "Yes, Beta sir." The Beta stood up and smiled.

"Well, there you have it," he said. "The bond is still alive, and as long as you complete the mate bond by the third full moon, then the rejection will be a silly mistake of the past." He clapped Colton on the back and then leaned over and kissed my forehead. "And please, call me Eric. We are family now."

"Wait, are you saying that you are expecting her to complete the bond and tie herself to this jerk for the rest of her life? And all within three months?" Tommy shouted. "Darren, really, are you going to allow this?" My dad glared at Tommy, his face going red, but it was the Alpha that replied.

"Thomas, I understand your concerns and admire your guardianship of your niece. But I assure you that the moon goddess wouldn't have paired her with Colton here if they were not a good match." There was something about the way he said guardianship that felt like more than just an uncle looking out for his niece.

"But you-" Tommy started, but my father interrupted him.

"Tommy, that's enough," he snapped. "If you have nothing productive to say, then you can just leave." Tommy stared at my father in disbelief before muttering something under his breath. He stalked over and pulled me into a hug.

"I'm sorry, kid," he said, and then looked at Colton and pointed a finger at him. "I'm watching you, very closely." Then he threw a nasty look at my father and stormed out of the room. I watched him go, feeling like I had lost my only ally. He had literally thrown me to the wolves.

It was the Alpha who spoke next, shocking me out of my death stare with the door.

"Well, I think we should give the new couple a little privacy," he said. "I hear there is cake!" He then headed around the desk, shook hands with Colton, and kissed my cheek. I was shocked to hear Colton growl, and there was something about it that caused a flutter in my stomach. He had just growled at his Alpha for getting too close to me. The Alpha just chuckled in response.

"Nice healthy wolf there, boy," he said and chuckled again before heading out of the door, followed by the Beta, who was frowning at Colton, and finally, my father.

The door closed, and we were alone. I suddenly felt extremely nervous. I looked at Colton and saw that he was staring at me, his eyes almost completely gold. I didn't know what emotion he was feeling, but our eyes only switched out to wolf when there was some strong emotion present. And a wolf's eye colour is a mark of rank. I had silver eyes, but when Colton and I completed the mate bond, my eyes would likely turn gold like all high-ranked.

Then it hit me; when Colton and I completed the mate bond. Oh crap! I was going to be mated. I felt sick and like I needed to sit down again. Colton must have noticed because he took my elbow and guided me to the chair behind me. He kneeled in front of me and looked at me with concern.

"Hey, Strawberries," he said, moving my hair to one side in a tender gesture. "Breathe." He ran his thumb in circles on my hand like he had last night. I felt the panic attack that was forming, subside, and he smiled. Last night! Last night when we had slept together, and then he rejected me! But now he was here, and I had a ring on my finger. The anger hit me like a wall, and I jumped out of the chair away from him.

"You bastard!" I hissed at him. "How dare you?" He stood up, an amused look on his face, and started to move slowly towards me as I backed up.

"You rejected me!" I yelled. "You didn't just reject me. You humiliated me!"

He glanced at the door and hissed, "Keep it down!"

I knew that no matter how loud I shouted; the office was soundproofed, which I always found strange, but my dad said that it kept sound out as well as in. I didn't tell Colton that, though.

"What's wrong, Colton?" I raised my voice, and he lost the amused look. "Don't you want everyone to know how you fucked me and then broke me?"

"I mean it Strawberries, you do not want to see me angry." He had got closer and suddenly felt so much bigger.

"And then you come in here and decide that you made a mistake. What, am I good enough to settle down with now, or did daddy tell you off?"

"Harper, I am warning you," he growled.

"Maybe I should just accept your rejection right now and break the bond for good."

He went very still. All emotion disappeared from his face, but pure gold surrounded the black centre of his eyes. His powerful beta aura blasted into me, sending my body cold.

"Bite your tongue, little one, else I do it for you." His words held a promise that had me shivering in fear. I should have stopped there, but of course, I didn't. I stood straight and glared at him.

"I, Harper Kirby, acknow-" my words were cut off as I was pushed against the wall, and his lips smashed onto mine. I tried to push him away, but his hands grabbed mine and pinned them above my head in one hand. He kissed me hard enough that I was sure my lips would be bruised. I stayed unmoving, not kissing him back despite everything inside me wanting to. I could feel the damaged mate bond and the overwhelming need to fix it.

Colton growled into my mouth, and his free hand ran down my body and landed on my ass before squeezing hard. I gasped, giving him access for his tongue to slip in and explore my mouth. My walls broke, and I found myself kissing him back. All the need and lust rushed to the surface and washing over me. Colton let go of my hands, and I wrapped them around his neck, and he lifted me and pulled me hard against his body. I wrapped my legs around his waist, and he groaned and ground into me. He moved over to my father's desk and sat me on the edge. My whole body reacted to him as I remembered the last night and the way our bodies melded together perfectly. The thoughts ignited a fire down below, and I could feel myself getting damp. Colton groaned as the scent of my arousal surrounded us.

Colton wrapped his hand in my hair, and I cried out as he yanked my head back, breaking the kiss.

"Now listen here carefully, Strawberries," he growled against my ear as he nipped at my neck behind my ear. "You belong to me. You have always belonged to me, and you always will belong to me. You are MINE!" I gasped as he snarled that last word, sending shivers down my body.

"And so help me, goddess," he growled. "If you ever try to pull a stunt like that ever again, I will mate you and mark you right where you stand."

My body reacted to the promise of the mark, and I couldn't help the moan that slipped out as his teeth grazed the very spot where he was to put his mark on me. Even Maia, my wolf, who had been silent since last night, suddenly made an appearance and yapped at the feel of him so close to me.

"Do you understand?" he growled, yanking my hair again, exposing my throat in submission, and bringing my attention back to his question. His eyes were pure gold, and his dominance played in overdrive, emphasising his anger. I involuntarily whimpered against the look in his eyes, but nodded.

"Y-yes, Colton," I stuttered, and he smirked in approval.

Suddenly his eyes bled back to their mostly hazel with the gold flecks, and his face rested into a flirty smile. He let go of my hair and hooked his finger under my chin, tilting it upward.

"Good girl," he cooed before brushing his lips gently against mine before pulling away. He smiled at me again, as if the past few minutes of aggression had never happened.

"Come on, baby girl," he cooed. "Let's go get some cake." He lifted me off the table and slipped his hand into mine. He laced our fingers together, pulling me towards the door and out of the office to our waiting families and cake. Well, at least there was cake.

CHAPTER 7

Harper

Everyone looked up as we walked into the dining kitchen. My mum's eyes zeroed in on Colton's hand wrapped around mine, and she grinned. I was thankful to see that Tommy hadn't left the house and was sitting in the corner of the room. He was glaring at Colton as soon as we walked into the room, but refused to meet my eyes.

The Alpha stood up and smiled.

"Here they are," he said cheerfully. "Come, take a seat, my dear. It is your birthday, after all." And then he held his chair out for me. Before I could sit down, though, Colton slid into the seat, and then I let out a surprised yelp as he pulled me down onto his knee. He wrapped his arms around my stomach and gently kissed my shoulder before looking around at everyone.

"I thought I would save a seat for someone else," he said with a shrug, and the Alpha started laughing.

"You do right, son," he said before sitting in the other spare seat.

I glanced across the table at Katie and Louise, who looked confused. Louise met my eyes and nodded toward Colton with a clear WTF expression on her face. I shook my head slightly, hoping nobody saw. Colton's arms tightened around me as an indication that he saw everything. I quickly looked down at my hands, and his grip loosened again. I looked up into the mirror on the walls behind the girls. Colton was watching me, and when our eyes met, he inclined his head, and a dangerous look flashed through his eyes.

Colton turned his attention away from mine, and I felt like I could breathe again.

"Oh, and apologies if you heard anything untoward just now in the office," Colton said, looking around the room, and the Alpha and Beta grinned. It was obvious what they thought he was talking about.

"Don't you worry about it, son," my dad said. "The office is soundproof. Nobody heard a thing." Crap! Caught. I couldn't help the mischievous smile, and glanced in the mirror again to see Colton glaring at me. He kept his eyes on mine as he leaned forward and whispered in my ear.

"If I had known that, I would have fucked you right there over the desk." I immediately went bright red, and Louise rolled her eyes.

"Well, everyone heard that untoward comment," she muttered, and Katie stifled a laugh while Colton glared at her.

"Darren, seriously!" Tommy burst out, his face set in a furious scowl. "Are you really going to allow this kind of talk?"

"Oh Tommy," my mum scolded. "They are a new couple in love. You'll understand when you eventually find your mate." I saw Tommy glance briefly at Louise, and she looked uncomfortable. I'd suspected for a few weeks that they were fated mates, but this confirmed it. Glancing in the mirror again, Colton had a sly grin on his face. He'd caught the exchange himself.

"Tommy, I have already told you once," my dad said in a warning tone, and Tommy stood up and growled before storming out of the room, stopping briefly and looking at me.

"Harper, could I have a word, please?" And then I heard him on the stairs. I went to stand up, and Colton's arms tightened around my waist. The Alpha laughed again.

"Let the girl go," he said. "You'll have your whole lives together." Colton growled low in his throat, but loosened his grip enough for me to stand up.

"Excuse me," I said to the room and headed out, following Tommy upstairs. He was standing in my room. I went in and closed the door.

Tommy still looked furious, but as soon as my door was closed, he rushed forward and pulled me into a hug.

"Shit, Kid!" he whispered. "I fucked up. I'm so sorry."

"I don't get it," I said, pulling away. "What happened? He was all for rejecting me and then suddenly, well... this!" I waved my hand with the engagement ring on around. Tommy went and sat on my bed and put his head in his hands.

"I told them," he mumbled. "I was all pissed off about what he did to you that I went storming up there. And then when I saw him gloating to his friends about it-"

"What!" I exclaimed. Oh, my goddess, all his friends were gonna know everything. How could I even show my face? Tommy looked up at me, sympathy in his eyes.

"I'm so sorry," he said again.

"Well, why did he change his mind then?" I asked, trying to stop the tears from falling, and Tommy shook his head.

"We were fighting, and the Alpha broke it up. I could tell that the little shit was going to get away with everything, especially since I was the one that attacked him, so I blurted out about him being your fated mate." He lowered his eyes at that last part. "After that, he was dragged into the office, and I felt pretty good that I had got him into trouble, until this afternoon when they all showed up here." The guilt on his face was evident, but I didn't blame him.

"I still don't understand why though," I said, sitting down next to him, and he sighed.

"Harps, there is so much about this little town of ours that you don't understand," he said. "It's not as quaint as it looks."

The town that our pack bordered was called Levington. It was a mid-size town. We had a cinema and a shopping centre. Pack members owned most of the businesses and the properties in town, and the pack bordered the edge. Most of us anyway. Like Katie and her family, some pack members lived in one of the apartment blocks that was owned by the Alpha, in and around the centre. This was mainly because omega-ranked pack members were not allowed to own property. It was a nice picturesque town with window boxes full of flowers and tourist awards and such. But I wasn't stupid. I knew that every town had a bad part.

I rolled my eyes at Tommy. He always saw me as sweet and innocent.

"Tommy, I'm well aware of the darker elements of town. I've snuck into Howlers before." Howlers was a seedy werewolf run bar. They had club nights on the weekends and were pretty much the only place in town. Despite the name, the humans in town still didn't know that a werewolf ran it or that we even really existed.

"Harps, it's not as simple as that." Tommy looked nervously at the door and lowered his voice to a whisper. "You haven't been told everything about our family heritage and how important it is to the town. There's a reason why it took so long for Susie to be able to move to Star Dawn with her mate, not until they realised it wasn't her."

"What are you talking about? What wasn't her?" He was talking crazy, and I was beginning to wonder if he had been injured in the fight last night.

He scratched his neck and stood up and put his ear to the door

"Listen, Kid," he said, turning to me. "If it were up to me, you would be out of this rotten town by now. I'm stuck here. I don't want you to be." He looked at me, and for a second, I swore his eyes glowed gold instead of their usual silver. "You're too important for that!"

I scoffed, "I'm not important." I'd been mostly invisible, happy to blend into the background my whole life. Susie enjoyed being the one everyone looked at with all the praise and attention. The very idea made me shudder.

"Oh kid, If only you knew," Tommy smiled. "You are more important than any one of us. I knew that from the moment you were born that you were-"

There was a knock on my door, and we both looked up. My mum popped her head in the door.

"Sweetie, Colton said he wants to go home," she said. Thank the goddess, I thought. Maybe I could get my head straight without him being around. Plus, I still needed to get ready for school in the morning. You'd think that becoming engaged to the future Beta might mean no more school, but there were only two more weeks left, and then it was done. Plus, despite it technically being legal in the UK to leave school at sixteen, our pack had a requirement that all pack members continued until eighteen, at the very minimum, within the compulsory pack training curriculum.

I smiled at my mum. "Okay, I will come and say goodbye." I went to leave my room, but my mum blocked my way.

"Harper, where are your bags?" she asked, looking around my room.

"Bags?" I asked, confused.

"Oh, you have got to be kidding me," Tommy muttered behind me, and I turned and looked at him, still confused.

"Sweetheart," my mum said. "You're moving into the pack house. You knew that, didn't you?" Erm, no, I did not! This was news to me. I knew that I would eventually be expected to move into the pack house, but not today, not straight away!

"What, mum, no!" I exclaimed. "It took Susie two months before she moved."

"Yes, I know, sweetheart, but you and Colton are engaged now. I mean, the engagement party will be this weekend!" My heart plummeted at what she was saying. They had already started planning the engagement party! Things were moving way too fast for me. I started to feel faint and sat down on the floor before falling down.

"Oh no! Harper, sweetie, what's wrong?" My mum started fussing, but her voice was faint. There was a loud rushing in my ears, and I felt like my eyes couldn't focus. It was all too much, and this was my way of shutting it all out.

Then I felt sparks across my cheek, and I was shocked back to reality. The room had got crowded, but my focus was brought to Colton, who was kneeling right in front of me, stroking my cheek. He even looked concerned and smiled when I focused on him.

"Hey, Strawberries," he cooed. "What's up, baby girl?" He leaned forward and grazed his lips against mine, and the sparks sent shivers down my spine.

"I think she's just a little overwhelmed with everything," my mum said. "She has panic attacks sometimes."

"Aw, Strawberries," Colton purred. "Why don't we get you home, and then I can take care of you properly?" There were awww's and ahh's from others, but I saw Colton's eyes as he said it, and the sinister look that flashed through them made me shrink away from him. I shook my head and moved further back.

"I-I have nothing packed," I stammered, hoping that it would be a reason to stay home. I was out of luck.

"Fine," he said, his tone clipped. "You have ten minutes, and then I want to leave." I could already tell that he was angry and probably tired of holding up the pretence of being the loving mate. I bit my lip to hold back the tears, and then Louise spoke.

"Colton, why don't you go home? Katie and I will help Harper pack her things, and then I will bring her home later." As the Gamma's daughter, Louise lived in the pack house alongside the Beta and the Alpha family. At least I would be living with one of my best friends. Colton glanced up at Louise and grinned.

"That sounds perfect!" he said and then looked back at me. "I will see you at home soon then, mate!" He leaned over and kissed me again, this time much harder, before pulling away and standing up. He headed out of my bedroom without a second glance, and less than a minute later, I heard the front door close. It was reminiscent of last night, and I couldn't help but burst into tears.

"Well," my mum said, uncertainty in her voice. "I will leave you girls to it," she added before she left the room. My dad stood in the doorway, smiled down at me, and then glanced behind me.

"Come on, Tommy," he said. "I think it's time we had a chat." Tommy stood up and headed out of the room, but stopped at the door.

"Don't worry, kid," he said. "I'll figure something out. I'll fix this shit." And then he left.

CHAPTER 8

Harper

I sat on the floor, not moving. If I moved, then I would have to pack, and once I had packed, then...

I didn't want to move to the pack house; I had lived here in this house my whole life. Even when I go to University in September, it will be a local one so that I can drive home every night and sleep in my bed.

"Harper, sweetie." I looked at Louise, who had kneeled beside me and was rubbing my back. "We should get started on some packing." I shook my head.

"I don't want to," I said, fresh tears welling up in my eyes, and Louise pulled me into a hug.

"I know, sweetie, I hate to say it, but I don't think you have any choice right now." She pulled away and smiled. "But plus side, we'll be living together." I smiled back and nodded my head. Louise helped me up off the floor, and I turned around to see that Katie had already pulled one of my suitcases out of my closet.

"I have put in some underwear so far," she said. "Although, Harper girl, we are gonna have to go shopping again pretty soon because your lingerie collection needs some work," she giggled, and I rolled my eyes. Katie loved to shop a lot! She also loved all that girly stuff, like makeup and clothes and nails. She always said one of the worst things about being a werewolf is that you couldn't wear acrylic nails because they popped off when you shifted.

"Katie, I think that sexy underwear is the last thing on her mind right now, don't you?" scolded Louise, and Katie stuck her tongue out at her.

"Well, it's not gonna be for Colton." Katie winked at me. "He was all over you just now, and now you will be living with him." I could feel the colour draining from my face.

"Oh my goddess!" I whispered. "I am going to be expected to have sex with him." I felt sick all of a sudden.

"Well, yeah, he's your mate," Katie chuckled to herself as she started folding the underwear she had pulled out of my drawers into the suitcase. "And Colton is a Beta. They have quite the insatiable appetite. In fact, you could probably skip clothes altogether. I don't think you'll be wearing them all that much!"

"Katie!" Louise snapped, and Katie looked up at her, shocked.

"What?" She looked between us. "I don't get it. You've slept with him already, haven't you? What's the issue?"

"Yeah, she slept with him, and then he rejected her," Louise said. "He showed his true dickish colours, and now she is being forced to mate with him, after what he did." I could tell she was getting angrier and angrier with each word she spat out. This would have been Louise's nightmare to have her choices taken away. This was why she hated the mate bond. She believed it took your choice of whom to love away. I put my hand on her arm, and she closed her eyes and took a breath.

"I'm sorry, sweetie," she said. "You don't need me and my issues right now."

"I'm sorry too," Katie said. "I was just getting excited. To be mated to a Beta, or another named rank would be life-changing for me." Katie was an Omega, and they were the lowest rank in the pack. They had more rules than the rest of us. They couldn't become warriors, and they weren't allowed to leave the pack territory and borders without express permission. Katie wouldn't be allowed to go to the University in the city like Louise and me. She wanted to run her own beauty salon, but Omegas weren't allowed to own property, and Katie had to settle for the local college in town and a job at her aunt's salon. Her aunt Sheila had ranked up when she mated with one of the warriors, but it was rare for an Omega to mate up the ranks unless fate deemed it. And unless they found that fated mate within their pack, then it was unlikely they would ever find them.

It was an awful system, one that got Louise angry all the time. I had heard that other packs had started an Omega exchange system where they could go stay in another pack for three months and work there, and hopefully, they found their fated mate and could stay there. Midnight Moon wasn't a part of the program. Our Alpha said that it went against tradition and gave people false hope, plus he didn't like strangers in his pack.

"Anyway," Katie said. "It's my eighteenth birthday soon, and you never know I might end up being Damien's mate. He was showing me attention at the party last night," she giggled, and I glanced at Louise, who half shook her head. But Katie saw the exchange.

"What?" she demanded, looking between Louise and me. "What's with the look?" I started to fidget and went to grab some clothes from my closet, so I had more than underwear to put on.

"Louise, Harper. Tell me." She knew that Louise wouldn't break, so she zeroed in on me, and I caved straight away.

"Damien was showing you attention, so you didn't see when Colton took me away from the party," I said. "Colton didn't want anyone to know we were fated mates," I explained. I didn't tell her that we knew this because Louise had overheard Damien and Colton boasting about it at the party afterwards. She didn't know I was the mate in question or that Katie was the filthy omega airhead that they were talking about.

Katie glared at me with tears in her eyes. "I can't believe you, Harper," she snapped. "Louise, I expected this from, but I thought you were better than this." I stood there dumbfounded. I had no idea what I had done. "Geez, you are mated to a Beta for less than 24 hours, and I am already not good enough for you, is that it?"

"Oh my goddess, Katie, no," I cried. "I never meant that at all." Katie stood up suddenly and headed towards the door.

"Well, don't let my lowly status drag you down, ladies," she growled and stormed out of the room.

"Katie!" I went to go after her, but Louise stopped me.

"Leave her, Harper," she said. "Let her calm down, and we can talk to her at school tomorrow."

"I didn't mean that, Louise," I said, getting upset again.

"I know, but it's hard for Omegas in this pack, so the rank is a sore subject." She hugged me again. "Come on, let's get this over with," she said and headed into my closet.

We spent the rest of the time packing, mostly in silence, breaking it occasionally to discuss whether I should take a certain item or not. I just had to pack what I would need in the next couple of days for now. Louise said that they would likely send a couple of Omegas to pack and move the rest of my stuff this week. It wasn't long before we had almost everything that I needed packed. I was getting a headache because Colton was trying to mind-link with me, and I was avoiding it, which was something that would have normally been impossible. The higher the rank, the more powerful your wolf is and the easier it is for you to overpower the lower ranks. I put my success at blocking it out to Maia being back asleep or something. My mum eventually came upstairs and told me she had received a mind link from Colton to tell me that dinner was ready in half an hour, and he expected me to be there. Louise rolled her eyes and said she had received the same link from her father.

I knew that named ranks had a tradition of eating together at most meals, and then Wednesday evenings were when the pack had its weekly meeting, followed by dinner in the great hall. It was voluntary for all, apart from omegas, who were often expected to work it or not entitled to go. But my dad always insisted on us going. I always found it a nice community event, and we sometimes got away with sneaking Katie in with us. But now, I suspect I would be at the top table for these events, and that was terrifying.

My mum looked over at my suitcase, which was now packed and waiting by the door, and smiled at me with tears in her eyes.

"My baby girl is all grown up," she said, hugging me. "I am going to miss our movie nights."

"Mum, I'm going to the pack house, not another country," I said, trying to wiggle out of her grip, "but if you want me to stay then-" My mum let go of me, cutting me off.

"No, of course not!" she exclaimed. "Your place is there now, with your Beta mate," she beamed proudly. "Oh, I can't wait to tell Susie when she phones later," she went on. My sister phoned every Sunday to update us on things in her life; especially now she was expecting her first pup.

We were stopped in our discussion by shouting downstairs. The door to the study must have opened, and Tommy was shouting at my father.

"I can't believe you really don't care, do you?" Tommy shouted. "As long as you get your cut, ain't that right, big brother?"

"I think you better leave." My father sounded just as angry.

"My pleasure." We heard footsteps as Tommy headed towards the door

"And don't come back. You aren't welcome in this family until you start showing respect."

"Whatever!" The door slammed shut. I put my hand over my mouth in shock.

"Oh my goddess!" I exclaimed. "Did dad just banish Tommy from the family?"

My mum shook her head. "Don't worry about it. They will both calm down soon, and they will be okay." She seemed so sure of it. I knew my dad and uncle argued but had never heard it this bad before.

I heard a sound on the steps, and shortly after, my dad popped his head in the door.

"Are you ready to go, pumpkin?" he asked. "I have an obviously lovesick Beta in my head demanding his mate."

I sighed. I guess I couldn't put this off any longer. My dad picked up my suitcase, and Louise and I grabbed a smaller bag each, and we headed downstairs to Louise's car. Both my parents gave me hugs and told me they were proud of me before getting into the car.

Louise sat in the driver's seat and looked at me with sympathy. "Are you ready?" she asked.

"No," I said, and she smiled weakly and squeezed my hand. I nodded to her, and she started the car and pulled away from my now former home. I looked in the side mirror, determined not to cry as we turned off the street, and I lost sight of my happily waving parents.

CHAPTER 9

Harper

Driving up towards the pack house felt a lot more daunting than it did 24 hours ago. It's hard to think that this time yesterday, I was so excited for the ball and finding my mate. And since then, so much has happened.

The house wasn't lit up like last night. Most of it was dark. This gave it an eerie feeling. As we drove over, Louise explained the basic layout. The ground floor was where the great hall was, as well as a pack's common area and a couple of spare offices. The 1st floor was all the main offices and where the majority of the pack businesses were run from, then the 2nd floor had the entertainment centre and gym which was strictly for named and high ranked as well as important visiting guests, who also stayed on the 2nd floor. The third floor was shared by the Beta and Gamma families. The top floor was the Alpha family living quarters, and the named ranked private dining room, where we would have almost all our meals. And then the live-in Omega quarters were in the basement with the laundry and other housekeeping rooms.

The grounds housed the pool house with the indoor pool. That and the surrounding gardens were private to named rank only. The rest of the grounds were open access to the pack. I was aware of the private pool and gardens, but had never seen them. Louise could have invited me in as my father was a higher rank than most pack members, but she was never allowed to bring Katie, so we decided to find somewhere more inclusive and less snobbish when we hung out together.

We pulled into Louise's parking space, and I had just about managed to unclip my seat belt when my door was pulled open, and Colton was reaching in to pull me out. I yipped accidentally as he pushed me against the car, buried his head in my hair, and took a breath.
"You took way too long," he growled, sending shivers down my spine. I tensed up, not sure what to do with this sudden display of affection. I glanced over at Louise and saw that Damien and Alex, Louise's older brother and Gamma heir, were also standing there grinning and witnessing this embarrassing moment.

Colton lifted his head, and his eyes were the full gold of his wolf, and he grinned at me. He grabbed my hand and started pulling me towards the house.
"Colton!" I exclaimed. "My things." I tried to turn back towards the car, but Colton kept dragging me towards the house.
"Leave them. Someone will bring them in," he snapped and kept dragging me along. He was taller than me, and his legs were longer, and I couldn't keep up with his pace and ended up tripping up over my own feet, running to keep up.
"Ow!" I exclaimed. "Colton, you're going too fast."
He growled again and turned and grabbed my arm. I assumed he was helping me up, but the second I was on my feet, Colton grabbed my waist, lifted me up and over his shoulder, and carried me into the house. The last I saw before we were inside was Damien and Alex doubled over laughing and Louise grimacing.

"Colton, put me down!" I cried, and he grunted in response and carried on up the stairs to the third floor, taking two stairs at a time. Once on the floor, he headed down one hallway, and to add to the embarrassment, I heard his mother coming in the other direction.

"Colton, dinner is in ten minutes," she said. I mean, he was carrying a girl over his shoulder, and that was all she said.

"Yep, mum. We'll be there," he responded. I was even more mortified when I looked up from my not-so-flattering position to see his mother looking back at us with a huge smile on her face.

Colton slowed to a stop at the door about halfway down and threw the door open, and walked into a dark room. He kicked the door shut and hoisted me off his shoulder onto something soft, which I quickly realised was a bed. Crap! I was alone with Colton in his bedroom! My heart suddenly started beating as I tried to fumble myself to a sitting position. A lamp came on beside me, and before my eyes had adjusted, Colton was on the bed, pushing his body between my legs. I went to say something, anything, when his lips crashed into mine, and I fell back to the bed.

My mind was suddenly blank as his lips massaged mine and the sparks of the mate bond hit me full force. I couldn't help but respond, wrapping my arms around his neck, pulling him in closer to me, and I could tell he was obviously pleased with my reaction and pushed his tongue against my lips, I parted them, giving him access, and he responded with a brief grunt. The passionate kiss went on for what felt like hours, but was probably only minutes. My mind began to cloud over a little as I got lost in the kiss, either from the lack of oxygen or the lust-filled wolf that was excitedly yipping in my head.

Eventually, Colton pulled away with a lazy smile on his face. His eyes were still gold, but there was also some of the hazel coming through.

"Welcome home, Strawberries," he purred and leaned down, kissing my nose. "I really want to progress this, but my father will skin me alive if we are late for dinner." He leaned in for one more kiss before pulling away and climbing off the bed. He held out a hand, and I took it automatically. He pulled me up quickly, and I had to put my hand out to stop myself, crashing into him. He wrapped his arms around me and bent to kiss me again, just as I heard his father's voice in my head. I could tell by Colton's reaction that he was also in on the mind-link.

"Dinner now!" Colton rolled his eyes and then winked at me.

"To be continued," he let go of me, but grabbed my hand again and headed out of his room.

As we walked quickly through the halls, although at a slower rate than before, I actually got a closer look at the place. I had only ever seen the ground floor before, which could be compared to the look of a five-star hotel. For some reason, I assumed that the decadence would be toned down in the private levels, but it actually felt more elite. The walls had dark wood panels and heavily patterned beige wallpaper with gold metallic accents, and the floor had deep soft coffee coloured carpets. Various paintings and decor items were at different points, each looking more expensive than the last. As Colton opened a door on the top floor, light flooded, and it took a couple of seconds for my eyes to adjust.

The room was huge! There were several large windows, all dressed with super heavy and luxurious-looking curtains in dark blue, and the walls were a powder blue. There was a large dining table in the middle of the room, which was already mostly filled with seated werewolves. I stuttered to a stop as we walked into the room, suddenly feeling really shy. Colton chuckled at my hesitation and began to rub circles on my hand with his thumb. I realised he had done this several times over the last couple of days, and each time, it had relaxed my nerves almost instantly.

I could feel the eyes of everyone in the room on us as he stood and stared into my eyes. He smiled, and my heart skipped a beat at the adoring look in his eyes.

"You okay, Strawberries?" he asked, and I smiled and nodded. "Good," he said as he turned and pulled me around the table into a seat next to Louise while he sat on the other side of me.

"Nice of you to join us," his dad, who was sitting next to him and at one head of the table, said. He scowled at Colton, but then smiled when his eyes turned on me.

"Ah, leave them be, Eric," said the Alpha, who sat at the other head of the table. Damien was on one side and the Luna on the other side. "You remember what it is like to find your mate, don't you?" The Beta inclined his head at the Alpha and then smiled at his wife, who was sitting opposite Colton. The Gamma fake coughed before speaking.

"Well..." He smiled at me, although it didn't reach his eyes. "It is a pleasure to have you as part of the family, Harper." I nodded a thank you, scared to actually say anything in case it came out as a squeak. He was sitting in the middle of the long table opposite Alex. The only other people at the table were the Alpha's twin daughters and the Gamma's youngest son. The one absence was the Gamma's former wife, who had left around six years ago. I had only just started being friends with Louise at the time, but remembered how much her mother abandoning the whole family had been on her.

The rooms suddenly filled with amazing smells as a door I hadn't seen opened, and four servers came into the room carrying food. I watched as plates were placed in front of the Alpha, Luna, Beta, and Gamma before leaving again and reappearing with more food. It wasn't long before a roast chicken dinner with all the trimmings was placed in front of me. The room lapsed into silence as everyone began eating. At some point during the meal, the wine glasses were swapped out for champagne glasses filled with sparkling bubbles. The Alpha stood up, holding his glass and everyone stopped to listen to him.

"I just wanted to take this time to officially welcome Harper to the family. May the moon goddess shine her blessings on you both." He raised his glass. "To the future Beta and Mrs Stokes." Everyone raised their glasses.

The Beta chuckled, "The far future Beta, I'm not ready to give up that title just yet, son." Colton frowned at him.

"Not planning on retiring yet then, dad," he said, grinning. "Spend your golden years with mum and all." Even I could tell the underlying message. Colton wanted the Beta title, and by the look on Damien's face, he wanted the Alpha title too. The Alpha laughed, which only infuriated Damien more, and the Beta inclined his head towards me.

"You can always get started on producing that heir, son. It'd strengthen your position when you claim it." I was taking a drink of the champagne at the time and almost spit it out everywhere, but still choking on it in the process. Everyone looked at me as I went bright red. I'd not even thought about pups, and as a named rank, Colton would be expected to have at least one heir. I was going more and more red just thinking about it. The Alpha laughed again, and the Gamma joined in while Colton rubbed my back.

He leaned in close and whispered, "And I want a big family, Strawberries." He kissed my neck, my stomach flipping in response. He leaned back in his chair, a satisfied smirk on his face, and his hand caressed my thigh under the table.

"Give the poor lass a minute to get settled in, maybe," the Gamma said, smiling sympathetically at me.

"Yeah, or three years or so, at least," Louise muttered, and Colton's head snapped up.

"What do you mean, three years?" he asked, the smile dropping from his face.

"That's how long university is, dumbass," she said, and Colton growled, and his hand tightened on my thigh.

"Oh, you got a university place?" The Beta asked happily.

I nodded. "Yes, sir."

"And what are you studying?" the Alpha asked. I was suddenly aware of two things. First, all eyes were on me, which made me want to hide. And second, for some reason, Colton was furious.

"Erm.." I was feeling more and more nervous as his hand gripped my thigh. "Childcare, Alpha sir." He nodded, impressed.

"No!" Colton said, and I turned and looked at him in horror. That one word held so much fury. "I do not give you permission."

CHAPTER 10

Harper

"What?" I ask in disbelief. Did I just hear Colton tell me I wasn't allowed to go to university?

"I said no!" he growled. "And that's final."

"Whoa!" Louise exclaimed. "She's your mate, not your property, and she has been working for this for years." She was getting angry, and so was Colton. The pressure of being sat between the two was almost unbearable.

"If you are worried about me going away, then I got accepted at Leeds University. It's only an hour's drive from here, and I was planning on travelling to and from every day, anyway." I smiled at him, hoping to smooth his fury. He just glared at me and tightened his hand on my thigh until his fingers dug in, and I winced with the pain. He leaned in close to me as I felt tears line my eyes.

"I said no!" he said slowly over pronouncing every word. A tear fell down my cheek, and he wiped it away with his other hand before leaning in and kissing my cheek. I lowered my head, trying not to let the other tears fall, knowing that everyone was currently watching us. Colton, finally satisfied, leaned back in his chair.

Everyone sat in awkward silence for a minute or so, and when I looked up, I met eyes with Colton's mum, who smiled sadly at me. Finally, the Beta coughed and smiled as if nothing had happened.

"Anyway, child, we thought that after you finished school, in what two weeks is it?" I nodded quickly. "Well, when you have finished there, then you could go and work with your father for a while, let him show you the ropes around the pack finances, so you are able to take over when he retires, that should give you plenty of time to start the next generation."

I felt sick! My whole life was being planned for me. I didn't want to work with my father. I wanted to study childcare and become a teacher.

"Well, before we even get to that, we have the announcement to arrange," the Luna said, and I stiffened. I saw Colton's mum perk up.

"Oh, of course," she chirped and then looked at me. "We will need to plan your dress and your makeup, of course." I looked between her and Colton, confused.

"I don't understand. What announcement?" There were chuckles around the room. Colton leaned in and kissed my cheek again. He moved his hand from my thigh and onto my back. I could feel his fingers trailing along the skin on my lower back as he slipped his hand in under my top.

Colton's mum smiled. "Why your engagement, of course. Eric dear, what was the timeline again?" The Beta grinned and leaned over to caress his wife's hand. I smiled at the obvious love in their eyes. I glanced at Colton, who was watching them too. He saw me looking and smiled and leaned in again, pulling me closer to him. His nose rubbed my neck, and I felt tingles running through me.

"I believe we agreed upon an official announcement at the pack meeting on Wednesday and then the engagement party on Saturday," the Beta said to his wife and then turned to us. "So I suggest that you have your public official, unofficial date tomorrow evening." I started to feel overwhelmed. There seemed to be a lot going on, and I was feeling very hot, and like I couldn't breathe. Everything started feeling like it was far away, and my eyes were blurring. Then I vaguely thought I had heard my name but couldn't tell where from. Everything started to move, and I was beginning to panic.

I felt hands on me, and everything was getting darker until it all faded to black and silence.

When I woke up, I was laid on a soft bed. Even before I opened my eyes, I could feel Colton laid next to me stroking my arm, the sparks travelling up and down following his fingers. I opened my eyes and saw that he held his head up with one hand and watched me. My eyes met his, and he smiled.

"Well, hello there, Strawberries," he cooed, leaning in and grazing his lips against mine. "You gave everyone quite the scare." At this point, I noticed we weren't alone in the room, and I looked around. Louise was sitting on the end of the bed, and the Luna and Colton's mum were standing at the end. Lastly, Doctor Roberts stood next to the bed, looking down at me and smiling kindly.

"Hello, Harper dear," he said gently. "Do you feel like you can sit up?" I nodded, and with the help of Colton, I got myself into a seated position against the headboard. I was able to see the room from my new position.

Much like the rest of the pack house, it looked like a room from a luxury hotel. The bed I was on looked to be a king-size four-poster bed with a deep red cover that looked to have gold threads sewn into it in an elaborate oriental style. The walls were a dusky pink with a subtle gold mottled effect, and the curtains, which were currently closed, were the same deep red and gold pattern as the bedding. All the furniture looked to be dark wood with an antique style, and there was a sofa in the same dark red which pointed towards a wall with a big television on it. There were two doors, one which was open and looked to be a bathroom. And the second one was closed, which I assumed led into the hallway. I could see that my suitcase and things were by that door. So I guessed that this was probably my room, or at least my temporary room.

The doctor examined me, looking in my ears and eyes, and doing all the usual things doctors did. He asked questions, like when I last ate, had I fainted before, could I be pregnant? Despite only losing my virginity yesterday, I still panicked on that last question. Everyone being werewolves meant that they embarrassingly heard my pulse quicken, and the doctor pushed for more information.

"When was the last time you had sex?" the Doctor asked, and my skin flushed, and I glanced at Colton. It was enough for Colton to chuckle, and he answered the doctor.

"It was last night, doc," he said, a tint of pride in his voice. I just flushed even redder since his mum and the Luna were both listening.

The doctor clicked his tongue and nodded. "Okay, and before that?" Everyone looked at me, and I kind of shrunk into myself.

I shook my head and whispered, "Never."

The doctor smiled. "Well, we can rule out pregnancy as the cause," he said. "That's not to say you're not pregnant if it was unprotected," he mused to himself. "Make an appointment with me in two weeks, and we will do some tests and discuss contraceptive options. They are limited for werewolves but available." I nodded quickly, hoping he would get off this conversation sometime soon.

I got my wish when he turned to Colton's mum and the Luna.

"I think we just have a case of overwhelm, mixed with the weakening that the rejection and subsequent actions caused to her wolf." Both the Luna and Colton's mum shot a disapproving look at Colton when he said that.

"Plenty of rest and fluids until her wolf fully heals, and I believe the fainting will be an isolated incident." He looked back at me and smiled. "I will check on you next week just to make sure, but for safety, no shifting, okay?" and I nodded my head again.

The doctor then excused himself, and the Luna saw him out. Colton's mum smiled at me.

"We have brought everything from the car to your room, dear. Make yourself at home. And there is a set of keys for you on the dresser." She then tapped Louise on the shoulder and headed for the door. Louise smiled at me and patted my leg.

"Get some rest," she said, and then glared at Colton before leaving the room and closing the door.

Colton nuzzled against my neck, whispering, "Finally, we are alone." I didn't know why, but his tone sent shivers straight down to my lower region, and I fought to keep my breathing even. Colton pulled my face to him and grazed his lips against mine again before adding pressure and pushing his tongue into my mouth. My body responded to him by instinct, and he used it to pull me back to a laying down position. He laid beside me, and his free hand that wasn't holding him up roamed my body. He slipped his hand under my top and into my bra and began palming my boob. The feel of his hands on my body felt so good and awakened a heat within me. I moaned into his mouth and felt him grin in response. He broke apart from the kiss and began kissing my neck while rubbing his pelvis against my leg. I could feel him hard in his pants as the scent of my excitement filled the room.

"Baby girl," he whispered against my neck. "I have been desperate to be alone with you all day." He rolled my nipple between his fingers and grazed his teeth against my neck at the same time. I couldn't help the moan that came out.

"That's it, baby girl," he grunted, and his hand left my bra and slipped into my pants.

Suddenly, memories from last night flooded my mind, and I froze. I started panicking and pulled away from Colton.

"Colton!" I cried, "I don't feel well."

"Oh, don't worry, Strawberries, I will make you feel real good real soon," he chuckled in my ear.

"No, Colton, stop!" I pushed him away from me, and he glared at me.

"What the hell, Harper?" he asked as I jumped off the bed.

"I'm too tired, and I don't feel well," I said and headed towards the door to let him out.

Before I knew what was happening, I was slammed against the wall, and Colton pushed himself against me.

"I didn't say you could walk away," he growled in my ear.

"Colton, please," I begged, and he leaned in.

"Let's get one thing straight right now, Strawberries," he hissed. "You belong to me. You are my mate, which means that you are mine, mind, body, and soul. And I will do whatever I want to what is mine, do you understand?" Before I could respond, there was a knock at the door. Colton growled before throwing the door open.

"What!" he growled. I glanced around to see Louise standing there.

"I thought I would help Harper settle in since the doctor told her to rest," she smiled sweetly at Colton, who just growled again.

"Fine," he said and opened the door wider. Louise came in, and Colton leaned into me. "Get some rest, Strawberries, because I will have you alone tomorrow night." He glanced at Louise before walking out through the door.

I took a deep breath and mouthed a thank you to Louise. She smiled and nodded. We quickly began our impromptu girls' night with movies and face masks.

I was just beginning to relax when a sudden wave of pain washed through my body. I cried out, unable to move. Louise looked at me in anger. But the anger wasn't at me. The anger was because she knew who was causing the pain and what he was doing to do so. I screamed again as more pain ripped through me. Louise pulled me into a hug as I spent the rest of the evening crying in pain.

CHAPTER 11

Harper

It was 2 am before I finally passed out from exhaustion. Louise had ended up staying with me all night as I screamed and cried in pain. At one point, she had gone storming down to Colton's room, but it was empty.

Eventually, Louise had called Beta Stokes, who I remember briefly glaring at me in disgust before storming out again. Mrs Stokes assured me that it was Colton he was angry at, not me. Doctor Roberts arrived after that and injected something into me. The pain was still there, but it was like I didn't care about it anymore. That was when I could pass out into blissful unconsciousness.

The next morning, I was woken by a knock at the bedroom door. I stumbled over to answer and found Louise on the other side. She had slipped out an hour or so ago to get ready for school. I pulled her into the room quickly, not wanting to see anyone.

"Give me ten minutes to get ready," I said and grabbed some fresh underwear from my suitcase.

"Are you being serious?" she asked, and I turned to see her looking at me with shock. "You went through hell last night. I think you can take the day off." I shook my head in response.

"I'm fine, honestly," I said, disappearing into the bathroom before she could say another word. Truth be told, I didn't want to spend any more time in the pack house than I had to. And after last night, I didn't want to run into Colton alone any sooner than was required.

I quickly showered and brushed my teeth. I applied some light makeup, mainly in an attempt to cover the bags under my eyes, and then headed out into the bedroom. Louise had got out my school uniform, which consisted of a silver, grey, and black plaid skirt, a white blouse, and a silver and black tie. The main school jumper was a mid-grey, but we had black ones since we were sixth formers. I dressed and put my hair into a French braid and then checked my appearance in the full-length mirror. I noticed the glint of the ring on my finger. Screwing my face in annoyance, I pulled the ring off my finger and put it in the bedside table drawer.

Louise quirked her eyebrow at me, and I shrugged. I didn't think it was appropriate school wear after all. I grabbed my schoolbag, and we headed up to the dining room, where I could already smell the sweet smell of bacon and coffee. We walked into the dining room to see the Alpha, the Beta, and Mrs Stokes all sitting at one end of the table. While, to my dismay, Colton was sitting at the other end with Damien and Alex. I glanced at Louise as I saw him, and she grabbed my hand and squeezed it in support. I felt Colton's eyes on me as we walked down the other side of the table, sitting in the middle. Louise put herself closest to the boys in a symbolic protective position. I kept my eyes down at the table in order to avoid Colton's stare.

Louise got us both a coffee and helped herself to breakfast while I suddenly felt sick, so I contented myself with taking sips of my coffee.

"Harper, dear," the Alpha said, "How was your first night in the pack house? I trust your room is comfortable." I glanced up and tried not to cry as I heard sniggers down the other end of the table. I didn't know how to answer his question, but I didn't have to, luckily.

"Well, she might have had a better night if she wasn't in horrible pain all night," Louise answered, while glaring at Colton. I saw Mrs Stokes also glare down the table and Beta Stokes watching me, his face expressionless.

"Am I missing something?" The Alpha asked, looking around the table. I noticed Beta Stokes mind linking him with the glazed-over look and saw the Alpha's smile disappear. Glancing down at the other end of the table, the boys had all gone quiet and looked uneasy.

The Alpha came out of the link and glared down the table.

"What have I told you about screwing the staff?" he spat. I shrunk back into my seat as his Alpha aura leaked into the room, making me want to submit even when I wasn't the object of his anger.

"If you want to act like children, you will be treated like children. Colton, there will be no more of this disgusting behaviour. You have a fiancee now, and you have a responsibility to her."

"Are you sure about that, dad?" Damien retorted, smirking at me. "I don't see a ring on her finger."

I glanced up in time to see Colton glance at my hands, and fury crossed his eyes. I pulled my hand under the table and focused on the tablecloth in front of me. I heard his chair scrape back, and he stormed out of the room. Everyone watched him go, and Damien and Alex looked at each other before bursting into laughter.

"I also think it is time you start looking for a mate yourself Damien," the Alpha said, still glaring, and Damien stopped laughing. "If you think I am going to allow you to take the Alpha role without a responsible woman behind you, then you can think again, boy." I looked up to see Damien glaring at me. Great, my future Alpha was going to hate me now.

"Don't look at her son," the Alpha snapped. "It is me speaking to you. Did you understand what I said?"

"Yes, Alpha," Damien growled, and I could still feel his eyes on me.

"Good, and I will see all three of you boys in my office by 10am." The Alpha stood up, walked around, and placed his hand on my shoulder.

"I apologise for the boys in this family. Hopefully, a good mate such as yourself can put some sense into that boy, and it will leak out to the imbeciles who are meant to be the leaders of this pack one day, so help me, goddess."

I smiled and nodded. "Thank you, Alpha," I said.

"Please, while we are in a private company, call me Daniel." His smile reached his eyes as they crinkled in the corner. "I will ensure that Colton puts extra effort in for your date tonight." With that, he walked out of the room.

Louise glanced at me and mentioned the time, so I finished my coffee quickly, and we also headed out of the room to leave for school. We were halfway down the hallway when I felt a hand on my arm, and I was pulled into a room with a yelp. The door was slammed shut, and I was pushed against it. I looked up to see Colton grinning at me. I barely opened my mouth to tell him to let me go when he crashed his lips to mine and pushed his tongue straight in. His hands started running up and down my sides as he pushed his body, with his very obviously excited state, against me.

One hand stroked down my leg and then pushed back up under my skirt and along my inner thigh. I tried to squirm away as his fingers brushed against my panties. I managed to break the kiss and push him away.

"What the hell, Colton?" I shouted.

"What the hell?" he asked, his eyebrows raised. "What the hell? You are my mate, and you have responsibilities to perform. Didn't you hear the Alpha?" he sneered.

"I think that was directed at you," I said, and he growled menacingly at me.

"Well, my dear, Sweet Strawberries, if you performed your responsibilities, I wouldn't have had to find mine elsewhere?" I looked at him in disbelief, tears falling from my eyes. I felt awful. How was this my life? How was I expected to continue like this? Your mate was meant to love you and cherish you, not reject you and betray you.

Colton's eyes softened, and he moved close again.
"Hey, hey," he said softly, and I flinched as he moved to lift my chin with his hand. I closed my eyes as he tried to make eye contact with me.
"Baby girl, look at me, please," he said and cupped my face in one hand and wiped away the still falling tears with his thumb. I knew he caused my tears, but the stupid bond had me leaning into his hand and welcoming the comfort.
"Come on, baby, please open your eyes." I complied, knowing that they would look glassy from the wetness and the blue-grey.
"There she is," he cooed and wiped away more tears. "I'm sorry, Strawberries. I didn't mean to do it. I'm just not used to having my mate, but that is no excuse for the behaviour or causing you this horrible pain," he said. "Could you please forgive me?"

Colton had such a sad, sincere look in his eyes, and I nodded before I even thought about it. Did I forgive him? Then his face lit up, and he smiled.
"Aw, Strawberries, whatever did I do to deserve such a beautiful angel for my mate?" He leaned in and grazed my lips gently, as if he was asking for permission, and I couldn't help but melt into the kiss this time. I wrapped my arms around his neck as he pulled me in tightly against his body and explored my mouth with his tongue.

He pushed me against the door again as he deepened the kiss and began caressing my hips with his hands again. I pushed my pelvis against him, and he groaned into my mouth and responded by grinding himself against me. I was deep into the kiss when there was a knock on the door, and I yelped in surprise.
"Erm Harper, we are gonna be late for school." Louise's voice floated in from the other side, and I quietly groaned and pulled myself away from the kiss.
"To be continued, Strawberries," Colton purred into my ear while nuzzling my neck. He pulled away, and I moved to open the door while straightening my skirt. Before I could open the door, though, Colton grabbed my hand.

"By the way," he said, "You forgot something." Then he slipped my engagement ring onto my finger. I glanced at him quickly, suddenly feeling guilty. "Do not let me see you take this off your finger again. Do you understand, Strawberries?" His stare was so intense that I nodded.

"Yes, Colton," I whispered, and he smiled and bent to kiss me on the cheek

"Good," he whispered in my ear. "Because I want everybody to know that you are mine!" he ended with a growl, sending shivers through me.

He moved away, and I fumbled with the door handle, finally getting it open and rushing through.

"Have a good day at school, dear," Colton called after me. "Oh, and Strawberries?" I glanced back at him. "I am looking forward to our date tonight," he said with a wide grin that looked like he wanted to eat me.

I nodded quickly and found Louise at the end of the hall, and, ignoring her raised eyebrows, we headed off to school.

CHAPTER 12

Harper

The ride to school was uncomfortable. I could tell that Louise wanted to say something. Most likely about how I was acting with Colton. We made it almost the entire way before Louise finally broke the silence.

"I'm sorry!" she burst out. Here we go, I thought.

"What the hell, Harper?" She glanced at me briefly before returning her eyes to the road.

"Please don't, Louise," I pleaded. I really didn't want to get into an argument on the patriarchy with Louise, certainly not when I felt as crappy as I did right now.

"Harper, how can you forgive him so easily?" she said. "Last night you were in so much pain that you practically had to be sedated, and all because he couldn't keep it in his pants and cheated on you."

"Well, I mean, technically, nobody knows we are even together yet. So does it count as cheating if we aren't official?" I was mostly musing to myself, but didn't miss the open-mouthed look that Louise had given me.

"Yes!" she exclaimed. "The second he put that ring on your finger and you accepted him, you were together, and he was cheating." Did I accept him? I thought to myself. I'm not sure I actually did. I just felt like I was going with the flow or being pushed down the flow. Is the lack of a refusal enough of an acceptance?

I glanced at Louise and shrugged. "Honestly, Louise, I don't know what is going on," I said, feeling the overwhelming despair fill my stomach with dread. "Two days ago, I was excited about going to the ball, and a fresh eighteen-year-old with romantic ideas forming in my head." I glanced at her and saw that her expression had softened. "And since then, I have found my fated mate, lost my virginity, been rejected, suffered mate bond betrayal pain more than once, got engaged, and moved out of my childhood home." Gosh, after saying it like that, I really had been through a lot.

"Oh, and the future I planned and worked so hard for is now shattered and replaced. Now, I'm becoming a pup factory and working in finance." I screwed my face at that. I hated Maths at school.

"Exactly," Louise said. "Colton is a class A dick, yet when you came out of the room just now, you looked at him with complete adoration in your eyes." I sighed because I knew she was right.

"I don't know, Louise." I felt so defeated. "I know what he is like, probably more than anyone right now. He is controlling and has a mean streak, and honestly, half the time, he scares me." I saw her frown. "But then something happens, and I don't know if it is the mate bond or something, but when he is being nice and caring, I wonder if he really does love me, and he is just struggling with all this too." I already knew what I was saying and how bad it sounded, and I watched Louise's face as she parked her car in the exclusive car park. She stayed silent, but her lips were in a thin line, and I knew she had a lot to say.

Once she had parked the car and turned off the engine, she turned to face me.

"Harper, I'm not going to lie. I'm really worried about you," she said, taking my hand, and I nodded as a few stray tears slipped down my cheek. "And I really fucking hate this mate bond crap. It is so demeaning." I glanced at her, knowing that she was struggling with her own mate bond issue, although she didn't know I knew.

"It's not all bad," I said, trying to reassure her. "The sex is amazing." I shrugged, and she laughed.

"Oh, please," she said. "You've had sex with one person, once. You hardly have a basis for comparison." I went bright red.

"Well, I enjoyed it." I lowered my eyes. "Well, until the rejection part." Tears slipped down my cheeks again.

I turned to face Louise fully. "It'll be ok, won't it?" I asked. "This is just a lot for both of us to get used to. Once Colton gets used to the idea, it will all be fine, right?" Louise smiled sadly and pulled me into a hug.

"Whatever happens, you still have me," she said, and I smiled into her shoulder. We finally pulled apart after I heard tapping on the window.

I looked up to see Katie standing there, looking nervous. I glanced at Louise, who smiled, and I jumped out of the car and pulled Katie into a hug. She hugged me back and started crying.

"Oh my goddess Harper, I am such a dick," she cried. "I can't believe I let my stupid petty issues get in the way when you needed your friends." I pulled away and saw she had tears streaming down her face. "Will you ever forgive me?" she said, and I laughed.

"Don't be silly," I said, wiping her tears away. "There is nothing to forgive." We hugged again. I glanced at Louise, who stood smiling at us, held out my hand, and pulled her into the hug.

The school bell rang, and we pulled apart, giggling and heading to registration. I walked happily, for now at least, with my two best friends.

"Oh," Katie said as we sat down in our usual seats. "Just a quick warning, Donna is on the warpath," she lowered to a whisper. "There is a rumour going around that Colton is off the market, and she is not happy about it." I cringed at this. Donna Tobbins was the school's Queen B, and she had a big thing for a named ranked position. Everyone knew Damien hated her after she cheated on him a couple of summers ago, so she had set her sights on Colton to get the ranking she felt she deserved.

"Do the rumours name me?" I asked. I knew that by the end of tonight, everyone would know. That was the point of the official unofficial date. To be seen in public together as a couple before the official announcement on Wednesday.

Katie shook her head. "No, but that rock on your finger might get some comments," she said, and I instantly shoved my hand under the table.

"Just take it off until after school," Louise said. "Not that I care about dirty Donna. I'll deal with her if she says anything." Katie grinned, and I smiled at Louise's fiercely protective attitude.

"I do think it would be a good idea to take it off," Katie said, and I nodded in agreement. Both girls looked at me like they were waiting for something.

"What?" I asked, confused, and Louise gave me a funny look.

"If you don't want to take off the ring, that is okay. You know that, right?" she said, her voice hesitant.

"No, I agree it would be better not to wear it, at least for today," I said and smiled. They both glanced at each other and wore almost identical concerned expressions.

"What is wrong with you two?" I laughed. "You are making me nervous."

"Harper, sweetie," Katie said, her tone careful. "Are you going to take the ring off?" I looked at her funnily. What was this obsession with taking the ring off? I had already said that I planned on doing so.

"Yeah," I said. "I already said twice I was going to. Geez, what is wrong with you two?" I rolled my eyes.

"Then take it off?" Louise asked, her tone flat.

Oh! I realised that I hadn't taken it off yet. I laughed nervously as I fiddled with the ring.

"I get you now. I must have spaced," I said and laughed again.

"Now, Harper," Louise said

"Huh?" I was confused again. "Now, what?"

"The ring, Harper. You said you wanted to take it off." Katie looked worried. "So, take it off now before everyone starts coming into the room." I looked at her and laughed. I was starting to feel a horrible feeling in the pit of my stomach. Something wasn't right.

"Harper, can you take the ring off?" Louise asked, and I looked at her worriedly. Of course, I could take the ring off, I thought to myself. Then why hadn't I? I fingered the ring with my other hand. All I had to do was slide the ring up my finger. Such a simple action, and yet it seemed to escape me. Then I remembered the conversation with Colton earlier this morning, where he had told me not to take off the ring. It was proof that I was his. Then it hit me what had happened.

I looked at the girls in horror. "I can't take it off," I said. Katie looked confused, and Louise looked sad. "Colton commanded me to keep it on."

CHAPTER 13

Harper

Katie gasped, and Louise had a disgusted look on her face. I glanced at the ring and felt sick. Colton had not only commanded me so easily; I didn't even know he had done it. Could I really trust him if he could hold that much power over me and use it so easily?

I didn't have too much longer to think about it as the gratingly high-pitched voice of Donna floated into the room, and she and her vapid fangirls walked in. She was ranting about the rumour and was declaring loudly that she would find the girl, although she didn't use that term and would make sure she disappeared for good. Donna was your typical bleached blond hair and fake-tanned stereotyped mean girl in all the teen movies. Her father was the pack's business manager, which afforded them a higher ranking among the pack, but everyone knew that wasn't enough for the spiteful, self-proclaimed princess.

She looked over at us and began stalking over, and I shrunk in my seat involuntarily. Did she know? Was she coming to make me disappear?

"Hey Louise," she started, and I breathed a sigh of relief and glanced at Katie, who giggled nervously. "You are looking great today. Did you do something with your hair?" Louise rolled her eyes at the fake compliment.

"Cut the crap, Donna," she scowled at her. "What do you want?" Donna smirked.

"There's a rumour going around that Colton is seeing someone, and it's serious." She glanced at me, and I looked away to avoid eye contact. "You live with him. Is it true?" Louise just shrugged like she was bored, but I could see the tension in her spine.

"Maybe. Why would I tell you?"

"I heard from Johnny that whoever the bitch is that she moved in yesterday," one of Queen B's fangirls spat in disgust, and Donna turned on her.

"What?" she shrieked and then turned back to Louise. "That means you will have met her." Louise glanced at me and shrugged again.

"If I had, I still wouldn't tell you anything," she said. I admired how calm and collected she was. I wanted to run and hide. "Now, run along and find someone else to bother." She waved her hand at Donna, who looked like she wanted to rip Louise's hair out. She was about to say something when Mr Henderson came in.

"Donna and girls to your seats, please," he said, and she began to argue, but he interjected, "Or I can have a note sent to the Alpha again." She immediately shut up, and with one last glare at Louise, she slunk away to the other side of the room. I knew she had been in trouble with the Alpha in more than one instance. She tried to rule the school by throwing her high ranking around. The big issue with this being that the school was a mixed school, and other than registration and Physical Education every afternoon, we mixed in with the humans in town. Mr Henderson was one of four teachers in school that were pack members and the school headmaster Mrs Gration who ensured that the rest of the town didn't know they were sharing it with werewolves. And all four pack teachers were also elite warriors for the pack and in charge of teaching the pack students how to fight. That was why it was mandatory for us to be in school until eighteen to get the required physical training.

Mr Henderson started taking registration, and when my name was called, I looked up and met Mr Henderson's eyes, and confirmed my attendance. He held my eyes briefly and then nodded his head to indicate he knew exactly who I was. I would soon be a named ranked member of the pack, which meant that my safety would fall under the elite warriors. Currently, Mr Henderson handled Louise's safety, and his nod just indicated that he was now responsible for mine. I glanced at Louise, and she smiled. She had caught the signal. Unfortunately, so had Donna, and I looked round to see her eyes narrowed at me.

After registration, everyone went to their individual classes, but Mr Henderson stopped me before leaving.
"Miss Kirby, can you stay back, please?" he asked as we began to file out. "Miss Bennet, you can stay too." We looked at each other and said bye to Katie as she left without us. When the class had filed out, Mr Henderson closed the door and smiled at me.
"Miss Kirby, I just wanted to say that it will be a pleasure to act as your guard, and if you have any concerns at all, please come to me."
I smiled politely, feeling a little awkward. "Thank you, Mr Henderson," I said, and he nodded.
"I was in school and trained with your uncle, so if you need any further assurance about my capabilities, I am sure he will tell you how I readily kicked his ass on numerous occasions." He grinned a bright grin that I couldn't help but return. "Also, I know we have two weeks left in school, but please, feel free to call me Greg." Once school was over, Mr Henderson, or Greg, would also leave school and continue, as Louise's and I guess, my private guard.
"One more thing before I let you girls go off to class." He picked a sheet of paper from his folder and passed it to me. "There have been a few changes to your class schedule."
"What?" I looked down at the revised timetable and saw that my classes had changed. All of my childcare-related ones had been stripped out and replaced with Political Science and Business Finance. I looked up at Louise, who took the sheet off me and hissed.
"Son of a bitch!" she swore. I knew exactly who had changed my classes. "I'm sorry, sweetie," Louise said, passing me the sheet back. "At least we have more classes together," she said, trying to find the bright side, I guess. I just wanted to cry.

"There are only two weeks left. Why change them now?" I asked in despair. Although, I knew exactly why. Political Science was actually Pack Politics and was taught by the Beta. All the named ranked kids and some of the high-ranked ones were required to take it. And Business Finances had never been taught in school before. I had my suspicions over who the teacher was, and it was gonna be confirmed as that was my first class of the day.

"Sorry, it's Alpha's orders," Greg said, although I knew full well this was Colton's doing. We left class, and I hugged Louise before heading to my first new class.

I walked into the classroom, which was empty, except for one person. I closed the door, and he looked up from the laptop in front of him and smiled.

"Hi, Dad," I said sadly, and he smiled sympathetically

"Aw, Pumpkin. Don't be like that," he said. "I know it's not what you want, but I promise it's important." I smiled weakly and sat down next to him as he went over the basics of the pack's finances.

By lunchtime, I was fed up. Political Science wasn't so bad, apart from the fact that Donna, who was also in the class, spent much of the class glaring at me. She was shamelessly flirting with the Beta when I walked in with Louise, and I could hear her trying to get information about his son's new girlfriend. The Beta looked up and smiled warmly at me, confirming her suspicions and hatred towards me.

At lunch, Louise, Katie, and I sat at a small table when Donna came stalking up and sat down opposite me and stared straight at me. I fidgeted uncomfortably under her piercing glare.

"Geez, Donna, take a picture. It'll last longer," Katie said.

"Shut the fuck up, runt," Donna shot back, and Katie cringed at the name. Donna and a few others in the pack considered the Omegas to be little more than servants and treated them awful.

"So, who would have thought that sweet little Harper would have had it in her, eh?" Donna asked as she glared at me and her fangirls, who were standing behind her, all sniggered. "Maybe it runs in the family. We all know what Tommy is like, and I had heard plenty about Susie being quick to spread her legs." I glared at her. My sister did have a few boyfriends before she met her fated mate, but she was by no means what Donna was suggesting. On the other hand, Tommy had a reputation that rivalled Colton's and Damien's for being a heartbreaker.

"Ha!" Louise laughed. "Talk about the pot calling the kettle black there, Donna," she said. "I distinctly remember you letting a few pack members climb between your legs. Including Harper's Uncle." I glanced at her when she said that, and the bitterness in her voice didn't go unnoticed elsewhere either. Donna growled at Louise, who just smirked.

"So what happened then, Harper? You turn eighteen, and your slut-o-metre kicked in?" Donna sneered at me. I went to take a drink and heard a gasp from behind Donna. She turned and looked, and I saw one of her fangirls staring at the ring on my finger. Oh shit! I had totally forgotten that it was there. Donna's eyes zeroed in on the rock, and I tried to pull my hand back, but she was quick and grabbed my hand in a vice grip.

"What the fuck is this?" she screeched. "Why are you wearing an engagement ring?" Half the lunchroom turned around in shock. The other half were werewolves and had probably already been listening in on the entire conversation.

"Donna, keep your bloody voice down, you idiot," Louise scolded, and Donna glared at her. Louise looked at me and mouthed sorry. She then lowered her voice to barely above a whisper. "And get your hands off your future Beta's mate before you get yourself into more trouble than even you can handle."

A gasp ran through the lunchroom, and a flurry of whispers started from the pack members who had heard everything. I went bright red as suddenly there was a lot of focused attention on me.

"No!" Donna hissed. "It's not true. Why would he pick you, of all people, as his mate?" She tightened her grip as I tried to pull my hand away. I wanted to get out of there before the tears that were threatening started.

"Look, she's about to start crying!" one of the girls behind Doona sneered. "How is she meant to be one of our leaders? She's so weak!"

Katie jumped up and slapped her, and everyone looked up, shocked.
"You call my friend weak again. I dare you!" The slap had been enough to distract Donna, and I pulled my hand away. I jumped up and grabbed my bag quickly. I needed to get out of here. I made it halfway down the hallway when I heard the lunchroom door slam open, and Donna yelled.

"Don't fucking walk away. I'm not done with you yet, you whore!" The next moment, I felt an impact and was thrown across the hallway and into some lockers. I landed on the floor in a painful pile. Before I could even comprehend what had happened, I felt a hand in my hair, and I was dragged up and slammed into the lockers again. Pain ran through my head as it hit the lockers full force, and I landed back on the floor, crying out.

"What the hell, Donna?" I heard Louise shout and looked up and saw enough to see that Louise and Katie were trying to get to us, but the fangirls and a couple of the pack boys that drooled over Donna, were blocking their way.

A shadow blocked the view, and I looked up to see Donna standing above me.

"Come on, you little slut," she sneered. "Fight back, or don't, and we can show Colton who really is the Alpha female here." I saw her hand curl into a fist and braced myself for the impact, but instead heard crashing and looked up and saw that Mr Henderson had Donna flat on the floor with his knee on her back.

"What the hell is going on here?" I cringed as I heard a bellow and saw the Beta standing at the end of the hallway.

CHAPTER 14

Harper

The Beta came stomping down the hallway, his authoritative aura surrounding him, making him appear even bigger than he already was.

"All of you out, unless you want to be involved in the punishment," he shouted at the students that were watching. They soon dispersed, and as soon as the block disappeared, Louise and Katie ran to me. I was trying to clear the blood that was pouring from a gash in my head out of my eyes, but it wasn't slowing. Louise pulled her jumper off and placed it over my head. My wolf was weak right now, so she wasn't able to heal me as quickly as she normally would.

The Beta got to me, took the jumper from Louise, and looked under and hissed. He then smiled at me.

"Just a scratch." I grinned, feeling a little woozy.

"I'm not sure I believe you on that," I said, and then covered my mouth with my hand. I had shown disrespect by not using his title and disagreeing with him in public. He just grinned and shook his head in amusement.

"I knew there was a spark of rebellion hiding in there somewhere." He gestured for Louise to take the jumper from him again. "You are going to be a fierce match for my son, just what he needs. No wonder the moon goddess paired you two." Despite myself and the pain I was in, I felt proud. There was a gasp from Donna, who I realised had not even thought of the fated mate bond being a factor. The Beta turned and growled at her. She still shrank back, even with Mr Henderson still holding her down.

"Louise..." The Beta turned back to us. "Could you take my future daughter-in-law to the office, please? We will be along shortly. And Katie, if you can go as well."

"Yes, Beta sir," they both said, and they each took hold of an arm and helped me stand up. I yelped as pain shot through the arm that Louise had a hold of, and she winced and moved to hold my side. The Beta saw this and turned to Mr Henderson.

"Greg, could you assist by transporting Miss Tobbins to the office, please?"

"Yes, sir," he said out loud, but I saw him lean in close to Donna. "Now maybe you're gonna get what you deserve," he growled, and I saw Donna whimper. I glanced at Louise, but she shrugged.

The Beta walked over to us and swooped me up off my feet, and started carrying me down the hallway.

"Come along, ladies," he said "Mr Henderson and Miss Tobbins will be along shortly." I glanced at his face and saw his eyes clear up from a mind link. I then heard a crack and a scream from down the hall. I glanced back to see Donna now standing but cradling her arm and looking terrified. I glanced at Louise and Katie, and they both had shocked wide-eyed expressions. There was obviously more to this than we all knew.

We had just got to the office, and the Beta had put me in a chair when I heard a car screeching outside and a door slamming. Only a minute later, Colton came smashing into the office, and his eyes fell on me. He ran straight to me and kneeled in front of me. He pulled Louise's jumper from my head, and I winced as part of it had dried to my head and ripped away.

Colton hissed when he saw what was underneath. He then gently took my hurting arm, and I cried out as pain shot up my arm again. He leaned his head down and kissed it ever so lightly, and I felt a flutter in my stomach.

The door swung open, and Mr Henderson all but dragged a crying Donna into the office. She appeared even worse for wear than when we had seen her a few moments ago. Colton growled and stood up. He grabbed her from Mr Henderson, lifted her by the throat, and slammed her into the wall, causing her to cry out.

"You dare to hurt my mate!" he screamed in her face. "You are fucking done in this pack, you and your whole fucking thieving family!" I glanced at the girls, and they were looking wide-eyed at Colton. I wasn't sure if it was because of what he just said or his very obvious display of protection of me.

"Colton," the Beta growled. "Put her down. The guards are here." Colton growled in her face one more time and then simply dropped her to the floor. She landed, and I noticed one of her ankles looked bigger than the other. It hit the floor, and she screamed and crumpled to the floor.

Colton came back to me and picked me up. His previous fury dissipated.

"Come on," he said. "Doctor Roberts is waiting for us at home." He nodded to his father and Greg, and then the girls, before walking out of the door. He made his way to the school exit. Once outside, I could see a red sleek sports car that he was heading to, and he opened the door and put me in the passenger seat. He put on my seatbelt, wincing as I cried out as my back hit the back of the car seat.

He closed my door once I was secured in and jumped in his side, and he set off back to the pack house. I was feeling dizzy again, and by the time we had got to the pack house, I felt like I was in very real danger of vomiting everywhere. Colton opened the car door and had to jump back as I did just that. I looked at the floor where I had thrown up and started crying all-out loud sobs.

"I'm so sorry," I cried. I felt like all I was doing was causing more mess and hassle. Maybe that girl was right when she said I was weak. Colton just smiled, eased me out of the car, and pulled me bridal style into his arms.

"Don't worry, baby," he said. "You have absolutely nothing to be sorry for." He kissed my forehead, and the sparks felt more comforting than arousing. I leaned my head against his shoulder as he carried me into the house. I thought I heard what sounded like a contented grumble from him, but it must have been the delirium from the bump to my head.

We got to my room, and Doctor Roberts was already waiting for us. Colton laid me gently on the bed and stepped back to let the doctor check me over.

"We have to stop meeting like this," the doctor said, and I giggled. Colton growled, and the doctor shrunk back a bit. I looked up at Colton and giggled again. It felt nice to see him being so protective over me. He looked at me and smiled a bright, adoring smile at me. It wasn't long before the doctor declared that I had a concussion, but thankfully nothing else was broken. He ordered bed rest and once again injected some sort of fast-acting miracle pain relief into my arm, and everything went all floaty.

After the doctor left, Colton disappeared for a moment and then came back with a bowl. He sat on the bed next to me and pulled a cloth from the bowl with steaming water. He cleaned the cut on my head, and I winced as the hot water touched it.

"Sorry, baby," he whispered every time I winced. "I just want to make sure you are clean before letting you rest." He worked lightly on my head and then pulled me to a sitting position before taking my jumper off and unbuttoning my blouse.

"What are you doing?" I asked as I tried to hold on to my blouse with my good arm.

"Calm down, Strawberries," he chuckled. "I just want to see your back so that I can clean it. Plus, you have blood all over your blouse." Oh, I felt a little silly as I let go of the blouse and let him finish opening it and undressing me. He pulled my skirt off, and I was left on the bed in my bra and panties.

He admired the sight for a couple of seconds and leaned over and kissed me.

"Even bloodied and battered, you are still the most beautiful person I have ever seen." I felt warmth spread through me from his comment.

"Baby, I need to turn you on to your front so I can see your back," he said, and I nodded as he slowly moved me around. I knew he was trying not to cause me pain, and I bit my lip to stop myself from crying out from the pain. Eventually, he got me on my front, leaned back, and hissed.

"I'm gonna fucking kill that skanky bitch," he growled, and I smiled to myself.

I felt the cloth once again across my back as he tended to those wounds. At some point, I felt my bra loosen as it was undone. The feel of the light touches of the cloth on my back lulled me into a deep sense of calm. And it didn't go unnoticed that Colton was leaving light kisses down my back. Every time I felt his lips on my skin, I shivered and felt a build-up in my lower regions. I felt the cloth graze the line of my panties just on the base of my back, followed by the feel of soft lips. I half gasped and half moaned. Colton groaned as the scent of my arousal filled the room. And I involuntarily lifted my hips against his lips.

"Baby," he whispered, his voice strained, and I felt his fingers graze my inner thigh. "Baby," Colton said again, his voice more croaked.

"Mmm," I sighed and lifted my hips again.

"Baby, tell me to stop if you don't want this." His fingers grazed the top of my thigh again, and I opened my legs to give him more access. Seeing this, he groaned and moved around the bed.

Colton positioned himself between my legs and ran his fingers along the outside of my panties. I moaned again as the feeling sent shivers through me. I felt a slight breeze as the cloth of my panties was moved to the side, and then I gasped as I felt Colton's fingers trace the outside before pushing through my lips.

He groaned as he felt how aroused I actually was.

"Fuck, baby, you are so wet." His fingers connected with my nub and slowly massaged it in circles. I pushed against his fingers, and he chuckled. I could feel the heat beginning to grow, and I hitched my pelvis towards him and then winced at the pain in my lower back. He pulled his hand away, and I moaned.

"Colton," I gasped, and he chuckled.

"Don't worry, Strawberries," he whispered. "I'm just gonna make you more comfortable." He flipped me onto my back. I cried out as pain radiated up my back again, but Colton quickly pushed my legs apart. He pushed the cloth on my panties aside again and pushed two fingers deep into me. My cries quickly switched from pain to pleasure, and I felt myself clench around his fingers, and he quickly pushed them in and out of me, each building upon the heated feeling that was taking over my body.

I felt his tongue circle my nub, and that was the final straw as I screamed as my body was overtaken with wave after wave of heated pleasure. Colton pulled his fingers free and gripped my hips, and latched his mouth on my mound as I bucked my hips to meet him. In the back of my mind, I could feel the pain in my body, but it was nothing compared to the pleasure that ravaged every never-ending. Colton kept on with the licking and the sucking as he prolonged my climax.

Eventually, I cried out, "Stop, please, it's too much!" He immediately stopped, and I collapsed back onto the bed, my body shivering with the aftershocks of what had just happened. Colton climbed up from the bed beside me and laid on his back, a grin on his face that rivalled the Cheshire cat. He swooped his arm under me and pulled me into him as I struggled to keep my eyes open.

"Rest Strawberries," he whispered and kissed the top of my head. "You can pay me back later when the painkillers aren't dulling your system." I snuggled down into his chest as his hand played along my back. My last thought before darkness consumed me was, if that was when my system was dulled, what would it have felt like without.

CHAPTER 15

Harper

I woke up in darkness. I was in bed, and I was alone. I moved to find my phone to get the time, and I hissed as pain radiated out through my body. It wasn't as bad as earlier. In fact, it was quite manageable. I fumbled on the bedside table for my phone when I realised I didn't remember even bringing my school bag home.

I pulled myself out of bed and made my way slowly towards where I remembered the bathroom was. I reckoned it was probably early hours in the morning from the dark of the room, although my tummy was making growling noises. Then again, I hadn't eaten since lunchtime, so no wonder I was hungry. I finally opened the bathroom door and was blinded by the bright light flooding in. I glanced at the window and saw that it was full daylight outside. Crap! How long did I sleep?

I quickly did what I needed and went to wash my hands. I stopped when I saw my reflection in the mirror. I looked paler than normal, apart from where the now-closed cut was on my forehead. Even though it was healing, it still had an angry red look and was surrounded by shades of black and purple. Well, makeup wasn't covering that anytime soon. Otherwise, my eyes had dark circles under them, and the rest of my skin looked sickly white. My grey-blue eyes looked dull and watery. I was wearing a t-shirt that didn't belong to me, and I think I vaguely remembered it being the one Colton was wearing when he brought me home from school. He must have put it on me after... well after... I thought back to the feel of Colton as he... a slow blush crept up onto my face as I watched in the mirror, and I felt the heat in my lower regions again. Well, I guess that put some colour on my face.

I took a deep breath and headed out into my room. I opened the curtains so I could see the room in case my bag had been brought in, but no such luck. I was still at a loss as to what time of day it was, so I hesitated as I left the room. I searched around the Beta quarters of the 3rd floor until I found Colton's mum in the shared lounge area.

"Harper, darling." She sounded happy to see me and had a huge smile on her face. "Please come in. How are you feeling?" I smiled back.

"I'm ok, still a little sore." She nodded, her eyes glazed for a few seconds, and then cleared again.

"I think it is absolutely terrible what that horrid child did to you." She shook her head. "Absolutely horrid." I just smiled, not really sure what to say.

"Erm, Mrs Stokes-" I started.

"Please, Caroline," she interrupted. "Or mum if you like."

"Caroline," I smiled. I didn't really feel comfortable calling her Mum. "Was my school bag brought home? Do you know?" She looked puzzled at my question. "It's just that Colton brought me home, but I don't think we had my bag. My phone is in there and all my books. I can't find it, and I don't even know what time it is." I started to feel the familiar feeling of a panic attack coming on and a simple sentence quickly turned into word soup.

"Oh!" Caroline said, and I breathed a sigh of relief that I wouldn't have to search for my bag anymore. "It's just after 1 pm, dear," she said, obviously very happy with herself. I just looked at her, confused for a moment, and then I slumped when I realised she had got excited because she knew the time, not where my bag was.

I felt the buzzing in my head that indicated someone was mind linking me. I opened the link and heard Colton's voice.

"Strawberries, my mum said you were awake." Oh, that would explain the brief glazing she did. "Could you come down to my office, please?"

"I'm only wearing your t-shirt," I responded, and he chuckled through the link. It felt strange to hear it in my head, but it still sent shivers in a beeline right to my core.

"Are you wearing panties?" His voice was curious and a little teasing and I blushed even though he couldn't see me.

"Yes!" I responded.

"Okay, good enough. That will work to prove our point."

"Huh?" I was confused. What point was he talking about?

"Nevermind. Come on down. I'll meet you outside my office."

"Sure, okay." I felt him shut the link off. I glanced at Caroline, who was reading a book.

"I, erm... need to go," I said. She didn't even look up from the book and smiled.

"Okay, darling, have fun." I shrugged and headed out and down to the first floor.

I felt slightly self-conscious about what I was wearing, but the place seemed deserted, anyway. Once I had hit the first floor, I headed right towards the main offices and almost bumped straight into Alex. He grinned at me and looked me up and down, lingering on my legs way too long.

"Alex," I snapped, calling his attention back to my face. "Colton asked me to come down," I said, and he grinned.

"Sure thing," he said. "He is waiting for you outside his office, just around the corner, darling." He winked. I smiled and shook my head as I headed around the corner. Colton was on his phone, leaning against a wall. He looked up as I came around and watched me as I walked over to him.

"Damn, girl," he said and whistled. "You look fine as fuck in my t-shirt." He reached out his hand, and when I grabbed it, he yanked me into him. I yelped and then hissed as my hurt arm hit his chest.

"Ah, shit, baby girl," he said and pulled me in for a kiss. His hands snaked around to my ass, and he cupped my cheeks, lifting me slightly onto my tiptoes while I wrapped my good arm around his neck. He broke the brief kiss and looked down at me, his eyes almost completely gold. He glanced up and growled, and I turned to see a man standing in the open doorway of the office. His eyes were obviously on my ass, and the t-shirt had ridden up slightly. He looked embarrassed to have been caught and then scared at the increasingly menacing growls from Colton.

"Beta, sir," he blurted. "I'm sorry. I didn't mean anything by it." He looked familiar, so I knew he was a pack member, but I wasn't sure who he was.

"Back in the room," Colton snapped and then let my waist go before taking my hand and pulling me towards the office.

"Wait, Colton!" I exclaimed, and he stopped and looked at me. "What's going on?" He grinned.

"It's your first official pack business as the future Beta wife. My dad tasked me and you to deal with this matter. He seemed to think that we would work well as a team," he smiled, although it didn't look genuine. "Plus, this matter directly involves you."

"Me, how?"

Colton grinned. "You'll see, Strawberries, come on." He pulled me into the office.

The office was of modern decor, in black, white, and glass. The big desk in the middle had a large black chair on one side and two smaller chairs on the other side. The man I had just met sat in one of the chairs and sat in the other was Donna Tobbins. She looked up at me and then at my hand in Colton's and then glared back at me. I growled before I knew why, but I was flooded with anger almost immediately afterwards, and I growled again. I knew instantly that the growl and the anger belonged to Maia, my wolf, and even as I allowed the anger to flow through me, I felt the constant dull ache disappear, and even my arm started to feel better. I felt something else as Maia prodded at the surface of my consciousness like she was trying to get out. But not like a shifting, something else entirely. I heard Colton gasp as he looked down at our hands and then back up at me. His mouth fell open, and he stared at me.

"What?" I asked, and he then just grinned in response.

"Okay, now I see it," he said with wonder in his eyes. He then turned to Donna and said, "now do you have any doubt that she is my mate?" he snarled at her, and she shrunk back in fear. Both Donna and the man were staring at me in shock, and I wondered if I had gained two heads or something.

"Colton?" I asked. "I don't get it. What's going on?" Colton just grinned more and turned me towards the wall. On the wall was a mirror in a black frame. I saw Colton and myself in the mirror and still didn't understand what he was so excited about. And then I saw it.

My face was no longer battered and bruised. It was back to my pale but healthy pink tint. And the large cut across my forehead had completely vanished. But that wasn't the most shocking thing that I saw. I moved closer to the mirror because I would have missed it otherwise. My eyes were glowing with my wolf's presence, but they were no longer the cold steel silver grey. They were now a beautiful pale gold colour. This was to be expected once Colton, and I had completed the mate bond, but that hadn't happened yet.

Nevertheless, I had officially ranked up. My wolf and I were now of Beta rank.

CHAPTER 16

Harper

I stared at myself in the mirror, fascinated by my new eyes. Upon closer inspection, I saw that the colour radiated several gold shades in a starburst pattern that seemed to shimmer.

"Strawberries." Colton drew my attention back to the room and the two waiting pack members. "Come here, please." Colton had settled himself in the chair behind the desk. I walked over, and he pulled me onto his knee and wrapped his arms around my waist.

"The reason why I have called you here, baby, is that Mr Tobbins and his daughter both currently stand accused of crimes against the pack." I glanced up at Donna, and the man, who I now knew was Richard Tobbins, and also the pack business manager. "The Alpha decided that the whole family would be held accountable for their actions. As you were physically hurt by one of the accused, you would be directly involved in deciding the punishment."

I looked at Colton in shock. "Me?" I said and looked to the two across the desk and then back to Colton. "But I can't do that."

"You can, and you will," Colton said. "This is all part and parcel of being in this family, Strawberries, so get used to it." His voice held a bitter tone, and I could feel his hands gripping the t-shirt tightly.

"Erm... Okay," I whispered. "I'm not sure what the procedure is, but I will do my best." I shrugged and noticed that Donna was glaring at me.

"So, what are the charges?" I asked, and Colton nodded in approval.

"Donna Tobbins is accused of attacking a named rank pack member," Colton started, but Donna interrupted.

"Wait, that's not fair," she exclaimed. "She wasn't even a Beta rank until a few moments ago."

Colton growled, and Donna shrunk back in fear.

"And Richard Tobbins stands accused of stealing from the pack businesses to the tune of just under half-a-million pounds." Colton finished.

"And what punishment would you normally give out?" I asked, and Colton smirked.

"Well, both crimes are punishable by death, if you so wish."

"What?" Mr Tobbins exclaimed. "It wasn't even me. I told you, you want to speak to Darren Kirby." Donna hissed at her father as my eyes widened in shock.

"My father is not a thief!" I shot at him, and he looked at me in shock, obviously not knowing who I was beyond the future Beta's mate.

"You're Harper?" Then he looked at Colton. "Well, it all makes sense now."

Colton sighed. "I have way more important things to do today." He turned to me. "Strawberries, my recommendation is banishment from the pack." I watched as both Donna and her father had a look of fear on their face.

"Please, Beta sir," Mr Tobbins said. "I swear, I will do whatever you want."

"I have a better idea," I said, and everyone looked at me. "How about instead of banishment, they have the option of being stripped of rank to Omega?" Donna looked horrified, but Mr Tobbins looked strangely happy about it. I turned to Colton to see what he thought and saw his eyes glazed over. They cleared up, and he smiled at me.

"The Alpha agrees and said it is a fitting punishment, well done, Strawberries." I blushed at the praise. He then turned to Donna and her father.

"Effective immediately, you will be stripped of high rank and will be awarded the title of omega and as such, have all your assets stripped and placed into the pack's claim." Donna began crying, but her father just nodded.

As Colton was finishing, the door opened, and two big warriors came into the room. Colton looked at the warriors and turned to Donna and her father.

"That will be all." He looked down at some papers on his desk as if they had already gone. Mr Tobbins stood and nodded to me before turning to leave. Donna glared are me and went to say something when her dad stopped her.

"Donna!" he snapped. "Now!" She glared at me again before lowering her head and following him from the room. And was closely followed by the warriors.

When the door clicked shut, Colton stopped staring at the papers and looked up at me. He smiled as he ran his hand up my thigh and under the t-shirt.

"You did great, Strawberries," he said as he nuzzled my neck. "I would like to show you how well you did." I felt his fingers play along the edge of my panties, and I squirmed away without thinking. Colton growled and held me tightly with his one arm before pushing a finger inside my panties and starting rubbing right over my sensitive area. I gasped as the feel of his rough fingers against my most sensitive area set something inside me on fire. I could feel his length harden under my ass, and I found myself rubbing, grinding against it while his words were on me.

We were both panting pretty heavily when Colton pulled his fingers away to my upset. He chuckled at my protest.

"Oh baby girl," he whispered in my ear. "I said last night that you could make it up to me." His hand slipped under the t-shirt and against my breast as he began rolling my nipple between his fingers, and I bit my lip, trying not to cry out as the sensation sent pulsing heat to my core.

"Right now, I want to see your pretty mouth work me, just like I did for you last night." He nuzzled into my neck, nipping and kissing.

"Would you do that, baby girl?" he asked. I wasn't sure what to say. I had never gone down on a guy, and I really honestly didn't know what to do.

"Baby?" he asked again. "What's wrong?" I smiled and shook my head.

"Nothing," I said. I stood up from his knee and turned to face him as he watched me expectantly. I kneeled in front of him, and he leaned forward and kissed my forehead. He then stood up in front of me, and I leaned forward to undo his pants and pulled them and his boxers down, allowing his member to spring free. I looked up at him, and he watched me with lust in his eyes.

I took a deep breath, held his member in one hand, and ran my hand up and down his shaft. I looked up again as he groaned, and then, confident that I couldn't get this wrong, I brought his member to my lips and ran my tongue around his head.

"Oh, baby girl," he groaned. "That's it, baby." I brought his head into my mouth and tasted the saltiness of his stuff. I then began to work my way down his shaft as I held the bottom to steady him as I worked on him. I wasn't sure if I was doing it right, but the groans I could hear from Colton made me think that I was doing a good enough job. Colton grabbed my hair and began thrusting himself deeper into my mouth.

"Oh goddess, yes!" He groaned and continued to work deeper into my mouth. The feel of his hands in my hair and the sounds of pleasure he was making were having an effect on me. I felt an ache in my lower regions. I reached down between my legs with my free hand, found my nub, and began rubbing circles and feeding the fire building inside me. I felt Colton's hand tighten in my hair, and he growled.

"Fuck baby girl, what are you doing to me?" He pulled out of my mouth and grabbed my arm, pulling me up. I was confused until he turned me to face the desk, pushed me down, and ripped my panties away. My breathing got shallow in anticipation as he kicked my leg to the side, making room for himself. I felt his fingers as they grazed my folds, and he groaned as he felt how excited I was.

"Fuck Strawberries." He lined himself against my entrance and thrust inside me hard. I cried out as my hips hit the edge of the desk with force, and his member hit something deep inside me that sent a shock wave of some feeling that I couldn't describe. Colton grabbed my hips and started to pound himself hard in and out of me, hitting that same spot each time. Soon the shock waves felt good, and then they felt amazing, and the pressure inside me was building to an almost unbearable level. Colton reached around to my front, found my extremely sensitive nub, and began working it with his rough fingers.

The pressure exploded, and I screamed as wave after wave of red hot pleasure ripped through my body. I started to buck under Colton as he continued to pound into me, and with each hit against that spot, a fresh wave of heat ripped through me. I wasn't sure how much more I could take when I felt Colton begin to lose the rhythm, and his grunting got louder before I felt as he came inside me. He collapsed over me, his member twitching inside me, and stayed still briefly before I felt his lips on my back. He groaned as I felt him pull away briefly before his arm wrapped around my waist and pulled me back and onto the floor. I ended up between his legs, leaning against his hard torso and his arms wrapped around me.
"I don't know where that came from, Strawberries," his voice almost a growl. "But damn woman, I'm up for a repeat event." He nuzzled into my neck, and I felt shivers down my full body. "In fact, many repeat events."
"I don't understand," I confessed. I mean, it was amazing. I could still feel the echo of the pleasure that had just happened, but I didn't understand what made it any different for him.
"Baby girl, I don't know what it is, but sex with your fated mate is just that much better. Maybe because I am the only guy you have had tend to your sweet needs, you have nothing to compare." I nodded. I guess that made sense.

"But baby, what just happened was something else. It was like I could not only feel your needs, but I had the uncontrollable urge to give them to you." I turned until I could see his face, and he leaned over and kissed my nose and smiled, "Maybe it's the spontaneous up-ranking, I dunno, but I sure as hell like it." He nuzzled back into me, and we stayed like that for a few more minutes. I don't know, maybe being the Beta's mate wouldn't be so bad after all!

CHAPTER 17

Harper

After I realised I was only wearing a long t-shirt and no panties, Colton helped me sneak back up to my room and then helped me out of his t-shirt. He never made it back to his office for the rest of the day. We just about managed to get dressed and make it to dinner, where both the Alpha and the Beta seemed super fascinated with my spontaneous up-ranking.

"So it just came on all by itself?" the Alpha asked, watching me with curiosity. Colton sat in the chair next to me, his arm held tightly around my shoulder.

"Yep," he said. "She saw that slut from school and growled. I watched as her wolf appeared, and then the silver in her eyes starburst into the gold." I listened with interest. I had no idea it had been such a display.

"And what were you feeling or thinking?" the Beta asked me.

I shrugged, "Angry, I guess."

"Yeah, she looked ready to rip that girl's throat out," Colton said proudly.

"This is interesting," the Alpha mused. "It's not uncommon for a wolf to up-rank on the marking, but you two haven't even declared your intentions yet." He watched me for a couple more moments. "Tell me, Harper, I forget, were you born in this pack?"

I nodded in response. "Yes, Alpha sir."

"Hmm, interesting indeed." Then his eyes glazed over, and I instinctively turned and looked at the Beta, who also had his eyes glazed. I glanced at Colton, and he just shrugged and smiled at me.

"I bet the sex is great!" Damien burst out, and I swear I saw his eyes travel my body. I turned and looked at Colton, who was grinning. He saw me looking, and his face dropped, and he threw a look at Damien.

"Not cool, bro, that's my mate you are talking about," he smiled and winked at me, and I blushed.

The rest of dinner went to normal conversation, and I noticed Louise being rather quiet. At one point, she got a text message, and the Gamma scolded her for bringing her phone to the dinner table. She glanced at me and then away again. I tried to get her attention, but she avoided eye contact for the rest of the dinner, and as soon as we were excused, she was out of the room and gone.

When I got back to my room, my school bag was on my bed, and I searched through it quickly for my phone. I had a dozen or so messages, and six missed calls from Tommy. There were a couple from Katie too, which mostly said that she missed me at school today.

I phoned Tommy, and he picked up just as Colton walked into my room.

"Harper," he said, sounding relieved. "Where the hell have you been?"

"Tommy, it's fine," I said. "I just had an incident at school and then took today off to rest." Colton started nuzzling at my neck, and I giggled.

"Oh, it sounds like you are busy," Tommy said, suddenly sounding distant. "I'll call you another time."

"No, Tommy, it's-" He had already hung up before I could get the sentence out. I looked at the phone, confused. But Colton quickly took my mind off it.

"Strawberries," he whispered in my ear as he ran his hands up and down my sides. "Come stay in my room tonight." I felt a shiver run down my spine as he said it, and I could already feel myself getting excited. Colton chuckled at the scent.

"I'll take that as a yes." He scooped me up into his arms bridal style, and I yelped and giggled as he headed down to his room.

Once in his room, he dropped me on the bed and immediately started to nuzzle into my neck.

"Oh, baby girl," he groaned into my neck, and my lower regions tightened at its sound.

He leaned back on his arm and looked down at me.

"Do you trust me?" he asked, a wicked glint in his eyes, and I gulped but nodded. I wasn't sure if I did, but I knew I should. He leaned over and kissed my nose and then turned and started rummaging in his bedside drawer. He turned back to me and winked.

"Put your arms above your head, baby," he said, and I complied. He leaned up and grabbed one wrist, and I felt something cold snap around it before some movement and then something cold around my second wrist. He moved away, and I looked up to see he had handcuffed me to the headboard. I felt a heavy feeling go through me and my heart sped up. I looked over at Colton, and he grinned. I took a breath but was suddenly filled with trepidation.

"Don't worry, baby girl." Colton moved down and unbuttoned my jeans and pull them and my panties down. "I got you." He ran his fingers along my hips, and I felt my body react despite my uncertainty. He leaned in and grazed his lips against mine before slipping his tongue in, and our kiss became heavy. He pulled away and looked down at me.

"You know I could do anything to you like this," he whispered. "And you wouldn't be able to do anything about it." Something like excitement, but stronger with an edge of fear, ran through me. I started to feel like I couldn't pull in breath quickly enough.

Colton's fingers had wandered to the top of my thighs and he lightly grazed between my legs before slipping one in through my fold. I gasped as he plunged a finger into my entrance and began pumping in and out. I couldn't help the moan that slipped from my lips, and Colton grinned. He nuzzled into my neck and nipped at my marking spot, sending lightning bolts of pleasure straight to my core. I panted with the anticipation of the orgasm that was already beginning to build. I tried to allow myself to fall into it but couldn't seem to shake the on-edge feeling that I had. I felt like something wasn't quite right.

I glanced around the room, and when my eyes landed at the door, I screamed. I saw Damien standing in the doorway watching us, and he rubbed his hand on the outside of his pants, where it was rather obvious that he was excited. He saw I had seen him and met my eyes and winked.

"Oh, my Goddess! Colton!" I exclaimed. Colton looked up. His eyes were lazy but confused. I glanced at Damien, who had an amused expression on his face. Colton glanced back and grinned.

"Oh hey, man," he said, not slowing his fingers inside me despite the audience. He pushed his thumb against my nub and rubbed circles quickly. I could feel the pressure building even though I tried to push it away. I glanced at Colton and Damien.

"Colton, please," I panted as I got closer to the climax. I could feel Damien's eyes on me and tried to struggle away from Colton's hand as his pumping got quicker, but the handcuffs held me in place. I could feel the edge of a panic attack chasing the impending climax.

"It's okay, baby girl, just trust me," Colton whispered. "Come for me, baby." I heard the command in his voice and felt myself flying over the edge into the Climax. Even as the waves of pleasure rushed through my system, I felt Damiens eyes on me. I looked up, and he met my eyes again and again winked.

"Just wanted to say good night!" he said and then disappeared from the door.

The waves of pleasure dissipated, then the shame and panic hit me full force, and I started to hyperventilate. Colton finally figured out what was happening and leaned into me with his free hand on my face, caressing my cheek.

"Baby, it's ok, calm down," he cooed as tears began to run down my face. I tried to pull away, but the handcuffs still held me, and the panic increased even more.

"Colton, please." I pulled on the handcuffs trying to yank my hands out.

"Hey, hey," Colton suddenly looked concerned, and he reached for something on his bedside table and then moved up the bed and undid the handcuffs. As soon as my hands were free, I scrambled off the bed and moved as far away as possible. I noticed my wrists were red raw from where the handcuffs had scraped them in my attempt to escape. I was still breathing heavily when I noticed a shadow over me.

I cried out as Colton came over and sat next to me.

"It's ok, baby," he said. "I told you that you could trust me, didn't I?" He pulled me onto his lap, and I tried to get away, but he held tight.

"Calm down now," he said, and I felt a calming sensation running through my body. I realised that he was using his Beta power on me, but at this point, I was so under it that I didn't seem to care anymore.

"That's it, baby girl," Colton whispered. "Nice and calm. Let yourself relax." My whole body felt heavy as I leaned into him and sighed. Colton lifted me up, carried me to the bed, and slipped me under the covers. My eyes closed, and I vaguely felt as he soon joined me in the bed and pulled me against him. I moaned, and he kissed my forehead.

"It's ok, baby girl," he whispered. "We've got plenty of time to play." Before I could figure out what he meant, I was swallowed into a dreamless sleep.

CHAPTER 18

Harper

The next morning at breakfast felt awkward. Colton had seated himself in his father's normal seat at the end of the dining table. He had put me in his usual seat, and Damien had sat himself opposite me. We were already seated in uncomfortable silence when Damien had sat down. He winked at me, and I looked down at my hands. The sound of their sniggers made me feel sick. I felt Colton's hand on my thigh and tried to pull away, but he gripped and squeezed hard. Hard enough for me to cry out. I looked up and saw the entire table looking at me, and I covered my mouth. I looked at Colton, who was glaring at me. I lowered my eyes again and heard him chuckle.

"Women, eh?" he said, and the men around the room chuckled. I glanced up again, and Colton began rubbing my thigh where he had previously hurt it.

"Harper dear," the Luna called from down the table. "Caroline and I were going to get ready for this evening's pack meal and announcement. Why don't you and Louise join us so we can ensure we are all looking our best?" She smiled, and I glanced at Louise, who rolled her eyes.

"Sorry," Louise said. "I have school."

"Not today, you don't," the Gamma said. "You can do the dress-up thing as requested by the Luna." He looked at me and smiled. "After all, it is for your best friend's benefit." I smiled back before looking at Louise with my best pleading eyes. I did not want to spend the day alone with the Luna and my future mother-in-law. Louise shook her head and rolled her eyes again.

"Fine!" she said grudgingly, and I contained the relieved squeal that was threatening to escape.

After breakfast, Colton pulled me into his room. He closed the door and pushed me against it. He immediately began kissing me, and one of his hands slipped inside my joggers and panties, finding my nub with accuracy. His other hand released the zip of his jeans before grabbing my hand and pushing it inside against his member. I pulled my hand out again and tried to push him away, but he growled, wrapped his hand around my throat, and pinned me against the door.

"Stay still," he growled into my ear and began rubbing circles on my nub. He nibbled around my ear, and I gasped as I felt the heat in my lower regions ignite and increase. Colton sped up as the scent of my arousal filled the room, and my breathing got shallow. I moaned as I felt myself on the edge of that sweet release that I had become familiar with within the last few days. I could feel myself start to tip over when Colton suddenly removed his hand. I cried out at the loss of his fingers and the ache that still burned unfulfilled within me. Colton grinned at me, his hand still firmly around my neck.

"You see, Strawberries," he hissed. "That's what happens when you are a naughty girl. You get punished."

"But, I didn't do anything," I choked out.

"You disrespected your Alpha," he said. "That's not just bad for you but reflects badly on me as your mate." He let go of my throat and stepped back just as there was a knock at the door. I jumped at the sound, and he chuckled as he pulled me out of the way. He opened the door, and there was a pissed-off-looking Louise and her brother Alex standing there.

"Seriously, Alex, get lost," Louise snapped at him and then looked at me. "Are you ready? Apparently, it takes all day to get ready for an informal pack dinner," she scoffed.

"Informal dinner?" Colton asked, a grin appearing on his face. "Is that what you consider your best friend's intention ceremony to be, Louise?"

"What?" I exclaimed, and Louise's eyes widened.

Colton turned to me with a mock innocent look on his face. "Oh baby, did I not tell you?"

"Tell me what?" I could feel the dread creeping in.

"Well, after you fell asleep last night, I went to see my dad and the Alpha and asked if we could move up our timeline," he smirked.

"But the intention ceremony!" Louise explained. "You have just become mates less than a week ago," Colton shot her a frustrated look.

"And in many cases, the mates would complete the bond that same night," he said. "In fact, if I remember correctly, our dear sweet Strawberries here begged me to complete the mate bond on our first night together."

I flushed bright red in the face. It felt like a lifetime ago, but I remembered being so taken by the bond that I wanted nothing more than for Colton to lay his mark on my neck. Of course, seconds later, he rejected me, but I wasn't going to bring that up now. I suspected Colton would consider it punishment-worthy if I did, and I could still feel the ache from the one a few minutes ago.

Colton tugged my hand and pulled me into him, and feeling his hands on me sent shivers right to my centre. I saw the quirk of his lips as he noted my reaction.

"Baby, I didn't do anything wrong, did I?" he said, nuzzling into me, and I sighed at his touch and couldn't help as I buried my head into his chest, drawing in his amazing scent. "Baby?" He sounded amused, and I pulled away so I could see his face. I realised I had gripped his shirt in my hands and was on the verge of ripping it away. I flushed again at my display in front of people. What the hell was wrong with me? It must have been the up ranking yesterday. I had seen a massive increase in rank, which meant a massive increase in my libido.

Everyone knew that an Alpha or Beta has seriously high sex drives, but it was less common knowledge that the females of the pack also increased in needs the higher their rank. The theory behind it is that their drive would need to match their mate's, so they are adequately eager to fulfil their mate's needs and provide a healthy heir.

If that was the case, I had just gone from a mid-level rank to a high named rank, so there were bound to be some symptoms. I tried to control my urge to touch him, but he wasn't having any of it and began kissing down my throat.

"Baby," he sounded amused. "You haven't answered me." Then he nibbled on my marking spot, which sent electric shocks right down to my centre, and I gasped and buried my head in his chest again. I tried to compose myself before I lifted my head away from his chest, but when I did, Colton gasped.

"Fuck me, baby," he said and whistled. "You are stunning." I looked at him in confusion until he turned me around to the mirror. I saw that my eyes were gold again, meaning Maia was just under the surface. And that only happens with anger or lust, and it was obvious that I wasn't angry right now. I closed my eyes and tried to calm myself down, mentally scolding Maia in the process. I opened my eyes, and they had returned to my blue-grey. However, I could see the gold specks in them. I took a deep breath and looked over at Louise.

"I guess we should go." I was desperate to get her alone to tell her about Damien last night. I really didn't know how to navigate the situation. And what was worse was that Colton didn't seem upset by it, or come to think of it, he didn't even seem surprised.

Louise smiled and nodded, "Sure, let's get this over with."

I smiled at Colton, and he pulled me into him again, pushing his lips against mine and wrapping his arms around me. The kiss was brief but hot and left me gasping for air.

"Now remember, Strawberries," he whispered in my ear. "Be a good girl, and I will make sure you get a good reward." I shivered at what I thought he meant.

We went to leave but stopped when Alex moved to leave, too. Louise stopped and looked at him.

"What are you doing?" she asked, glaring at him.

"Coming with you," he said. grinning

"What the fuck for?" she countered, and Alex looked at Colton.

"I've assigned Alex to protect Harper," Colton said, and I looked at him shocked.

"What, why?" I exclaimed. I didn't want to have Alex following me around all the time.

"First off, you have just up-ranked, so you are more vulnerable to the side effects while your system adjusts." I wondered if he meant the extra lustful feelings. Did he think I would sleep with someone else?

"Second, you have already been attacked once since becoming my mate. This will prevent that." He pulled me against him from behind. "And third..." He leaned in and whispered, "Alex will be watching to make sure you are being a good girl." He growled the last part, and goosebumps raised along my arm, and he chuckled.

"I don't think I need Alex to follow us, and I don't want to put anyone out," I said quickly.

"It's no bother at all, Harper." Alex smiled at me, and I blushed. It was only a few years ago that I had developed a bit of a crush on Alex. He had been responsible for driving Louise around before she got her licence, which meant he was around a fair bit. We had even shared a brief, chaste kiss one night when he had dropped me off home after hanging out with Louise. Nothing had happened after. In fact, he had been rather distant. I just assumed that it was because I was a bad kisser, and he regretted it. I glanced at Colton, watching me with his eyebrows raised, and I blushed even more.

"It's non-negotiable," he said, his voice firm and clear, ending the discussion. I half smiled and nodded. I guess I would have to be more subtle with my conversations with Louise.

I turned to Louise, who looked annoyed, but I shook my head, and she sighed. She linked her arm into mine, and we headed from Colton's room and up to the top floor, with Alex quickly behind us, where we had planned to meet with Colton's mum and the Luna.

CHAPTER 19

Harper

The day was filled with awkwardness. Colton's mum and the Luna obviously knew about the change to the intention ceremony, and both seemed to be very excited about it.

"Isn't it a little quick?" I asked as the Luna held up different dresses to my body.

"Or a lot quick," Louise said, which earned her a glare from the Luna.

"Louise dear, I'm not sure you can understand the want to be connected to your fated mate once you find them," Caroline chastised, and I glanced at Louise, who blushed. She saw me looking and looked away. I knew already that she had found that fated mate, but she still wasn't admitting it to herself, forget anyone else.

"Now, Harper dear," Caroline said. "I know it can feel a little fast, but it is quite an acceptable time frame."

"And didn't I hear that you asked to be marked on your first mating?" the Luna asked, and I blushed. Oh my goddess, did everyone have details on mine and Coltons first time. The Luna took my blushing as a good sign and smiled.

The door opened, and Damien walked in. I was standing in just my underwear, and he took his time observing my body.

"Oi! Pervert," Louise called, glaring at him, and he glanced at her briefly before turning to Alex and whispering something. Alex looked over at me as Damien relayed his message, so I didn't have to guess the topic of the conversation. I glanced at Louise, and she met my eyes and shrugged.

"Damien, dear," the Luna said. "Don't be so rude." Damien smiled at his mother. He crossed the room and kissed her on her cheek.

"My apologies, mother," he said with a smirk. "I was just relaying some information regarding a surprise that Colton is cooking up and also to deliver this." He nodded to the door as it opened, and an omega walked in with a large white box. He put the box on the table and quickly scurried out again.

Damien walked to the box, opened it, and pulled out a dress. I couldn't help my gasp. The dress was beautiful. It had a solid grey underdress, which looked quite short, but the over layer looked to be spun from silver. It was an elaborate lace pattern that started in a fitted bodice effect and then flared out and fell to the floor. As Damien moved towards me, it sparkled in the sunlight from the window, and the long skirt portion moved like it was feather light. He held the dress up to my body and smiled.

"Colton is right," he said, looking into my eyes. "You will look beautiful in this." I felt a heat rising to my face. Was Damien flirting with me? I wasn't the only one who thought so.

"Hey jerk, get your own girl," Louise called. "Stop hitting on your best friend's mate." Damien rolled his eyes and then winked at me before turning to Louise.

"How about you, Louise?" He grinned, and I saw something crossover Alex's face. I couldn't tell what it was, but it wasn't pleasant.

"Hmm, no thanks," Louise smirked. "I'd rather fill my mouth with hot coals." Damien laughed.

"Well, maybe another time." He glanced at the Luna, and they shared a brief look before he turned back to me.

"There are shoes and accessories in there too, with compliments from your mate." He half bowed and winked again.

"Good day, ladies. I will see you this evening," he said, and with a nod to Alex, he left the room.

The rest of the day was mostly uneventful and spent getting ready for dinner. Around half an hour after Damien's visit, a mass mind link went out from the Alpha informing everyone that tonight's pack dinner was mandatory and formal dress. I was sure that by now, everyone would have heard that Colton had found his mate, although I highly doubted anyone knew who I was. It didn't matter because by 7 pm tonight, everyone would know. The thought made me want to run and hide and maybe throw up a little. I could imagine the judging stares from the girls who hung off of Colton at any chance they got. They would think that I wasn't anyone special and certainly not good enough for the future Beta of the pack.

But it didn't matter because 7pm quickly rolled around, way too quickly for my liking, and I was standing by the double doors to the grand hall awaiting the announcement. My dark hair had been straightened and pinned to the side, so it flowed over one shoulder. The dress, which fitted perfectly, sparkled in the dim lights of the entrance hall. The accessories included a silver-coloured arm cuff, and a diamond clustered clip in my hair, and the silver sandals were thankfully only an inch high on the heel. My makeup had been done similar to the Mid Summer ball with soft silvers and white and a pretty pink lip stain. I had been told that the pack would gather at the tables in the grand hall, and then the Alpha would speak. Then Colton would leave his place at the head table and come to the back of the room and present me officially.

I was all alone except for Alex, who stood by my side. He smiled at me as I trembled at the thought that every pair of eyes in the room would see me when those doors opened.

"Don't worry, you'll do amazing," Alex whispered in my ear. "And you look beautiful." I blushed at the compliment, raised my head, and took a deep breath.

I listened as the Alpha cleared his throat, and the room descended into silence. The Alpha talked about the connection between the fated mates and how finding that mate in this big world and finding them in the same pack was such a rare occasion. He then announced that Colton had been so lucky and obviously destined for greatness to have been given such a rare gift from the moon goddess.

"I am beyond pleased to announce that not only is young Beta Colton's new mate a prominent member of our pack." I scrunched my face at that. I was hardly prominent.

"But she has already proved her worthiness by activating the up-ranking prior to the marking ritual." There was a hushed murmur that ran through the crowd. "Which is why we have agreed to the couple's decision to make tonight's pack dinner into their Intention Ceremony." The Alpha finished proudly. There was another wave of noise from the pack, this time louder and with a sense of anticipation. The room slowly quietened down to an almost silence again before I heard the Alpha speak again.

"Colton Stokes, future Beta of the Midnight Moon pack." I heard a chair move, as I guess Colton stood up from his seat. I suddenly went from nervous to very nervous and felt like I couldn't breathe.

"Please do us the honour of presenting your goddess-given fated mate to the pack." I heard more murmuring and movement as Colton made his way down the stairs and to the back of the room. The doors to the room opened, and Colton stood in front of me and looked me up and down. I watched as his eyes switched from the light hazel into the pure gold as he whistled low in appreciation. I took in his appearance as I smiled shyly at him. His black suit and silver tie looked amazing against the white shirt. He stepped out of the room and up to me and bent to lay a gentle kiss on my cheek.

"You look stunning, mate," he whispered against my cheek. "I hope you have been a good girl because I really want to take this dress off you later." I closed my eyes and focused on anything, but what he was saying. The last thing I wanted was for a room full of werewolves to be able to smell how much his words excited me.

He took my hand and began his signature rubbing of circles with his thumb until my breathing evened out again, and then turned and gently pulled me into the room.

We stood at the entrance with everyone watching us. Colton squeezed my hand and smiled at me before turning to the room.

"Alpha Sir, and fellow members of the Midnight Moon pack, may I present Miss Harper Kirby as my mate."

CHAPTER 20

Harper

A murmur went through the room as I quickly glanced around. My eyes rested on my mother and then my father. Both of them looked so proud. I smiled weakly at them. I could see Tommy next to my father, but his back was to me. In fact, he was the only person in the room who wasn't looking at me. I wanted to hide behind Colton; I was never one for attention, and the amount directed my way was way too much.

Colton tugged gently on my hand and began rubbing circles with his thumb again. I looked up at him, and he smiled. I hadn't even noticed, but my breathing had shallowed with my anxiety. I smiled back as I regained my breath, and Colton began leading us down the centre of the room towards the stage. I tried to compose my nerves as we mounted the stairs onto the stage where the master table was. I glanced at Louise, who met my eyes and forced a smile. The Alpha stood in front of us and smiled as we neared the centre stage.

The intention ceremony was a small but formal affair, especially when it involved a named rank pack member. We stood to one side of the Alpha as he spoke about the rarity and importance of a fated mate and how this was a gift from the moon goddess. He mentioned that the discovery of the fated mate bond falling on the summer solstice was another sign that Colton and I would be a powerful asset to the pack. Lastly, were the vows and the token bond gift.

"Beta Colton Stokes," the Alpha boomed. "Do you swear that you have been blessed with the gift of the fated bond to Miss Harper Kirby? And do you intend to honour that bond into full completion?" Colton looked at me, smiled, and then looked back at the Alpha.

"I, Beta Colton Stokes, swear that I have been gifted with the fated bond with Miss Harper Kirby, and I do intend to honour it to completion." The Alpha nodded his head and turned to me.

"Miss Harper Kirby, do you swear that you have been blessed with the gift of the fated bond to Beta Colton Stokes? And do you intend to honour that bond into full completion?" I nodded my head quickly and tried to speak clearly, although you could still hear the quiver in my voice.

"I, Harper Kirby, swear that I have been gifted with the fated bond with Beta Colton Stokes, and I do intend to honour it to completion." I let out a breath, glad that I had got everything out correctly. Again, the Alpha nodded and turned to Colton.

"When do you intend to complete the bond, under the eyes of the moon goddess?" We hadn't actually discussed when we would actually do the mating ritual, but I knew it needed to be done within the next three months because of his rejection. But then again, we hadn't discussed doing this ceremony so quickly or anything, really. Colton had made all the decisions.

"I intend to complete the mate bond ritual before the next full moon," Colton said proudly, and my eyes widened as I looked at him in shock. The next full moon was just over a week away. Was Colton really expecting me to be mated and marked by then? He squeezed my hand tight enough that I had to stop myself from crying out. I got the hint and looked down, knowing that he had seen my look just now and that he wasn't happy. The Alpha noted the exchange. And when I looked back up, he smiled at me with sympathy.

The Alpha turned back to Colton.

"Do you have the bond intention gift?" Colton nodded. He pulled out a black velvet box from his pocket and opened it. He turned it to face me, and I couldn't help the gasp. Inside the black material were a delicate silver chain and a circular pendant with a flat black surface around a silver crescent moon. There were tiny diamonds set into the black to look like stars to finish it. I knew, of course, that it wasn't real silver, but a silver compound that gave the impression of silver without the lethal quality that silver has to werewolves. The whole pack owned jewellery made with this stuff. It didn't take away from the beauty of it, though. Colton took the necklace out of the box, put it on the table behind him, and looked at me expectantly. I turned around, and he placed the necklace around my neck and whispered in my ear as the crowd cheered.

"This officially makes you mine now, Strawberries." A shiver ran down my spine at his words "Mine to do whatever I want with." He stroked his finger down my neck and onto my shoulder, and I clenched my hand, digging my nails into my hand to try to control my thoughts and emotions. I glanced out to the cheering pack and searched for my Uncle Tommy, but the seat beside my father was empty. Colton took my hand and turned me to face him, pulling me into a kiss, and wrapped his arms around me. I melted into the kiss as the pack cheered more.

Next was the pack dinner, which was pretty much the same except this time I was sat up on the stage with the rest of the named ranks and not with my parents. I could see Katie sitting at the back of the hall with her father. She grinned when she saw me looking and waved. I waved back and smiled. Colton looked in the direction I was smiling and frowned.

"I think we will need to look at the list of people you associate with from now on," he said to my shock. "I have a reputation to uphold, which extends to you now." My jaw dropped as I looked at him. Did he mean I couldn't be friends with Katie anymore? I was about to argue, but he grabbed my knee under the table and squeezed. I whimpered at the pain, and he shot me a look that clearly said not here. I let it go for now, but I wasn't going to let Colton decide who my friends were.

After the dinner was a brief informal reception which allowed pack members to offer congratulations and the such. My parents told me how happy they were and that my sister passed on her congratulations. I asked after Tommy, but my father just brushed it off and changed the subject. About an hour into the reception, Colton came over to me as I was talking to some school friends and took my hand.

"My apologies, ladies," he said with a charming smile, to which they all swooned. "But I must steal my mate away from you now, I have a surprise planned, and it is getting late."

"Aw, that's so sweet," one of the girls cooed, and I smiled and said my goodbyes.

Colton led me out of the grand hall and into the front courtyard. Alex was standing by one of the many cars that I had learned the Beta family had and opened the back door when he saw us coming. I climbed in and over to the other side as Colton climbed in after me. And after closing the door, Alex ran around the car and jumped into the driver's seat. Colton took my hand and leaned in to kiss my cheek before nuzzling into my neck. I gasped as his hands quickly began to roam my body.

"Colton!" I exclaimed as he began unzipping the outer layer of my dress. "Alex can see us." He grinned.

"Then we better put on a good show, baby." He pulled at the dress, so the top layer slid down my body. I was left in the short grey dress underneath, and Colton looked me up and down. He grazed his hands along my thigh and up under the dress. I giggled and pushed his hand back down. He growled into my neck and nipped at my marking spot, and I gasped. I pulled myself up from the seat, and Colton grabbed me and pulled me onto his knees, so I was straddling him and leaning in to kiss him. He wrapped his hand in my hair and deepened the kiss. His other hand travelled up my thigh again and pushed under my dress. I gasped into his mouth as his fingers rubbed against my panties. I tried to pull away, but his hand left my hair and landed on my ass, and he held me firm.

"Colton, please," I whispered and turned and looked at Alex, who was focusing a little too hard on driving. Colton groaned against my chest but moved his hand.

"We are here anyway," Alex called back, making it obvious that he was fully aware of what was going on.

"Here?" I asked, looking out the window into the dark. "Where's here?"

Colton chuckled. "You'll see, Strawberries."

Alex turned off the engine, jumped out of the car, and opened the car door. I pulled myself off of Colton's knees and climbed out of the car. Alex offered me his hand as I got out so I wouldn't fall, and I thanked him. Colton then climbed out with his eyes on Alex, and even though they weren't mind linking, I could see that some unspoken communication was going on between them.

Colton turned and smiled at me and started leading me down a dark path. We were in the middle of the countryside, but I honestly didn't know where. After a couple of minutes, I saw a light up ahead. As we got closer, I saw that the light was coming from a gazebo of sorts. There were fairy lights all around it and what looked like a blanket inside with a basket. I looked up at Colton with a happy smile.

"A night picnic?" He smiled and nodded. I was so happy. This was such a romantic gesture. But my happiness was short-lived when I saw what else was in the gazebo. Standing there holding two wine glasses was Damien Chambers.

CHAPTER 21

Harper

I stopped short when I saw Damien. Colton turned around when he felt I had stopped and pulled my hand slightly.

"What's wrong, Strawberries?" he asked, and I shook my head.

"What's going on?" I asked. I looked behind me and saw Alex standing in the path behind me. Colton pulled me into his chest and wrapped his arms around me. I tried to move away, but he held me tight.

"Don't be naughty, baby," he whispered in my ear. "I'd hate to have to punish you." I shivered as he ran his hand down my spine. He cupped my chin and lifted it, meeting his lips to mine.

"Don't worry, baby, if you are a good girl, we can make you feel really, really good." I pulled away and looked at him.

"We?" I asked. I glanced behind him and saw Damien was staring at me like a predator would prey. I started to back away. "What do you mean 'we'?" Colton growled and grabbed my hand.

"Just come and sit down, have a drink, and I'll explain." He stepped closer, and I stepped back, straight into Alex. "Come on, baby. I promise I'll be good." He pulled me into him again and whispered in my ear, "Unless you want me to be bad."

I shivered again but let him lead me into the gazebo. Damien smirked at me and handed me a glass of wine. I had to use both hands as they were shaking so much. There was a pile of blankets on the floor, and Colton pulled me down to sit on the blankets. He sat leaning against the gazebo wall and pulled me to sit between his legs. Damien went and sat on the other side. He sat watching me like I was something to eat. I saw Alex standing in the doorway, and he at least looked a little uncomfortable.

Colton pushed my hands up, encouraging me to take a drink from the glass, and ran his hand down my arm. I saw Damien move forward as I took a gulp of the wine and swallowed it down.

"The thing is, baby," Colton started. "I have certain tastes when it comes to..." He waved his hand around like he was struggling to find the right words. "Intimacy." He pulled me against him, so my back was against his front, and kissed my shoulder.

"Do you remember when we..." Another kiss against my shoulder. "...made love for the first time?" I wouldn't call what happened making love, but I nodded anyway.

"When I said those words... when I rejected you..." I felt a horrible feeling in the pit of my stomach. I could never forget that. "Well, you know what followed? The beautiful mix of pain and pleasure as they chased each other around your body?" I stiffened. Damien had been moving closer as I was paying attention to Colton, and now he was sitting by my feet, his hand stroking my leg.

"The pain is what makes the pleasure so mind-blowing." He leaned in and grazed his teeth against my neck, and I whimpered. Damien was still stroking my leg, only now the strokes were longer, as he ran his hand up and down my leg.

"Baby, I want to feel that again," Colton breathed in my ear. "I want to feel the pain and the pleasure mixed together."

"I-I don't understand," I stuttered. I felt him nod, and Damien pushed my legs open and pushed himself between them so I couldn't close them again.

"Colton, please..." I tried to move away, but Colton wrapped his arm around my waist.

"It's ok, baby," he cooed in my ear. "It's not really like cheating, Damien and I have shared before." Damien winked and leaned down and kissed my leg. My body reacted to the touch, and the scent of arousal hit the night air.

"There you go baby, just let me and Damien make you feel real good." Colton kissed my shoulder again as I felt a rush of heat through my body. "That's a good girl." He started to kiss and nip at my neck while Damien moved up my leg. I tried to form some sort of thought through the betrayal of lust running through me. I didn't want this, but it felt nice. I tried to relax for Colton. He was my mate, and maybe this is the compromise that mates made for each other.

I felt Damien's fingers skimming along the edge of my dress, and it pulled me from whatever state I was in. I suddenly realised that Colton was using his Beta command. I shot up from where I was sitting, surprising them both.

"No!" I exclaimed. "No, I don't want to." I shook my head. Colton glared up at me, and I could feel the command before the words came out of his mouth.

"Harper," he commanded. "Sit back down now!" I could tell he was angry, and it took everything I had not to do as he said.

"No!" I said, my voice shaky but clear. He got up from the floor and started to move slowly towards me. I matched his steps backing up, trying to keep the distance between us.

"Harper, you will do as you are told or so help me goddess, you will not enjoy the consequences." I backed up and hit Alex again. I whimpered as I realised I was trapped here with the three of them.

"Alex, grab her," Colton said, and I felt Alex's hand around my arms. I struggled to rip myself away from him and somehow managed to go flying outside the gazebo into the path in the woods. Alex stared down at me and caught my eyes with his. He glanced to the side, into the woods, and back again. I looked into the woods and back at him.

"Alex, for fuck's sake, grab her!" Colton shouted. I pulled myself up and ran as fast as I could into the woods as Alex advanced towards me.

I was running blind but kept pushing myself forward as the branches, and twigs scraped against my body. I could hear shouting behind me as I ran.

"HARPER!" I heard Colton shout, "Get back here right now, you little slut!" I tripped over a root or something and went flying into a tree, banging my head pretty hard. My head ached as I tried to get up, but my coordination wasn't working, and I fell back down.

"Fine, you little bitch," Colton shouted. "You will regret this, and you can find your own way back!"

I realised I had run almost a half-circle and could see the car that we had come in.

"Alex, come on," Colton called.

"Shouldn't we look for her? She could get hurt?" Alex looked down the path we had gone.

"No, the bitch can suffer. Get in the car now," Damien called, and I saw as they all climbed in, and soon the car was speeding off into the night.

I waited until I couldn't see the headlights anymore before pulling myself from the woods and onto the path. I had no idea where I was. I didn't have a phone or anything, and my dress was ripped from the run. I tried to pull it down as much as possible and tried to get my bearings. Maia whimpered in my head. She was upset at what our mate did and how he could so easily turn nasty. I tried to shake off her sadness. I had to find my way back home, or at least to civilization. I had no idea what I was going to do. Colton was clearly mad at me, and there was no way I could go back to the pack house.

First things first, get myself to a phone or something and then figure out what I needed to do next. I set off walking down the road the car had gone, one thing clear in my mind. There was no way I was going to stay with Colton. I had to find a way to accept his rejection. Maia whimpered at the thought, but I couldn't live with that man. Not like this.

I had walked for I don't know how long when I started to feel a familiar pain in my heart.

"Oh goddess, no!" Not here. I knew this was his way of punishing me as the pain increased. Suddenly, the pain slammed into me full force, and I screamed as I fell to my knees. I pulled myself into the bushes, so I was hidden from the road as I felt the darkness of my unconscious mind pull me under.

CHAPTER 22

Harper

The sound of a car woke me up, and I was unsure of what the hell was going on for a moment. I woke up in a ditch in a ripped dress, and my body felt like I had been hit by a truck. Then it all came back to me. Oh goddess, what was I going to do about Colton. There was no way I could go back to the pack house. But I had nothing on me, and everything I owned was there.

I was trying to get my body to move without crying out in pain when I heard another car. Only this one slowed to a stop right by me. I froze as I heard the engine shut off and the car door open and close. I heard someone moving towards me and then felt hands on me.

"Goddess Harper, I have been looking for you all night!" I looked up to see Alex pulling the bushes aside. I growled at him and tried to back away.

"Get the fuck away from me." He stopped, looking shocked, and then he grimaced. He moved towards me again, and I kicked out at him, sending pain shooting through my body.

"Harper, calm down, will you?" he snapped as my foot connected with his knee. "I'm trying to help you here." I glared at him and growled again. There was no way I was going to let him near me. I wasn't going back to the pack house. I would fight first.

Alex sighed and backed off. He watched me for a minute as I glared at him. I didn't want to take my eyes off the bastard for even a second. He looked towards the car and glanced back at me and then walked away over to the car. I used the moment to pull myself up and tried to run back into the woods. I fell and cried out in pain and heard Alex swear, as he probably saw I was trying to escape again. I tried crawling, but he was on me in no time, and I felt something cover me fully. I realised he had used a blanket to hold me, but I still fought to kick, scream and hit him as he scooped me up and carried me to the car. I screamed more as he pushed me into the backseat, and as soon as the door was closed, I crawled to the other side to try to get out there. I got the door open, but Alex was already there.

"I didn't wanna do this Harper, but it's for your own good," he said as he pushed a needle into my arm.

"What the fuck did you...." I started to feel floaty and fuzzy. Oh crap, it was the painkiller that Doctor Roberts had given me. I tried to fight it, but the drug mixed with exhaustion took over, and I passed out.

I woke up again, only this time I was in bed, in fresh clothes. But it wasn't my bed or my clothes. I struggled to sit up, wincing at the pain when I heard voices. They were coming from the other room. My door was open a tiny bit, and I could see a line of light.

"I swear to the goddess. I will fucking kill him!" I recognised that voice and instantly felt my body relax, knowing I was safe.

"Tommy, calm down!" That was Louise. "Remember the last time you went all caveman and stormed up there?" I smiled as she chastised him.

"Listen, you should figure something out," Alex's voice floated in. "He's already out searching for her. I dunno how long I am going to be able to hide that I know where she is."

"Alex, you can't tell him," Louise said.

"What do you want me to do, Louise? It's not like he won't be able to smell her on me the second I hit the pack house." There was a pause and then, "And you know it won't be long before he comes looking here either."

"Yeah, I know. I'm trying to figure something out," Tommy snapped.

"Also, Louise, you need to stop spending the night here. Dad is gonna figure it out," Alex said, and for a second, I got excited. Tommy and Louise!

"Like I care," Louise sneered. "What's he gonna do? Lock me away?"

"After mum, I wouldn't put it past him," Alex said.

I pulled myself out of bed and made my way to the door. I winced at the pain that just moving caused. I knew they had heard me moving and, as expected, they were all looking as I opened the door. Louise was cuddled into Tommy's arm on the sofa while Alex sat in one of the chairs. I smiled weakly as I moved to the other chair and let myself drop into it. Relieved that the pain had dulled now, I stopped moving.

"So..." I said, looking around the room. "What are we talking about?" I said with a grin or as much of a grin as possible. The tension in the room visibly relaxed, and Tommy chuckled at me. Louise untangled from Tommy, grabbed a blanket, and put it over me. I grinned at her as she did.

"So, Tommy, huh?" I said, and she flushed red.

"Shush!" she said, and I giggled.

"How are you feeling?" Alex asked. I looked at him, and he couldn't meet my eyes.

"Like I have been repeatedly run over with a truck," I said with enough edge to my voice that he flinched. "Did you know what he had planned when you drove us up there?" I asked. The look on his face answered for me, and I felt the sting of fresh tears.

"What could I do, Harper?" he asked. "Say no? He would have just got one of his buddies to do it instead, and they wouldn't have thought twice about joining in."

"Wait, what?" Tommy sat up. "I am missing something here!" I glanced at him. "What happened?" He looked between Alex and me.

"Colton took me to someplace in the middle of nowhere. At first, I thought it was sweet, like a midnight picnic, but Damien was waiting when we got there," I said. Tommy's face was set in a frozen fury.

"Waiting for what?" he hissed, and I shrank back at the power rolling off him. I had never seen this from him before. Louise put her hand on his shoulder, and I saw as he relaxed slightly.

"Colton s-said that they... erm... s-share," I stuttered. I really struggled to say it without fear washing over me again. I had my head down because I felt shame in what had gone on.

"I think he used his Beta command to coerce me into...." I fiddle with my fingers. "Anyway, I realised, and I said no, that was when he got angry." Tommy growled, and I looked up in shock. He was glaring at Alex, his eyes shining silver. Louise was looking between us in shock.

"And you took her there?" Tommy snarled at Alex, who stood up slowly, and backed around the chair.

"Tommy, he helped me get away," I said quickly. "And he brought me here, right?"

"Not good enough," he snapped, and I shrunk back as tears fell down my face. "I should rip your throat out where you stand." He began to rise from his seat. Louise jumped up and stood between the two of them.

"Alex, go home," she said. "Do not tell anyone where she is. I mean it!" Alex nodded. He slowly moved to the door and looked back at me.

"I'm really sorry," he said, and Tommy growled.

"Just go," Louise said, and he slipped out.

Louise wrapped her arms around Tommy and whispered something in his ear, and slowly he relaxed against her. He pulled her into him and buried his head in her hair. I knew that the scent of your mate was enough to induce a relaxed state, but to see it actually happen was fascinating.

"I should go too," Louise said. "He's right. Dad really is going to notice that I'm not home." She turned to me and smiled. "I'll come back when I can, but I suspect I will be watched for a while, so it might be a bit." I nodded.

"Just be safe," I said, and she smiled again. She and Tommy said their goodbyes quietly and sweetly at the door before he let her out and locked the door.

Tommy turned and looked at me and smiled.

"Hot chocolate?" he asked, although it clearly wasn't a question as he headed to the kitchen and began filling the kettle. By the time the drinks were made, and I was cradling mine in my hands, I was already feeling sleepy again. Tommy noticed and took the mug from my hands.

"Get some rest, kid," he said as he tucked the blanket around me. "I am going to make some calls." I nodded sleepily and drifted into sleep almost instantly.

I slept all day, although I had dreams of being chased through the woods. I woke up with a start and looked around for Tommy. He was on the phone, and I could tell he was angry.

"I told you, Darren. I haven't seen her. Did you check with Susie? Maybe she went to visit her." He paused and glanced up at me. "Well, she's your bloody daughter, maybe you should know what is happening to her." He made another pause as he screwed his face in frustration. "Ok, fine, if I see her, I will let you know." He ended the call and swore under his breath with his eyes closed tightly. He then took a deep breath and opened his eyes and smiled at me.

"Hey, how are you feeling?" he asked, and I pointed to the phone in his hand. "My dad called you?" I asked.

"Yeah, I've been ignoring his, and well, everyone's mind links" then he looked a little sheepish. "Well, apart from Louise's." I grinned at him. He rolled his eyes and sat down on the sofa.

"Listen, there is a full-on search party out for you right now. Louise said Colton's going crazy. When she got back to the house, she saw him kicking the shit out of Alex."

I gasped, "Oh my goddess!" I exclaimed, "Is he ok?" and Tommy nodded.

"He's a werewolf. He'll be fine," he shrugged. "Apparently, it took Damien and a few warriors to pull Colton off. He could smell you on him and demanded to know where you were. Louise said Alex didn't spill, so that's good at least," he said.

"I don't like this," I said, getting annoyed at the fresh tears. I was sick of crying. "People are getting hurt because of me."

"No!" Tommy said. "People are getting hurt because of him. Do not blame yourself for this." He stopped for a minute, and I could tell he wanted to say something.

"What is it, Tommy?" I asked.

"Louise linked me an hour ago," he shuffled. "Colton has declared that he plans on completing the mating ritual Saturday night after the engagement party." I couldn't help the sob. If the mating ritual went ahead and mine and Colton's bond were completed, he would have complete control over me. I wouldn't be able to resist his command. The wolf with the higher rank automatically becomes the stronger one in the relationship, and even with my up level, he was still stronger than me. I couldn't let it happen.

"We need to get you away from the pack as soon as possible. You need to accept his rejection and leave the pack," Tommy said. "That is the only way I can see this going." I nodded in agreement.

"Listen, I have a friend. I contacted him and told him what was happening, and he said-"

He was interrupted by a knock at the door. We both looked at each other and then at the door. He stood up and signalled for me to go into the bedroom. I quickly moved in there and closed the door, all but a little bit, and listened. Tommy opened the door and sighed.

"What can I do for you, Greg?" he asked as if he was bored.

"Cut the crap, Tommy. He knows she's here." Greg Henderson, my old teacher and elite warrior, stood at the door. "I've come to take her home."

CHAPTER 23

Harper

I saw Tommy shrug through the gap in the door.

"Dunno what you are talking about, man," he said. "I'm alone here." I heard Greg sigh. He obviously didn't believe Tommy.

"One, I'm not stupid. There is nowhere else she could go," Greg said. I could tell from his voice he was getting impatient.

"Two, I can smell that she's here. And three, Colton knows. He was all ready to come storming down himself, and he will if I don't return with her. And you know that's going to end very badly for you."

"Tell him to bring it on, the arrogant little prick," Tommy snarled.

"Tommy, just be reasonable, please!" Greg pleaded.

"Reasonable!" Tommy growled, "Do you know what he did to her?"

"No, and it's not my place to know. My place is to ensure she is safely brought back home." Greg pushed the door open and stormed into the apartment. I watched as he looked around until his eyes settled on the door and then met mine.

"Come on, Harper," he said, slowly walking towards the door. "No one needs to get hurt, but they will if you don't come with me now."

"Greg!" Tommy stood in front of the bedroom door, blocking my sight. "We are friends, and we grew up together, don't do this."

"I am doing this because you are my friend. Otherwise, you'd be unconscious now. I was given orders, any means necessary."

"Then use them because I'm not letting my niece go back to that monster," Tommy spat.

But I knew Greg was right. Colton wouldn't give up, and people would get hurt. I opened the door and stepped out around Tommy.

"Harper," Tommy exclaimed. "What the hell are you doing?"

"Stopping you from getting hurt," I snapped. I looked at Greg and took a deep breath. "Tommy is kept out of this," I stated, and he nodded.

"You come now, and Colton doesn't go all homicidal on the town." I nodded. I gave Tommy a hug, and he just stood there stiffly, his hands clenched. Eventually, he hugged me back and whispered in my ear.

"Be ready. When I get everything sorted, I'm coming for you." I nodded again.

Greg had moved to the door, patiently waiting for me. I walked over, still dressed in the oversized t-shirt and bare feet, and gestured for him to lead the way. He took hold of my arm, and we headed out of the apartment. We got to a black SUV, and he opened the back door for me to get in. I climbed in, and the door closed and locked at the same time. Greg got into the driver's seat and glanced at me in the rear-view mirror.

"Seatbelt," he said while buckling his own.

"What's the point?" I snapped. "Maybe I'll get lucky, and we'll crash." He just stared at me in the rearview until I rolled my eyes and then pulled on the seatbelt. I watched as his eyes glazed over for a couple of seconds and then cleared as he started the engine.

"Who did you link? Colton?" I asked, and he ignored me and started to drive back in the direction of the pack house.

Ten minutes later, we pulled into the driveway of the pack house. The first person I saw standing in the doorway was Colton. He watched as the car pulled up and pulled on the back door handle before Greg had even turned the engine off. The car door opened, and he met my eyes and growled. His eyes flashed gold, letting me know his wolf was also angry. He undid my seat belt and pulled me out of the car. He then pulled me into a tight hug.

"Thank the goddess, Harper," he exclaimed out loud. "I'm so happy you are safe." Then, under his breath, "You have been a very, very naughty girl." I scrunched my eyes shut, and my stomach felt like it dropped, and there was now a dark lump of fear in its place.

He picked me up bridal style and turned and walked into the pack house. The Luna and Colton's mum were standing in the entrance, and both smiled at me as Colton walked past. And Alex was standing a little way back by the stairs. His arm was in a sling, and he had fading bruises all over the parts where his skin was uncovered. He was looking at the floor when we came in but glanced up at me briefly before I heard Colton growl, and his eyes returned to the floor. Colton made his way up the stairs, and I noticed when I looked over his shoulder that Alex was following us.

He took me straight to my room and walked in, slamming the door shut behind him. He dropped me unceremoniously onto the bed before switching on the lights. I shrunk back when he turned to look at me. His eyes glowed the gold of his wolf as he stalked slowly towards the bed. I backed up until I was against the high wooden headboard and had nowhere else to go.

"Please," I begged. "Please don't hurt me." He sneered at my comment and climbed up the end of the bed. He stopped just short of me and grinned.

"Why, Strawberries, why would you think that I would hurt you?" he asked, a smirk growing on his face. "I'm just so happy that you returned home to me safe and sound."

His hand shot out and wrapped around my ankle, and yanked me down onto the bed. I yelped as he pounced on top of me and pinned my arms above my head. His lips crashed down onto mine as he roughly kissed me, forcing his tongue to explore my mouth. I tried to resist, to pull away, but he held me firm underneath him. Colton growled when I didn't reciprocate his kiss, and one hand let go of my arms to graze down my body. He found the edge of the T-shirt and ran his hand back up underneath, and palmed my breast briefly before squeezing my nipple between his fingers. I yelped at the pain, and he grinned into the kiss and did it again. This time, my yelp became more of a moan as I started to feel heat rise in my lower regions. My own body was betraying me again. Maya was excited at the touch of our mate, and soon Colton chuckled as the scent of excitement started to fill the room from me. He grinded his body against me, and I gasped as he worked his legs between mine, pushing them apart.

"You need to understand, baby girl, that you are my mate, you are mine. And I will always know where your buttons are. I will know where to press to make you do exactly what I want you to do." He grinned down at me and let go of my arms to move some stray hair from my face. I glared at him and struggled to push him off me. I was shocked that he had let me. I jump off the bed, away from him.

"Well. I'm sure that would be true if you didn't have to use your Beta command on me," I spat, and his face dropped. I grinned, suddenly feeling confident.

"Didn't realise that I knew?" I said. "Like how I can't seem to take this damn ring off my finger." I waved my hand around. "Well, I broke out of it last night, and I will again, and I'll find some other way to get this damn band off my finger, I promise you."

Colton moved like lightning, and I felt the sting across my face before I realised that he had backhanded me hard enough to send me flying into the floor.

He smirked down at me as I rubbed my burning cheek and glared up at him. He kneeled down, and I went to move away when he grabbed my hair and yanked my head back. I cried out at the pain, and he yanked again. I saw his wolf shining in his eyes as he got in my face and growled low in his throat.

"So Strawberries has claws, does she?" he smirked. "That's fine, baby girl, you can scratch all you like but remember, I like the pain. It gets me off." He licked up the side of my neck and nuzzled into me. He then yanked my hair again and twisted until we had eye contact.

"If you think you have even had a taste of my command over you, then you have another think coming." His other hand grabbed my wrist, and he pulled it up. "Clever girl might have figured it out, but let's up the stakes." He fingered the ring and smirked. "This ring does not leave your finger ever. I am telling you how much pain you would feel if it did. Do you understand me?" I found myself nodding before I felt the command this time. The last times he had used it had been subtle, but this time wasn't. The full weight of his command felt like it forced its way into my mind and rewired everything it needed. He smiled and tugged on the ring. Immediately, a sharp pain ran through my head, and I cried out and clenched my fist so he couldn't move the ring. He grinned as I felt the horror of what he had done.

"Also, dear sweet mate of mine," he said, letting go of my hair and standing up. "If you think that this is anything to go by, just wait until we complete the bond. I will own you: mind, body, and soul." I started to shake. I had underestimated him, and now I could tell he wouldn't play nice anymore. He held out his hand to me, and I glared at it. He tutted, leaned down, grabbed my arm, and yanked me to my feet. He pulled me in closer and whispered.

"This can go one of two way's Strawberries, you can comply and be the good little mate and do everything I say and reap the rewards, and being the Beta's mate has many rewards if you allow it." He ran his finger down my arm. I shuddered, knowing he was talking about his arrangement with Damien. "Or I can make you comply, and there will be punishments." He bit my earlobe before sucking it into his mouth. I cried out and then couldn't help the moan that followed. "And even if I can't hurt you directly, there are plenty of people in your life that could suddenly get accident-prone. I have already ensured that your wolf is too weak to do anything against me for the next few days, but by then, we will have completed the mate bond ritual." Use my wolf against him. He meant to accept his rejection. After he had sex with someone last night, Maia was once again too weak to do much of anything, let alone break the mate bond, not without risking her dying altogether.

He let go of me, and I stumbled back, tears in my eyes. He held everything over me, and I was trapped. He stood staring at me, a look of satisfaction in his eyes.

"You shall remain in this room until Saturday evening," he said. "All your meals will be delivered here. Alex or Greg will stand guard on your door, so don't even think about trying to unlock it." He crossed the room to me and stood right in front of me again, and ran his finger down my cheek.

"Then Saturday evening, you will attend our engagement party with me. You will smile and accept all congratulations with great joy and excitement. And then after the party, we will move into our suite together, and I will take you to our new bed. I will mate you, and then I will mark you as my property. And you will willingly and enthusiastically enjoy it. And you will be mine." I stared in horror as he detailed the exact scenario I wanted to avoid. I shook my head, unable to form words.

"Oh, baby girl," he said, his face suddenly softening, and he pulled me into his chest. "I don't want to have to hurt you, but don't you realise I only do it because I care about you." I felt as he kissed the top of my head, and I couldn't help but clutch his shirt as his scent felt like home. I closed my eyes, and tears once again fell down my face.

CHAPTER 24

Harper

Colton picked me up and put me on the bed. I laid there crying with him curled around me, stroking my hair and whispering that it was going to be okay. I was getting whiplash from his personality shifts, but even though he was the one who was making me so upset, his scent still gave me some comfort, and I clung to that comfort.

At some point in the evening, I fell asleep, and when I woke up again, it was pitch black. I stumbled around for a light, once again cursing the need for table lamps, and eventually found the wall switch. I had no idea what time it was and no idea where my phone was. I hadn't taken it to the pack dinner and had left it in my room. But a quick look around told me that it wasn't here anymore. I could only assume that Colton had taken it. I sighed and went to open the door to ask him. The handle turned, but the door didn't move. I was locked in. I pulled on the door a few more times, just in case it magically opened, but I was locked in. I sighed in frustration, trying not to let the tears start again. I huffed and headed to the bathroom. I looked in the mirror and could see I looked pale, more than usual. My dark hair was a mess, and I was still covered in all the dirt from my escape attempt, and I was still wearing Tommy's t-shirt. I put on the shower, turned it to hot, stripped out of my clothes, and climbed in. I spent as long as possible in the shower, allowing the water to beat down my skin. Eventually, I washed my hair and body and climbed out. Afterwards, I brushed my teeth and hair and put my hair up into a French braid while it was still wet, and found some comfy nightclothes.

I opened the curtains and looked out the window at the very beginning of daylight. I could see the pack house estate, and I surveyed immediately below my window. We were on the third floor, which, even for a werewolf, would be quite the drop. I guessed my only way out of here was through the door. I just had to figure out how to get it unlocked and get out. Colton had said that I would have either Alex or Greg on the door, meaning there was no way I was getting through unnoticed. I went and laid back down on the bed in frustration and soon felt myself drifting back off to sleep.

The sound of the door opening woke me up this time. By my guess, the room was now flooded with morning light, which made it around 8 am. This was confirmed when the door opened, and Colton walked in holding a tray filled with amazing-smelling food. I smiled as I saw the food, and Colton's face lit up, and he smiled back at me.

"Good morning, Strawberries," he said brightly, putting the tray down on the bed. I mumbled an acknowledgement as I briefly surveyed the full English-cooked breakfast before digging in.

Colton chuckled at me. "Quite the appetite this morning," he said, sitting down on the bed. "I wonder what else you have the appetite for?" His hand grazed up my thigh and under the leg of my shorts, then brushed against my panties. I rolled my eyes and pushed his hand back down.

"Colton," I said, my mouth full of food. "I'm eating." He sat and watched me with a curious expression.

Eventually, I ran out of food, and at least felt sated in the belly. I wiped my mouth with one of the napkins and pushed the tray away. I looked at Colton, waiting for him to say something, but he continued watching me. Eventually, I caved. I hated the silence.

"I can't find my phone," I said, and he raised an eyebrow. "Do you know where it is?" He nodded.

"It's in my room," he said, all matter-of-factly. "Phones are a privilege. You'll get it back when you earn it back." I looked at him open-mouthed.

"How am I meant to talk to my family or my friends?" I asked. I was getting annoyed. This was my property, not his. He raised an eyebrow again and growled low in his throat.

"Careful Strawberries, I don't like your tone," he said. "I am your family now, and maybe a reassessment of your friends will be a good thing, anyway." I wanted to argue, but I could tell by his sudden tense body language that things wouldn't go well for me. I looked down and started picking at the bedding and felt as he leaned in and kissed my head.

"Good girl," he whispered, and it took everything I had not to snap at him.

Thankfully, there was a knock at the door, and Colton got up to answer it. The door opened, and on the other side, there was an Omega holding a white box and several bags. Colton let him in, and he placed the box on the table by the sofa and the bags on the sofa. While the door was open, I saw Alex looking in the room. Our eyes met, and he smiled weakly at me. I couldn't bring myself to smile at one of the people holding me captive, so I just glared instead, and Alex eventually broke the contact and looked away. Colton saw the exchange and grinned as he closed the door behind the exiting omega.

"Don't blame Alex," he said, "he really did try to stop me finding you, took quite the beating, and still didn't spill." He walked over to the sofa. "I would have been impressed if it wasn't for the fact that it was my mate he was keeping away from me." He opened one of the bags and pulled out a pair of silver shoes.

"Now come over here and look at what I have bought you for tomorrow night." He looked up at me expectantly, and I rolled my eyes but got off the bed and walked over. He spent the next hour showing me the dress, various accessories, and lingerie that he said I would be wearing later. I barely took notice. The dress was a beautiful silver silk piece, but I had no interest in wearing it.

"I have also allowed Louise to come by this evening," Colton said, frowning. "She said that you should have a girls' night before the party."

"Thank you," I said and smiled at him. "I appreciate that a lot." I watched as his face lit up at my smile, and I wondered for a moment if he actually cared about me and thought he was doing the right thing for us. He pulled me into his body and kissed my nose before letting me go again.

Colton stayed until after lunch. After showing me the clothes, he told me about our new suite and how it had been decorated especially for us. He told me about the preparations for the engagement party and other random pack business. He seemed almost gentle in his manner, with the occasional touch now and then. Eventually, he excused himself to do some work and said he would come by with breakfast in the morning. He kissed me on the cheek and left with a smile. I felt confused at the exchange and spent the rest of the day trying to figure out my own conflicting feelings. I tried to talk to Maia about it, but I hadn't heard anything from her since Wednesday night.

Later on, as it started to turn to dusk, Louise arrived with bags full of movies, plus snacks and drinks. And lots of pampering products. She grinned as she walked into the room and started setting everything up. Despite her upbeat outer appearance, I could tell there was a nervous energy about her, and the few glances she shared with her brother seemed to convey some sort of hidden meaning.

"I tried to convince his almighty to let Katie come too, but he wasn't allowing it," she said as we sat down to watch the first movie.

"I don't think he approves of Katie," I said, and Louise frowned.

"Bloody snob," she said. We both knew it wasn't Katie. It was the rank she held that was the issue.

We settled into the movie, and I was drifting off to sleep when Louise suddenly jumped up.

"Harper, we gotta move now!" she said, pulling me up. She grabbed a bag that she hadn't unpacked and passed it to me.

"Wait! What's going on?" I asked. I had an awful feeling.

"We are getting you out of here, but we have to do it now." She tapped the door and waited.

"No, you can't, he'll find me, and if not he'll come after you," I said. "I'm not putting you in harm's way."

"Don't be silly. I'm the Gamma's daughter. He won't do anything to me." The door opened, and Alex poked his head in.

"Seriously, if you are doing this, you have ten minutes before I raise the alarm," he said, and I looked at him in shock. "Don't look at me like that, Harper. I couldn't stand by and do nothing, now come on."

Louise pulled me out of the room, and Alex closed it and locked it again. We headed down the back servant stairs and into the now empty kitchen. We made it out of the house and off the grounds without seeing anyone.

"Tommy is waiting at the border, but we have to be quick," Louise said as we rushed through the woods. "It would be quicker if we shifted, but I'm guessing that isn't an option right now for you." I shook my head.

"I can't hear Maia at all. She's too weak after Wednesday," Louise growled at that as we continued.

I could see headlights in the distance. When Louise cursed.

"Fuck!" she exclaimed. "It's too soon!" We burst into a clearing, and I saw Tommy and Katie standing by a car with someone I didn't know.

"They already know," Louise shouted, and Tommy nodded.

"Yeah, I already got a strongly threatened link from the dick," he growled.

"Harper, listen to me," he said, turning to me. "This is Aaron. He is a good friend from when I did warrior training at the council." I looked at the stocky guy, who smiled brightly at me. "Aaron still works for the council, and he's going to take you and hide you there for a bit. It's the only place that Colton won't dare to look, okay?" he asked, and I nodded. The council was the law for ours and other supernatural species. Most trials and punishments were dealt in-house for packs, but if it involved more than one pack or species or the council saw fit, they would get involved.

They were known for being ruthless in their actions, and their word was law regardless of any pack law.

"I promise as soon as it is safe, I will let you know, and you can come home," he said.

"What if it's never safe?" I asked, my voice breaking, and he pulled me into a hug. He pulled away and looked at me.

"Kid, you are going to have to renounce the pack, so they can't lay claim on you." He then looked at Louise and back at me. "And you need to accept Colton's rejection; otherwise, he's gonna be able to find you straight away."

"But Maia, she is too weak," I cried, and he hugged me again as tears fell.

"I know, kid, I'm sorry."

"Dammit!" Louise exclaimed, "Alex just linked. He's got a search party out in the woods." She looked at me. "Harper, I love you, but we are running out of time." I nodded and hugged her. I turned to Katie, and she smiled even though she was crying.

"I am going to miss you so much," she said, and we hugged.

"Harper!" Tommy said as he searched the woods frantically. "Katie, get out of here. They are close." And with one last look, Katie shifted and dove into the woods. Louise pulled her clothes up and bundled them into a second car.

"Harper, it's time," Tommy said, and I nodded.

I took a deep breath and said, "I, Harper Kirby, renounce any loyalty and claim on the Midnight Moon pack and accept that I am now rogue until such time that I swear loyalty to this or another pack." I felt the snap instantly. It felt like there was something in me that was set free. At the same time, I felt lost and like I couldn't catch my breath. I glanced at Louise and Tommy, who both wrinkled their noses. I knew that to them my scent would change. I took another breath and looked at Tommy. He smiled in encouragement as I began the next statement that would almost definitely kill off my wolf. My voice was shaking as much as my body was.

"I, Harper Kirby, acknowledge the rejection of Beta Colton Stokes and accept it now, breaking our bond in the eyes of the moon goddess." I gasped as another snap jolted through my body, followed by a wave of intense pain. I screamed and fell to my knees. It felt like I was ripping away a part of myself. I curled into a ball as the pain raced through me and around me. I was vaguely aware of a harrowing howl and knew which wolf it belonged to. Colton had felt the rejection go through as well, and my only consolation was that he was probably in as much pain as I was.

I felt a strong pair of arms pick me up from the ground, and I was put into the back of the car and a blanket was put over me.

"Don't worry, little pup," the guy that Tommy called Aaron said. "I'll look after you, I promised your uncle." He closed the door, and I saw Tommy and Louise through the window. I felt the engine start and the view out of the window change as the car moved.

"Sleep, pup," I heard the man say from the driver's seat. "We have a bit of a trip ahead of us." I didn't want to sleep, but the intense grief I felt coupled with the pain that was still echoing through me was enough to send me into a deep, dark unconscious hole.

CHAPTER 25

Harper

Ten Years Later

I clenched my thighs around the head between my legs and wrapped my fingers in his blond hair as he worked at my clit with his tongue. I could feel the pressure rising as he pumped two fingers deep inside me, curling them to hit just the right spot. I bit down on my lip to stop myself from moaning as I got closer. Just as I started to feel like I was about to burst, I reached to my left finger and tugged on the damn ring. Pain shot through my body and sent me over the edge as pleasure chased it, and I cried out. I tugged on the ring again as he pulled out his fingers and ran his tongue across my entrance, drinking in his reward, sending another jolt of pleasure through me.

I sighed and leaned back against the wall, sated. I looked down at the cute blond warrior sitting on the floor with a smug grin on his face. He looked up at me and winked. I chuckled and shook my head and glanced at my phone. The time read 1:54 pm!

"Shit!" I exclaimed and jumped down from the shelf that I was sitting on. I grabbed my tight black jeans and pulled them on quickly.

"Thanks, Mark," I said as I found my boots and started putting them on and doing up the side zip. The blond frowned at me.

"It's Paul," he said, jumping up from the floor, and I shrugged.

"Oh, yeah, Paul," I smiled. "Well, that was good, maybe again sometime." I grabbed my bag and headed for the door of the Janitor's closet.

"Hey, wait, where are you going?" He grabbed my arm. I looked down at his hand and then back up at his potentially imposing 6ft4 broad frame. I smiled and narrowed my eyes. He glanced at his hand and quickly removed it. I nodded. A wise move.

"Sorry, dude," I said, "I got a meeting with Nathanial in...." I looked at my phone. "Fuck, two minutes."

"Well, what am I supposed to do with this?" He pointed at the hardened impressive-sized bulge in his pants. I nodded in appreciation and grinned.

"Got two hands, don't you? Take your pick." I looked down again. "But feel free to catch up later, and I can make it up to you." I winked as I opened the door and slipped out into the hallway.

I closed the door behind me and headed down the hallway of The Council UK Branch. The hallway was flanked on either side by offices and training rooms and I headed up the stairs to the second floor, where the Council Elders held their offices. Each of the twelve Councils around the world had twelve Elders. Those twelve Elders comprised three representatives from the four main supernatural categories, Shifter, Immortal, Faerie, and Magic Worker. Each of the categories had subcategories. One of my responsibilities as an Elite Officer of The Council was to know them all and their strengths and weaknesses inside out.

I knocked on the door of Elder Nathaniel Bethrinton, one of the UK Branch's Shifter representatives and my mentor, and didn't wait before walking in. I was greeted with two pairs of eyes, one being my mentor and the second being Drake Valcoin, one of the representatives for the immortals and the Branch High Council Elder. The High Council was made up of one Elder from each Branch and was led by The Sovereign.

Other than the title, any information on The Sovereign was a strictly guarded secret.

Nathaniel looked up at me from behind his desk with a disapproving look. His greying hair was the only potential indication of his age, which was somewhere in his mid-fifties, although the rest of him could pass for the late thirties. He wore a traditional professional three-piece suit, and other than when we were training, I never saw him in anything else. In stark contrast to Nathaniel, Drake grinned when he saw me, and I raised my eyebrows as he shamelessly checked my body out before finally meeting my eyes. Drake was the very definition of a Greek god. His olive skin tone held the hint of an ethereal glow and his very dark brown hair matched his so dark they were almost black eyes. I knew from experience that the body underneath the black shirt and dress pants was built up of a well-defined and sculpted muscle set.

"Harper!" Drake exclaimed, "How lovely it is to see you." I smiled and nodded.

"I'm sorry," I said and then looked at Nathaniel. "I thought we had a meeting. I can come back," I started to back out of the room.

"No, no, Sweetheart," Drake purred and stood in front of me in the blink of an eye, damn vampire speed. "You come on in. I was just on my way out." He took my hand and smiled, a mischievous look crossing his face. "Unless I could steal you away for a bite." I pulled my hand out of his and smiled politely.

"Thanks, Drake, but it's not going to happen," I said and stepped to one side.

He grinned, "Don't deny yourself, sweetheart. You know I can make you happy." I blushed and then frowned, annoyed as he laughed at my reaction. I had made the mistake of thinking I could handle the three-thousand-year-old vampire eight or so years ago and found out the hard way that vampires, especially the old ones, could be dangerously addictive. If it wasn't for Nathaniel, I might have ended up one of Drake's blood whores.

Nathaniel coughed, "I think we are done, Drake," he said, and Drake nodded, his eyes still on me.

"Of course, Nathaniel," he said in amusement. He turned to walk out the door and stopped. "By the way, Harper dear, interesting work in Cornwall." I cringed and looked at Nathaniel, knowing this was why I was in his office right now. Drake laughed as he opened the door. "Very inventive indeed," he chuckled to himself as he closed the door behind him.

I turned back to Nathaniel and grinned. He promptly looked back down at the papers on his desk as if I wasn't there. I rolled my eyes and went and sat in the chair opposite him and swung my legs onto the desk. He looked up sharply at my legs, and I debated pushing it a little, but I was already in a shitload of trouble, so I put my legs down on the floor again. Nathaniel nodded before going back to looking at the papers on his desk. We sat there for five minutes in silence before I couldn't take it anymore.

"Okay, I know I fucked up, but really, what choice did I have? I mean, it was clear he wasn't going to come quietly, and what did you expect me to do? I wasn't going in unarmed." Nathaniel didn't react to one word, and I was starting to get annoyed. "I mean, come on. He was a psycho who was planning on killing me, creatively!"

"Four hundred and sixty-eight thousand pounds," Nathaniel said, cutting my rant off.

"Huh?" I looked at him, puzzled

"Four hundred and sixty-eight thousand pounds, numerous more property damage and an unsanctioned kill," he finally looked at me. His piercing blue eyes seemed to bore right into me. I glared right back.

"He was using his fucking glamour to coerce those girls. Did you really think I was going to sit back and watch what he was doing while we waited on fucking paperwork," I spat out. "I acted in the best interest of his victims with the knowledge and experience I had."

Nathaniel slammed his hand down on the desk, causing me to flinch. "Goddess dammit Harper, you had no proof!" He glared at me. "No warrant, no proof, and no official reason to even fucking be there." He stood and paced the room.

"So what!" I shot back, "I was supposed to ignore everything because he was some jumped up little rich faerie? Would this have been an issue if his family wasn't loaded?"

"No, probably not, but they are." Nathaniel went and sat behind his desk again. "And in addition to that, they also know three members of the High Council," he said. "That's what Drake was just in here for. They want you brought up on charges." I rolled my eyes.

"So is that it, Nathaniel," I said. "Goodbye, Harper, you know I know it's bullshit," I said. "Drake won't let that happen while he thinks he can get back into my pants," I said, and Nathaniel glared at me. "Also, if that wasn't enough, how about the fact that I am the best damn Elite Officer in this branch. And I'd be happy to go toe to toe with anyone who disagrees."

"Yeah, I know you are good," Nathaniel said. "I have watched you grow from that scared and broken girl that arrived here almost ten years ago. I watched as you threw yourself into training and smashed through the ranks to become the woman you are now." I smiled despite everything.

He was right. It had been the early hours of the morning when Aaron had brought me to the Council. I was broken and quickly slipped into a deep depression after my wolf Maia never returned. I had spent three months in bed constantly crying and a further year or so terrified that they, or more, that he was going to find me and drag me back. Aaron kept me up to date with the reports. He had searched local packs first and then all over the UK. I spent my days scared of my shadows, which was how Nathaniel met me. I had been on a walk at Aaron's insistence when Nathaniel had surprised me, and I freaked out. I had a breakdown right there in the courtyard. After getting me to calm down, Nathaniel got Aaron to tell him everything. That was when Nathaniel suggested I train with the warriors, and despite still not hearing from my wolf Maia, I quickly excelled in training. It was shortly after meeting Nathaniel that Aaron told me that the search for me had ceased, and I felt like I could rest easy again.

It was in my mentorship with Nathaniel that we began to realise that I could funnel my anger into my training, and after another year, we began to see evidence that Maia hadn't gone. My eyes bled to the Beta rank gold on one occasion, and Nathaniel declared that this was evidence that I still had my wolf, although, to this day, I still haven't shifted and still haven't heard anything from her.

I looked at Nathaniel and smiled. "So no charges then?" I asked hopefully. He scowled at me but shook his head.

"No, no charges now." He reached into a drawer and took out a brown folder. "But that's because I have a mission for you, one that you are uniquely qualified for."

CHAPTER 26

Harper

I took the standard case folder from him and opened it to look at the contents. The first thing I saw was a picture. It was obviously a stakeout shot from the angle it was taken. The man in the shot looked to be of medium build, with mid-brown hair that had a golden undertone and lightened a bit at the ends. It was one of those short messy styles that are meant to look like they don't care, but probably took longer than my whole morning routine. This was carried into the designer stubble with the slight, oh, I forgot to shave today, stubble. That was where the messy look stopped, though. The three-piece suit he wore was obviously tailored to him, and he held himself with a confidence that could be seen a mile away.

"Cute!" I said, and Nathaniel scowled at me.

"Dangerous," he said sternly.

"Even cuter," I replied with a wink, and he rolled his eyes.

"His name is Elias Owens," Nathaniel said as I thumbed through the attached case report. "Not much is known about him, and what we do know isn't good." I glanced up at Nathaniel briefly. He seemed genuinely concerned about this guy, which was not normal for Nathaniel at all. I looked back down at the papers.

"Werewolf, Alpha rank," I read from the front sheet. "Thirty-Five years old, no known information on his family." And then I saw the list of pack names under the ownership. I counted seven names and looked up at Nathaniel, confused.

"Why are there seven different packs under ownership?" I looked back at the list again. "He can't be Alpha of seven different packs, surely," I said in disbelief, and Nathaniel shrugged.

"That list isn't up to date. It's eight now," he said.

"Eight!" I exclaimed. "How does someone become the Alpha of eight packs?" It was not unheard of for Alpha's to fight over territory. Still, if the victorious Alpha already had a pack, it would normally be a neighbouring territory, and the two would be merged together into his original pack. The pattern of these packs made no sense. I knew of two of them, but not the others. The map attached showed that all seven packs were spread across the country.

"And is the eighth pack connected to any of these?" I asked, and Nathaniel shook his head.

"Owens appeared on our radar almost five years ago," Nathaniel said. "Just out of nowhere, no connection to a pack that we can find, no lineage that we can find." He pointed to the case file, and I passed it back. He searched through before pulling out some papers.

"Ah, here it is," he said as he thumbed through the report. "Owens rushed the border patrol of the Red Rock pack with around fifteen wolves, all assumed to be rogues. He quickly took control of the pack after killing the Alpha in cold blood." I stood up and walked to the window, looking out onto a group of warriors who were mid training session as he spoke. So far, it was all standard.

When a werewolf doesn't have a pack, he is considered a rogue. Other rogues will gravitate towards him when an Alpha wolf doesn't have a pack. The only reason it wasn't considered a pack is the lack of territory. Rogues are considered the lowest of the low, especially to pack wolves, and living in a pack would have you believe they are not all that common. But the fact is that there are more rogue werewolves than there are pack wolves. They still gravitated towards a pack-like structure, mostly in cities, but were not recognised. So, for Owens to have a small assault of fifteen wolves was certainly not uncommon. What was interesting, though, was that he was able to take down a pack with such few wolves.

"This is where it gets interesting," Nathaniel said, drawing my attention back to him. "Owens then spends approximately six months in the pack before setting up a stage Alpha, someone who holds the title for the pack, but Owens stills holds ultimate control over the pack. He sets up the hierarchy from a mix of his own men and one's from the existing pack that seems to pass some sort of test of his. Once he has done this, he moves on to another pack."

"But he still holds control, and the pack remains as is?" I asked.

"Mostly, there are some movements between packs from what we can see." He looked back down at the file. "The packs that he attacks all seem to be run down, smaller and more isolated packs," Nathaniel continued. "The ones who don't have alliances to call upon to help defend themselves. And every one of those packs suddenly began to see abundance and revitalisation before Owens moved on."

"That's a good thing, though, right?" I asked. Surely a pack doing better would be a positive.

"Yes, in general, the pack doing better is a good thing." Nathaniel looked up at me. "But we have reason to believe that the sudden upturn in prosperity comes from a not-so-positive source."

That piqued my interest.

"What do you mean?" I asked. Nathaniel shuffled the papers around and then looked up at me.

"We believe Owens is a high-level member of The Circle." I couldn't help the look of shock on my face. The Circle was well known within the Council. They were an underground criminal organisation that dealt with trafficking drugs, guns, and people. They mainly worked within the underground supernatural world. Still, it bled into the mundane world, and I had heard stories of female werewolves being taken and sold to rich sick bastards because of the amount of punishment their bodies could take. Or for vampires and certain fae to be bled dry and their blood sold to the highest bidder for drugs. I knew the Council had been investigating the Circle for longer than I had been here. There had been rumours that the Circle had infiltrated areas of the Council, so work on those cases was on a strictly need-to-know basis and limited to Council Elders and Councilmen.

"Wait, so why are you talking to me about this?" I asked. Even as an Elite officer, I wasn't qualified to be working on a Circle case, despite how much I would have loved to be involved in taking these scumbags down.

"We believe that Owens has been using the packs to set up distribution centres and transit routes for the Circle's activities. I looked back at the map and saw how the layout of the packs, now under his control, could create quite the opportunity for concealed travel. Some were close to high international traffic areas and some to seaports.

"Ok, sure," I said. "But again, why am I sitting here discussing this?" I asked.

"Owens is very clever," Nathaniel said. "Once he takes over a pack, his guards go up. We have tried to infiltrate his operations on numerous occasions, and each time we have been blocked."

"Nathaniel?" I was getting a bad feeling about where this was going.

"You understand that to bring this to someone of your position is a big violation of the rules." I narrowed my eyes and looked at the map again. "Of course, it would mean that if you were successful in obtaining the information we needed, it would all but guarantee you my last Councilman position." I looked up at Nathaniel. He knew without a doubt that this would pull me in. I had been hinting very strongly about that position, and it was one that previously had never been filled by a woman. I knew I was good enough, but the position came with the chance of promotion to Council Elder, too, and thus was never given lightly.

"Nathaniel," I snapped, and he looked at me quietly. "Why am I uniquely qualified for this case?" Those were the words he had used, and now those words scared me.

"Because you have a genuine reason to visit the latest pack he has taken over," Nathaniel said, his eyes not leaving mine. I felt a drop in my stomach that I hadn't felt in such a long time.

"And what is that?" I didn't want to know, even though I already knew.

"To grieve the death of your father." I shook my head in denial. No, not there, anywhere but there. My father had passed away five months ago. I had received word through Aaron, as I hadn't spoken to my family since that night.

"Harper, the pack he has taken over is the Midnight Moon pack!"

CHAPTER 27

Harper

I felt like I was going to be sick. The feeling of dread in my stomach intensified as I sat back down in the chair opposite Nathaniel.

"No," I said and shook my head. Nathaniel inclined his head and gave me a surprised look.

"No?" he asked.

"No!" I said clearer. "I can't do this, Nathaniel. Please don't ask me to do this."

Nathaniel looked down at the papers and back up at me. The look of sympathy crossed his eyes.

"Harper, I'm not asking you to take this case." His face dropped into a blank expression, and I closed my eyes. I knew that expression. It was the one he had when there was no discussion to be had. "In this matter, I am telling you that you will be taking this case."

I shook my head again and opened my eyes.

"I can't go back there. Not now, not ever," I pleaded.

"Harper, the only reason why you are getting away with not being dragged up in front of the High Council and the Sovereign himself is because you are the only one that could even get close to this," he said. "At this point, you have fucked up so much that no amount of skill and talent, no amount of sweet-talking, will get you out of this."

"I would rather become Drake's puppet again," I spat, and Nathaniel scowled at me.

"No, you wouldn't, and you know that," he scolded. "But if he had his way, you would be, and he is High Council, so you are lucky he hasn't sanctioned the request already because I assure you it is on his mind."

I shrank down in my seat and closed my eyes again. I felt a tear slip down my cheek.

"So my choices are death by trial, blood whore, or go back to the place that ruined me?" I asked rhetorically.

"Harper!" Nathaniel walked around the desk and came and crouched down in front of me. I looked at him as he took my hand and squeezed it softly. "You are not ruined! Not even a little bit." He had a fierce look in his eyes. "You are one of the strongest people I have ever met. Yes, you make questionable choices in your love life."

I snorted at that. I didn't have a love life. I had a sex life. After coming to the Council, I had attempted a relationship, and my fucked up brain wrecked it and almost ruined an important friendship for me. I chose to keep people at a distance and could lose a few fingers and still count on one hand the number of people I trusted.

"You can do this. You are not that scared little girl who arrived here almost ten years ago." Nathaniel smiled at me. "Come on, sweetheart, I think of you as my own daughter, and I wouldn't ever put you in a situation that I didn't think you couldn't take." I smiled back. Nathaniel had really provided the father figure role to me these last nine or so years that he had been mentoring me in a way that my real father never seemed to be able to do, and I was ever grateful for it. I never even realised that it was a role that I lacked or that my own father had always operated from a more self-serving space until I met Nathaniel.

I sat up and wiped away the tears, and Nathaniel patted my hand. He stood up, walked back around the desk, and sat back down. He looked at me again, and I could tell by the grimace that there was more that I wasn't going to like.

"Owens has a set way of doing things from what we have gathered," he said, his tone all business again.

"When taking control of a pack, he kills the Alpha and, in most cases, the Beta and Gamma." I nodded, keeping my face blank, but inside hoping that meant that the one person I didn't want to see was on this criminal's hit list. I immediately felt bad for thinking that, but if anyone deserved it, then it was him.

"In this case, it looks like he did just that. Alpha Daniel Chambers, Beta Eric Stokes, and Gamma Stephen Bennet were all found dead outside of the territory's boundaries." I looked up, shocked. It was one thing to know that this new person was ruthless, but another to have known the people on his list. The Alpha and Beta had been nice to me, and, although I had limited contact with the Gamma, his daughter Louise had been my best friend for years.

"What about their families?" I asked, hoping that the ruthless reputation of Owens wasn't as bad as it could be. Nathaniel started to look uncomfortable, and I didn't like it.

"What?" I asked, the feeling of dread coming back.

"After Owens clears out the named ranked, he fills those roles with a mix of his own men and existing pack members. I can only assume that this is to establish authority and keep the familiarity that makes the pack compliant." Nathaniel pulled out a sheet of paper and read through it before looking at me.

"The Gamma role was already free as the death of the Gamma left no heir due to an incident with the Gamma heir some years back." The gamma heir, that was Alex. My heart hurt a little. Was the incident related to me escaping?

"That role has been assigned to one of Owens' own men, a man by the name of Marcus Farwell. What we know of Farwell is limited to his time here. He trained as a warrior before something happened, and he disappeared. He was an exceptional warrior." Nathaniel grinned at me. "Someone who probably could have gone toe to toe with you." I scowled at this.

"Owens has Alpha control in the current setting, but their report suggests that the original Alpha heir, Damien Chambers, is unaccounted for after fleeing the pack in the initial attack, although his wife was seized and is currently incarcerated in the pack cells." I cringed at the thought that Damien had found a wife, poor lass. And for him to run away and leave her behind as well, well, that sounded like he hadn't changed one bit.

I noticed that Nathaniel had stopped talking and was looking concerned. "What?" I asked.

"As I said, Owens always instals one existing member of the pack into the named rank positions." He handed me the report he was reading from, and I quickly scanned down the words. It was an update report from an independent scout. I looked for the latest information and saw where Nathaniel had been reading from.

"Ok Alpha, Elias Owens assigned his own man Marcus Farwell into the role of Gamma and original pack member and Beta heir-"

I stopped dead at seeing the name in print right in front of me. I resisted all the urges to scream or cry or the panic attack that was pushing at my carefully constructed walls. I took a breath and passed the sheet of paper back to Nathaniel.

"I'll take the offer from Drake," I said, keeping my expression as blank as possible.

"The hell you will," Nathaniel snapped. I looked up at him, and his eyes were the silver of his wolf. Despite being a Council Elder and my mentor and, for all intents and purposes, my boss, he was a lower rank than I was. I was never a rank snob. The majority of the Council Elders and people within the Council had the silver eye rank. It didn't matter here, and not now, because Nathaniel still exuded confidence and power without the rank status. Even now, seeing him glaring at me made me want to shrink back and hide.

"I told you, Harper, you will be taking this case." I returned his glare, but he just ignored me.

"I have made arrangements for your entry into the pack territory. Aaron has already spoken with Thomas Kirby, your uncle, I believe." I nodded, feeling kind of numb.

"Kirby has petitioned for you to enter the pack territory because you are there to grieve the loss of your father, Darren Kirby. You will be required to meet with Owens at his request."

"Meet with him. Why?" It was common for outsiders to be granted limited access to territories, but not so common for the Alpha to demand a meeting.

"Like I said, he closes the borders in the six months he is in a pack. He is almost paranoid about it. My guess is he will want to feel you out to ensure you aren't a spy."

"But I am a spy," I said.

"Yes, well, I am sure you are able to convince him otherwise," Nathaniel said. "You got the highest scores in the undercover practices exam in the last twenty-five years. I am sure you can manage this." Nathaniel grinned, and I couldn't help returning that grin. I knew he was particularly proud of that achievement of mine.

"The mission needs you to get close to Owens. Find me something I can use to bring this bastard up against the High Council. Anything that will help us get some dent in the armour that the Circle has, and I swear that you will be returning to that Councilman position."

Nathaniel had a determined look on his face, and I knew he wouldn't send me in unless he had to. I sighed and looked back down at the paper.

"When do I leave?" I asked, and Nathaniel seemed to visibly relax at my silent agreement to take the case.

"Tomorrow," he said, "So you need to pack."

I nodded. I knew I looked like I was focusing on reading the report, but I couldn't take my eyes off of that one sentence. That one name that still sets fear in my heart.

Original Pack member and Beta heir, Colton Stokes, as the acting Beta.

CHAPTER 28

Aaron

"She wasn't too happy when she left here, and she knows you knew, so be warned." I groaned as Nathaniel relayed his conversation with Harper earlier. I appreciated the phone call to warn me, but I would have appreciated not being pushed under the bus even more. Harper's temper was notorious around The Council, and not many would face her when she was on a warpath.

"Yeah, thanks for that," I said sarcastically. I pressed end on the phone and sighed. If I had known sooner, I would have brought doughnuts. That would have at least eased the beating I was in for. Despite being a slight build, the girl trained hard, and she could take down guys bigger than me with a smile and a flick of her hair. But here I was at the door of our shared apartment empty-handed and ready for the worst.

I put my key in the lock and opened the door ajar. It was unsettlingly quiet. There was rarely a time that Harper didn't have some rock or metal band playing loud. Maybe she wasn't home. I was lying to myself in hope since I could already smell her scent, and it was fresh, although it was mixed in with the scent of fermented grapes. Great, she had been drinking. I took a breath and pushed the door open, only to pull it back again when I saw the shadow of something flying at the door. I heard a smash against the door and winced. I listened for any more objects that may be headed my way when I heard a sigh.

"It's fine. You're safe." I let go of a breath I didn't know I was even holding and eased the door open again.

"For now," she said, and I hesitated with the door half open when she giggled. Oh man, she was drunk. This was not going to be good.

I opened the door all the way and looked into the apartment's living room. Harper was sprawled across the sofa facing me. Her eyes were closed, but I knew she knew my exact movement. I stepped over the pool of wine and broken glass at the door and looked back up at her to see she was now watching me. I nodded down to the glass and raised my eyebrows. She shrugged in return and closed her eyes again. I closed the door and moved to place my briefcase on the side table by the door, still watching her with caution. I took off my coat and shook out the water from the rainstorm outside before hanging it up.

"You've been drinking," I said. She opened her eyes, and I nodded to the two empty bottles of wine at the foot of the sofa. She followed my gaze and shrugged.

"I can handle a bottle or two," she said and closed her eyes again. She was right. As werewolves, it took us a bit more alcohol than your average mundane to get a good buzz, but she wasn't acting or smelling like she had only had two bottles. I walked into the kitchen and sighed as I saw three more empty bottles. I grabbed them and walked back into the living room.

"And these?" I asked. Her eyes opened again, and she giggled again.

"Those were the ones I handled," she said with a wink. I shook my head and put the bottles in my bag. I would put them down the recycle shoot on my way out tomorrow.

I turned and saw she was watching me and ran my hand nervously through my hair. The tension in the room had suddenly gone up a few notches.

"I bumped into Paul earlier," I said. "He wasn't happy."

"Who?" she asked with a smile, and I rolled my eyes. He said she had forgotten his name. I didn't have the heart to tell him she never forgot anyone's name. She just pretended she did when she was only interested in getting laid.

"I've asked you before not to sleep with the newer warriors. They don't understand your ways." It wasn't the first time I had some jilted fresh warrior. Harper was undeniably beautiful and a formidable warrior and officer, but she was damaged, and she took her damage out in mindless fucking.

I went and sat in the armchair and rubbed my tired eyes. I had been putting in a lot of hours in the classroom where I taught Parapsychology for the first years. I sensed Harper's presence before I felt her hand stroking up my leg. I opened my eyes and looked down to see her on her knees in front of me with a mischievous grin on her face.

"Why? Are you jealous?" She winked and continued to push her hand up my leg, getting close to my groin. I stopped her hand and glared at her.

"Don't," I said sternly but already knew she wouldn't listen. She got up from her knees and climbed onto my lap, straddling me and leaning close to my ear.

"Come on, Aaron," she whispered as she ran her hands through my still damp hair and pushed her torso against my hardening dick. "You look like you need to blow off some steam, and you know I know how to please you." She nibbled my ear, and I groaned automatically. I wanted nothing more than to take her into my room and show her that she didn't need to fool around with the first years, that I could do a much better job than they ever could for her.

We had tried a relationship before. After I had picked her up as that scared little eighteen-year-old girl, I had taken her in. We had got very close, and I felt unbelievably protective towards her. At first, it was very platonic. She hated to be touched at all, and the nights were filled with nightmares and fears. The only time she let me near was when I held her as she clung to me in tears.

After she had fallen for the charms of that dick Drake and got deep in his sordid world, it was like something had clicked in for her. She had come out of that situation a lot different, and although she never talked about her three months at the Castle, a mansion owned by Drake which was basically 24/7 blood and sex games, I knew it had affected her greatly and likely added to the trauma that she already had from that ex-mate of hers. With Nathaniel's help, I had got her from Drake's grips and brought her back home.

That was when our relationship had developed from just friends to something deeper. And it was going well for a year or so, I really saw a change in her, and we were happy, despite Tommy telling me he was going to kill me the next time he saw me. I wasn't bothered about that, though. The guy hadn't left the borders of his town in almost fifteen years, not since we had trained here together.

Things with Harper had taken a darker turn, and her interests in the more taboo sex practices had got too much for me. I didn't mind playing with the handcuffs now and then, but the things she wanted to experiment with were beyond my comfort level, and I couldn't stand the idea of her wanting me to hurt her. I'd called the relationship shortly before eighteen months together, and we had agreed to be friends. It had killed me to do it and broke my heart, but I knew I wasn't what she needed. Every now and then, I slipped, and we found ourselves back in bed together, and I regretted it every single time. Sure, the sex was great, amazing in fact, she was right when she said she knew what turned me on, but the heartache after knowing that she was never really mine was too much.

Harper had moved to kiss my neck and was grinding against me, and I felt myself wanting to slip for a second more before I pulled myself together. I grabbed her around the sides and stood up, lifting her off me and putting her down on the sofa before walking off into the bathroom, aware that she was sulking behind me.

I washed my face as I tried to compose myself and stared at myself in the mirror. Harper appeared in the reflection behind me, and we just watched each other before she broke eye contact.
"I'm sorry," she said and looked back up at me. I smiled slightly to let her know I wasn't mad.
"I just..." she said and waved her arms around. "I feel like I am falling right now." She sat down on the closed toilet seat and looked up at me with

unshed tears in her eyes. "I don't think I can do this, Aaron." She wiped at one tear and then looked at the offending wetness on her hand in disgust. "I can't go back there. I can't see him again." More tears fell down her cheeks, and I turned and reached down and pulled her in for a hug. She clung to me like she did in the early days, and I kissed the top of her head.

"Harps, you are one of the strongest people I have ever met. I have every faith in you being able to do this," I said, and she looked up at me.

"I haven't seen anyone since that night, not even spoken to Tommy." Her eyes lit up. "Can't you come with me? We can say you are my boyfriend." She looked excited all of a sudden. "Surely two agents are better than one?" Her face fell as I shook my head.

"Sorry, Harps, I already tried. Tommy originally requested two entry passes, one for you and your boyfriend, but the second one was denied, and he didn't want to push it." She nodded and went silent. Her fingers toyed with the buttons of my shirt as she stared off into space. I sighed and leaned in, and picked her up off the floor. Her hands moved around my neck, and she snuggled into me as I carried her into her room.

I pulled her covers back and put her into bed before taking off her jeans and then pulling the covers back over her. Her eyes had already closed as the emotions had really taken it out of her. I turned to go back into the living room.

"Aaron?" she asked quietly. I could tell that sleep was trying to claim her.

"Yeah?"

"Do you really think I can do this?" she asked, and I smiled.

"Harper, sweetheart," I said, turning to face her again. "You have faced countless challenges, criminals, and the likes of. I have no doubt that you can handle one small pack jerk." I saw her smile, her eyes still closed, and went to turn again.

"Aaron?" she asked again, this time quieter.

"Yeah, darling?"

"Please don't go." I smiled sadly. The pain and fear in her voice wouldn't show to most other people, but I knew her, and I knew she needed not to be alone right now. I sighed and closed her bedroom door. I slipped off my shoes and clothes down to my boxers and climbed into the bed behind her. She turned and snuggled into me, and her breathing evened out as she fell asleep. It wasn't long before the comfort of her scent relaxed me, and I fell asleep.

Harper

I woke up with a slight headache, and Aaron's arms wrapped around me. I snuggled into him again for a few minutes, internally cringing at how I behaved last night. I loved Aaron. He was my rock, and I didn't want to hurt him. I had wished for so long that I could be the girl he wanted, but I still had so much work to do, and it wasn't fair on him to drag him through it.

Eventually, I sighed and grudgingly pulled myself out of his arms and went into the bathroom to shower. By the time I was done, I could smell bacon cooking and walked into the living room to see Aaron by the door cleaning up the broken glass from last night.

"Whoa!" I said, wrapping the towel around my body. "You can't cook bacon and do something else. You'll overcook it." He stood up and rolled his eyes before walking into the kitchen to throw away the broken glass.

"Don't worry, princess," he said with a grin. "This one is mine. I'll make your raw one in a couple of minutes, so get dressed." I scowled at the frying pan with the burnt bacon crisping before heading off into my room. There was a suitcase open on my bed, and I saw Aaron had already packed most of the clothes I would need. I grabbed some panties and bras from their drawers without even bothering to look in the suitcase. Aaron knew me well enough to pack for me and cook my bacon right, and I knew him well enough to know that he refused to go into my underwear drawers.

After breakfast, we headed down to Aaron's car, and as he was putting my suitcase in the boot, I saw Nathaniel walking up. He handed me a brown envelope.

"Proof that you have been working as a secretary for the last three years in London, and then as a waitress before then." I nodded and tucked the envelope under my arm as I climbed into the car. Aaron joined me and started the car. Nathaniel waved as we drove off, but I couldn't bring myself to wave back. I suddenly felt very nervous.

The drive to the pack border took four hours, and I had fallen asleep somewhere around hour three. I felt as Aaron shook me awake a bit later. I sat up, rubbed my eyes, and looked around. We were at the side of the road on a grass lay-by, and I could see another car a few metres off. Sitting in the car was one person who I hadn't seen in almost ten years. I looked at Aaron, and he smiled encouragingly as I got out of the car.

I walked up to the unseen border and smiled shyly at Tommy. He looked much the same as he did the last time, older obviously but not bad older. Aaron handed me my case, and I hugged him.

"You got your phone?" he asked, and I nodded. I turned and stepped over the border, feeling the shift as I entered pack territory.

Tommy took my suitcase and placed it in the back seat before turning and pulling me into a hug and whispering, "Missed you, kid." I rolled my eyes and smiled and hugged him back.

That was when I noticed another car had pulled up a little further on. I glanced at Tommy, who followed my gaze before growling low in his throat.

"Come on, let's get out of here," he said, and I climbed into the car. I looked over at Aaron one last time, glaring at the other car. He glanced my way and then smiled and waved before getting back in his car. Tommy turned our car around and drove down the road that led into town. I tried not to look as we passed the other car, but the pull to glance up was too much, and I did just as we passed by.

My heart leaped, and I felt fear run through my system as I clearly saw HIM behind the wheel of the car staring at me. Our eyes met for a brief second before we passed by, and I pulled my eyes to my knees. I felt as Tommy reached over and squeezed my hand.

"Don't worry, kid," he said and smiled as I looked up at him. "I got your back."

I had a feeling from the way he looked at me in that brief second that I was going to need all I could get at my back.

Welcome home, Harper. Welcome home indeed.

CHAPTER 29

Colton

I sat with my head in my hand, feeling nothing as the redhead on her knees in front of me wrapped her mouth around my dick. I wanted to relax and enjoy the feeling as she ran her tongue down my shaft and rolled her eyes up to look at me as she did it. I closed my eyes, grabbed her hair, and thrust myself into her, down to her throat. I pulled a picture up in my mind of HER as the sounds of the redhead gagging with each thrust filled the room. I imagined it was her on her knees in front of me, begging my forgiveness for daring to leave me. I began to get close to bursting with each thrust. I tightened my grip on the hair in my hand as my breathing got heavier, and I teetered on the edge of my climax as I imagined her beautiful-

A knock on the door pulled me out of my dream, and the pleasure dissipated instantly. I looked down at the redhead, whose face was stained with tears and mascara. I let go of her, and she fell back on her ass on the floor.

"Geez, Colton," she snapped. "I don't mind the rough stuff, but give me a warning the next time." I glared at her, and she shrunk back in fear.

"That's Beta to you. Now get the fuck out of my office." She looked down and pulled herself off the floor.

"Yes, Beta, sir," she mumbled and turned towards the door just as there was another knock. More like a pounding, so I already knew who it was.

"Fuck sake!" I exclaimed. "Come in." The door flew wide open and slammed against the wall.

Marcus stormed into the room with a big grin on his face. He looked the redhead up and down and then glanced at me and rolled his eyes.

"Hey there, darling," he said, and I watched as she blushed.

"I don't have all day, Marcus," I snapped. "What do you want?" Marcus turned towards me as the girl scurried out.

"Boss said to bring you these files." He put a pile of brown folders on my desk.

"Seriously? Like I don't have enough to do." I looked at the mounting work and shook my head. I wasn't leaving this place anytime soon.

"Take it up with the boss, dude." He shrugged and then grinned at me. I knew he was trying to bait me into some sort of fight. He had been doing it since they had got here. The guy was a brute with more tattoos than bare skin. He acted dumb and carefree, but I recognised the eyes of a hunter and kept a close eye on him.

"What?" I asked, and his grin widened.

"You sound awfully stressed for a guy who just got off," he said, and I glared at him.

"If you hadn't interrupted, I might have, but now it's not just your mere presence that irritates me."

I looked down at the files and sighed.

"How the fuck does he expect me to do all this on top of my usual stuff?" I suddenly found myself with three times as much work three months ago when his almighty Elias Owens took over the Midnight Moon pack. I was happy to finally get the Beta position my father had been gripping hold of. But I didn't want to get it as a result of seeing my father's throat ripped out along with the Alpha's. Things had changed drastically in the time that Elias had moved in. I had to be careful with who I talked to as more and more people seemed to be either disappearing or publicly siding with Owens.

I didn't care if he was technically the new Alpha. He wasn't my Alpha. I just hoped I could keep everything running until Damien gathered help. He had left a message through a secured line saying that he had, and it was on the way. He seemed rather happy about it, saying it would blow my mind. The guy sounded drunk, though, so I took his shit with a pinch of salt. In addition to all the usual pack business, Elias had me going through every pack member and property holdings files. He wanted my opinion on everyone. I didn't, for one second, believe he did. I think he was also trying to get me to break.

"Well, if you had more help, you would get through things quicker," Marcus said, thumbing through the files, and I scowled at him.

"Are you offering?" I asked, and he shook his head.

"No can do, fella," he said. "But I'm sure if you knew where that chicken shit friend of yours was, he could help you." I glared at him again. "Where's Damien, Colton?" I rolled my eyes. It was the same every day. They were so keen to get their hands on him. But despite the fact that he was hiding like a scared rabbit, he was still my best friend, and I wasn't about to rat him out.

"You know the answer to that. I don't know," I snarled. "Now get out of my office. Can't you see I have work to do?" I looked down at my papers and ignored him.

"Sure thing, dude, I think I'm gonna go find that piece of ass that was just in here, show her what a real man is like." I rolled my eyes again.

"Sure, be my guest," I said without looking up. I could feel him staring at me but continued to work through the file that I had open on my desk. After a couple of minutes, he eventually got bored, and I heard as he turned and left without another word. I looked up at the door that he had just slammed shut and grinned. I was taking that as a win.

I finished the file I was working on and went to grab the next file when I saw a red tag sticking out of one of the files. I pulled it out to see it was a temporary entry request. A few of these had been requested since Elias had taken over, but they had all been denied. I had heard that was standard for his operations, so I was intrigued when this one had an approved stamp on it. I opened the file, and my eyes widened as I saw the name on the front page.

Harper Kirby.

It felt like an electric shock had run through my whole body. She was coming back. She had requested to come back, but why now? After all this time. Did she think I had forgotten about her? Or did she crave me as much as I craved her? Was she coming back to me? If so, why didn't she reach out? My head was awash with questions and scenarios. I needed answers.

I grabbed the file, left my office, and walked two doors down to the Alpha's office. I resisted the urge to slam the door open and demand answers. Instead, I knocked and waited.

"Come in." The clipped voice of our new Alpha called through, and I opened the door. The room was the same as it had been when Alpha Daniel had it, apart from the personal pictures that had all been removed and the addition of the heavy-duty safe pushed into the corner by the bar. The man himself sat behind the desk and, as always, dressed as if we were in a corporate office in the city with his three-piece designer suits. This one was grey with a black tie. He wasn't wearing the jacket, and the arms of his shirt were rolled up, showing his arm ink. He looked up at me from his paperwork and looked a little pissed off at the interruption.

"What is it, Colton?" he asked. I put the file on his desk, and he glanced at it before looking up at me.

"What of it? It's an entry request from a former pack member."

"Harper Kirby," I said, and he looked up again. "Did she state the reason for the request?"

He took the file and looked through it. Towards the back, there was a picture of Harper from her school file. Seeing her beautifully sweet face hit me hard in the heart, and I stopped breathing for a second.

"She didn't," Elias said. "The request came through Thomas Kirby, her uncle, I believe."

I couldn't help the growl that sounded in my throat, and Elias glanced up at me before carrying on. "He requested that she visit due to the death of her father, from a heart attack, it says here." Yeah, heart attack, sure. Very few people knew what happened that night, but that piece of shit Kirby got what he deserved, that's for sure.

"The request had originally been for two, so her boyfriend could accompany her, but I denied that."

I growled at that. Her boyfriend! She had a boyfriend? The idea that another man would dare to touch my Harper sent fury to run through my veins. Elias quirked an eyebrow at my reaction.

"So I was right?" he asked. "She's that Kirby." I looked at him in shock. "You know?"

"What? That your mate rejected you and ran away from town?" He sounded amused. "Of course, I knew. I make it my business to know everything going on in this town."

"Well, you got one thing wrong," I snapped. "She didn't reject me. I rejected her." His head tilted slightly like I said something extra interesting.

"But according to my records, you were one day off of your mate bond completion when she left."

"Where the hell are you getting this information?" I demanded, and he raised an eyebrow.

"Check your tone, Beta," he said, and I lowered my eyes. It was important that I stayed on his good side, for now at least.

"And as far as my sources are concerned, that is just that. They are mine." He looked back down to his desk and carried on. He was obviously done with the conversation.

"When is she getting in?" I asked, trying to keep my voice even, and he looked up again and sighed. He looked at the file and then at the clock.

"I would say in about twenty minutes, Kirby is meeting her at the southern border. Now can I please get on with my work?"

I nodded. I was done. I had somewhere to be. I went to grab the file, and he picked it up.

"No, it's ok. I'll keep hold of this one." He had that dangerous look in his eyes, the one he had just before I saw him rip out my father's throat. I nodded and backed away. He nodded and then put the file in his drawer, locked it, and then looked back down at his work. I took that as a signal that I had been excused.

I headed out into the hallway and stopped by my office to grab my car keys before heading out of the pack house. I jumped into my car and headed towards the southern border. I arrived and saw Tommy's red heap of junk and another black car. I could see the other car was just beyond the border. The car didn't have my main attention, though. I was more drawn to the two people standing in front of it. They were in an embrace that made me want to jump out of my car and race down and smash his head. The guy looked big, but I was sure I could take him easily enough. But the woman in his arms, and by the looks of her lean frame, she had grown into a beautiful woman indeed. She was everything I remembered her to be. And nothing the same. Her beautiful, dark golden brown hair still held the natural golden highlights and flowed down her back. She wore tight black jeans and a tight black vest top that showed her breasts had filled out nicely. Just remembering her perky little ones already made me hard, and I was looking forward to introducing myself to the upgrades. She walked confidently across the border, and I swear I felt as she entered the territory. She hugged Tommy, and even though I knew he was her uncle, I still didn't like his close contact.

She glanced back to the probable boyfriend, who I could tell was staring in my direction. Harper followed his gaze, and I saw that as her eyes hit the car, something I couldn't quite place crossed over her face. She got into the car, and Tommy got in the other side. I saw the boyfriend get in his car and start to drive away. That's right, man, drive away. Don't expect to see your girlfriend again. She's mine now, and I'm not letting her go this time. I watched eagerly as Tommy's car drove alongside mine, and, for just one shining second, I saw her. Our eyes met, and I saw her flinch. A smile crept on my face. Oh yes, she is most definitely mine.

I watched as the car disappeared up the road in my rearview mirror and then grabbed my phone and dialled the number. The phone rang a few times before the familiar feminine lilt answered.
"What do you want, Colton?" I ignored the blatant disrespect. I would deal with that later.
"Tell Harry you aren't coming in to work tonight," I said, "and get ready for me. I'll be there in half an hour." I ended the call, not bothering to wait for a reply, and started my car.

One good night of getting my frustration out, and then I was going to get my mate back and make her mine once and for all.

CHAPTER 30

Harper

The sound of kids' cartoons and banging pots and pans invaded my sleep. I opened my eyes to see two small faces watching me with open curiosity. I groaned, pulled my blanket over my head, and tried to turn over on the uncomfortable sofa.

My mum had been so excited to see me yesterday when Tommy had brought me home. She began crying and was hugging me in a death grip. I had hoped I could grab a room at the motel in town, but my mum had insisted that I stay at the house. It might have been okay, but it turned out that my sister Susie had moved back home three years ago. Her mate had been cheating on her, and when she finally confronted him, he had got abusive. I was told in great detail how caring Alpha Daniel had been. He had arranged with her Alpha to have her and her three pups transfer back to Midnight Moon, and the Alpha of Star Dawn had banished her mate as punishment for what he had done.

This meant my old room had been turned into a kids' room for the nine-year-old and the six-year-old boys, and Susie had taken her old room that she shared with the four-year-old little girl. This made for a very busy house, and the only space for me was on the lumpy sofa that had been here since before I had left.

"There's no point trying to sleep now." I heard my sister's voice and groaned again. "You might as well get up before they start jumping on you." I heard giggling before I felt the weight of two small children hit me, one over my head and the other on my stomach, knocking the wind out of me.

"Fuck!" I exclaimed as I did my best to untrap myself from the covers.

"Harper, watch your language!" Susie scolded, and I rolled my eyes.

"Auntie Harper said a bad word, mummy!" One of the pups sang while the other one ran off shouting, "Fuck."

"Great, just great," my sister groaned. "Jackson, you are not to repeat that word." My sister's voice faded as she chased the younger boy around. I finally got free of the covers and sit up on the sofa. I looked for my phone, which I had left on the table, and saw it was halfway across the room on the floor.

I retrieved my phone and groaned again as I saw that it was barely 7am.

"Seriously," I said to myself. "I need to stay somewhere else."

"You're leaving again?" My mum's voice startled me from behind, and I turned to see the hurt expression on her face. She had changed so much. She was thinner and looked tired. Susie had told me after mum had gone to bed last night that the effect of dad's death had really messed her up. She had been with mum when he died. They had been out shopping, and suddenly mum screamed in pain and fell to the floor crying uncontrollably. She knew instantly, and by the time they got to the pack house where dad had been in a meeting, he was being rolled away in an ambulance. Mum had gone into a catatonic state for about a week after, and when she came to, she was never really the same.

The death of a mate was known to drive the surviving mate to insanity or death due to breaking the bond. It was like losing a piece of your own soul. I knew the feeling. When I had accepted Colton's rejection, I had felt like my world was ending, and I didn't know who I was. I had cried in despair for weeks after. I knew that what I went through was nothing compared to what my mum had gone through, not even close.

"Mum," I said. "I'm not going anywhere. I'm just thinking that the house is overcrowded. I could stay in town and still be here every day." Well, apart from when I was trying to get the information on this Owens guy, I added silently to myself. My mum looked like she was visibly relaxed, and she smiled sadly.

"I have just missed you, Harper dear," she said. "And you look so different. I feel like I don't know anything about you now." She headed off into the kitchen, and I sighed and followed her. The third kid, and the eldest, was sitting on a mobile phone at the breakfast counter, ignoring everyone.

"James, you know the rule about phones at the table," my mum said and pulled the phone out of his hand.

"Hey!" he exclaimed and stood up to say something, stopping when he saw me glaring at him. He tried to hold my stare before losing eye contact and huffing before storming out of the kitchen. I shook my head and grinned. I turned back to watch my mum as she emptied and loaded the dishwasher. I was going to ask if I could help when the back door opened, and Tommy walked in.

"Hey Linda," he said, kissing her cheek and then looking at me. "Hey Harper, how was your first night back home?" I shook my head and grimaced.

"I was ready to give that damn sofa all my secrets by 2 am," I said, rubbing my still aching back, and he laughed.

"Yeah, I feel you, kid," he said. "The odd night I stay over, I get the torture treatment from that old thing, too." I looked at him in surprise.

"You stay over?" I asked, and he nodded.

"I help out around the house, you know, since..." his voice trailed off, and he glanced at my mum, who was now pulling an armful of food out of the fridge.

"More like hinder," my sister said as she walked in carrying her daughter on her hip, who, as soon as she saw Tommy started bouncing and holding her arms out to him.

"Uncle Tommy!" she exclaimed in her sweet little voice, and Tommy's face lit up as he took her from her mum's arms.

"Come here, Gracey," he said and swung her around the room while she giggled manically. I smiled at the scene as my sister moved to help my mum with the breakfast preparations. It, at least, looked like they were a solidish family unit. I had missed my family a lot while I had been away, but I knew I couldn't get in contact with them. Certainly not at the beginning, when Colton had still been looking for me. I knew he would probably have had them watched, just in case. Then, after he had stopped looking, it had just felt too hard to reach back out. The longer it got, the more difficult it was.

Tommy sat on the stool next to me with Gracey on his knee and smiled at me.

"Remember, Kid," he said. "You have a meeting with Alpha Elias this afternoon." I nodded as I took a bite out of the slice of toast put in front of me.

"Yup, I remember," I said.

"What!" my mum exclaimed, looking between us in horror. "What do you mean you have a meeting with the Alpha?" I glanced at Tommy and then at Susie in confusion.

"It was a condition of her being able to come to visit Linda," Tommy said, and my mum shook her head.

"No, nope, absolutely not," she said. "My daughter cannot go see that monster. You know what he's like." My confusion grew. I had obviously missed something.

"Mum, don't worry," my sister said. "Harper has nothing to hide, and maybe when this probation calms down, she could even stay." I glanced at my sister and frowned. I had no intention of staying in this town any longer than I had to. I wanted to get back to the Council and planned to do so as soon as I had got enough evidence on this jackass.

"No, he killed your father," my mum started hyperventilating as the obvious signs of a panic attack set in. "He killed Alpha Daniel and Beta Eric." She looked at me in fear and started crying.

"Harper, please don't go. I don't want him to kill you too. He can't find out who you are." I glanced at Tommy. Did my mum know why I was here? As far as I was aware, only Tommy knew I was here on council business. He shook his head as if he read my thoughts while my mum continued to cry and mutter something about crown and child and stuff. My sister was trying and failing to calm her down, so I rushed around the counter and grabbed her hand, finding a certain point between the thumb and forefinger and pressing down. I rubbed circles in a clockwise direction, and my mum's breathing slowed down, and she became calm again, apart from the odd sniffles.

I guided her to a stool and helped her sit, smiling at her.

"Better?" I asked, and she smiled, her eyes still shiny with tears. I nodded and looked around for some tissue to wipe her eyes. Both Tommy and Susie were staring at me as if I had just sprouted wings.

"What?" I asked, and Tommy laughed.

"What the hell did you just do?" Susie asked, and I threw her an amused look.

"She had a panic attack," I said. "I just used a pressure point to relieve it. Remember, I used to suffer from them." I showed her where the point was on her hand while she nodded.

"Where did you learn that?" she asked, looking at me in wonder. I grimaced at the question.

"Colton," I said quietly. "He would do it when I started panicking. After I left, I wanted to know why it worked on me and found out that it was a common point on werewolves for anxiety." I didn't add that I had also learned where the points were for rendering various species of the supernatural incapacitated too.

"Harper, honey," my mum said, "You have to be careful with Alpha Elias. He's dangerous." I smiled at her.

"I'm sure I can handle one Alpha," I said, and Susie scoffed.

"Oh yeah," she laughed. "When was the last time you even saw an Alpha, especially while working as a receptionist for an insurance company?" Oh yeah, that's right, I thought—cover story. According to my records, I lived and worked in London for the last six years and in a diner before that. I smiled at my sister and shrugged.

"You wouldn't believe the pig-headed alpha types that think they run things in corporate," I said, and she laughed.

"I'll bet, but just be careful. There is something different about this Alpha." I nodded. I looked over to Tommy, who was being quiet and nodded to him. He got the hint and followed me to the living room, putting Gracey down.

"What did mum mean about Owens killing my father?" I asked quietly and turned up the TV so my sister and mother couldn't hear. Tommy shook his head and frowned.

"Elias had nothing to do with Darren's death." He looked at me. "He's a decent Alpha and not as nasty as everyone thinks," he said. "But he doesn't know that you work for the Council so I would keep that and whatever business you have to do here away from him." I nodded again just as my sister walked in the room.

"So, what do you plan to do while you wait for the meeting with the tyrant?" my sister asked and grinned. I smiled in return.

"Well, I thought I would catch up with Katie and Louise first. They are both still here, right?" I noticed Tommy's face darken as I mentioned Louise's name.

"Yeah, they are still here," Susie said, glancing nervously at Tommy. "Katie lives in the same apartments as she did, although a different number. I can find out for you." I nodded.

"And Louise?" I asked, and Tommy growled.

"You won't be able to talk to Louise," he hissed. "She's still locked in the cells until her spineless piece of shit husband is found."

"Wait! What?" I asked, confused. Louise and Tommy had seen each other in secret after finding out they were fated mates. Did she reject him? "What do you mean by her husband?"

Susie glanced at Tommy again before looking at me again

"Harper, after you left the pack, Louise mated with Damien. They have been mated and married for nine years."

CHAPTER 31

Harper

I stared at Susie. Did she just say what I thought she said? I looked at Tommy, and he looked away.

"I'm sorry, what did you say?" I shook my head. "No, Louise wouldn't agree to that." For one, I knew she hated Damien.

"Well, she did," Tommy hissed. He looked me in the eye and then indicated to Susie, and I nodded. He didn't want to talk in front of her.

"I'm gonna get ready and then head into town," I said. "Tommy, I don't have a car. Can you give me a lift?" He nodded.

Susie eyed me suspiciously. I knew I seemed to let it go a little too easily, even for the Harper she knew. But I smiled pleasantly, and she eventually shook her head.

"Well, just be sure to be home by 6pm. Mum wants a family dinner, and I'm not spending half the day in the kitchen for you to be late. That includes you too, Tommy," she said, pointing at Tommy. He rolled his eyes and then grinned.

"Careful there, Susie," he said. "You're starting to sound like your mum." Susie growled at him before playfully slapping his shoulder, causing him to laugh.

"Okay, kid, let me know when you are good to go, and I'll be your taxi service," Tommy said, turning to me with a grin on his face. I smiled, nodded, and then headed off upstairs to get ready.

Half an hour later, I was dressed in my trademark black skinny jeans and a low-cut black vest top. It was a warm day, so I opted for a cut-off black and red plaid shirt paired nicely with my combat boots. I let my hair hang loose and air dry and put on some light makeup, and I was done. I said bye to mum and Susie before Tommy and I headed out to the car. As soon as we were off the street, I turned to him.

"What the hell!" I exclaimed. He shook his head, glancing at me briefly before returning his eyes to the road.

"Not while I'm driving, let's get a drink," he said and then he fell silent. I could see his hands gripping the steering wheel hard enough for his knuckles to turn white. I nodded and turned and looked out of the window at the passing town as we drove through it.

It was never a bustling metropolis, but I expected more people than the two, maybe three that I saw, even at 8am. But all the shop windows were dark, and the streets were empty.

"What the hell happened to this place?" I asked, and Tommy shrugged.

"Many of the mundanes moved on when Elias took over three months ago. I guess his men have a heavy vibe from the outside." I looked at him, and he shrugged again. "We've had a curfew in place too, so I think that probably scared many people off." I continued looking out of the window as Tommy pulled into the carpark of Howlers, the local dive bar. This place was the opposite of the town. Doors open, neon lights glowing, and even at this time, a good handful of people.

"Seriously, Howlers?" I asked, looking at him, and he grinned.

"Yeah, when the diner closed a few years back, Harry took it upon himself to branch out. Before 7pm, this place is a family place." I got out of the car and looked around. There was a funny feeling about the place, and I swore I had the feeling of being watched as well.

I followed Tommy into the bar and was pleasantly surprised at the changes. The dance floor was still at the back with the tiny stage and DJ booth, and the bar still ran along one side. But the rest of the place had comfortable-looking tables and chairs with a row of booths running along the back wall. It was reasonably busy, with a few of the tables taken by a range of people. Some business suits, some workman wear and even a couple of families. Tommy walked up to the bar and ordered himself a coffee, and I ordered a diet coke from the pretty-looking blond behind the bar, who winked at Tommy as he paid. While we were waiting, I heard a voice behind me.

"Well, isn't this a sight for sore eyes, Harper Kirby? Is that really you?" I turned to the voice to see a grinning Alex standing behind me. I breathed a sigh of relief before grinning and walking over and hugging him. After reading the report stating the incident with the Gamma heir, I had been scared to ask in fear that Alex had been killed.

"Damn girl," he said, pulling away to look at me. "You have certainly grown in all the right places." I heard Tommy growl behind me and laughed.

"It's great to see you too, Alex," I said and hugged him again. His grip around my waist tightened, and I swear I felt him sniff my hair. Finally, I pulled away, and he grinned before looking behind me.

"Sal, I'm gonna take a break, okay?" I looked around to see the blond glaring at me before smiling at Alex and nodding her head.

Alex glanced at Tommy, who now had our drinks, and nodded towards the other side of the room. Tommy headed over to one of the booths, and I followed, with Alex at my back. I slid in one side, and Alex slid in next to me, despite the disapproving look from Tommy. I rolled my eyes at him. I wasn't upset with how close Alex was. The guy had filled out a little since I last saw him, but it was obvious that it was all muscle, and his arms were decorated with what looked like Norse tribal tattoos. His dark hair was cut pretty close to his head, not completely short but not enough to grab when you... I blushed at the thought that popped into my head. I looked up to see them both looking at me and shrugged. Alex grinned again, and Tommy rolled his eyes.

"So, you work here at Howlers?" I asked Alex, and he nodded.

"Yeah, mostly nights, but the odd morning too."

"Nights?" I asked. "Can't be too many of them with a curfew," I said, and Alex laughed.

"Yeah, it's not a full curfew, is it? If you get the seal of approval, then you are good to go as normal." He shook his head and smiled. "But enough about me and this place, I wanna hear about you," he said, and I narrowed my eyes. I knew he was purposely being evasive.

"Erm nope, I wanna know what the fuck went on here after I left." Alex looked taken aback by my assertiveness. I had to remember that I was known as the timid, sweet girl, not the woman I had become. I smiled sweetly at Alex, and he smiled again. He looked at Tommy, who took a drink from his coffee.

"Louise," he said, and Alex growled.

"Okay, come on," I said. "Why would Louise mate with Damien, and what the hell happened with you?" Alex grimaced and looked around the bar before looking back at me.

"Honestly, it felt like you leaving was a big catalyst in this place," he said. "Colton lost it; I mean, really lost it. He knew I had been involved in you escaping, and I ended up in the hospital for a while."

"Yeah, he damn near beat him to death," Tommy said. "Seriously, we weren't sure he would survive,"

"Oh my goddess, what?" I was horrified and felt guilty. Alex got hurt helping me.

"Yeah, I ended up with damage to the brain and was put in a medically induced coma for some time," he said. "When I woke up, the Alpha came to see me. He said my trial had taken place, I was proven guilty, and I had been stripped of my Gamma rank. I was lucky that I wasn't getting any more severe punishment." He sighed and looked down at his hands and then back at me. "I was in the hospital for another two weeks, and in all that time, not once did I see my dad or Louise. I had been frozen out. It was Tommy who got me set up in town and told me about Louise." I looked at Tommy, who was glaring into his coffee. "What about Louise?" I asked, and he looked up, his eyes hard with pain.

CHAPTER 32

Harper

"Her dad found out we were fated mates and told her to reject me," Tommy said.

"Did she?" I asked. I knew Louise wasn't a fan of the whole fated mate thing, but I thought she liked Tommy. He shook his head and looked back at the table.

"No, but she was told to stay away, and the next I heard, it was announced that she and Damien were to be mated." He looked up at me, his eyes shiny with unshed tears. "I tried to get to see her but was blocked at every point. It wasn't until Greg Henderson managed to get a message to me telling me that Louise was under strict twenty-four-seven protection." Alex scoffed at that.

"More like imprisonment." Tommy glanced at him before looking back at me.

"They had completed the mate bond within two weeks of you going." He looked at me, a haunted look on his face. "It was one of the most painful experiences of my life, feeling the fated bond ripped away like that. I felt so guilty for making you do that too."

I bit my lip to stop the tears from falling. Even when a fated bond isn't complete, it creates such a powerful connection that you simply feel like you can't live without the person. I felt it with Colton, even though he was so possessive and nasty to me. I still cried every night for months from the pain and loss.

"I don't understand, though. Why would she agree to it?" I asked.

"It had always been the plan," Alex said. "After Damien rejected his fated mate because she was an omega just after they turned eighteen, the Alpha and my father had agreed that Louise would mate with Damien. I found out about six months before everything happened and was trying to figure out some way to block it."

"Still, it's Louise here," I said. "She hated Damien."

"They threatened to kill Alex and me," Tommy said. "After the mating, Louise managed to get out and came to see me. They told her that if she didn't go ahead with it, then both Alex and I would be found guilty of treason and be put to death."

I closed my eyes as a tear slipped down my cheek.

"And that was why she was kept under lock and key until the mating happened because the Alpha didn't want what happened with you to happen with Louise," he said.

"Because of me, because I left," I said. I couldn't believe the pain my leaving had caused. "I am so sorry. I should never have gone. This is all my fault."

"Hey, no!" Alex exclaimed, grabbing my hand, and I opened my eyes to see him looking at me. "This is not your fault, trust me, these things have been in motion long before you knew what was happening." He reached up and wiped a tear away from my face with his thumb. "And I would have done it all again to make sure you were safe." I leaned into his hand, feeling the warmth of it against my cheek. He smiled at my reaction, and I smiled back, feeling a little flutter in my stomach.

Once upon a time, I had the biggest schoolgirl crush on Alex, and he had certainly improved since then. We had shared an accidental kiss one night when I was sixteen, but then he had got evasive, and I assumed it was because he had decided he had made a mistake and I was too young. Looking into his eyes now, I wondered if there had been another reason all that time ago.

Tommy growled again, and I glared at him.

"Seriously," I snapped. "What is your problem?" He shook his head and then glared at Alex. Alex looked away, and I sighed.

"Listen, Harper. You need to be careful," Tommy said. "We know that Colton knows you are here, and I have heard from one of my sources that he is planning something." I rolled my eyes but couldn't help the sinking feeling in my stomach.

"Don't do that. The guy was pretty obsessed with you. That much was evident after you left. He ripped this and many other packs apart looking for you. Just because he stopped looking on the outside didn't mean he wasn't doing quiet searches."

"I can handle myself, don't worry," I said to him, and maybe to reassure myself. Tommy shook his head to show he wasn't convinced but dropped the conversation.

We changed the subject to more pleasant ones. I told the boys about my fake life in London. Tommy knew it was all a lie, but Alex seemed none the wiser. They told me about different things that had happened in town and with different people. We talked for the next couple of hours, and throughout that time, I would feel Alex's hand against my thigh, or his arm would hang on the back of the booth behind me for a bit, and I would feel him playing with my hair. It felt nice, and I had made up my mind to visit him at the bar when Tommy wasn't around being overly watchful.

I noticed the bar had picked up and looked at my phone. It had just passed 11am, and Alex needed to excuse himself for the lunch shift. I took that as an opportunity to excuse myself, too.

"I'm gonna go and see Katie," I said, and Tommy went to stand up. I threw him a funny look.

"I can manage this alone," I said with a grin. "Chill, okay? It's not your job to protect me." He looked me dead in the eye with one of the most serious expressions I have ever seen on him.

"Yeah, but it is, though," he said, and I stopped and looked at him again. What the hell did that mean? I shook my head and laughed.

"Well, don't worry, I'm not as breakable as I used to be," I said. "I can manage the walk to the apartments." I smiled again and stared at him until he huffed and sat back down.

"Okay, but just be careful, okay?" he said, and I nodded. I said goodbye and waved to Alex, who waved back and I left the bar. I headed across the parking lot and down the short alleyway into the apartment complex. It was one of two in the town. This one was more run-down than the other one, where Tommy lived. This one was housing for the Omegas in the pack, and you could tell that it didn't get the care and attention that the rest of the town had got.

I headed up the stairs towards the apartment number Susie had given me. And was just coming out of the stairwell when the door opened. I ducked back a bit and watched as Colton walked out. He looked around like he was looking for something and then turned to the door. He said something in hushed whispers. I kept myself hidden in the shadows, hoping that my speeding heart wasn't as loud as it felt. I was ready to make a run for it if he headed this way, but to my relief, he headed the other way down the open landing. What the hell was Colton doing at Katie's place? Surely they weren't seeing each other. The thought hit me harder than I thought. I mean, it didn't matter to me who he was seeing, so why was I feeling annoyed.

I waited until I was sure that Colton had disappeared and my heart had resumed to normal speed before I relaxed enough to move out of my hiding place. I took a deep breath and went to walk around the corner when I felt a movement behind me. I went to turn towards it when I was painfully slammed face-first into the wall. I cried out automatically. My arms were grabbed from behind and a warm body pressed against me. I could already tell who it was before he spoke. It felt like my body relaxed against him all by itself.

"Hello, Strawberries."

CHAPTER 33

Harper

I closed my eyes as his hand crept around and wrapped around my throat, squeezing ever so slightly.

"You still smell like strawberries," he said as I felt him nuzzle into my hair and take a deep breath. "Just as sweet as ever." I struggled to push him away, but I was at an awkward angle and couldn't get the leverage I needed. He chuckled in my ear, and I tried not to let the sudden trapped feeling overwhelm me. This wasn't working. I needed to get a better advantage.

"Colton," I whispered in my best whiney voice. "Please." His hand around my throat loosened a little, and I relaxed a bit.

"Oh baby girl, I like it when you beg," he muttered and twisted my arm further behind my back. I cried out again, but this time it was all fake. If I acted like the old weak Harper and got myself into a better position, something, I could work with.

"Please, Colton, that hurts," I whined and rolled my eyes at the same time. To be honest, it did hurt a little, but I found it a little hot and had to resist the urge not to rub my ass against his groin, which I could tell was already hard.

Colton chuckled again and dropped my arm long enough for him to spin me around, slam my back against the wall again, and grab my arms, pinning them above my head. Again, he pushed himself against me and grinned down at me before using his free hand to swipe my hair to one side and bury his face in my neck. Fireworks went off in my brain as he kissed my neck and my body remembered his touch like it was only yesterday. I bit my lip to control myself as my breathing grew heavier. Colton's free hand glided down my body, brushing against my breast before sliding down and gripping my hip.

"Mmmm, baby girl, I have missed you, and I can tell you have missed me too," he whispered between kisses, and I wanted to pull away in disgust. I needed him to let go of the tight grip on my wrists, so did the first thing that I thought of. I played along.

"Oh, Colton," I moaned, and he growled in appreciation, grinding his hard member against me. Just as planned, he let go of my wrist so he could grab my other hip to pull me against him. I let my arms fall onto his shoulders and then wrapped them around him. I fought the rising lust trying to take over my senses and manoeuvred us until he was in the exact place I wanted him to be. I felt him relax into me and smile as I pushed against his shoulders and brought my knee up swiftly between his legs, hitting him right in the jewels. He cried out, probably in a mix of shock and pain, and doubled over. I didn't waste time and kicked his legs out from under him, and he went face-first to the ground. I had him pinned with my knee pressed into his back and his arm yanked behind him in under a second.

He might have been bigger and heavier than me, but I had extensive combat training designed to work against supernaturals bigger and stronger than him. I leaned down close to his ear as he struggled.

"What's up, Colton?" I whispered. "I thought you liked a bit of pain."

"You fucking bitch!" he spat. "I'll fucking kill you when I get my hands on you."

"Sure you will, sweetheart," I said, laughing. "Now listen here, you disgusting piece of trash." I got serious again. "I am here to visit my family. I will be doing just that, and you will stay the fuck away from me. Do you understand?" Colton grunted, and I twisted his arm further up his back. "I said, do you understand?" and he nodded his head.

"Be aware I am not that same scared, little, innocent Harper that you fucked around with back ten years ago. Your days of being able to manipulate me are over," I snarled, and I felt my eyes shifting to their gold, knowing that my strength would increase with the shift. I was surprised when Colton laughed.

"Oh yeah, I can't manipulate you, can I?" he said. "Then why are you still wearing my ring!" Fuck I forgot he would see that. Even after almost ten years, I still couldn't shift the damn thing off my finger.

"Face it, Strawberries, you still belong to me, and you always will," he gloated, and I growled.

I grabbed his arm and his shirt and yanked him up by them, taking him by surprise, and then I pushed him against the open bannister, slamming his hips against it and kicking his legs out, so he leaned right over, giving him a view of the two-story drop to the pavement below. As a werewolf, he would survive, but it would certainly hurt a lot. He screamed and tried to cling to something with his free hand.

"Let's get one thing crystal-clear right now. I belong to nobody other than myself. And don't think I won't hesitate to let go of you and let gravity do the rest," I growled.

"You fucking psycho bitch," he shouted. "Pull me back up. I'm the Beta of this town. You can't do this to me."

"I don't care what your rank is. You fuck with me again, and they won't find enough body parts. You hear me? I have taken down bigger and more dangerous supers than you!" I wasn't sure if it was the look on my face or the growl in my voice, but Colton suddenly looked like he believed every word. He nodded his head quickly, and I stared at him for a minute longer before pulling him up and letting his feet find the floor.

He looked like he was going to say something for a second, but I growled again, and he backed away. He watched me as he backed up the stairs and then turned and ran down them. I watched as he appeared downstairs in the carpark and rushed across to the car that I had seen him in yesterday. He looked up at me before getting in the car and quickly driving off. I hoped that would be the last of any trouble that I would have from him, but the look he gave me made me think otherwise. I couldn't quite put my finger on it, but he seemed more confident than I would have liked down there by his car.

"Harper?" I turned to the voice calling my name and saw Katie standing there with a big grin on her face. She was still the same as when I saw her last, slender frame, ample breasts, and blond hair, although it was currently flat and wet, which I guessed was from the shower. She was wearing a silk looking short black robe that barely covered her ass. She ran over in her bare feet, threw her arms around me, and hugged me.

"Oh my goddess Harper, it's so good to see you," she said. I pulled away and gave her a confused look.

"Katie, why did I just see Colton, of all people, coming out of your place?" I asked, and a hurt look crossed her face before she grinned again.

"Well, hello to you too," she said jokingly.

"Katie?" I asked again, and her face fell in defeat.

"Okay, you better come in, and I'll explain everything," she said and turned and walked back to her apartment door. I followed her into the apartment and looked around. It was tiny and seemed a bit dark and dingy, like the light couldn't get in. Although the accessories were several shades of pink, the furniture was all mismatched, telling me that not much had changed about Katie.

"Do you want coffee?" she asked as she headed to the side of the room that housed the kitchen. I shook my head.

"Water will be fine," I said, and she shrugged and pulled out a glass from the cupboard and poured some water from the tap. I knew she was avoiding sitting down. I could read her nervous energy as she busied herself with the kettle and several other things.

"Katie!" I finally said, and she looked around at me and sighed. She put down the plate in her hand and walked over to the sofa, sitting down.

"It's not what you think," she said.

"So you're not sleeping with him?" I asked, and she blushed.

"Okay, it is what you think," she muttered. "But it's not like I want to."

"What!" I exclaimed. She stood up and disappeared into a room that I assumed was the bedroom and came back out with a white box. On the side of the box, the word Harper was written in black marker. Katie put the box down in front of me, and I looked at it as she spoke.

"When you went, Colton went crazy, like rip-the-town-apart-crazy," she said. "He would disappear for weeks on end and then come back more frustrated than ever. Then one night he turned up at my door with a bag." and she gestured to the box, "This stuff or a variation of some of it was in the bag." In the box, there was some body spray that was strawberry flavoured, some of my old clothes and a brown wig.

"He was super drunk, ranting about how the other girls couldn't get it right, and they weren't convincing. He said I knew you better so I would know how to be you." I looked at her, horrified.

"Are you meaning to say, he dressed you up as me to have sex with you?" I felt sick as she nodded, looking down at the floor, shame all over her face. "And you did it?"

She looked back up at me. "That first time, I was terrified. He had already killed a couple of pack members earlier in the year when he was in a rage. I was scared he was going to kill me." I gave her a sympathetic look. I had seen a taste of Colton's temper before I had left. I knew how scary it could be.

"Then I felt kinda ok with it, and I surprised myself that I was able to act like how I thought you would act. I realised after that he had used a command on me, and I hadn't realised." She shrugged and looked at me. "The next day, the Beta came to visit me. He said that I had helped a lot, and Colton was the calmest he had been in over a year." She looked at the floor again, shame creeping back on her face. "Things were hard, Harper, hell, they still are. Howlers don't pay enough and I can't get a job anywhere else."

"What did he do?" I asked, although I already knew.

"He offered me money. Every time Colton needed to visit, I would be paid £500." I hissed at her words. "He also said that my dad and brother would have problems if I didn't agree to it," she said, and I suddenly wished that this new Alpha hadn't already killed the son of a bitch.

"It isn't so bad, though, even the times Damien came with him. And it's less and less since the new Alpha took over." I was looking at her in open shock.

"Damien?" I asked, my memory flashing back to that night. "What did Louise say about all this? Surely she wouldn't have agreed or stood for this." Katie laughed.

"Harper, Louise and I have barely spoken three words to each other since you left."

"What?" I exclaimed. She shrugged again.

"She disappeared, and the next I heard, she was mating with Damien, and then it was like we had nothing in common. I was annoyed that she would hurt Tommy that way too." I shook my head. I couldn't believe how much destruction had been left because I couldn't deal with my asshole mate.

Katie quickly changed the subject when she saw my expression, and I smiled as she told me about her brother and his new wife and their new baby. She asked about me, and I kept it vague. I told her the story about London, and the subject turned to guys. She asked about Aaron, stating that he was hot, and I told her how we had dated for a while, but were still good friends. Before long, it was getting to 1 pm, and it was at least an hour's walk from here to the Pack House where I was due to meet with the new Alpha at 2:30 pm. I said goodbye to Katie and said I would visit at least once before leaving town again.

I took a slow walk most of the way to the pack house, enjoying the warm sun. I got to the pack house with ten minutes to spare and walked through the main entrance. I was hit by serious amounts of flashbacks, as nothing had changed, other than being a little worse for wear here and there. And it was empty like nobody was around at all.

I assumed this meant that the layout was the same and made my way up the stairs to where I remembered the Alpha's secretary would sit. And I was right. Sitting behind the desk was a pretty redhead. She was busy flirting with a big guy, who I recognised from the picture in the case file back at the Council. It was the Gamma Marcus Farwell. He turned his head slightly and watched as I walked up. The redhead smiled at me.

"I have an appointment with Alpha Owens," I said, and the redhead just smiled again and then tapped on the keyboard in front of her for a bit.

"Okay, Miss Kirby," she said. "The Alpha has just stepped out, but you can wait in his office. Do you know the way?" I nodded and then narrowed my eyes.

"How did you know who I was?" I asked, and she blushed.

"Everyone has heard about you, darling," Farwell said. He had a strong cockney accent and a cheeky grin on his face. I grinned back, thinking I wouldn't mind checking this one out for some evidence at some point.

"I hope it wasn't all bad," I flirted with a wink, and his grin widened.

"Well, depends who you ask, but anyone who can piss Stokes off is alright in my book," he said, standing up. "He's just been ranting at the Alpha. I pissed myself laughing when he said that you knocked him to the ground." He looked me up and down. "If I had known you were this tiny, I would have still been laughing."

I smiled and shrugged.

"It's amazing what a couple of self-defence lessons can do." I looked Farwell up and down myself. This was the guy Nathaniel said would be able to give me a challenge. I was certainly willing to give him a chance.

"Well, I would be happy to show you some more self-defence tricks at some point," he said with a wink, and I grinned again.

"I might have to take you up on that," I shamelessly flirted. If I could get close to the Gamma, I could maybe get some evidence. The quicker, the better, and then I could get out of this damn place.

I excused myself with a smile and a promise to meet up later and headed down the corridor towards the Alpha's office. Farwell had said that the Alpha wasn't in, so I didn't bother knocking. I opened the door to walk straight in and came face to face with Colton again.

CHAPTER 34

Colton

I leaned against the wall behind the Alpha's desk, watching Harper. She was sitting on one of the chairs on the other side of the desk. She looked like Harper, my Harper. The sweet and innocent Harper who I had known all that time ago. Her appearance, hair, stunning, slender frame, and those grey eyes that felt like they pierced my soul. All the same, but the subtle differences, the clothes she wore, the way she held herself, and the smirk that she was throwing my way right now, were all indications that my Harper had long since gone.

I was a fool to reject her in the first place. If I had just listened to my wolf Canyon, then maybe things would have turned out differently. We would have been mated with pups of our own. I wouldn't have this big gaping hole inside me that no amount of sex or whisky could fill.

I had known there was something different about her since just after my 18th birthday; I had seen her at school, and Canyon had perked up immediately. You aren't supposed to know who your mate is until you are both eighteen. But I swear he knew. But she was a quiet and shy fifteen-year-old then, and I had no interest in having to fight the virgin wards to get what I wanted at the time.

It got worse when she and Louise became friends. She was around more, and Alex had started sniffing around her, too. When he had come home one night a year or so later, smelling of her, I had almost ripped his throat out where he stood. I told him then to stay clear of her. I then managed to avoid contact with her for the next couple of years, keeping an eye on her and keeping a distance. The day she turned eighteen, the day of the Midsummer Ball, I felt the bond smash into me. It hit me so hard just after midnight that I couldn't sleep. I wanted nothing more than to go storming to her house and claim her right there and then. But I held off until the ball that evening. I knew she would be there; it was mandatory for all pack members to be at the ball.

But I listened to Damien. He had rejected his mate a few years before. She was an Omega from a visiting pack, and he refused to lower himself to that level. He said that the pain from the rejection had been amazing, and he only wished that he had been fucking her at the time. He said I should do that, and then neither of us would be trapped by our mates because mates make you weak. I believed him. I saw how my dad would bend over backwards and drop everything for my mum, how even in her state of mental decline, she still controlled him. And how he hurt her in the process. I wasn't about to be controlled by anyone, certainly not a weak, timid creature like Harper. But more importantly, I knew I would destroy her too, and somewhere deep down, I didn't want to do that.

So I did it. Damien helped me to set it up. He would run a distraction so I could get her away without anyone seeing. I would deflower and then cut off my beautiful sweet strawberries. And what a night it was. That night was the best sex of my life, nothing compared. Everything was amazing from the moment I slid my hand into hers right up to when I exploded my seed in her. I knew it was exactly as it should be. And when she had called out and begged me to claim her, I almost did. My canines were already out in full, and I was seconds away from sinking them into her neck when I remembered the plan and said the words. Damien was right, though. The pain that came along with it, and the way it meshed with the pleasure, was something so mind-blowing that I didn't regret it for a second. Until later that night.

I had been back at the party for a few hours boasting to the crew about what I had done and how fucking amazing it was. Not before being accosted by Donna and dragged into the kitchens for a quickie. I had Canyon sulking; he kept repeating how much I had made a big mistake. So I was distracted when Tommy Kirby attacked me. He got a few hits in before I could easily get the upper hand. My father and the Alpha had come over kicking off. Although I wasn't bothered, I didn't expect to get in any trouble. I mean, Kirby had attacked me, not the other way around. Then he opened his big mouth. Again I didn't think it was an issue until I saw the shift in my dad's and the Alpha's faces.

It was only when I had been ordered to the office, and it was explained to me exactly who the Kirbys were and, more importantly, who Harper Kirby was that I realised how much I had fucked up. It made so much sense why I could feel her before her eighteenth, why I had felt the pull to be with her. My father had screamed about how important it was that the Kirbys' were looked after, why Tommy Kirby never left town after he had come back from Council training and why Darren Kirby had been so tightly woven into the pack operations that it would be impossible for him to leave. Also, a year previously, there had been so many issues about Susie Kirby being allowed to leave to join her mate's pack, but even she was back now.

Again I was resolved that I did the right thing, but then the other guy took over and my father and the Alpha had fixed everything that night. They had pulled Darren into the office, told him how much of a mistake I had made, and had him agree it was in my and Harper's interest to clear this up. Not to mention the good of the pack. I heard Darren had already turned his back on the Order, but the additional promotion in the pack businesses certainly helped to sway his decision.

And that week, with Harper by my side, it was heaven. Even from my place in the dark, I felt the bond repairing and growing stronger. But I was frustrated. She was guarded with me; she wasn't giving me everything, and I couldn't risk losing her when things were so fragile. Showing her how much I already loved her by introducing her to the edge of the pain and pleasure and sharing her with Damien and Alex was never intended to be seen as bad. I knew that if she just trusted me, saw how amazing it could be to have three attentive lovers, she would understand that what I was giving her was a gift. I only used the command to help her relax. It wasn't my fault she took it the wrong way, or that Alex had got cold feet. As soon as she knew that her place was at my side, she would understand the magic we could create.

Just thinking about it, thinking about how much we fit together so well, how she felt when she was in my arms when I was sliding inside her, was starting to do things to me. I felt myself hardening, but it brought attention to the pain I was still feeling in my balls from a few hours ago when she had kneed me. I winced at the feeling and tried to discreetly adjust myself, but she caught the action and raised her eyebrows, and smirked again. I wanted to wipe that smug look off of her face so badly. I wanted to push her against the desk and make her remember that one time in my office. I could almost picture her screaming my name as I pounded inside her, making her mine again.

I winced again as a sharp pain in my nuts shot through my body. She shook her head and chuckled. I could only glare back at her. I would have to make her pay for what she had done at the apartments. And I would make her pay real good, real soon. I had made the mistake of telling Elias what had happened. I was furious, and the anger had me bursting into the office, demanding that she be punished for assaulting a ranked member of the pack. Elias watched me with mild amusement, which only annoyed me more. Marcus, on the other hand, was a condescending fuck.

"You mean to tell me you were overpowered by a girl," he said before he started laughing. I wanted to punch him right in the face. I had argued that she clearly caught me off guard.

Elias seemed uninterested in everything. I knew that if I was going to get Harper back; I needed to restrict her movements in the town. Undoubtedly, that uncle of hers would be trying to get in the way, and I had already received word that she was at Howlers with the traitor Alex this morning. So I tried to reason with Elias that maybe she should be watched. If he moved her to the pack house, then I could catch her unawares. Elias had shut me down, stating the pack house wasn't a hotel, and maybe if I stayed away from her, she couldn't pick on me. This had Marcus in stitches again, and I was ready to walk out there and then.

But I knew Harper was due for her vetting, and I wanted to be here when he did that. It was shortly after that Elias had received a phone call. Whatever it was, it pissed him off enough to swear. He stormed off, saying he would be back soon. Marcus soon got bored as he did and wandered off. I don't know where.

At least I got these few minutes to study Harper. She was still sitting in the chair, relaxed and checking her phone, when I noticed her body stiffen. She looked up to the wall next to me, and her face lost the smug expression for something more like fear. Just then, the door opened, and Elias stopped in the doorway like there was some sort of barrier. His eyes shifted to gold, and he was staring at Harper from behind with a lustful hunger in his eyes.

"Oh goddess, no!" Harper muttered and then glanced at me before closing her eyes. I looked up at Elias just as he sniffed the air. Then he uttered one word that shattered my world.

"Mate!"

CHAPTER 35

Elias

"Fuck!" I leaned against the wall outside the entrance to the cells and closed my eyes. I didn't know how long I was going to be able to deal with that infuriating woman. I could still hear her shouting obscenities at the guards. All I wanted to know was where her husband was and that she was willing to cooperate, and then I would let her go, under a watchful eye, of course. This entire pack was a mess. Three months in, and I still doubted almost every single one of them. There was maybe a handful who I felt confident to recruit. The rest of the pack, well, they would have to be dealt with in the usual ways.

I heard a beep and looked down at my Rolex and sighed. I had a meeting with the Kirby woman right now. I was all set to deny her request for entry into the territory, especially since the first request included her boyfriend, Aaron Jacen. It took me a while to remember where I knew that name from. It was Marcus who told me that he was a Council warrior. I had spent a brief time in the Council when I had turned fifteen, but I had hated all the rules. I was never a fan of rules, unless they were my rules, of course.

I denied the original request, but Tommy Kirby had come and put in a second request for just his niece alone. It was then that he had told me she knew Jacen through him and how he had sent her to the Council to hide for a while. He told me about Stokes being her mate and pretty much being an abusive dick to her, which didn't surprise me. I already knew of his crazy blow-up ten years ago. It turned out it was about her. I had Marcus arrange an extensive search on the girl, but everything came back pretty boring. She had spent six months at the Council and then moved to London and worked as a waitress for a while before doing administration or something in insurance. There was a mention of a romantic occurrence between her and Jacen, but that was recorded as ending some time ago. Kirby told me that his niece and friend had stayed friends, and Jacen had offered to come back with her, so she didn't get shit from Stokes. He said that was why it had taken her four months to even request to come back. It all seemed to line up.

But you can never be too careful with the Council. They had been sniffing around my operations for some time, and they could cause real issues if they found out what we were doing. I approved Kirby's request but insisted on a meeting so I could feel her out myself. You don't get to where I am without being good at judging people and then making the hard decisions.

I set off back to the pack house feeling tired. My wolf Jax had been on edge all day. It had started yesterday just after Stokes had burst into my office and then stormed off again. Jax was normally pretty calm, but since yesterday, he had been so active. I even went for a run last night to try to drain some of the restlessness, but we ended up circling one particular housing estate for hours, and Jax wouldn't say why. I made a point to investigate that area later. Maybe he detected a threat. He was good at that.

I was heading into the pack house when I bumped into Marcus, who was grinning wildly. He had been flirting with Kylie, my receptionist, so I was guessing he had scored.
"Dude!" he said as he walked up to me. I raised my eyebrows.

"Dude?" I questioned. We were good friends, but we were in public, and I didn't want people to see weakness in my operations.

"Oh yeah, I mean Alpha," he said, although I detected a mocking undertone and rolled my eyes.

"What do you want, Marcus? I'm late for my meeting."

"That's what I wanted to talk about," he said. "I just met her, the Kirby chick," he said excitedly. Strangely, I felt annoyed at the terminology he was using, but I logically knew he meant no disrespect.

"Did she like being called a chick?" This time, he rolled his eyes.

"I'm not that stupid," he said. "But seriously, she's hot! I mean, seriously, she had this whole flirty, badass vibe about her. I'm gonna meet up with her later for drinks or something." He wiggled his eyebrows. I shook my head and grinned at him. The guy was unbelievable. In the three months we had been here, he had slept his way through half the single women in the pack. So, of course, he would find the new person interesting.

"Well, I am sure to find out for myself in the next couple of minutes," I said, and he grinned again as I patted his back and turned to walk up the stairs.

"She's a feisty one," he called up after me, and I waved my arm in acknowledgement.

I passed a sullen-looking Kylie on the desk and headed down the hall towards my office.

Jax was suddenly very excited. He was jumping around inside my head.

"Seriously, dude, what the hell?" I chastised inside my head, and he howled in response. Then it happened. I was hit with the most fucking amazing smell of strawberries. I never really cared for strawberries, but right now, I could have bathed in a tub of the delicious juicy red fruit. I threw my office door open and stood at the entrance. Sitting in one of the chairs with her back to me was the source of the heavenly scent. Everything narrowed down to her. I didn't need her to turn around to know that she would be the most beautiful woman I had seen in my life, but at the same time, I desperately wanted her to turn around so I could feast my eyes upon her beauty. Jax was chanting in my head over and over one word.

"Oh goddess, no!" she uttered. What did she mean? I took in that beautiful scent one last time before I said the word Jax was repeating.

"Mate!"

I swear she flinched as I uttered the word. Why was she not as happy or as excited as I was, and why would she not turn around and let me see her? I noticed Stokes was still in my office, and he looked shocked. He was looking between the two of us. Then he met my eyes, and the shocked expression changed to anger. Why was he angry again? Then it hit me. This was the mate that Stokes had hurt and abused. The one that was so scared that she left her pack and family and ran for her life, and it had taken her four months after her father had died to come back to grieve him. And it was all Stokes's doing.

Jax growled in my head as I saw red and launched myself at the man that had abused my mate. I smashed him against the wall before slamming my fist into his surprised face. It didn't matter that she wasn't my mate then. It didn't matter that she had been his mate. As decreed by the moon goddess, she was my mate now, and it was my duty to protect and care for her.

I saw red as I continued to punch Stokes over and over. I would kill him for this. Stokes surprised me by responding with a sucker punch to my stomach, causing the air to expel from my lungs with force. I recovered quickly and went to punch him again when I heard the door slam shut.

I looked around to see the chairs and the room now empty.
"Mate gone," Jax huffed in my head, and I growled. "Go find mate."
"Fuck!" Stokes gasped and started to move towards the door. I grabbed him and shoved him back against the wall.
"Stay away from her," I snarled, and he laughed.
"Not a chance." He shoved me away and made it out of the door before I could get to him.
"Shit!" I exclaimed and then opened a mindlink to Marcus.
"Marcus, find the Kirby woman now. Don't engage. Just watch and do not let Stokes anywhere near her." It was less than ten seconds before he responded.
"Aye, aye, captain," he said. "What's up, she not what she says she is?"
"No, she is my mate," I replied. And just like that, it sank in. I found my fated mate. At thirty-five years old, I was beginning to lose hope that it would happen at all.
"Fuck dude, congrats!" he said, and then, "Aw fuck dude, then I guess drinks are out of the question." My responding growl was enough to get

him laughing down the link. I knew he was yanking my chain, and he was probably the only one who could do it. It didn't matter now. All that mattered was finding my mate.

CHAPTER 36

Harper

"Nathaniel, I swear to the goddess if you don't phone me back right now, I am going to...." I didn't know what I was going to do. But I did know one thing. I was getting the hell out of this place right now. I was almost home after running out of the meeting. I had phoned Nathaniel five times and Aaron three times. Why wasn't anyone picking up their damn phones? I got to the house and ran upstairs to where my suitcase was stored. I pulled it out of the closet and opened it up on the floor. I then went into the bathroom to collect the cosmetics I had used this morning.

I was just collecting them when my phone rang. I glanced at the screen and saw it was Aaron. I pressed to accept the call.
"Aaron, thank the goddess!" I exclaimed.
"Harper!" he called down the phone. "What's wrong?"
"I can't do this, I can't, I have to get out of here, please come and get me." I was close to a panic attack, the first real one in years.

"Harper, you need to stop!" I heard Aaron's tone change, taking charge. I stopped instantly and sat on the floor next to my suitcase. I noticed Susie had followed me up the stairs and had her phone in her hand.

"Okay, now breathe, sweetheart," Aaron said, and I closed my eyes and took a deep breath, "Feel better?"

"No," I said truthfully. "But I feel calmer."

"Good, now tell me what is happening." I looked up at Susie and hesitated. She didn't know that I was Council or why I was here. I also wasn't sure I wanted anyone to know what had just happened. Just then, the front door opened and slammed shut.

"Susie!" Tommy shouted, and she looked down the stairs before heading down.

"Aaron, I can't do the assignment." I whispered, "Between Colton and the Alpha, I just can't do it."

"What happened? Did that fucker do something to you?" he asked, his voice rising in anger. "Because if he did, I don't care. I will cross the territory line just to kill him." I smiled despite everything. Aaron was always there for me, no matter how much shit I had caused him. If the moon goddess really saw fit to give me a second-chance mate, why couldn't it have been him?

"No, well yes, he did try, but I put him on his ass," I said, turning into the phone. "It's Owens, that's the big problem."

"The Alpha! Did he find out who you were?"

"No, he's...." I hesitated again. I really didn't want to say the next part out loud. "He's my mate."

"What!" Aaron exclaimed.

"What!" I turned around to see Tommy looking at me in shock. Oh shit!

"Harper, you can't come back yet. Drake is pissed off that you went in the first place. He said if you fail then-" Aaron carried on while I stared at Tommy. His eyes widened when he heard Aaron mention Drake.

"Aaron, shush!" I interrupted him, but it was too late, and Tommy snatched the phone out of my hand.

"What the fuck, Aaron!" he exclaimed. "Why does Drake even know who she is? I thought you were protecting her."

"Whoa!" I said, reaching for the phone, but Tommy countered and slapped my hand away. He grabbed my wrist, hauled me up from the floor, and dragged me into my old bedroom. Shutting the door, he then put my phone on speaker.

"Aaron, I trusted you!" he snarled into the phone. I sighed. It didn't occur to me that Tommy would know Drake or that he wouldn't have known what happened. Aaron was quiet on the other end of the line, and I giggled. Tommy glared at me, and I shrugged.

"It wasn't his fault," I said. "I got involved with Drake before I understood who or what he was. If it weren't for Aaron and Nathaniel, I would have still been there."

"You don't have to cover for me, Harps," Aaron finally said. "He's right. I should have been more protective. It doesn't change the situation, though."

"And what exactly is the situation?" Tommy snapped.

"Drake has been sniffing around Harper since we pulled her out, he's been keen to get his claws into her, and this mess with the fae has given him a chance."

"What mess with the fae?" Tommy asked.

"I killed a pervert," I said.

"You tortured and then killed a son of a noble fae family without a warrant," Aaron sighed.

"He was still using his compulsion to violate women," I snapped. "Oh, and not to mention he had a gun to my head."

"Be as it may, Drake used it for his own means," Aaron said. "It wouldn't surprise me if he had set the little bastard up, and you along with it." That made sense. I didn't understand why Drake had such a fascination with me in the first place. Anyone knew he could have anybody he wanted with the click of his fingers. So why did he keep coming after me?

"If you turn up back at the Council without completing the mission, he will force Nathaniel's hand," Aaron carried on, and I knew he was right. I was trapped in this place until I could gather the evidence I needed to prove Owen's involvement in the Circle. I smiled in defeat at Tommy.

"Fine," I said with a sigh. "I'll complete the mission, and then I can leave this cursed place." Tommy looked thoughtful for a bit, and then he smiled at me.

"Harper, you know not everyone gets a second-chance mate," he said. "Elias is a better man than Colton." I rolled my eyes at him.

"A pile of steaming dog shit is a better man than Colton," I said and shook my head. I knew the chances of the goddess giving you a second-chance mate were seriously rare, but really why did the goddess see fit to pair me with not one but two jackasses? I wasn't playing that game again, that was for sure.

Tommy excused himself, telling Aaron he would phone him later, which was code for. "I'm gonna verbally kick your ass. But not in front of Harper." I then spent the next couple of hours talking to Aaron on the phone. He had a great way of calming me down that no one else did. I told him about how I had kicked Colton's ass and about all the things I had learned today, and he told me about some tests he was writing for his third-year classes. You wouldn't know it to look at him, but the guy was a geek, and he knew more than anyone I knew about the supernatural community. I listened quietly as he detailed some new law that the witches were bringing in. Eventually, we were interrupted by my sister telling me that dinner would be on the table in ten minutes. I said my goodbyes to Aaron and ended the call before leaving the bedroom. I saw my suitcase had been taken from the hallway as I headed down the stairs.

I got to the dining room as Tommy, and my mum argued about something. They caught my entry and stopped talking before I could get anything, but I had a feeling that the conversation was about me. Tommy looked angry, and my mum looked uncomfortable. I shrugged and sat down at the table and noticed that there were five settings. That meant there were either one too many plates or a few short. I glanced up at Tommy.

"Are the kids not eating with us?" I asked as Susie walked in with a dish of vegetables.

"Oh goddess, no," Susie said. "They won't eat this. I fed them an hour ago, and now James is attempting to earn his phone back in the living room." I chuckled, poor kid.

"So, who's the extra plate for then?" I asked, and Tommy growled. Just then, the doorbell rang, and my mum smiled wide.

"I'll get it!" she said and rushed to the door. I was already putting two and two together and getting an answer I didn't like.

"Oh, fuck no!" I said when my mum walked in, followed by Colton. "Are you fucking kidding me?" I exclaimed, and my mum and sister looked at me in shock.

"Harper!" my mum scolded. "Manners!" Colton grinned and then winked at me. He had many roses, which he presented to me like this was some sort of fucked-up date. My mum and sister both squealed, and I rolled my eyes.

"I'm gonna need a drink," I said, and Tommy moved from his corner and disappeared into the kitchen before returning with a couple of glasses and a bottle of chilled wine. He put one in front of me and poured the wine. I grinned at him, and he grimaced back. My mum managed to arrange it, so I was sitting next to Colton at the table. I sat there as Colton, my mum, and my sister made polite conversation. Colton tried including me in on the conversation a few times. Asking what it was like to work in London and did I miss my friends. I met his questions with a glare. I didn't want him to know anything about my life. Not even my fake one.

"I mean, it must be tough for your boyfriend, seeing that you are still wearing my ring," he said just as I was taking a drink. I almost spat it back out everywhere. I had been careful to have the stone turned inwards, so no one saw, and by the looks on my mum's and sister's faces, they hadn't noticed I was still wearing it. I growled at Colton, and he threw me a smug look.

"You have a boyfriend?" Susie asked. Colton was obviously referring to Aaron as he had tried to get entry for both of us and posed as my boyfriend.

"Oh, what's he like?" my mum asked, and I grinned. Two could play this game. I glanced at Colton first.

"Oh, he's amazing," I said. "He is so kind and intelligent and so strong too." My mum looked pleased. Colton did not. And I wasn't done either. "He is such a virile lover, too," I carried on with a smirk at Colton. "Easily the best I've ever had."

Colton looked like he was going to explode, the look of anger etched on his face. My sister looked between us before scowling at me and swiftly changing the subject. The tension slowly eased, although I noticed Colton kept glancing over at me before looking away again. When I was finishing my second glass of wine, I noticed that Colton's hand had started creeping my way. I watched as he went to place his hand on my thigh. I grabbed his wrist before leaning in, and knowing that everyone would still hear, I whispered in his ear.

"If that hand touches any part of my body, I will rip it off and serve it up to everyone for dessert!" I then let go of his hand and sat back in my seat as Tommy was trying hard to cover his laugh behind a cough and my sister and mum looked mortified. Colton had gone a delightful shade of red as he snatched his hand away.

"Harper!" my mum scolded again. "What has got into you?"

"It's okay, Mrs Kirby. I was maybe rushing things a little." Colton smiled at her. "I mean, if I am going to win back the heart of my mate, then I have to remember it will take time." My mum and my sister both made aww noises at him and smiled. I couldn't believe they were falling for his charm. I rolled my eyes and stood up.

"I've had enough of this. I need a real drink." I walked out without waiting for a response and grabbed my jacket before heading for the door.

I opened the door and jumped when I saw the Gamma Marcus standing there, looking like he was about to knock. I smiled seductively at him and bit my lip.

"Good timing," I purred. "Are you ready to take me for that drink?" I saw a genuine struggle on his face as he was clearly here for another reason, and my offer was tempting enough to forget everything else.

"Sorry, princess," he said, his face set into a determined expression. "No can do. I'm here on orders to escort you to the pack house." I groaned in frustration as he said, "Alpha wants to see you."

CHAPTER 37

Harper

"Sorry, darling," I said as I brushed past him and walked out into the street, knowing he would be following on my heels. "I have no plans to follow through with that shit show of an idea." His hand circled my wrist, and he yanked me around to face him. I was expecting it and threw my weight into it to pull him off balance. But he was also waiting for my move and laughed as his grip on my wrist tightened, and he pulled me into his chest.

"Dammit," I whispered more to myself, and his grin widened.

"Don't worry, princess, I got you. Wouldn't want any damage to come to my new Luna now, would I?"

"Not your fucking Luna," I hissed and pulled away from him, trying to twist out of his grip on my wrist.

"You can take that up with the boss, not my place."

"What the hell is going on out here?" I heard Colton's voice and groaned. "Gamma, release her at once!"

"Not your call, Stokes," Marcus said without taking his eyes off me. "Although you'd be happy, Alpha now agrees that this firecracker should stay at the pack house, just like you suggested." I glared at the two of them.

"Like fuck I am!" I snarled and kicked out at Marcus, but again he seemed to counter it, and he swept my one-planted leg out, and I landed on my ass.

"Son of a bitch!" I exclaimed.

I looked up to see Marcus grinning down at me. I really wanted to wipe that smirk off his face so badly. Colton seemed to have the same idea, and Marcus was knocked from my view, as they both went tumbling down the drive. I took the chance while I had it to jump up and set off running down the street. I was already rounding the corner and diving into the woods before the two testosterone-filled brutes stopped their fight, long enough to notice that I had gone. I grew up in these woods. Even after ten years away, I still knew them like the back of my hand. I quickly found the path I used to take to town and headed down it.

After ten minutes of quick pace walking, I came out by Katie's place. I headed past the apartment building and into the car park of Howlers which was packed out, as was Howlers itself. I could tell the dinner crowd was ending, and the night crowd was starting up. Perfect, just in time to blow off some steam. I headed to the entrance and was met by two large, unfamiliar werewolves. One of them glared at me while the other leered, his eyes travelling up and down my body. The scowly one elbowed the other in the chest before his eyes glazed over. Crap! He was mind linking someone, probably Marcus, or, worse, Colton. His eyes cleared, and he sneered at me before moving to the side and waving his arm towards the door. I glared at him, knowing my time was limited. Chances were the Alpha already had guys on the way. They were super possessive that way. I remembered one case where two Alphas had gone to war over one poor woman they claimed was their mate. They had literally burnt a town to the ground fighting. And this Alpha had a reputation for being brutal. Which once again begged the question of why the moon goddess decided to mate me with not one but two nasty pieces of work.

I sighed and headed into the bar, past the two slabs of muscle. I obviously didn't have much time to have fun before company arrived. I could have slipped out of the back, but at this point, unless I left town, I suspected I would be found, eventually. I headed up to the bar and saw that Katie was serving at the end. I waved to get her attention, and her face lit up as she grinned. She finished with the customer and made her way down the bar to me.

"Harper!" she exclaimed. "What can I get you? On the house." It was good because I had left my bag with everything in, at the house.

"Nice!" I nodded. "I'll have a double rum and coke then." She grinned and turned to prepare my drink. She soon had it ready in front of me and winked.

I took a drink as I saw a door behind the bar open, and Alex walked through carrying two boxes of bottled beer. He was wearing a black shirt that looked so tight that it left not one part of his solid eight pack to the imagination. Katie followed my stare and grinned as she saw who I was drooling over. Alex looked up and saw me, and I bit my lip and winked. He took a deep breath and looked around, and I thought for a second that he wasn't interested, but then he walked around the bar and grabbed my hand. Before I could say anything, he pulled me towards the end of the bar and into a room marked office.

The door was barely closed before he pushed me against it and his mouth was on mine, pushing his body against me like he couldn't get close enough. I laced my arms around his neck and pulled him even closer. My lips parted, allowing his tongue access, and he took delight in exploring all the corners of my mouth while my own tongue chased his. He broke the kiss sooner than I would have liked and looked down at me.

"I have been wanting to do that ever since I saw you this morning," he said. "Geez, Harper, how are you so fucking beautiful?" I blushed slightly at the compliment and smiled at him.

"What else did you want to do to me?" I asked in the most innocent tone I could muster, especially with the aching that was starting between my legs. Alex groaned as I leaned up to nibble against his neck.

"Aw sweetheart, I'm not sure there are words for what I want to do to you that could be said in the company of a lady," he growled, and I felt heat flush through to my core in excitement.

"Good thing there aren't any ladies around her then, isn't it?" I purred, and he growled again. He grabbed my waist, lifted me, turned towards the desk, and sat me on top of it. I wrapped my legs around his waist and pulled his face down to me again. He began to trail kisses down my throat, and his hand unbuttoned my jeans. I pulled his top off so I could get a good look at the raw goods underneath when Alex stopped. He froze mid-action and then hissed.

He stepped back, untangling himself from my legs and arms, and I frowned at him.
"What the hell, Alex?" I snapped. "I was starting to enjoy that." He scowled at me.
"Tell me it's not true," he growled. His eyes were full of lust and his hands clenched by his side.
"What?" I asked.
"Tommy is just fucking with me, right?" He looked towards the door and then back at me. "Tell me I was not about to sign my fucking death certificate by screwing the Alpha's mate." I closed my eyes in frustration.
"I'm not his mate," I said defiantly. "I belong to me, no one else." Alex groaned.
"Fuck, Harper!" he exclaimed. "He is going to fucking kill me. He's killed others for less."
"I told you, I'm not his mate," I said, jumping down from the table and fastening my jeans back up. "But if you're not interested, I'll find someone else to have fun with." I walked past him to the door, but he grabbed my arm before I reached it.
"Harper, I am saying this as a friend," he said as he moved in close and took in my scent. "Watch out for this guy. He's not Stokes. I've seen some of the things he has done that have earned him the reputation he has." Alex pulled me in close to him. "I hate to say it, but if he decides you're his, then get used to it." I pulled away from him and watched his face to see if he was trying to mess with me.
"Fuck this shit!" I said, "I know he's a bad guy already. I have no plans of being involved with him any more than I have to." I turned towards the door and pulled it open before Alex had time to say anything else.

I was halfway down the hall when it registered that it was unusually quiet for a bar. The music and chatter had stopped. I rounded the corner into the main bar and stopped dead. The place was deserted. There must have been over a hundred people in here before. But now I could see Katie standing behind the bar looking nervous, the two goons I had encountered on the way in, and Marcus standing by the DJ booth with a new black eye and a wide grin. But all of those people faded out as I met the eyes of the man standing in the middle of the room with his arms crossed. I didn't get a good look at him in the office, but I had seen enough pictures of him to know who he was, even if my body wasn't reacting to the scent of mint and sea salt. I knew the man in front of me was Alpha Elias Owens.

I felt Alex come up behind me and swear as he saw the scene. But I couldn't rip my eyes away from the man in front of me. Despite being the smallest frame of all the men in here, and dressed in a three-piece suit, everything about him screamed pure dominant Alpha. He narrowed his eyes slightly and tilted his head as he watched me. His face was completely devoid of any expression. But the look in his eyes said everything. He was, without a doubt, a hunter, a predator, and I was his prey. Alex was right. In his eyes, I was already his.

I felt breathless as just his look felt like it woke something up inside me. Something that stretched and growled inside my head. Then I heard the voice of someone I hadn't heard in almost ten years. I felt as my wolf Maia recognised the wolf staring back at me through the man's eyes as she said what I already knew.
"Mate!"

CHAPTER 38

Harper

Owens continued to trap me with his eyes for a few moments longer before breaking the contact. He glanced at Katie behind the bar, and she shrank back in fear.

"Bar is closed for the night, Miss Harsen. Go home." Katie glanced at me and then back to Owens before bowing her head. Owens was already back looking at me.

"Yes, Alpha," she whispered, and she disappeared into a room behind the bar and came back out with her bag and jacket. She headed around the bar towards the exit and then glanced back to Owens, looking petrified.

"Erm... well..." she hesitated while Owens didn't even acknowledge her. "I was just wondering if I would still get paid for my shift, but if not, then that's ok too. Oh, I'm sorry, it doesn't matter, I shouldn't have said anything." I grimaced as she was getting more flustered the longer she spoke. Yet Owens still stared at me. I looked around him briefly before returning my eyes to meet his.

"Yeah, you'll still get paid," I said confidently. "At his expense too." Katie's eyes popped in shock. Owens raised an eyebrow, and the corners of his mouth twitched.

"Oh, well..." Katie started again.

"Goodnight, Miss Harsen," Owens said, his tone as flat as his expression. Yet both sang with so much information in their blankness. His voice felt like a cool breeze along my skin, and his eyes continued to burn into my soul.

Katie squeaked and headed out through the door as quickly as she could. I rolled my eyes before returning my stare to the Alpha in front of me. I started to get annoyed at him and returned the stare. I had faced some pretty scary characters. I could deal with a self-entitled Alpha prick. I crossed my arms, mimicking him, narrowed my eyes, and glared at him. He raised both eyebrows this time. I could tell he was fighting off his amusement. That's right, buddy, you just keep underestimating me now, I thought to myself.

Owens glanced behind me towards where Marcus was standing and gave a half nod. I heard a scuffle behind me and then a snap, followed by a cry of pain. I turned around to see Alex cradling his hand. I rushed to him, and he flinched away.

"No, Harper, don't!" he said through gritted teeth. From what I could see, two of his fingers were broken and swelling fast. I growled and whirled around on the Alpha.

"Are you fucking crazy, you psychotic bastard," I snarled as I rushed at him. I reached to punch him straight in his pretty-boy face, and he grabbed my wrist before it connected and twisted it around. I was sent off guard by the burst of sparks that exploded over my body from his touch. He spun me around and crushed me against his body, his other arm circling me, trapping my arms and body against him. I struggled to get out of his grip as he leaned in and ran his nose against my neck, taking in my scent and whispering in my ear, the sensation causing my breath to quicken and heat to flood my core.

"Behave." His tone held so much dominance and command that it took everything in me not to do as he said and melt into him like a good little girl. Meanwhile, Maia was not helping the situation as she yapped excitedly in my head and tried to encourage me to grind my ass against his crotch. I did everything I could to keep tense, so he knew the second he relaxed his grip, I would rip myself away from him. He moved his head away from me, and I almost groaned from the absence of his touch.

"You understand the consequences for touching what is mine?" Owens said to Alex, who met my eyes briefly before looking back at Owens and nodded.

"He didn't even know, you son of a bitch," I snarled, and his arm tightened around me, and he growled.

"Why do you think it was his fingers and not his neck, sweetheart?" He nuzzled back into my neck again. "And don't worry, we'll get to your punishment later," he whispered, and my heart skipped a beat as dread filled my body. The guy was clearly a psychopath, and I felt the promise in his statement in my bones.

He nodded to Marcus again. Marcus nodded and then called behind us.

"Davy, take Casanova here to the hospital and make sure his fingers are set right. Anders, bring the Alpha's car around." I heard the doors to the bar open and close again. One of the two guys walked past us and grabbed Alex's arm. Alex shrugged him off and glared at him, but started walking, anyway. He glanced at me as he passed and winked.

"Still worth it," he muttered under his breath, and I smirked. Owens tightened his grip on me even more and growled. I rolled my eyes in response. Even though he couldn't see it, Marcus could, and he grinned at me.

"You got yourself a handful here, boss," he said, and Owens growled again.

"Wait outside," he ordered, and Marcus mimed, tipping an invisible hat before heading past us.

When the door closed again, I became all too aware that we were now alone in the bar. A shiver of excitement ran through my body at the very thought of it. Owens relaxed his arm holding me to his body, but before I could take action, he spun me around and pushed me against the bar, the edge digging in my back. He caged me in with his body and one arm on either side and leaned in to take in my scent before moving to make eye contact again. This time, there was something different to him. His body was more relaxed, and humour danced in his eyes. Even his calm expression softened his face and held a hint of flirtiness. It was as different to a few moments ago as chalk was to cheese. I glanced at him up and down, confused. This unsettled me more than the bad boss-type he held just now. How easy he seemed to be able to switch between the two.

"It appears we got off on the wrong foot already," he hummed, and his voice still held that fresh touch along my body.

"Speak for yourself," I said. "I got interrupted before I had a chance to get off at all." He laughed. Not like a smarmy evil boss man-laugh, but a full, genuinely happy laugh. I blinked at him in surprise. Who was this guy?

"Don't worry, darling," he said, his eyes filling with lust. "I am very happy to help with that." I gulped at the raw tone in his voice. "Nevertheless, I am looking forward to getting to know you, my little mate," he cooed, and I shook my head.

"I'm not your mate," I said, as confident as I could. "You don't just take a whiff and decide you can keep the shiny new toy. You gotta earn that shit, and I don't care who you are."

"Well, I will have plenty of time to earn everything you have and more, sweetheart. We will be spending quite a bit of time together," he mused. "Starting with you moving into the pack house."

"What!" I exclaimed, what is it with these dudes and that damn pack house? "No, I can't." I tried to keep a straight face, but I couldn't face the idea of being so close to Colton. "Please, I'll behave or whatever."

"And probably run out of town the first chance you get?" He raised his eyebrows. "Not happening, sweetheart. I'm keeping my eye on you."

"I won't run, I promise." I couldn't, anyway, without becoming one of Drake's blood groupies, but he didn't need to know that.

"Your track record goes against you," he stated.

"Seriously, he was an abusive prick, and I was eighteen. What was I supposed to do, stay and mate with the bastard?" I snapped at him, and he smirked.

"And this afternoon?" he asked. I looked at him in shock. The only people who knew I was planning on leaving this afternoon were Aaron and... Oh, of course, I should have known.

"Tommy!" I exclaimed. "He told you I was gonna leave?" He nodded. I wasn't sure if I should have just been angry or hurt.

"Who do you think warned me that my Beta had gone against my direct command and was sitting at your dinner table?"

He then tilted his head again.

"Is that it?" he asked. "Is that why you won't come stay at the pack house? Are you worried about Stokes?" His voice had taken a tender tone, and I nodded. He growled low in his throat before hooking a finger under my chin and lifting it until our eyes met.

"Well, rest assured, my little mate, I will always keep you safe, no matter what." Everything from his expression to his voice and his body language screamed that he was speaking the truth, and I found myself nodding again before I realised what I was doing. Dammit, I needed to get my head back in the game. I pushed him away from me, and he let me. I moved out of his space and turned around to face him.

"Fine, but I want my own room," I said. "And far away from Colton." He nodded.

"You'll have your own room on the top floor. There is only Marcus and me up there, and it is secured from anyone else."

"Okay, and this doesn't mean I agree to be your mate. I only agree to do this because my mum's sofa is terribly uncomfortable," I stated, and he nodded again.

"I am not obliged to stay or anything," I went on. "I am here to do what I need to, and then I am out of here, and you won't stop me." He tilted his head again.

"And what is it that you need to do?" he asked, and I cursed myself in my head for slipping on that.

"None of your goddess damn business," I snapped, and he grinned. "What the hell are you grinning at?" I snapped again.

"Marcus was right. You are gonna be a handful," he chuckled, and I looked around for something to throw at him.

"Fine, I will agree to your demands, but I have one of my own," he said, getting serious.

"Well?" I asked.

"Give me a chance," he said, and I looked at him in shock. "Contrary to popular belief, I can be a nice guy." I frowned at him.

"Tell that to Alex while they reset his fingers," I shot at him, and he shrugged.

"Us Alpha types tend to run a little possessive, I'm afraid." I quirked my head at that, and he looked at me confused.

"What? What did I say?"

"Colton said something very similar to that the first night we... well, you know," I said, blushing a little. He tutted with a cheeky grin.

"Now, now, sweetheart, if you can't say it, you shouldn't be doing it," he chuckled, and I rolled my eyes.

"Fine, the night we fucked!" I said, and he took a deep breath, his eyes filling with lust again. I rolled my eyes again. Geez, and I thought I was horny.

Owens cleared his throat and held out his hand to me.

"Come on then, my dear, let us go home," he said. I hesitated. I wasn't sure I liked the hungry look in his eyes, and I was sure I was making a big mistake. But at least I was going to be as close to the man as anyone could get. Surely I would be able to find the evidence against him a lot quicker this way. I reached out and let him take my hand in his before guiding us out of the bar and into the car waiting outside. As we drove towards the pack house, I couldn't help but have a horrible feeling that I was making a big mistake.

CHAPTER 39

Harper

The pack house came into view as we drove up the driveway. Owens pulled the car up to the entrance and jumped out, and was around my side of the car before I had even got my seatbelt undone. He opened the car door and offered me his hand. His face held the blank expression that I was starting to think was more of a mask. The big, tough, bad boss showed no emotion as he ruled his empire. I took his hand, and he helped me out of the car. He kept my hand in his grip as he turned to walk into the house.

I half turned at the sound of another car and saw Tommy driving up the driveway. I stopped and waited until he pulled up behind Owens' car. He got out of the car and met my eyes for a second before heading around the back to open the boot. He came back into sight, holding my suitcase and my bag. I hissed at the sight, traitor! Owens nodded to an omega, and he ran up and took the suitcase from Tommy and headed inside the house. Tommy walked over to us and held out my bag.

"Your phone is in there too," he said, and I glared at him. "Don't be like this, Harp, I think it's for the best."

"What about what I think?" I spat at him, and Owens' grip on my hand tightened. I glanced at him, and he glared at me, clearly not happy with my tone. Well fuck him, I thought, rolling my eyes. I returned my glare to Tommy and snatched my bag off him before turning and walking into the pack house. Owens kept my pace and got to the main door to hold open for me.

I walked into the entrance hall to see Marcus, Colton, the; I guess now former Luna, and Colton's mother all standing there. Behind them I could see some other people, which from the guess of the identical blond women and the young man who resembled Alex, were Lisa and Lily Chambers, and Jamie Bennet.

Colton met my eyes as we walked in, and then his eyes slipped to my hand, which was still being held by Owens. He growled and stepped forward, but Marcus held his arm out, blocking him.

"Stay," he said with a warning tone in his voice. He then turned to Owens. "The bedroom next to yours has been set up." Elias nodded. He then turned to the group as a whole.

"Harper will be staying here, for the time being. She is here as my guest, and I expect people to treat her as such." He pulled me close to him and wrapped his arm around my waist, and stared directly at Colton. "Mine, I mean!" Colton growled again and pushed away from Marcus, and stepped in front of Owens. Both of them stood staring at each other. I rolled my eyes at the stench of testosterone that was circulating the room and pulled myself out of Owens' grasp. I stepped around them and looked at Marcus, who watched the exchange with an amused grin that made me wonder if he had even tried to keep Colton away.

"Marcus, be a dear and show me to my room while the children play," I said, and one of the twins started laughing while I saw a twitch of a smile appear at the corner of the former Luna's mouth.

Marcus turned his smile on me and held out his arm in a grand, sweeping gesture.

"Of course, m'lady," he said. I linked my arm in his, and he guided me up the stairs. We were barely halfway when Owens called up.

"Marcus, hands," Marcus chuckled but let go of my arm. I rolled my eyes again but followed as he moved ahead of me. As I got to the top, I looked back down the stairs and saw Owens and Colton staring at me with identical possessive predator gazes. I guess I was going to have to show both of them I wasn't the prey that they expected.

Marcus and I continued to the top floor of the pack house, and I followed him down a hallway I had previously never been. The only time I had been on the top floor was for meals in the named rank dining room. I wondered if that was still a thing under this Alpha.

"Marcus?" I asked as we got to a door and he pulled out a key to unlock it.

"Yes, darling?" He opened the door and stepped back for me to walk in first.

"Do the named ranks still have meals together?" I asked. It was probably the best part of being here.

"Yes, ma'am," he said. "Every evening at 6 pm on the dot." He leaned down by the door and picked up my suitcase that had been left outside. I watched as pain flashed over his face, and he winced. He carried the suitcase into the room and put it on the bed.

"What's wrong?" I said with a grin. "Did Colton win the fight?" He laughed.

"Nah, darling, that turd couldn't fight his way out of a paper bag." He pointed to his eye and his side. "This was from Elias."

"What?" I exclaimed and rushed over and lifted his shirt before he had a chance to stop me. He tried to pull it back down, but I batted his hand away and glared at him. He raised his hands in surrender as I returned my inspection of his torso, which was very finely sculptured. But it was also decorated in crude black, blue, and purple welts and bruises. I growled at the sight of it and prodded one of the welts. Marcus hissed in pain.

"Geez, woman," he exclaimed.

"Why did he do this?" I asked.

"He gave an order, darling. I didn't complete it." He shrugged like it was the most normal thing to happen.

"What was the order?" Marcus looked at me and raised an eyebrow, and I closed my eyes in realisation. "It was to bring me back here." This, much like Alex's fingers, was all my fault.

No, scratch that shit. This was the Alpha's fault.

"You are way bigger than him. I'm sure you could have taken him," I said, and Marcus laughed again.

"Aw darling, don't let the expensive suit and the well-groomed hair fool you," he said. "The Alpha is a well-oiled killing machine. He is brutal and unforgiving when he has to be. And I am good, I'll give you that, but he would wipe the floor with me in a heartbeat." I looked to see if he was joking, but his face was serious.

I looked back down at his body again and was about to say how much of a bully the Alpha seemed when there was a cough at the door.

We both looked up to see the bully himself standing in the doorway with his hands in his tailored dress pants pockets.

"Any reason why you are showing my mate your body, Marcus?" he asked. I would have reminded him that I wasn't his mate, but he had a look in his eyes that screamed danger to any sort of defiance. Marcus stepped back, and his shirt pulled out of my hand, allowing it to drop and cover the brutal display.

"Sorry, boss, the woman couldn't keep her hands off me." He shrugged and then winked at me.

"Dick!" I muttered, and he laughed. Owens seemed to relax as well and nodded to Marcus. Marcus grinned at me and then turned and headed out of the room, closing the door behind him. And once again, I was alone with Owens.

He stepped towards me, and I stepped back. He stopped, and a hurt look crossed his face.

"Did you really do that to Marcus?" I asked. He looked like he was deciding if it was a good idea to answer or not, but then he looked at me and nodded.

"I expect success in every action," he said.

"So if they don't do what you ask, you kick the shit out of them?" I had seen a fair amount of violence as an Elite Officer, but this wasn't the same. This was exercising authority with cruelty.

"The punishment is always fitting the crime." He was slowly moving towards me. I was trying to keep the distance between us, but I was running out of space. Before I was backed into a corner, I could see it happening, but I couldn't seem to change it.

"And me?" I asked. "If I misbehave or don't follow an order, do you plan on decorating my body with bruises?" The look of genuine disgust crossed his face. I had backed up into the wall, and a slight upward tug of the corner of his lips said that he was fully aware I was trapped. He moved quicker, right up to me, close enough to feel his breath against my cheek. His scent hit me hard, and I closed my eyes as it washed over me.

I felt his hand on my chin and opened my eyes to meet his as he tilted my chin upwards.
"I would never intentionally hurt you. You are my exception," he said. He was so close that I felt his breath on my skin, and I was able to see his eyes clearly. They were a brilliant sky blue but had a distinct inky blue ring around the outside. They held secrets I wanted to dive into and drown. I felt Maia shift inside me, and a fire lit my stomach. My eyes flickered to his plump rosy lips, and for a moment, I wondered what it would be like to kiss them. Would it be a gentle caress or fierce, passionate, hard embrace? The more I thought about it, the lower the fire got, and I saw the corners of his mouth twitch upwards again. He leaned in close to me, his lips almost touching mine.
"Unless, of course, you wanted me to," he whispered against the thinnest layer of air that separated us.

I felt the tension in his body, holding himself back. He was making it clear. This was my decision. I would have to make the final move. I felt a little dizzy, like I couldn't get enough oxygen to my brain, and realised I had been holding my breath. Everything inside me screamed to close the gap, and I couldn't think why it would be wrong. I tilted my head slightly higher and brushed my lips oh so lightly against his. That was enough for him, and with a growl, he pushed his mouth against mine and pulled me into a dark abyss of passion as I wrapped my arms around his neck and pulled him in closer. Close enough to consume me. It was like every nerve ending was lit up as I felt his hands on my body. I was vaguely aware of him lifting me off my feet and moving us until I was pushed against something soft and sat on the bed.

Owens never once took his lips from mine as he pushed me back up the bed and crawled up between my legs as my head hit the covers. Finally, when I wondered if I was going to pass out from lack of oxygen, did he break the kiss. I was laid on my back with Owens on top of me, and I could feel his excitement as he pushed against me. My own excitement didn't go unnoticed, the fire had now turned into an inferno, and I gasped with need as I felt his hand against my jeans. He buried his head in my hair, and I felt as he ran his nose against my neck before his lips made contact, and he started kissing and nipping down to my shoulder.

I ran my hand against his body and growled in frustration at the layers of clothes that stopped me from making skin contact with my own hands. I wound my fingers in his hair as I felt his tongue against my marking spot just as he slipped a hand into my panties and expertly found my clit. I cried out from the touch of his rough fingers against my most sensitive area as he began massaging it in circular motions. I could feel the pressure rising with every rotation of his fingers.

I was suddenly pulled back to reality when I felt his teeth graze my marking spot, and the cold realisation of what was happening cleared my mind, pulling away from the fuzziness.

"No!" I exclaimed as I pushed my hands between us and against his body. Caught off guard, he moved back with ease, his hand slipping back out of my panties, and I scrambled out from under him and jumped off the bed. His own lust-filled haze dissipated, leaving a confused expression on his face.

"What? What's wrong?" he protested. What was wrong? I had one rule, don't get close. Sex was sex, but that was it, no emotions, no attachments. As long as I controlled that, I controlled my heart, stopped it from getting hurt, stopped me from being vulnerable ever again. That was my only rule, and in the last ten years, I had broken it exactly once. With Aaron, I had allowed myself to fall for him, but he couldn't handle the darkness inside me, and even though I hid it well, I was crushed beyond belief when he ended things with me. So the rule stayed. The thing is, the mate bond. It doesn't follow the rules. It feeds on emotion and vulnerability. Where the mate bond is concerned, emotions will always be involved. But how could I explain to Elias Owens, my mate, that the mate bond was a pure poison that I refuse to allow run through my veins?

CHAPTER 40

Harper

"I can't!" I said, shaking my head as I backed away from Elias. He stood up from the bed, and I held my hand out to stop him from coming closer.

"Harper, please," he pleaded. "I don't understand."

"You were going to mark me," I cried. "I mean, come on, it's been less than twelve hours, and you think you can lay claim on me just like that." Elias looked shocked and then horrified. He stepped forward, and I shook my head.

"Harper, please listen to me." He held his hands out, as if he was trying to talk me off a cliff edge or something. "I swear, I had no intention to mark you. I wouldn't, not without your consent."

"Well, don't expect that, ever!" I spat. I could feel tears burning my eyes. I knew I was overreacting, but I couldn't seem to get a grasp on myself.

Elias stopped and looked at me. His expression shifted to something unreadable.

"What do you mean, ever?" he asked in a slow tone that was edged with danger. I shook my head again.

"I'm not completing the mate bond, not with Colton and not with you!" I wiped away the tears that had begun to stream down my face.

"But we are fated. The goddess paired us for a reason. The mate bond is a sacred gift." A hysterical laugh escaped my lips.

"A gift!" I exclaimed. "It's a curse, a heavy weight that will drag you down and drown you."

"Why would you say that?" he asked. I had edged around the room towards the door. If I could get out the door, I could get out of the forsaken place.

"Why?" I looked at him like he was crazy. "How about my mother, who is slowly going insane because her mate is dead?" I cried. "Or my sister who suffered years of abuse and pain at the hands of her fated mate. Or even my uncle, whose mate you happen to have locked up in your cells right now!" Elias' eyes widened.

"Wait, what, who?" he asked.

"Or if that isn't enough, how about this!" I held up my left hand, showing the damn engagement ring that was still on my finger after ten years. Elias rushed forward and grabbed my wrist before I had a chance to move away. He glared at the ring with hate.

"Is this... Why the hell are you still wearing it?" he snarled, his eyes switching gold. I tried to pull my arm away, but his grip was ironclad. He reached up and pulled on the ring. I screamed as pain shot through my body, overwhelming all my senses. I felt like I was on fire and was being stripped raw. It was different from when I did it to chase the pleasure. I had the control, but this, this was unbearable.

I vaguely felt as my arm was released and the floor rushed forward, as I fell face first. The pain continued to rush through my body in waves. I felt something cold against my skin and heard shouting as the pain became too much, and I slipped into darkness.

"Seriously, dude, what were you thinking? You can't go grabbing shit off people. I'd told you he was gloating about it." I heard an angry whisper.

"Yeah, I know, I saw red. I'm a dick." Another voice.

"Yeah, well, it's one thing to kick the shit out of me to prove a fucking point, but she's your mate. You need to learn some respect."

I tried to open my eyes, but they felt heavy, and it took a couple of tries until I managed it. I was laid in a bed, and by the looks, I was in the room I had passed out in. I could just about see two figures through the blur and the darkened room. They were standing at the end of the bed, arguing. Or one was telling the other off. My eyes cleared, and I saw it was Elias and Marcus. Shockingly, it was Marcus telling Elias off. I tried to lift my hand to get their attention, but my body felt like it was about six times heavier or something.

I finally croaked a cough out, and they both turned and looked at me. Elias rushed to the side of the bed and placed a hand on my forehead, and smiled at me. His hand felt cold and soothing against my hot skin. Marcus stood at the end of the bed and grinned.

"Geez princess, you gave us quite the scare there," he said with forced cheer.

"What happened?" I asked. I remember that Elias had flipped over the ring and tried to take it off, but it didn't make sense. I had never felt pain like that. Well, I had, but that was almost ten years ago.

"It was my fault," Elias said, bowing his head. "Stokes had been gloating over the fact that you were wearing his ring. I guess I saw it and lost my temper. You tried to pull away and I dunno, I should have let go." The look of guilt was all over his face. "I didn't understand. I still don't understand. But the doc said that you had gone into shock from the pain."

"It's commanded," I croaked. "Colton commanded me to keep it on. He said if I or anyone tried to take it off, I would feel immense pain, or something like that." To be honest, it had been ten years, and I had worked to block that time out. I had also tried several ways to get the ring off my finger, but all had resulted in pain. I looked up at Elias, and his eyes shone with fury.

"I want him found and thrown in the cells now!" he hissed. Marcus grimaced and looked at me before looking at Elias.

"Boss, don't get me wrong, I agree, but you know…" he glanced at me again. "I mean, if you want to…."

Elias sighed and rubbed his eyes. He cursed under his breath before looking at me again and forcing a smile on his face.

"The doc gave you something for the pain," he said. I blinked at the sudden change of topic. I guess we'd finished that one then. "Get some rest, and we can talk in the morning." He leaned in and kissed my forehead before moving away again. He stood up from the bed and smiled again before heading for the door. Marcus grinned at me before turning to follow Elias. He stopped at the door and looked back at me.

"Don't worry, princess, as Gamma, it's my duty to protect you. And I take my duty deadly serious."

"I can protect myself," I said defiantly, and he grinned.

"Sure, I believe you," he said. "Well, then call me back up," he said with a wink, and I smiled. He closed the door, and the room fell into darkness apart from one dim lamp on a chest of drawers.

I laid there for several moments, not sure what I should do. Eventually, my eyes started to close again, heavy with tiredness, and I shuffled onto my side, wincing at the pain, and clutched my pillow and allowed myself to drift off to a dreamless sleep.

The next morning I woke up feeling like an elephant had trampled me. My whole body hurt, and I groaned as I tried to pull myself to a sitting position. I managed it on the fourth attempt and looked around the room. It was still dark, but the clock on the bedside table announced it a little after 7 am. I would have gone back to sleep, but my bladder had other ideas, and I dragged myself out of bed towards the only other door in the room, hoping it was the bathroom.

While there, I showered and otherwise get ready for the day. I knew yesterday was tiring, and I had found myself in the pack house of hell once more, but I had to look at this as a positive. Despite my dislike of the mate bond, it could really help me right now. Elias would have his guard down around me more, which could afford me more ease when trying to find the evidence I needed. I felt a pang of guilt at the idea of investigating my mate but quickly shoved it to the side. It wasn't my fault that he was a criminal mastermind. That was on him, and he had to deal with the consequences of his actions.

I was back in the bedroom towel drying my hair when I remembered I had heard Maia yesterday. I stopped and closed my eyes.

"Maia!" I called in my head, and I felt something shift, but there was no response. I wondered if the issue with my ring last night had weakened her again. But at least now I knew she was still here, which was more than I knew twenty-four hours ago. I finished getting ready and then turned and looked at the door. I walked over, half expecting it to be locked, but it opened up easily, and I looked out into the hallway. I was surprised to see Marcus sitting in a chair a little further down. He looked up and grinned as I poked my head out.

"About time, princess," he said, getting up and stretching. "I'm starving." I gave him a confused look.

"What are you talking about?" I asked.

"Told you, I take my role seriously," he said, and I remembered what he said last night.

"You were waiting for me?" I asked, my eyes widening, and he nodded.

"Of course. A gamma protects the Luna." I went to speak, and he raised his hand. "Or in this case, backs up his Luna."

"But I'm not your Luna," I stated, and he rolled his eyes.

"Sorry princess, you are fated to my Alpha, and until such time as you break that bond by rejection or some other means, in my eyes, you are Luna." He stood proud as he said so, and I smiled at his determination.

"Well, okay, but I'm not the Luna," I said. "But I am hungry, so where can a girl get some breakfast around here?" Marcus grinned.

"Now you're talking sense. This way, princess." He made a sweeping motion, and I laughed and followed him down the hallway.

I realised barely steps before we reached the doorway that we were headed to the shared named rank dining room. I hesitated at the hum of conversation inside, and Marcus turned and looked at me and pointed to himself.

"Back up, remember." And I smiled at him, suddenly very grateful for his presence. He opened the door, and I walked into the room to see it was pretty full. The former Luna and Caroline Stokes sat in the middle of the table. The twins were giggling opposite them, and Jamie was reading a book next to the twins. Sitting down at one end of the table where the Alpha sat was Elias, and right up at the other end, in the Beta's seat, was Colton.

I noticed they had been glaring at each other, but as I entered the room, they both stood up and watched me expectantly. I stood in the doorway as everyone went quiet.

I felt Marcus lean down behind me and could tell he was grinning.

"It's showtime!" he whispered with glee. I sighed and closed my eyes. Oh yeah, I thought sarcastically, this was going to be real fun.

CHAPTER 41

Harper

I looked around the room as everyone watched me, probably waiting for me to make a move. The former luna smiled at me as I considered backing up out of there.

"You know what," I said. "I suddenly don't feel so hungry after all." I glanced at Colton, who smiled when our eyes met. "In fact, I feel quite nauseous." Colton's face fell again as I scowled at him.

"Nonsense!" Marcus said, pushing me further into the room. "You are not a coward, so grow a backbone." I glared at him, but he just grinned in response and grabbed my hand and pulled me around the room, passing Colton on purpose, until we got to the other end of the table where Elias stood and held out the chair next to him.

It wasn't lost on me that it was the chair that the Luna used to sit in, and I glanced at her as I stood there. She was already watching me and smiled brightly and nodded her head. I sighed and sat down.

"Suits you nicely," she said, and Colton growled at her. Caroline glanced at him and then to her friend and back to Colton in confusion.

"Colton dear, don't sit in your father's chair. You know how he gets," she said and then carried on talking to the Luna. I glanced between them, and Colton watched his mother with a sad look on his face. He noticed me watching and glanced up at me before looking away.

When I lived here, it had been rumoured that the Beta's wife was compromised with her mental health. That was ten years before the loss of her mate, so it wasn't shocking that things would have progressed. I glanced at Elias, who was watching Caroline with concern. He met my eyes and grimaced. We broke contact as a plate was placed in front of me, and the smell of bacon reminded me of how hungry I was. I grabbed my fork and began to dig into the English breakfast on my plate.

I half-listened to all the conversations around me as I ate, catching snippets here and there.

"Alpha Elias," one of the twins purred at him, smiling brightly. "Would Lisa and I be able to steal a piece of your time later today so that we can go over the final preparations for the ball this weekend?" I looked up in interest. I glanced at the twins and then Elias.

"Ball?" I asked, "You are still holding the Midsummer Ball?" I asked, and Elias nodded.

"I wanted to continue some of the pack's traditions," he said. "It seemed the balls and the weekly dinners are something that the pack values." He shifted in his seat, suddenly looking fidgety.

"Which reminds me," he said, looking over at Marcus. The latter was grinning at his Alpha's sudden discomfort, "The weekly dinner is tonight, and well…" he hesitated before looking at me. "I would like you to sit with me at the top table." I felt my stomach drop as he said it, "Please," he pleaded as he took my hand in his, and I glanced down the table as Colton growled. My eyes met Colton's, and he glared at me. The last time I had been to the pack dinner was our announcement and intention ceremony. It was also the night when he and Damien tried to force me and then left me alone in the cold, dark night and in pain. He had no right to be pissed off at me, or anyone, for that matter. I smirked at him before turning back to Elias.

"I'd be honoured," I said, and he glanced at Colton and then back to me and smiled. He knew I was doing it to spite Colton, but the look on his face said he didn't really care.

Elias looked back at the twins with a smile on his face, although he didn't let go of my hand.

"And of course, Lily, why don't you and Lisa come and see me this afternoon." Both girls nodded enthusiastically. I smiled to myself as I took my hand back to finish my breakfast. Elias looked disappointed for a minute but then smiled and stood up.

"You will all excuse me. I have some work to do," he said and motioned for Marcus to follow. "Beta, I'd like to see you in my office at your earliest convenience," he said, and Colton scowled at him but nodded. Marcus grinned at me before getting up.

"See you around, princess," he said with a wink, and I rolled my eyes as he followed Elias out of the room.

"Harper dear," the Luna called, and I looked down at her. "Would you please give us the pleasure of having lunch with Caroline and me?" She glanced at Colton, who seemed to have a permanent scowl on his face. "I would like to talk with you about something." I smiled and nodded.

"Of course, I have something that I need to do this morning but can certainly find you after," I said. Maybe I could get some information from her about Elias while I was at it.

"Amazing, we will be in the 3rd-floor sitting room from midday," she said with a delighted smile. Colton stood up suddenly, scraping his chair back loudly, and stormed out of the room. I watched him go and then glanced at the Luna, who seemed to have a smug smile on her face. There was obviously something going on between them. I was hoping that I could maybe get that from the Luna in our little talk later.

Soon everyone drifted out of the room, and I was alone when I finished my breakfast. An Omega came into the room to clear my plate, and I thanked her as she scurried off. I got up to leave the room and headed back to my room. I had plans for my morning and wanted to grab a couple of things before I went. I opened the dining-room door, and leaning against the wall immediately opposite, was Colton.

I stared at him straight in the eye, keeping my expression blank, as he kicked off the wall, crossed the hall, and blocked my way out. He tried to back me into the room, but I held my ground despite him getting right in my personal space.

"What do you want, Colton?" I asked with my best, bored tone, and he grinned at me. I knew he wasn't buying my calm exterior. My heart was beating really fast, and werewolf hearing meant that he could hear exactly how fast.

"I wanted to remind you of something, Strawberries," he said as he leaned in to sniff me. "Just because that jumped up piece-of-shit Alpha thinks that he can lay some sort of claim on you. You always have, still do, and always will belong to me." He grabbed my left hand and tugged on the ring quickly. I hissed at the shock of pain that ran through my body, and he smirked at my reaction. I was starting to get seriously pissed off with this guy. I glared at him as I pulled my hand out of his and slapped him across the face. His head rocked back with the impact, and he growled at me.

"Bring it on," I growled back, and he took a step forward, so we were practically touching. I pushed my hand between us and pushed him back again.

"Let's really get one thing clear," I growled. "You are right. The Alpha doesn't have a claim on me, but then neither the fuck do you!" I pushed him again until he was out of the door frame and I could get out of the room.

"The only person that holds a claim on me is me!" I pushed hard one last time and slammed him back into the wall. "Do you understand Beta Stokes?" I didn't wait for a response before storming past him and down the hallway. I was sick of everyone thinking they could decide for me.

I made it to my room and grabbed my suitcase. I unzipped the secret compartment in the back, pulled out my favourite hunting knife in its sheath, and slid it into my boot. I left the room and headed down the stairs and out of the pack house. I made my way halfway down the drive and then left the path and headed into the woods. I had been itching to do this ever since I had found out yesterday, but it had suddenly become very busy. I found the little wood path that I only knew about because of Tommy and followed it all the way up to the solitary stone building. I circled the building three times, taking in the cameras surrounding it. I tried to gauge if they had any blind spots that I could use to my advantage between them.

I looked at the double steel doors to see if there was a magical button that would allow me entry because, of course, they would leave the entrance to the pack cells open for all to visit, right? I scoffed at myself. I knew I had to get in since I heard Louise was being kept here. But I also knew that it had always been forbidden for pack members to even be in this area.

I circled the building again, trying to formulate a plan. I would need to come back at night and bring some tools. The electronic keypad could probably be hacked if I had enough time. I was mentally making a note of everything I needed as I rounded the corner to the front of the building again and stopped dead in my tracks. Elias was standing right in front of me, his face expressionless, just like it had been at the bar yesterday. Marcus was leaning against the door with a big grin on his face. I glared at him, which only caused his grin to widen, and then returned my look to Elias. His lips twitched as he watched me squirm, trying to think of a feasible excuse for why I was here.

"I wondered how long it would take for you to show up," Elias said with a satisfied smile.

CHAPTER 42

Harper

I glared at Elias and that smug look on his face. I took a deep breath and turned around, and started walking down the path again. Fuck! How the hell did he know I was going to be there?

"Hey," he called after me, but I didn't stop. I felt his hand on my arm as he pulled me to a stop and then pulled me against him. He ran his nose through my hair and whispered in my ear.

"Wait, don't go." I closed my eyes and tried to focus on anything other than the feel of the sparks that danced along my skin. He let go of my arms, running his fingers down them before I stepped forward out of his space. I turned around to look at him and smiled. I was aiming for sweet and innocent, but the look on his face told me he wasn't buying it.

"I was just walking," I said innocently and batted my eyelashes. He raised an eyebrow while Marcus fake coughed back at the building.

"Bullshit!" Marcus coughed around, and I shot him a glare. He just started laughing.

"So you just happened to walk by this building?" Elias asked, and I nodded.

"And so you thought it was interesting and decided to investigate?" he carried on. I nodded again.

"Yep, exactly," I said with a smile.

"So it's a complete coincidence that you found yourself by the entrance to the cells, the very same cells that your friend happens to be in?" I knew he knew I was lying through my teeth.

"Oh?" I said in mock surprise and widened my eyes. "This is the entrance to the cells?" And he shook his head.

He grabbed my hand and pulled me back to the entrance and then jerked his head to Marcus as we got there. Marcus winked at me before walking off around the corner, leaving the two of us alone. Fine protector, he was, but I guess that didn't include protection against his own Alpha. Elias positioned me at the door in front of him.

"I get it," he said, standing behind me. "You are concerned for your friend. He ran his hand along my shoulder and swept my hair back, so my shoulder was bare.

"You could have come to talk to me about it," he moved closer, so my back was completely against his front. It felt nice, so I wasn't in a rush to move.

"And you would have let me in?" I asked. He chuckled against my skin, and I felt the vibration run through my body.

"No," he said. "Not without asking for something in return." And there it was. I turned around to face him and scowled.

"And what exactly is it that you want in return?" I arched my eyebrow, ready to slap him for whatever vile thing he was thinking of. He leaned in close to me and whispered in my ear.

"A chance." I stepped back and looked at him in shock.

"Let me show you what the fated mate bond is really about."

"And how do you propose to do that?" I asked sceptically.

"Tomorrow is your birthday, right?" he asked, and I nodded. I guess my birthday would have been in my records. "I want to take you to dinner, a date."

"A date?" I asked. "That's it? I go on a date with you, and you let me see Louise?" He nodded.

"If you agree now, I will open the door and take you down to her right now." He tucked a piece of my hair behind my ear, and I felt prickles along my scalp. "Do you agree, Harper Kirby?" I nodded quickly. I could handle one date. Plus, if I could get him to really trust me, then I could get close. That would make it easier to get what I needed.

Elias smiled and stepped back. I moved to the side and looked at the door expectantly. Was it really this easy? He stepped forward to the door, and I watched as he typed the code into the keypad, and the door opened. He glanced back at me with a cheeky grin.

"Did you catch that?" he asked, and I feigned innocence again. He turned into me, grabbed my hips, and pulled me against him.

"Tell me, Harper, what number did I just type in? I know you saw." I tried to steady my breathing as I felt a shift inside me.

"Mmm, don't tell him. Maybe he'll pull us closer." Maia shocked me by speaking. I shook my head in surprise.

"You're back again," I stated.

"Yeah, we are still weak, but his beast pulls me out, gives me strength," she sighed. Oh, that wasn't good. I wanted Maia back, but not because of Elias.

"I'm waiting, sweetheart," Elias cooed against my shoulder, and I shivered as he kissed it. I took another deep breath.

"Seven, one, nine, six, four, one," I breathed each number as he moved kisses onto my throat.

"Good girl," he breathed against my neck, and I felt another rush through my body. I shifted to clench my legs together, despite the obvious aroma of my excitement embarrassingly making itself known. Elias chuckled again and stepped back. It took every ounce of strength not to follow him and close the space between us again. He moved to one side and gestured with his hand towards the door.

I headed in through the door, and he followed close on my heels. Marcus appeared a few seconds later and grinned at me again. I rolled my eyes at him and then turned to face the door in front of me. Elias pressed a button, and I heard a whirling and realised it was an elevator. The doors opened, and I walked in. Once we were all in, Elias opened a keypad and typed in a different number. This one I didn't get. The elevator went down, and the doors opened. Elias walked out first, and I followed with Marcus at my back. The room was stone everywhere. There was a desk, and one guard sat behind it. He looked up as we walked in but stood to attention as soon as he saw Elias. There was something familiar about him, but I wasn't sure what it was.

"Alpha, sir," he said, and Elias waved at him to sit down.

"I am taking Miss Kirby here to see Mrs Chambers," he said, and the guard looked me over.

"Kirby?" he asked. "Tommy Kirby's niece?" I nodded. He continued to watch me as Elias filled out the pretty sparse visitors' sheet. I narrowed my eyes at the guard. I was starting to get annoyed at the attention.

"Do you have a problem with me?" I snapped, and Elias looked up at him.

"No, ma'am," he said with an acidic tone to his voice.

"Spit it out, soldier," Elias responded. "It's clear you have something to say." I saw his body language stiffen and could hear the challenge in his tone. The guard looked uneasy suddenly, and I remembered where I knew him from. He was one of Damien's and Colton's group from before I left. Which likely meant that he was one of the ones that Colton had bragged to after our first night together.

"Nothing, sir," he said and glanced at me before lowering his eyes with a smirk on his face.

"I said spit it out," he growled, his Alpha command coming through clearly. The guard attempted to struggle before he stuttered.

"I-I just remembered C-Colton telling us how g-good she was in b-bed," he said, and he looked up in fear at Elias. I glanced over and saw the gold shine of Elias's wolf. His hands were clenched like he was holding back. I glanced at Marcus, who was also glaring at the guard.

"Boss, take your girl to see her friend," he said and then looked at me. "Round that corner," he said and pointed down a hallway. I nodded and grabbed Elias' hand. He glanced down at my hand in surprise and then back up to me, his eyes still gold.

I pulled him around the corner that Marcus had directed me to. He resisted a little, but I managed to get him out of sight of the guard. We got around the corner, and he stopped.

"I should go and snap his neck," he growled, and I tugged on his hand.

"Leave it," I pleaded. I could see the murderous look in his eyes.

"And I am going to fucking kill that bastard too," he snarled. I could see he was getting riled up again and was seconds away from turning back towards the guard. So I did the only thing that I could think of at the moment. I pushed him against the wall and smashed my lips against his. He didn't respond at first, but there was a fine line between anger and lust, and thankfully, his wolf chose the latter. He growled into my mouth and returned my kiss with such force that I was sure that my lips would be bruised. Elias gripped my body and pulled me into him as close as humanly possible. There was nothing gentle as he took control of the moment and spun us, so my back was against the wall. His mouth left mine and found my neck, and I gasped as my body exploded with the need to touch, be touched, ride, and be ridden by the furious passion coursing through my veins.

Elias found my mouth again just as I heard a noise and a scream of pain from around the corner. There was another cry of pain and then a loud bang before a second bang. And then the sound of metal clanking. Everything went silent, and I pulled away from Elias. He growled in protest but let me. He leaned his forehead against mine as we both regained our breath. Elias grinned at me, and his eyes sparkled blue again. I heard movement to the side of us.

"Aw, Harper, I was looking forward to calming his ass like that," Marcus fake whined, and I laughed and looked over at him.

"You're a dick. You know that," I said, and he grinned in response.

"Is it sorted?" Elias asked, and Marcus nodded.

"I've linked for a replacement," he said, and Elias nodded. He grabbed my hand, smiled at me, and then kissed my nose, which I scrunched in response.

"Come on, let me take you to your friend," he said and tugged me further down the hallway.

We got to the bottom, where a heavy-duty-looking metal door was. I was starting to wonder if I would have been able to get in by myself at this rate. Elias flipped a panel and typed in a code, blocking it from my view. The door opened, and he walked through. I followed into another corridor. Only this one had doors on each side as we walked. The doors were metal with small windows. Some were dark, and some were lit up. I wondered who else was down here. We made it to the end of the corridor, and Elias tapped another keypad, and the light next to it turned green. He opened the door and walked in. I smiled as I heard a familiar voice.

"Oh great, what the fuck do you want so soon?" Louise ranted from inside the room. "And before you ask, no, I don't know what the schedule is, or who is involved, and no, for the last fucking time, I don't know where the hell the spineless piece-of-shit husband of mine is. Satisfied, you arrogant bastard?" Elias looked over his shoulder at me with an eyebrow raised, and I pushed past him into the room. It was a standard cell room—toilet and sink in one corner and a single metal bed against the wall. Louise sat on the bed, her back straight and a furious look on her face. She looked at me, and confusion crossed her face before she realised.

"Oh my goddess Harper!" she gasped. She jumped off the bed, and I met her halfway as we hugged. "Why did you come back? It's not safe for you!"

CHAPTER 43

Louise

Three Months Ago

I screamed as the orgasm ripped through me, and I transcended into complete bliss, my whole body alive with the fires of passion. I looked down at Tommy as I continued to ride him, not wanting this perfect, amazing moment to ever end. Tommy's hands held my hips in a firm grip as he guided me over and over. I could tell he was lost in his own ecstasy too. Eventually, I collapsed onto his chest, panting and sweating and happy. Tommy's arms circled me, and he growled contentedly into my ear.

"Fuck me baby, that was amazing!" he whispered, his voice hoarse.

"Don't call me baby," I responded automatically, and he chuckled. The truth was, I liked when he called me that. I liked the idea of being his. I didn't just like it. I loved it. I was so unbelievably in love with Tommy. Despite the last ten years of pain and misery, he was always a beautiful, strong shining light in everything.

A single tear slipped down my cheek onto his chest, and he lifted his head to look at me. He wiped away the trail that it left behind. I smiled sadly, and he kissed my head.

"Can you stay tonight?" he asked, and I shook my head.

"Damien is being really annoying lately," I scowled. "He keeps going on about spies or something like that." Tommy scowled at that but didn't push. He knew that things at the pack house were a mess. Something had gone wrong in the pack businesses, and tension was high.

Damien was fully aware of where I was. Our marriage was a horror show right from the beginning. I never wanted to marry him. I would have broken the forced mate bond long before now if it wasn't for him threatening that he would have both Tommy and my brother Alex killed straight away. I knew he would, too. I could see it in his eyes when he said it. My husband was unhinged, but he was nothing compared to his best friend and Beta Colton. I feared the day when they took over this pathetic excuse for a pack.

The pair were immature and maniacal and had way too much power to go with it. But Colton was something else entirely. After we managed to get Harper to safety, he had lost it big time. He had put Alex in the hospital and killed several of the warriors who he blamed for not getting to her in time. Of course, he knew that Tommy and I were a part of her escape, and he paid me back by telling my father that I was sleeping with Tommy. My father had gone mental at that and demanded I stop seeing him. It got worse when he found out that Tommy was my fated mate.

He told me right there, not two days after Harper had gone, I would be mating with Damien. I had refused, of course, but they kept me locked in my room, and the next thing I knew, it was announced that we were to be mated. That was when the first threat came. My own father saying that he would kill his own son while he lay in a coma was one of the coldest things I had seen. But it was nothing on him holding me down while I screamed as Damien completed the mating ceremony, shattering my bond with Tommy. The weeks that followed were just as bad as I was introduced to the perverse nature of the people I had lived with my whole life.

I knew what had happened with Harper and half expected it when Colton joined us in the bedroom. But the hate that Colton had for me for helping Harper leave him was so evident in his actions, and I would often have to spend days in bed recovering from it as Damien would tell me that it would be alright. He never once lifted a finger against his friend.

Colton had somewhat calmed down in his anger after a while, but there was a more sinister thing about him. He kept saying he would bide his time until his mate returned, and he knew she would come back soon. I prayed to the moon goddess every night that I would never see my best friend again because if I did then, I couldn't even imagine what Colton would do to her.

It was three years into this nightmare that I finally snapped. Damien watched as Colton worked himself inside me, not knowing that I had got my hand on a steak knife from the kitchen. I slipped my hand under the pillow and felt for the handle. I closed my fingers around the hilt and pulled it out with every intention of sinking it into Colton's throat. But Damien had realised and jumped in the way, and the blade went into his arm instead. They were both furious, and I ended up beaten and locked in a cell overnight. The next morning my father, Alpha Daniel, and Beta Eric all visited me in the cell, and my father added to the bruises that were already decorating my now weakened body.

The Alpha declared that I needed to be conditioned to the role of a Luna and learn my place. I told them I would kill them all in their sleep if they ever let me out and to just put me out of my misery. Of course, they didn't. But our Luna, Alice, had suggested that the appearance mattered, and as long as the pack believed that we were a strong unit, it didn't matter what happened in reality. Negotiations had started there. There would be no more sharing with Colton, but I would agree to produce an heir for Damien and attend all the functions and events as the dutiful future Luna. In return, I would be afforded some freedom, although I knew I was being followed everywhere I went.

The first place I went when they let me leave was Tommy's. I hoped to the goddess that he hadn't left the pack or moved on to another mate. It was selfish of me to want him to wait for me, but I was ready to be selfish.

I knocked on Tommy's door, and when he opened it, I threw myself into his arms in tears. Things got better after that, and after his initial outburst of murderous rage, I was able to calm him down. Despite our shattered bond, it was still there, in pieces, at the bottom of my heart. Over the next seven years, we slowly rebuilt our bond. We spent occasional nights together where we could, and Tommy helped me deal with and heal from what I had suffered.

I still wasn't fully healed, and living in the house, sleeping in the bed with some of the worst monsters I have ever known, was still wearing on my soul. But Damien and I had slipped into a weekly arrangement in the interest of producing this heir, while I added the hope that I would never fall pregnant to him to my list of prayers to the moon goddess.

Tommy squeezed me in his arms, bringing me back to the present, and I sighed. I glanced at the clock on his bedside table and groaned. It was just after 5 pm, and I had to be at the laughable pack family dinner by 6 pm. I climbed out of bed and the warm embrace of my lover and hunted around for my clothes. I could feel Tommy's eyes on me as I moved about the room.
"It's rude to stare," I said as I looked over my shoulder with a coy smile, and he grinned.
"Can't help it, baby, when a piece of heaven is walking around my room, I have no choice but to worship." I rolled my eyes at the cheesy line, but my heart fluttered a little too.

"You have dinner tonight, right?" he asked. He had long since been banned from the pack dinner after several threats against Damien. I was shocked that he hadn't been dragged off to the cells or banished with the stuff Tommy did. He always said they wouldn't do the first and couldn't do the second. Not while his idiot brother continued to turn his back on the family name. I asked what he meant, but he just smiled.
"So it's minimal warriors on duty then?" Tommy asked, and I looked at him puzzled.
"What are you up to?" I asked, and he shrugged.
"Absolutely nothing, baby. Are you sure you can't miss the dinner?" I shook my head. It was part of the agreement that I put a united face on at the pack events. I didn't also add that tonight was the night I spent

with Damien. He knew it happened but didn't want to know when. Thankfully, our bond was still fragile enough that he didn't feel it, or if he did, he never said it.

I leaned in to kiss him before leaving and heading up to the pack house. I got there just as the first pack member was approaching, and Damien caught hold of my arm as soon as I walked into the building.

"You are late," he hissed as he pushed me up towards the main hall. "And you stink of that mutt." I glanced at my phone.

"I have fifteen minutes," I declared, and he growled at me. He was even worse today, and I decided not to push my luck as we made our way up to the main table. I sat down next to Alice, and she smiled at me. Her hand reached under the table, and she squeezed mine ever so gently. I smiled at her in return, grateful for the saving grace she had been during these years.

We were just beginning the first course not half an hour later when the main hall doors flew open, and many unknown wolves flooded into the room. In the centre of them, looking like the very essence of dominant Alpha, stood a man in a black suit with a red shirt. He smiled as he watched all of us, his eyes finally landing on Alpha Daniel.

"Alpha Daniel Chambers, I Alpha Elias Owens challenge you to the ownership of the Midnight Moon pack."

CHAPTER 44

Louise

I looked over at Alpha Daniel, who was staring at the other Alpha, a look of fury on his face. A large man walked into the room and handed something to the Alpha. He looked down at it as pack members began to panic. I watched as the warriors were quick to reseat anyone who looked to be standing up or causing trouble.

"I'm still waiting for your response," Alpha Elias said to Alpha Daniel without looking up from the papers.

"Who the hell do you think you are?" Beta Eric bellowed, and I glanced down the table as he and my father jumped up. My father moved in front of the Luna and me as if to protect us. The Alpha finally looked up from the papers and sighed. He looked positively bored with his surroundings.

"Do you accept the challenge or not, Alpha Daniel?" he asked, and I looked past Luna to the Alpha again. He looked absolutely terrified. I shook my head in disgust. His pack was under attack, and the man looked like he was about to faint.

"Fine, we'll do it the hard way." The other alpha turned to the man next to him and nodded towards our table. "Him and the heir, and their Lunas too." And there was a sudden swell of activity in the room.

Alice turned to me and smiled and gripped my hand as two warriors roughly removed us from our seats. We were ordered to move out into the court in front of the pack house. I followed along behind Alice with Damien behind me. As we were forced to our knees, Damien grabbed my other hand.

"When I say so, run." I looked at him in shock. I knew he was a weasel, but I guess all his bully posturing was for nothing, even when his family was concerned.

"I would rather die right here on my knees than go anywhere with you," I sneered at him and he glared at me.

"Fine, you slut, you've made your choice." I was seconds away from informing the warrior behind me that my husband planned on running when there was a fight of some sort behind us. I turned to see Colton shifted into his wolf and trying to rip through a warrior or two. Damien took that moment to run. He had shifted into his wolf form before he hit the trees. The Alpha shouted commands to subdue Colton and to find Damien. He walked over and stood in front of me. The look of disgust on his face as he looked down at me.

"Where did your husband go?" I smiled as I looked up at him.

"I wouldn't know," I said. "And I don't care either." He shook his head and turned to the crowd that gathered.

"As your Alpha, the supposed protector of your pack, has refused to accept my challenge, I have no alternative but to take control of the pack by force." He walked over to Alpha Daniel and pulled a dagger from his pants. With one swift movement, he sliced the knife through the air and the Alpha's throat. Gasps ran through the air as the Luna screamed and doubled over in pain as her mate died.

"As the blood spilled by my hand soaks into the ground, so does my claim on the Midnight Moon pack." I felt as the bond to Alpha Daniel shifted into something unfamiliar.

"Return to your homes, nobody is permitted to leave the territory, and you will all be processed and required to swear loyalty in due time." The warriors jumped to life and steered the crowd down the drive. The Alpha started barking orders as I tried to comfort Alice. It wasn't until I looked closely that I realised she was laughing and not crying.

The Beta and my father were dragged in front of the Alpha and forced to their knees. The big guy that had given the Alpha the papers whispered something in his ear. Whatever it was pissed him off something strong because he snarled as he looked down at the two. He didn't even say a word when he sliced through the Beta's throat.

"Please, I'll do anything you want," my father started begging, and the Alpha shook his head.

"You should have thought about that before this," and he shoved the papers at my father. My father's eyes widened, and he started sobbing. I watched closely as the Alpha slashed his throat too. I leaned forward as my father dropped forward to the floor, and his eyes stared blankly ahead. I felt a calm come over me knowing that monster was dead.

A now sedated Colton, still in wolf form, was carried away somewhere. The Alpha nodded behind me, and I was dragged to my feet. The Alpha stood in front of me again and looked me up and down.

"Now, my dear," he sneered. "Let's try this again. Where did your husband go?"

"Hopefully straight to hell," I spat, and I felt a sharp sting across my face as one of the warriors stepped forward and slapped me. I struggled against the hold that the other warrior had on my arms.

"Try that again when your buddy isn't holding me back, you impotent mutt," I snarled at him, and the warrior stepped forward again. The Alpha put his arm out in front of the warrior and shook his head.

"Take her to the cells until she co-operates," the Alpha called and the warrior holding my arms started dragging me backwards.

Present Day

"And I've been here ever since," I said, glancing up at the man who killed my father. He was leaning against the door, his face impassive as if he wasn't listening. But as I told Harper my story, I noticed shifts in his body movement that said he was listening and wasn't happy. I looked back at Harper, who had tears in her eyes and fury on her face.

"I swear to the goddess I am going to kill Colton," she hissed. I couldn't believe the difference in her. She was my Harper, my best friend. She looked exactly the same as she did the last time I saw her, maybe leaner at most. But she held herself completely different, and the spark in her eyes was not the timid, sweet girl I had known all that time ago.

"I would rather you just leave and get out of here," I said, "You can't underestimate Colton. He kept saying you would be back. Like he knew!" Harper shook her head and glanced at the Alpha before looking back at me. I looked down and noticed the gold band on her finger.

"Don't worry about me. Trust me. I can take care of myself," she said.

"Really?" I asked and snatched her hand up to reveal the stone of the engagement ring that Colton had given her. "Take this off then," I said, and she growled and pulled her hand away. She then glanced over to the Alpha again and back to me.

"Ok, it's complicated," she sighed.

"Why did you come back?" I blurted out, and she grinned.

"What? Not happy to see me or something?"

"No, I am. I would prefer to see you outside of this damn place," I glared at the Alpha again, and Harper looked around at him, and he finally made eye contact with her. His usual expressionless features slipped into something close to how Tommy looked at me. I looked between the two of them. I could tell they weren't mind linking, but something emotional was going on.

The Alpha sighed and then looked at me. He shook his head and walked out of the cell, and Harper got up and followed him. I heard them arguing in hushed tones outside, and then it went quiet. I sat and watched the open door. Finally, a head popped in through the door, and I recognised the man who had been with the Alpha that night.

"Hey, you've made bail," he said with a big grin, and I looked at him confused. "Well, are you coming, or should I shut the door again?" I jumped up quickly and rushed out of the door into the hallway. I stopped short when I saw Harper and the Alpha down the hall, locked in a full-on make-out session. The man stood next to me and sighed dramatically.

"I'm feeling left out again, guys," he called, and Harper pushed the Alpha away and grinned.

"Ok, Marcus, you can have him back." The Alpha rolled his eyes before turning and walking off down the hall.

The man, Marcus, and I caught up to Harper, and she linked arms with me as we walked out of the cells towards the exit.

"Erm, Harps?" I asked, and she smiled.

"Oh yeah, Elias is my second-chance mate," I couldn't contain the shock on my face as she laughed.

"Yeah, I might need to catch you up on a few things," she said and laughed again.

CHAPTER 45

Harper

"You will stay in sight of one of my men or your room at all times." I twirled my hair, quickly getting bored with Elias' conditions for Louise's release. "You are not permitted access to a computer with internet access, mobile phone, or any other method of communication at any time."

"Okay, we get it," I scowled at him. "She's still a prisoner, yada-yada." Elias scowled back at me. "I have agreed to have lunch with the Luna-"

"Former Luna," Elias interrupted me, and I rolled my eyes.

"Former Luna. I want to take Louise with me," I said, and Elias shook his head.

"No, not this soon." He looked at Louise. "I need you to stay here right now." She nodded.

"Why?" I asked. I didn't want to leave my friend on her own after she had spent three months or so locked up.

"Because I have arranged a personal guard for her, and he will be here soon," he said, his tone clipped. I narrowed my eyes and glanced between him and Louise.

"And who might that be?" I asked.

"Me" I looked over to the door where Tommy was standing. Louise gasped and ran to him, throwing herself into his arms. Tommy captured her, his arms surrounding her, and buried his head into the crook of her neck. Louise burst out crying as she hugged Tommy tight.

"It's ok, baby," he cooed. "I got you now." I smiled at them and then looked at Elias, who was watching me with a look of desire in his eyes. Our eyes met, and he smiled before looking away.

"Okay, everyone out, let's give them some time." The two warriors, who were standing by the door, left, and Marcus followed them. I walked to the door, following Elias out of the room. I stopped at the door and looked back at Tommy and Louise. He guided her to the sofa and whispered things in her ear as she curled up against him. They both looked so relaxed and calm.

I felt his breath on the back of my neck as Elias moved in close behind me and whispered in my ear.

"See the beautiful power of the fated mate bond?" His hand slipped down my side and pulled me against him. He ran his nose up the back of my neck, and I shivered as sparks flew through my body. I pulled away, closing the door and giving them the privacy they deserved. I turned toward Elias, took hold of the collar of his shirt, and smiled.

"That was a very nice thing you did there, Alpha," I said as he began backing me up against the wall.

"It was the least I could do," he said. "I didn't know that she was Tommy's mate. I just saw her as the future Luna and thought that she could help me get Chambers." I nodded. He smiled down at me and backed me up against the wall. I tutted at him and shook my head.

"Nah-ah," I said as he kissed down my throat. "I told you I have plans." He chuckled against my throat.

"As much as I want to pick you up, take you into my bedroom, and make you forget those plans ever existed, over and over again....." I found myself biting my lip as images of what he wanted rushed through my mind. "Alas, I also have important work to do. So please enjoy your lunch plans." He leaned in and whispered, "and maybe I will eat later," he purred the word eat, and I stopped breathing for a second. Elias smirked at the reaction he was getting and kissed my cheek before walking away down the hall, leaving me almost panting at the wicked thoughts that he had put into my mind. Dammit, I was used to being the one that left them reeling in a lust-filled frenzy. I was starting to think that this mate bond would be the death of me in a whole different way.

I gathered myself, pushed away from the wall, and headed down the hallway and down to the next floor. I was a little later than planned but headed into the 3rd-floor living room where Alice Chambers and Caroline Stokes were sitting on one of the sofas chatting. Caroline looked up and smiled brightly.

"Harper darling," she said excitedly. "How lovely of you to come. Did you bring Colton with you?" I stopped and narrowed my eyes at her, and Alice shook her head at me and looked over at Caroline with concern on her face. She leaned over and took her hand.

"Caroline, honey, Colton is working, remember?" Caroline smiled.

"Of course he is. Bless him. He is so keen to get his poor dad to retire. I keep telling Eric that he promised when you had the pups." Caroline continued in her own dialogue while I stared at her, confused.

"Please, Harper, come sit down," Alice said, cutting Caroline off. I smiled and walked over and sat on the opposite sofa. Alice passed me a plate, and we lapsed into silence as we ate sandwiches.

We were just finishing up when Alice put down her coffee cup and looked at me.

"Harper, I want to apologise," she said, and I glanced up at her. Her eyes glistened like she was about to cry, but otherwise, her face was calm, not devoid of emotion, but if pleasant was an emotion, I could imagine this is what it looked like.

"When I found out that you and Colton were..." she trailed off, "Well, I prayed to the moon goddess that you would find a way to escape the cruel fate that some of us couldn't." My eyes widened as the realisation hit with what she was saying. A tear slipped down her cheek.

"Are you saying..." I trailed off and looked at the women. Alice nodded,

"Yes, the rotten apple doesn't fall far from the tree at all. It was the reason Julia Bennet left. She escaped like you did. Although, there are rumours that she didn't escape at all." I couldn't believe what she was telling me. Especially after I had heard what Louise had gone through.

"But Harper dear, that's not the important part," she looked up at the door and then back to me. "When Daniel and Eric found out that Colton had rejected you, they got very upset." I had always wondered what had happened for him to go from rejecting me to going mental when I left.

"What with your family being a bloodline of The Order and all, it wasn't enough for them to have your father in their chains, not with what he did and the strained relationship with Tommy-" Alice was talking, but I didn't understand what she was saying.

"What are you talking about? What's the Order, and what did my dad do?" Alice gave me a confused look.

"Harper, do you not-" she stopped suddenly and looked up behind me. I turned around to see Colton standing in the doorway. He was glaring at Alice, his eyes showing the gold of his wolf.

I couldn't help the growl that escaped my lips, knowing what he did to Louise. And he glanced at me in surprise before returning his furious look to Alice. I looked back at Alice, and she was staring at Colton with a smug smile on her face. I had the feeling that what she had said was something Colton didn't want me to know about, which made me instantly curious.

"Harper," he said, not taking his eyes off Alice. "The Alpha has asked to see you." I glanced between the two, uncertain.

"Go, my dear," Alice said. "We can talk another time." I nodded and stood up, walking to the door that Colton held open. I glared at him as he smiled at me.

"Oh, Colton," Caroline called, "While you are both here, could we discuss your 10th-anniversary party. Harper, would you like me to see if Alpha Daniel will allow some pink in its colour scheme? I know how much you love pink. And we should start early so the pups could attend for a little bit." I looked at Caroline, even more confused. I turned to look at Colton, and he was watching his mum with a sad look in his eyes. He saw me looking and shrugged.

"We can talk about it later, mum, I promise." That seemed to appease her, and she turned to Alice to talk about this supposed party. Colton gestured to leave the room, and I walked into the hallway.

He followed me out, closing the door.

"What the hell was that?" I demanded, and he shook his head, the sadness still written all over his face.

"She's got a lot worse since my father died, but she started declining steadily way before that." He looked at the door and then back at me. "In her mind, you never left." He moved towards me, and I moved back. "We got married, and we have two pups." My back hit the wall. Colton leaned in, his arms on either side of me, caging me in. "In her eyes, we are madly in love with each other. I sometimes sit there and listen to her talking about the life that she can see." He leaned right in to whisper, "Do you ever wonder what it would have been like if you never left me? Because I do. Every day."

"And where does sexually assaulting my best friend fit into all of that," I hissed, and he stepped back, shock written all over his face. "Because from what I heard of that, I don't think our lives would have been remotely happy." Colton quickly returned to his arrogant mask and smirked at me.

"From what I hear about your exploits over the last ten years, I bet you would have quickly learned to love what we did." It was my turn to look shocked. How did he know what the last ten years were like for me?

"Oh yeah, Strawberries, I know everything. The blood games with the vampire and the many not so forgotten names," he leaned in again, "and especially, I know the secret of who you work for and why you came back." Dread gripped my stomach. How could he know?

"So if you don't want your new lover to find out, and I can assure you he doesn't take betrayal well, you and I better come to some mutually beneficial arrangement."

CHAPTER 46

Harper

I glared at Colton as he rubbed the now reddened skin on his cheek where I had just slapped him.

"You disgust me!" I spat. "And I don't care what you threaten to do or say. I will never do anything that will remotely benefit you ever!" I was furious. Who the hell did he think he was, to think that he could even suggest that after what I had just found out. I didn't care what he wanted. I wasn't interested. I turned to walk away from him and heard him chuckle.

"Never say never, Strawberries," he called after me. "It might have been ten years ago, but I remember when you not only didn't say never, but you begged me to take what I wanted and more. You begged me to claim you!"

"Yeah, well, feel free to say never now," I called back without looking. "Because that girl is dead!"

"Do you know what your new dear mate does to people who disappoint him?" I felt Colton following me down the hall. "Do you know what he would do to someone who betrayed him like this? Someone who only got close to him so that they could take him down?" I stopped at the end of the hall and knew Colton was standing right behind me. I could feel his breath on the back of my neck.

"People have gone missing from this town since he arrived," Colton said. "How many young she-wolves have you seen in town since you got here? Do you really think this curfew is for anything other than thinning the herd, taking what he wants, and disposing of the rest? I know that you have read the file on him. You will have seen what he has done in other packs, to other people." Colton leaned right into my ear, and I shivered as he whispered,

"What would a man like that do to a member of the Council elite guard, sent to spy on him and ruin the empire he is building?"

I hated to admit it, but I had read the report. The background on Elias was that he was ruthless and unforgiving. But I had met the man underneath. I had seen a nicer, more caring side to Elias. Did that mean that he wasn't a bad guy? No. I was here to find evidence that we could use against him to prove that he was a part of the worst underground criminal organisation that the world didn't know existed. The mate bond couldn't change that and couldn't change the type of person he was. No matter how much I was starting to have feelings for the man.

I leaned against the wall and closed my eyes. Why did everything have to be so fucking complicated? I opened them again to see Colton watching me with a smirk screaming to be punched in his face.

"Don't worry, Strawberries," he said. "I'm not going to make you do anything you don't want to. In fact, I will help you get what you need to take Owens down." I looked at him and narrowed my eyes.

"Why?" I asked. "Why would you want to help me, knowing that once I have what I need, then I'm gone?" Colton looked around and then back at me.

"Because I want the bastard gone too," he said. "With him gone, I will finally be able to take control of my pack."

"Your pack?" I asked, surprised. "But you're not an Alpha. It would be Damien who would take back control. Wherever he is." I raised my eyebrows in question, hoping for an answer, and he chuckled, moving in close to me.

"Nice try, Strawberries," he said, "I'm not giving that bit of valuable information away. It doesn't matter, though, because that spineless piece of shit was never going to be the Alpha of this pack. It was always going to be me." I stared at him, not quite sure what to say.

I was so shocked by what he was saying that he caught me off guard, grabbed my wrist, and spun me, slamming me face-first into the wall.

"Fuck!" I exclaimed in pain. "Get off me now, Colton." He chuckled in response. I struggled to get out of his grip, and he pushed my arm up to my back.

"And how I get the rank I deserve, well, that's where you come in, baby girl, you and your Order," he purred in my ear. I growled in return.

"Because, my beautiful goddess-given mate, you will never leave this place. I won't let you go this time." I threw my head back, aiming for his nose, when he grabbed my hair and yanked it further back. I cried out in shock rather than pain.

"You can go straight to hell, Colton," I hissed. "I'd rather risk Elias than help you get your sick twisted hands on the pack."

"Well, we will see about that, Strawberries." He let go of my hair, and I almost whacked my head on the wall with the sudden change in force. "You have until dinner tonight to decide. If you agree to work with me, turn that pretty ring around on your finger so the stone is showing."

"You are delusional if you think I will agree to that," I spat and pushed off the wall with every ounce of strength. I don't know if I caught Colton off guard or if he let me move, but either way, I got free of his hold and turned on him, ready to punch him. He stepped back out of reach, grinning at me.

"If you don't agree, I will not only tell your dear Alpha mate who you are and why you are here, but I will also tell him how Tommy knew as well." I felt a knot of dread in my stomach. "You might be able to sweet-talk your way out of it, but I doubt Tommy would be able to do the same. Are you really willing to risk his life, even if you are willing to risk yours?" He smirked again, and I growled.

Tapping his wrist like there was a watch there, he turned away.

"Tonight's dinner, Strawberries, or I'm spilling all the secrets." I glared at his back as he went.

He was right; I was good at getting myself out of this type of thing, but if Elias thought that Tommy knowingly brought me here to take him out, he wouldn't hesitate to kill Tommy, not according to his file. My only hope was to get ahead of this, tell Elias myself first. Come clean and hope that he wasn't who the Council thought he was.

I headed down the stairs to the first floor, where all the offices were, and headed to Elias' office. I saw the door was open, and I walked slowly up to the door when I heard Elias' voice.

"Do we have confirmation that the schedule is in place?" he asked.

"Yeah, I got confirmation from Taylor yesterday." I recognised Marcus as the other voice.

"And is the shipment the standard, or are there any special orders?" Elias asked.

"No, standard only, no report of living orders this time," I heard shuffling papers.

"Okay, tell Taylor to keep our men on it. I need this to reach its destination."

"Yes, Alpha," Marcus responded.

"Did the Luca family get relocated?"

"Yes, relocated with a cover." Marcus chuckled, "And I confirmed that Alex Bennet is healing after last night too."

"Good, he was a good show of strength, so people know we mean business," Elias said, "What about-" then he stopped, and I heard a chair move and footsteps.

I stepped back just as Elias walked out of the office and looked in my direction.

"Harper," he smiled at me, and his eyes twinkled like he wasn't just talking about beating people up and shipments, probably filled with drugs and weapons. "What are you doing here? Not that I'm not happy to see you." he stepped closer to me and then stopped and growled.

"Why do you smell like Stokes?" he asked, his voice low, and the twinkle stripped from his eyes in seconds. I rolled my eyes.

"Because he's a delusional dick," I said. "He was waiting for me at lunch with his mum and the Luna."

"Former Luna," he corrected, and I rolled my eyes again.

"Yeah, that," I waved my hand dismissively. "Did you know that Caroline Stokes thinks that we are married and all that?" He growled.

"Yes, I was aware of her ramblings," he said sadly, "I have offered to have her go somewhere where people will help her, but Stokes wasn't having any of it." He rubbed his eyes like he was tired and then looked up at me again.

"Anyway, what can I do for you?" he asked, taking my hand.

"I erm... just wanted to know how I am expected to dress at dinner." I said, "It's been so long since I have done one and all that," I rambled, and he raised his eyebrow at me.

"There's no dress code," he said and pulled me in close to him, the scent of mint and sea salt invading my scent like the most amazing smell in the world. "Whatever you wear will be beautiful." He kissed my forehead, and I felt the sensation down into my toes and fought the urge to shiver. I nodded my head and smiled.

"Well, ok then, I will see you at dinner." I turned to go, but Elias didn't let go of my hand,

"Harper," I turned back to him, "I'll pick you up from your room. I would like us to enter together." I smiled and nodded, and he finally let go of my hand.

I turned and rushed down the hallway. I needed to get out of there fast and back up to my room. I needed to call Nathaniel. If anyone were going to sort the mess I was in, it would be him.

CHAPTER 47

Harper

I rushed up to my room and grabbed my phone. I dialled Nathaniel's number by heart and prayed for him to answer. He finally picked up the third time I phoned.

"Harper, I am in a meeting," he growled down the phone. "What is so important?"

"I'm found," I said. "Someone knows everything." I paced my room as I spoke.

"What?" he exclaimed, "Ok give me details." I spent the next few minutes detailing the conversation and the threat from Colton. When I had finished, I waited. The other end of the line was silent, and I half wondered if we had got cut off mid-rant.

"Nathaniel?" I asked,

"I'm thinking," he said sharply and then lapsed into silence again.

Eventually, he spoke again.

"So you decided to go and tell Owens everything?" There was a harsh tone to his voice which was reserved for when he was angry.

"What else was I supposed to do?" I asked. "I have my psycho abusive ex-mate trying to blackmail me!" I exclaimed, "I panicked."

"I have to say, Harper, I am rather disappointed in you." Ouch! That stung. "I expected better from you, not to fold as soon as things got a little difficult." I opened and closed my mouth, unsure what to say and fighting the sting of tears in my eyes.

"This isn't a little difficult," I said. "This is the person who every nightmare I have is based on." I tried to defend myself. But it didn't matter. I was already upset that Nathaniel thought so little of me and that I could let him down so much.

"A proper Elite Warrior can compartmentalise that sort of thing. If required, you should be able to maintain a pleasant relationship with your worst enemy. Even an intimate relationship is sometimes required to get the job-at-hand done." His words continued to hit me hard. The idea of being intimate with Colton turned my stomach. Hell, even the idea of being pleasant left me with a nasty taste in my mouth.

"Never mind that, we have damage control now," Nathaniel said. "What happened when you told this to Owens?" I shook the self-pity out of my head to focus on trying to get this mess cleaned up.

"I didn't tell him," I said. "I got there and overheard a conversation that he was having with his Gamma about a shipment."

"So you haven't actually revealed who you are to him?" Nathaniel asked.

"No, but I-"

"No, this is good," he interrupted. "We can work with this. You need to accept the help from this Beta. You should be easily able to get what we need to take Owens down between the positions that you both have."

"What position do I have?" I asked, already knowing where he was going with this.

"Harper, you know the power of the mate bond. Owens will trust you quicker and tell you things that he might not tell others," Nathaniel said. I couldn't mistake the excitement in his voice.

"So you suggest I sleep with him and then use that to get information out of him?"

"Well, it's not like you haven't done something similar before," he said, like I was being unreasonable.

"True, but those people didn't share a mate bond with me." The more intimate I got with Elias, the stronger the mate bond would be.

"How much do you want this Councilman position Harper?" Nathaniel snapped. "More importantly, are you going to let something like that get in the way of the hundreds of she-wolves that are going missing because of the Circle and your mate?" he spat out that last line harshly enough that I felt like I had been slapped. I felt raw from the discipline and knew I had to fall in line.

"No, sir," I sighed. "I'll get the job done, I promise."

"Good," he said. "You know what to do, don't let the Council down now, Harper."

"Yes, sir," I replied, and we ended the call. I sat staring at my phone for about ten minutes feeling deflated and helpless. I didn't want to give Colton control of the pack, but I also couldn't let Elias or the Circle get away if I could make a difference.

I sighed and noticed that it was getting late in the afternoon, and since I was going to be walking into the dinner tonight with the Alpha, I thought I better get ready for it. I headed into the bathroom, turned on the shower, and started to get ready.

Two hours later, I was just putting the finishing touches on my makeup when there was a knock at my door. I glanced at the clock and saw it wasn't quite time for Elias, so I was curious when I went to the door. I opened the door, and Louise was standing on the other side. I smiled when I saw her and pulled her into the room.

"You're looking nice," she said, and I smiled. I was wearing a simple black dress that went to the knee. I wasn't sure how to dress and thought I couldn't go far wrong with this.

"Thanks, I hope it's okay. I'm pretty nervous about going to the dinner as the Alpha's guest." She smiled.

"It's not that, Harper. You aren't the Alpha's guest. You are the Alpha's mate," she said. "Which means people will be looking at you like you are the Luna," I glared at her.

"Way to add the pressure," I said, and she rolled her eyes at me.

"From what I have heard from Tommy, you can handle some pressure," I sighed and sat on the bed.

"Harps, what's wrong?" she asked. I looked at her with a strained smile.

"I don't know how much I can tell you," I said, and she gave me a quizzical look, and I sighed again. "Things are a little more complicated than they originally seemed." I stopped and looked at her as she patiently waited for me to carry on. I felt bad that I didn't know if I should or even could trust her enough to tell her what was going on.

"I didn't just come home to grieve for my father. In fact, I didn't come home to do that at all." I said. I took a deep breath.

"I work for the council," I said, and her mouth fell open. "I'm an Elite warrior, and I am here to investigate the Alpha for some serious stuff."

"Oh my goddess Harper, please be careful!" she exclaimed. "I know that Tommy says the Alpha is a good man and all, but he wasn't in the cells the last three months hearing him interrogating people from the pack." My eyes widened at that. "I mean it Harper, if he really is the bad guy you are investigating then please you need to be careful because that man has a nasty temper." I took a deep breath. I really didn't know what to do. Could I trust Colton to actually help me, and what did I do with his threat? It was clear that I couldn't go to Elias about this. I needed to get this evidence and trust that I could get myself out of this mess.

There was another knock at the door, and we both looked over at it. I glanced at Louise and went and opened the door. Elias was standing there with a smile on his face.

"Wow, you look amazing," he said, leaning in and kissing my cheek. "Are you ready to go down? People are arriving." I smiled and looked back at Louise, who had an obviously worried look on her face. I took a breath and smiled at Elias again. I guess I was in this for the dangerous game.

"I'm ready," I said, and he looped his arm for me to hook mine through.

"We'll see you down there, Louise?" Elias asked, and she nodded.

We headed out into the hallway, and as I closed the door, I fumbled with my left hand twisting the ring round, so the stone was showing. I knew full well that I was going to seriously regret this.

CHAPTER 48

Harper

The next morning I woke up to banging on my bedroom door. I stumbled half-asleep to the door, thinking about the dinner last night. I didn't know what to expect, but people seemed happy to see me walking in with Elias, and a fair few came up to me afterwards to offer condolences for my father and say they were happy to see me back. I recognised some of them, but not others. My mother and sister were sitting in the main dining area, along with my sister's kids, and when they saw me, they waved. I had been happy to see Louise walk in with Tommy on her arm, and they both sat at a table in front of the main table, along with Alice Chambers and Caroline Stokes and their families.

The only people sitting up at the top table were Elias and me, Marcus and Colton. Elias had arranged it, so I was sitting between him and Marcus, so my evening was filled with jokes and laughs as the pair recalled stories from their time together. I found out they had been friends for at least fifteen years, and Marcus had followed Elias from pack to pack. My heart hurt a little at that. Did that mean that the sweet cheeky Marcus was also a part of the Circle? I had pretty much resigned myself to the very likely scenario that Elias was an evil criminal mastermind guy, but I was really struggling to see Marcus in the same light. On the other side of Elias, Colton sat quiet and alone. I could see him as he kept glancing over at me. I purposely kept my hand hidden just in case there was some miracle that rode in on a white horse to save me.

It was towards the end of the evening, just as the plates were being cleared, when Colton turned in his chair and grinned at me.

"Alpha, do you mind if I have a word with you?" he asked, looking at me.

"Can it not wait, Stokes?" Elias replied, not even looking at him.

"It's pretty important. I think you would want to know this," Elias tutted and shook his head.

"Fine," he said, going to stand up. I felt panic set in and grabbed Elias' arm. He looked at me, shocked, and I smiled and leaned in, pressing my lips against his. I felt him smile on my lips as he eagerly responded, pulling me closer. I wrapped my hand around the back of his neck and glanced at Colton to make sure he had seen the ring on my hand. He met my eyes and nodded his head to show that he had seen it, and we had an understanding before I closed my eyes again and allowed myself to melt back into the kiss with Elias. Elias pulled away eventually and smiled at me before turning to Colton.

"Well, come on then," he said, and Colton shrugged.

"On second thoughts, it can wait till tomorrow," he said, leaving Elias to glare at him. The rest of the evening was less stressful and soon wound down with Elias walking me back to my room and leaving me at the door with a chaste kiss and a wish of sweet dreams.

Another knock at the door brought me back to the present. I opened the door to see Louise grinning on the other side.

"Happy birthday!" she called out, and I groaned. She pushed past me and held the door open when I tried to close it. I realised Tommy was following with a box in his arms.

"Happy birthday, kid," he said and winked at me.

"One, not a kid," I said, pointing at Tommy. "And two, it's not even 8am yet."

"But it's your birthday, and we have lots planned," Louise said as she took the box from Tommy and began to pull things out on the coffee table by the sofa.

"Like what," I asked, suddenly feeling worried. Louise pouted at me and then shook her head.

"Nope!" she exclaimed. "It's not only your birthday, but it is the first day in three months that I haven't woken up in a tiny cell. I deserve this as much as you do." I held my hands up in defeat, and she grinned for victory. Tommy soon excused himself when he saw Louise pull out the ingredients for a facial. He wished me a second happy birthday and disappeared.

I was never one to really enjoy my birthday, certainly not after what had happened ten years ago on this very day, and thankfully Louise kept things low-key. We did pampering in the morning, which included a special breakfast sent up to my room at Elias' request with a promise of an evening to remember later. Seeing that made me nervous, I had pretty much forgotten about the date that I had agreed to go on, but it was now brought back to my attention again. In the afternoon, I visited my mum and sister and was surprisingly delighted to get homemade gifts from the pups while my mum served us cake and tea. The closer to the evening we got, the more nervous I felt. And it wasn't long before I was back in my room with Louise, stressing about what I was going to wear.

"I have no idea what to wear," I groaned as I lay face down on my bed, "Why the fuck do I care what I will wear?" I asked, only frustrating myself further.

"Because you like him," Louise said, like it was the most obvious fact in the world. "He's your mate, and you can't just fight that and be okay." I sat up on the bed and glared at her.

"I don't need this getting any more complicated," I said and picked up a top Louise threw at me from my suitcase.

"Why is everything still in your suitcase?" she asked.

"Because I don't plan on staying, that's why," I replied, pulling the top over my head. "I'm only here to get what I need, and then I'm going back to the Council. Hopefully, as a Councilman."

It was about an hour later when Elias knocked on the door. I was dressed in skinny black jeans and a dark red silk low cut top. My brown hair was straightened and fell across my shoulders. I had gone for light make-up everywhere, but my lips were a deep red to match my top. I opened the door and smiled as Elias handed me a bunch of roses. He was in a pair of black jeans himself and a fitted grey t-shirt that looked so out of place on him compared to the suits he wore daily.

"Happy birthday," he said, and I smiled. Louise took the roses from me, and I accepted Elias' looped arm before heading down the hall and the stairs. When we got out of the pack house, Elias guided me to the side of the house to where a small black sports car was waiting for us. Once in the car, we set off out the gates and were soon speeding into the darkening night down country roads.

Something about the journey felt familiar, and I was getting a bad feeling in my stomach. Elias made small talk while he drove. He told me about his day and random pack business. He casually mentioned that Colton had been around all day, and Elias had kept him busy so that he didn't come up to bother me. I thanked him for the kind thought before lapsing back into silence.

After about 20 minutes, Elias pulled into the side of the road by the entrance of a woodland path. Everything felt familiar at this point, but I couldn't place my concern. Elias helped me out of the car and guided me down the path leading to the woods. I was a little way down the path when I saw lights up ahead and suddenly realised where we were.

I stopped dead and stared at Elias in fear before looking back down the path at the stone structure ahead of me. We were back at the gazebo Colton had brought me to all those years before.

CHAPTER 49

Elias

I walked into my office and sat down at my desk, keeping myself very still. The fury raging inside me was at the point of almost tipping over into a destructive warpath. Marcus followed me in, watching me carefully.

"Hey, boss," he said. I could tell he was keeping his tone even so as not to trigger me. If anyone knew my temper, anger and the monster that lived inside me, and I didn't mean my wolf Jax, it was Marcus. He was the one who knew the other monster lurking inside and was the one who had seen him in action. I did my best to keep that side of me, the bloodlust side, firmly under wraps. Only since meeting Harper, since finding my beautiful mate, that monster felt both sated whenever we were around her and instantly hell on earth furious the second anything dares to hurt her.

"How much did you hear?" I asked, looking up at Marcus. We had just been to the cells. I had found Harper snooping around the entrance in what suspiciously looked like she was casing the place. She was trying to get access to get her friend, who we had locked up. Louise Chambers was an odd one. I saw as her husband made a run for the woods, and she made no move to follow him. And then, when I killed the former Gamma of the pack, I expected to turn around and see her screaming, crying, anything that would express the grief that she should have at seeing her own father killed right in front of her. But no, she was staring at her father with such anger and rage that I knew there was more to that story.

This was why I didn't treat her like the other detainees, despite her husband being one of the people listed on my list of being responsible for this whole thing. I needed to get Damien Chambers in a cell to get everything I needed to ensure this pack benefited from our operations. I believed Mrs Chambers when she said she didn't know where her husband was, but I couldn't be certain. So she stayed in the cells until I knew for sure.

I really thought allowing Harper in to see her friend scored me some brownie points and that maybe Chambers might let something slip that would help me find her husband. So I listened. I stayed right there in the cell as the women talked. What I heard set my blood on fire. The torment and torture that the poor woman had endured at the hands of the people that were meant to be protecting the pack, one of them being her own father, sickened me. I held it together but almost lost it when I realised that because of who she was originally mated to, this could have very likely been the fate of my own mate. The monster inside me howled for blood, and Jax joined in. In fact, for the first time in my life, the three dominant parts of me were in complete agreement.

The least I could do was agree to let Chambers out and set her up still on the top floor, away from the people who hurt her the most. Finding out that she and Tommy were mates was also a shock and led me to wonder what else Tommy was hiding. So after allowing him to spend some time with his mate, I planned on speaking to him about what else he was hiding from me.

"I heard it all, boss," Marcus said, pulling me back to the room and my fury, "But we still have to be careful. We need Stokes to ensure the transition is a smooth one." I growled even though I knew Marcus was right.

"I never liked that slimy mutt," I growled. "And I see how he looks at my mate, and after what he did to her..." I felt the monster rise, and I saw the red haze setting in before I could grasp control. He had already taken control of my body, and I was helpless to rein him in. I blinked and forced myself to push forward to take control again. Once I breathed through the rage and came back to myself again, I looked up at Marcus in relief. Which quickly turned to shock and then shame.

The room was trashed. My computer was laid in pieces across the room, and the desk was empty, the original contents now scattered across the floor. Two of the bookshelves were also laid on their sides, with their contents littering the floor. Marcus was standing with his hands outstretched, with a guarded look on his face. I closed my eyes and dropped my head into my hands.

"How long?" I asked, and I heard Marcus blow out a relieved sigh.

"About 20 minutes. Not bad this time," he said with a nervous laugh. I looked back up at him, and he smiled and shrugged his shoulders.

"Did he say anything?" When the monster came out, he sometimes had a message to give before I was able to reseal him back up in his box, or whatever it was that kept him simmering with rage inside me.

"He demanded that I command Stokes to come here now and said that he will burn in the fires of hell for all eternity, you know the usual flowery crap you expect." I chuckled at his definition of flowery and shook my head.

"You didn't call him, did you?" The last thing I wanted was for Stokes to see this mess. Thankfully Marcus shook his head and grinned.

"But I did call for a couple of Omegas to come and clean up," he said, and I nodded my head.

"I want to talk to Tommy about Harper and her experience with Stokes," I said, and Marcus raised an eyebrow.

"Is that a wise move?" he asked, and I grinned.

"I promise he will be on his best behaviour."

The Omegas arrived looking shocked at the mess, but I allowed Marcus to direct them while I decided to take a short walk around the grounds. I was half tempted to take a trip up to the third floor to see how Harper was doing with her lunch but instead left her to it. It wasn't long before Marcus was calling me back to the office. And the room was spotless when

I got there. Not at all like someone had lost their shit an hour before. I sat at my desk as Marcus passed me some documents, and I started to look over the manifest in front of me. It was a Circle report of the latest merch runs.

"Do we have confirmation that the schedule is in place?" I asked him, looking through all the different descriptions.

"Yeah, I got confirmation from Taylor yesterday," he said, and I looked up at him.

"And is the shipment the standard, or are there any special orders?"

"No, standard only, no report of living orders this time." I nodded in relief. The last thing I needed was to deal with a truckload of panicked she-wolves.

"Okay, tell Taylor to keep our men on it. I need this to reach its destination."

"Yes, Alpha," Marcus responded.

"Did the Luca family get relocated?"

"Yes, relocated with a cover." Marcus chuckled, "And I confirmed that Alex Bennet is healing after last night too."

"Good, he was a good show of strength, so people know we mean business. What about-"

That was when I smelt the overwhelming scent of strawberries and knew that my mate was lingering nearby. I jumped up from my desk to find her. She was standing in the hallways, looking uncertain. I got a sense of unease from her like her mind was conflicted. I hated we hadn't mated because I couldn't mind link with her yet but knew better than to try to force my mark on her. In fact, the growling that happened inside my head from both the monster and Jax told me they would risk killing themselves to rip me apart for doing such a thing.

"Harper?" I gave my best disarming smile, although it did little to settle her unease. "What are you doing here? Not that I'm not happy to see you." I moved closer, hoping my own scent would help calm her down, but caught the strongest scent of that mutt Stokes, and it was all over her. A growl slipped from my lips without warning.

"Why do you smell like Stokes?" I growled and then chastised myself for being so possessive. Thankfully, it didn't seem to phase her as she rolled her eyes.

"Because he's a delusional dick. He was waiting for me at lunch with his mum and the Luna."

"Former Luna," I pointed out. She didn't hold that title, and I wanted Harper to realise that she was destined to be my Luna. Not of this pack, that was only temporary, but of the entire empire that I was building.

"Yeah, that. Did you know that Caroline Stokes thinks we are married and all that?" She asked, and another growl slipped from my lips.

"Yes, I was aware of her ramblings." It was so sad to see the woman lose her mind but worse to see that useless son of hers encouraging it. "I have offered to have her go somewhere where people will help her, but Stokes wasn't having any of it." I was struggling with keeping my cool just thinking about that dick, and I rubbed my eyes to hide the flash of gold that was Jax threatening to break out.

"Anyway, what can I do for you?" I took her hand to help keep myself calm.

"I erm... just wanted to know how I am expected to dress at dinner. It's been so long since I have done one and all that." She was so sweet when she rambled, and it took all my effort not to chuckle.

"There's no dress code," I said and pulled her in close to inhale her beautiful fruity scent. "Whatever you wear will be beautiful," and I laid my lips on her forehead and could feel the slightest tremor in her when I did it.

"Well, ok then, I will see you at dinner." she turned to go, but I didn't want this to end. I had the feeling she was pulling away from me.

"Harper." She looked at me, the nervous look returning to her face. "I'll pick you up from your room. I would like us to enter together." She smiled, and I finally ran out of excuses to keep her here with me, so regrettably, I let her go. I watched as she walked down the hallway until she turned the corner and disappeared from sight. I took a deep breath, hoping to catch the remnants of her beautiful scent.

"Okay, lover boy, back to work," Marcus called from the office, and I muttered under my breath how much of a dick he was. He laughed out loud to indicate he had still heard me.

"I have Tommy on his way down in a few minutes," he said, and I grimaced. Good, I was ready to hear the ugly truth about the time that Colton had my mate under his possession.

CHAPTER 50

Elias

"Elias, calm down!" Marcus shouted over the roar of rage in my head. "Control it, for fuck's sake."

"I am going to find him and rip the bastard limb from limb!" I snarled. "Now get out of my fucking way before I make you get out of my way." Marcus widened his stance in front of the door stopping me from going on a rampage to find the abusive little mutt.

"Elias, don't let him take over," Marcus growled.

"Oh, this isn't him. This is all me. I am the one to do this, not him," I growled back.

I felt a hand on my shoulder and whipped around, smashing my fist into the person's body and realising a second too late that I had just knocked Tommy flying. He jumped up, his eyes shining gold and then bright white. That was enough to break me from my rage for a second and enough for me to breathe through and control it.

"What the fuck was that?" I exclaimed as his eyes bled back to their normal colour.

"My wolf," he said a little too dismissively. It was a sure sign that he was hiding something. I narrowed my eyes at him, and he just shrugged again and picked up one of the fallen chairs and sat in it like his Alpha hadn't gone completely berserk on him. I shook my head and turned to Marcus.

"You need to ensure that piece of shit stays away from me, and especially stays away from Harper." I thought for a second and then looked at him. "In fact, your job from now until further notice is guarding Harper. You understand me?" I asked, and he nodded, a grin on his face.

"Yes boss, I can break him enough that he is still fulfilling his uses if he steps out of line," he said, and I nodded, satisfied.

I knew Marcus would protect my mate with his life. He was a Gamma from a long line of Gammas, and since he swore loyalty, his primary duty would be to protect my Luna from everyone, including myself. Not that it would ever be the case. Marcus had been itching to get on Luna duty since he found out that Harper was my mate.

"There's just one problem with keeping him away from you," Tommy said casually. "Well, probably not one, but one in particular." I watched him waiting for his answer.

"Well?" I snapped, and he glanced up at me, amused.

"The dinner tonight," he said simply, and both Marcus and I groaned at the same time. He was right. Stokes would be at the dinner and sitting at the top table at my side. I growled when I realised that Harper would be sitting on my other side. I fully planned on making sure we were seen as a unit. Not just for the people but also for Harper herself. The quicker she started to see the power of the mate bond, the quicker she would accept me as her mate.

I shook my head. I would have to block him to a minimum and get through it, just get through these next few weeks, and then we would be done here, anyway.

"Fine," I sighed. "Marcus, you are on Harper duty. And Tommy, I need you to watch Colton."

"I'm banned from the dinners," Tommy said.

"Well, you're not now. In fact, your mate was one of the ranked families, so you can sit with her at their table." Tommy nodded with a smile on his face. I nodded back, satisfied.

I thought back to what Tommy had told me about that one incident with the picnic, coupled with what I knew about the ring that Colton had sealed on Harper's finger. I knew ring was something that kept her attached to not just the little shit himself but to the trauma he caused her ten years ago. If I could get her to start healing, then I could get her to release the hold on the trauma and everything that went along with it. That needed to start with breaking down her walls. I stopped and thought, suddenly I had a good idea for our date tomorrow night. It would be risky, but it could be major if I played it right. I glanced over at Tommy.

"Ok you need to tell me everything, in detail about that night," I said and then looked at Marcus "Get Bennet up here too." He nodded, and his eyes glazed over as he contacted Alex Bennet.

A few hours later, the four of us had a plan of action to keep Stokes under close eye and also keep Harper safe. I was satisfied enough to leave and go and collect my mate for the pack dinner. I knocked on the door, and when she opened it, I was struck dumb for a second by how beautiful she looked. She was wearing a black dress that hugged her stunning figure, and her hair flowed straight down her back.

"Wow, you look amazing." I kissed her cheek and revelled in her amazing fruity scent. "Are you ready to go down? People are arriving." She smiled at me and then looked back into the room when I noticed Louise was there. They both looked nervous for some reason. I was about to question it when she looked at me and gave me that beautiful smile again, and my concern melted. I felt so at ease around her. It was literally the only time that everything was quiet inside me.

"I'm ready," she said, and I offered my arm, which she took, and tingles ran through my body, even through my clothes. I glanced back at Louise, who was still looking nervous. I guess I couldn't blame her. I had locked her up for three months. I would need to find a way to show her that I wasn't going to hurt her friend.

"We'll see you down there, Louise?" I asked, and she nodded quickly. I smiled at that and headed down to the main hall with my beautiful mate on my arm.

Walking into the hall on previous dinners was always tense. I would see the pack members almost take a collective gasp like I was going to order their deaths right there and then. But tonight was different. The pack recognised Harper, and I wondered if seeing her at ease on my arm helped them see me in a different light. People approached Harper and me, mostly talking to her but still being friendly with me. I was happy to see Marcus flag us as soon as we walked into the hall, watching everyone with suspicion.

We finally made it to our seats, and I purposely put myself between Stokes and Harper. She looked relieved when she saw that. I could still tell she was nervous, so Marcus and I told her stupid stories from our early mis-endeavours and did our best to make her laugh and, more importantly, block Stokes out away from her. I still noticed the glances she sent his way, and I could feel the nerves rolling off of her. Stokes had tried to speak to me at one point, claiming he had some important information or something. I almost gave in, but Harper had pulled me in for an amazing kiss. It had started slowly, but then I felt her ease down and allowed herself to be taken by the kiss. I had to break it and allow us both to come up for air, although I didn't want to. Whatever had happened to her during that kiss, though, Harper seemed more relaxed and enjoyed the rest of the evening. I dunno. Even Stokes was being less sulky. But the rest of the evening passed quickly, and I was sad to be walking her back to her room.

When we reached her door, I wanted to carry her in and take her as my own. I wanted to fall to my knees and beg her to allow me to worship her. Or, at the very least, I wanted her to see how I looked at her and how much I knew I was already falling in love with her. Instead, I didn't push it. I didn't try to impress her. I kissed her cheek lightly and wished her sweet dreams before allowing her to close the door. I leaned against the door, really hoping that she would have sweet dreams and that I would play a starring role in them.

I headed back to my room, and mind linked to Marcus. I was checking that everything was in place for tomorrow. I wanted it to be absolutely perfect and for Harper to be completely relaxed. Marcus laughed and told me to stop bothering and go to sleep. I didn't know how to go to sleep, though, because a lot was riding on tomorrow. If I messed this up, then I knew that I would have no chance with Harper trusting me again. I stripped to my boxers, carefully laying my clothes onto the ottoman at the end of my bed before sliding into my covers. I laid there awake for some time before finally falling asleep.

In my dream, I was running through the woods, chasing something. But I wasn't alone. To my left, Jax ran and to my right was a shadow. We all matched each other in every way. If I verved, then they verved, and if I sped up, so did they. We were mirroring each other, and I enjoyed the feeling of freedom you get when you run at speed. Slowly the forest gave way to fires, and everything around me was on fire. The hotter it got, the more difficult it was to breathe. The lack of oxygen caused me to slow down, and Jax along with me. The slower Jax and I got, the quicker the shadow got. It was like it thrived on the heat and the destruction.

Then up ahead, I saw a bright white light that looked to be at the peak of a hill. The shadow ran towards it. I pushed against my aching muscles towards the light. As I got closer, I saw a figure in the light. The figure had long dark hair and a long, flowing white dress. The dress had small stones on it that seemed to reflect light from somewhere and was what was causing the ethereal glow that I could see. As I got to the top of the hill, I saw the shadow standing tall next to the figure, and both were looking down into a massive crater. I stood at the edge and looked down into the crater to see what looked like a big battle going on. I could make out bodies, but they were blurred like they weren't really there. I looked up and noticed three other sources of lights around the edge of the crater, each with its own person looking down onto the battlefield. I glanced back at the figure beside me when I realised the person was Harper. She smiled at me and went to speak when suddenly I felt something hit me in my gut, and I was knocked back. As I landed on my ass, everything went black, and I shot up in bed.

I looked around the room, now lit up with the morning light, until I saw Marcus grinning at me. I then noticed one of my shoes on the bed and growled. I looked back up at him.

"Did you just throw a shoe at me?" I asked, and he grinned again.

"Yeah, because I'm gonna wake you up the regular way," he said and rolled his eyes. I laughed and threw the shoe at him.

"I'm not that bad," I muttered to myself.

"Sure, you're a cupcake of sweetness," he replied sarcastically as I headed towards my bathroom to get ready.

Once I had showered and got ready for the day, I walked back into my room to see Marcus still there. He was flicking through one of my random magazines.

"You don't have any place to be?" I asked, and he shrugged his shoulders.

"I sorted a breakfast for your girl and set Stokes a list a mile long," he said. "He won't have time to pester her today." I nodded my thanks.

"And everything is ready for tonight?" I asked. "This is really important. It can't be messed up." Marcus grinned and nodded his head.

"Don't worry, boss, everything is set up. I got people out at the location today, and it will be ready for you."

Satisfied knowing that there wasn't anything I could do but wait, I decided to get some work done. We were almost complete with the plans for this pack, and I wanted to map out the next pack we were going to take. We had a few to choose from and scouts at all, but I was conscious of certain organised elements watching us and wanted to be as strategic as possible for maximum impact, if not anything else.

I spent the day pouring over maps and plans with Marcus while liaising with various scouts. I had decided to leave Harper alone for the day. I knew that she was with Louise, and Tommy had told me they were doing some girly self-care thing, so I was happy that Harper was at least content in her day. It wasn't long before I was back in my room, getting ready for the evening. The plans I had required a more casual approach, so I put aside my usual suits and wore jeans and a t-shirt. I headed over to her room with the roses I had bought in hand. I knew roses were cheesy, but I didn't mind a little cheese. I had a weight in my stomach from the nerves. This was crucial, and if it worked, it would let Harper know that she could count on someone other than herself.

I knocked on her door and was floored when she opened it. Again, her hair was straight and down her back, and she wore the amazing jeans that hugged close enough to her body that I felt jealous of the amazing material. The top she wore was a deep red shade that complimented her skin perfectly and was enhanced by the deep red that adorned her lips. I wanted to cancel the whole thing right there and then and just take her back to my room. I was speechless and held out the roses to her like an idiot without even saying anything. I shook myself to get my head back in the game.

"Happy Birthday," I finally said, and she smiled, and I held out my arm once more for her. She took it after handing the roses to Louise, who was standing behind her eyeing me suspiciously.

Harper and I headed out of the pack house into the courtyard, where I had one of my cars waiting for us. I helped her into the car, holding the door open for her, then ran around the other side and jumped in. We set off down the drive, and I sent a quick, silent prayer to the moon goddess that this would actually work.

CHAPTER 51

Elias

My nerves got stronger as we drove closer to the location. There was every chance that this would go wrong. I tried to draw Harper out by making small talk. I mentioned I had made sure Stokes wasn't ruining her birthday by bugging her, and she smiled and thanked me. She kept looking out the window, and I readied myself in case she realised where we were heading and reacted badly.

I pulled to the side of the road where I was directed and saw the pathway we were to take. I glanced over at Harper, who was looking out the window. She seemed uneasy in herself, but when I helped her out of the car, she smiled at me. We began down the path, and just as I saw the lights decorating the gazebo come into view, I felt Harper stiffen and then gasp behind me. I turned quickly, and she was staring at me with terror in her eyes. I felt like such a bastard at that moment, and there was a din in my head as both the monster and Jax chastised me for what I was doing.

I reached out to Harper, and she backed away, shaking her head.

"No!" she whispered, and she turned around to go back down the path. I reached out again and grabbed her arm, trying to stop her so I could explain. She whirled around on me, and I felt her fist slamming into my face before I even saw it coming. And she packed one hell of a punch. She immediately gasped and covered her mouth with her hands.

"Oh my goddess, Elias," she exclaimed. "I am so sorry, but you don't understand this place-" I grabbed her arms as I felt her panic setting in.

"Harper, I know," I said, stopping her mid-sentence, and she looked at me, shocked. Then the fear in her eyes turned to anger.

"You know?" she asked slowly. "What do you know?"

"Alex and Tommy told me everything," I said. "That's why I brought you here."

"Why?" she asked. "Why would you make me relive this? They were right. You are not a good person at all," she hissed at me, and I was taken aback by the viciousness in her words. I wanted to ask who was saying this, but I knew it had to wait.

"You're right. I am a bad man," I said. "But right now, I am trying to help you." I gripped her arms firmly and made eye contact. "Please, Harper, I am begging you to trust me just this once." She glanced behind me and then back to me.

"You don't have Colton in there waiting?" she asked, and I shook my head.

"Absolutely not," I growled. "Not unless the bastard is buried under the thing." Harper's eyes widened. "When I heard what he and that spineless piece of shit had almost done, I wanted to hunt them both down and eradicate them from the surface of the earth."

"So why bring me here?" she asked. I pushed a stray hair from her face.

"Please trust me?" I asked again. She looked into my eyes for what could have been forever before finally nodding her head. I breathed out a relieved sigh.

I took her hand and slowly guided her towards the small building. She gripped my hand like it was her only lifeline as we got closer. I walked her to the entrance of the gazebo, and I felt her resistance again. I looked around at her, and she took a deep breath. Her body was shaking slightly, and I saw the woman I had met just a few days ago crumble in her eyes.

The gazebo was set out almost exactly like it was that night almost ten years ago. I had got help from Alex, who, after I heard he was there that night, was lucky that he was still alive. I wanted to create as much as possible the same scene. In humans, this could be dangerous, but for fated mates, we were able to pull from the bond, share our hearts and minds, and heal the damage that had been caused. That is why when we lose our mate, we lose a part of ourselves that is no longer able to heal. And it is why, even when we reject the bond, we still crave to connect and rebond with that one person. I may hate Colton Stokes, but I understood why he had the desperate need to go after my mate.

"Harper," I said, drawing her attention as she looked around the gazebo like a wide animal looking for its way out. "I want you to understand that I am doing this to help you. You are avoiding this town, and our bond, because of the trauma you have received in this town and this place." She looked up at me, and her eyes were laced with unshed tears.

I walked into the gazebo and picked up the only thing that wasn't there that night.

"But the thing is, that pain you feel is inside you, not here. And I know that you are a strong, amazing woman, so maybe it's time you showed you the same thing." I opened her hand and placed the sledgehammer into it. She looked down at the sledgehammer in her hand and then back at me.

"I don't understand," she said, her voice trembling a little. "How is this meant to help?"

"Because by smashing this place to pieces, you will see that it can't hurt you and that the memory of it can't hurt you either," I said, and then I grinned a little. "And if that doesn't work, then at least you'll get a workout." I shrugged, and she laughed. It was only a small laugh, but it was enough.

Harper lifted the sledgehammer, swinging it above her head before bringing it down right smack in the middle of the gazebo, smashing the picnic plates and three champagne glasses. She seemed uneasy until that first hit, and something snapped inside her. I saw the light turn back on inside her eyes as she swung the hammer again against one wall. Slowly but surely, each hit became rawer than the last. It was like every one of the hits broke an additional link in the chain that had been holding her to this trauma. I stood back and watched as she laid waste to the little building that led to her leaving this place. She administered hit after hit and reduced the building to a crumbling mess for two solid hours and then some. By the time the building was a pile of broken bricks on the floor, Harper was screaming into each hit, and her face was streaming with tears. She was covered head to toe in dirt and ran herself to exhaustion. I moved in after the last hit and placed my hand on her arm. She flung me off and went for another hit.

I wrapped my arms around her waist and trapped her arms at her side. She struggled to get away from me for a bit until I whispered into her ear.

"You can stop now!" I whispered, and she stopped fighting and leaned into my body, the tears streaming still. "You see, I have you. I will always have you." I felt her knees give way, and she collapsed to the ground. I followed her down and pulled her into my lap, and she clung to me, sobbing. We stayed like that for another hour until her sobbing quieted, and she finally settled apart from the occasional sniffle here and there. Her fingers curled around my T-shirt, and I rocked her gently, whispering in her ear that everything was going to be ok. I could feel the bond strengthening and feel its tendrils moulding us together.

I picked up a sound in the trees and saw Marcus head down the path. He walked slowly up to us and smiled down at Harper.

"Next time I want a demolition man, then I'll just hire you, darling," he said, and I looked down to see her rewarding his foolishness with a small smile. Marcus leaned down to take Harper from my arms, and I actually growled at him.

"Easy there, boss. You can have her back once you have got yourself up off the floor," he said, and I jumped off the floor and dusted the dirt from my clothes. I reached out for my mate, and Marcus passed her back to me. She slipped her arms around my neck and nuzzled into me, and I could feel as her breath tickled my neck. We walked away from the demolished building while Marcus muttered something about sending some omega's out to clean the place up.

By the time we had reached the car, Harper had already fallen asleep. I climbed into the back of the SUV that Marcus had driven up, and Marcus closed the door behind me. I was fine with leaving my car there and would have someone come to pick it up in the morning. Marcus drove us up to the pack house, and I walked in, still holding my sleeping mate in my arms. I glanced briefly to the side and saw Tommy and Alex standing talking to Jamie Bennet, Alex and Louise's little brother. Tommy nodded to me as I walked past, and I nodded an acknowledgement back.

"What the hell?" Stokes shouted from the other direction, and I moved on, trying to ignore him and getting Harper away from him as soon as possible. Marcus intercepted and told him to stand down. I saw a vague movement as if he was going to continue, but both Alex and Tommy moved around me and blocked him.

I made my way up the stairs to my room, where Louise had run a bath ready for us. She smiled at me as I carried Harper into the bathroom. It was the first genuine smile I had ever received from her. Harper had woken up on the way up the stairs, and I placed her gently on her feet and headed out of the room while Louise helped her undress and cleaned up. I went into Marcus' room and jumped into his shower, quickly washing myself. My mind was full of everything and also full of nothing. I knew things would be different tomorrow, and the same would happen with Harper. The numbness would wear off, but hopefully, it would have a healed heart or part healed in its place.

I headed back into my room to see Louise helping Harper into my bed. She smiled at me again and nodded before she left the room, leaving Harper and me alone. I smiled at her and stroked her hair as her eyes closed again. I leaned down and kissed her forehead before I moved towards the sofa. I had already decided that I wouldn't be leaving the room tonight.

"Elias?" Harper's voice floated over, a little more than a whisper. I turned and looked at her. "Please stay with me." I nodded my head and smiled. I quickly turned off the lights, slipped into the covers behind her, and gently pulled, and she shuffled back into me. I wrapped my arms around her, and she murmured something I didn't quite understand before her breathing was steady as she had fallen fast asleep again. I thought I would be wide awake, but it wasn't long before I joined her in a deep slumber.

CHAPTER 52

Harper

I woke up enveloped in the warmth of arms wrapped around me. Elias' scent surrounded me, and I felt a peace inside me that I hadn't felt in a really long time. If ever at all. I laid there, not wanting to break the spell. And I knew that there was some small part in me that wanted to hold on to this feeling like my life depended on it. And yet there was a bigger part that was scared, scared of allowing me to be taken in, to trust someone else fully with that broken part of me. To see beyond the shield and see how fucked up I really was. Because what if they saw that and they rejected me? What if they decided that there were too many pieces to fix and what if, after showing them the truth about what I was, they left me there, exposed to my own feelings? And no way to know how to build my wall again.

Or worse, what if they stayed? What if they were really in for the long haul? They come armed with emotional superglue and diligently work to piece every part of me back together. What would that look like? I had been fucked up for so long that I didn't even know what healed and healthy Harper actually looked like. Could I really be her? Would I even still be me? Am I the sum of all my broken parts? And do I fear losing who I am because I don't know what I will become? That part of me wanted to get out of the bed now, grab my things and get the hell out of here. But another part, maybe the little part, she was ready to be healed. She was ready to look past the bullshit with Colton. And even before that, I always felt like I didn't quite fit anywhere. The parents hid more than they revealed. There was always something not quite right about my life. I was just able to ignore it.

Elias moved behind me, and his arms tightened around my waist. He snuggled in closer, and I felt his nose rub against my neck while he muttered something incoherent. I found myself melting into his touch more and closed my eyes against the feel of his skin on mine. I had never woken up in bed with someone other than Aaron before; I had never allowed myself to get close enough to them. By instinct, I reached for the ring on my finger and pulled on it, bracing myself for the now-familiar pain to shoot through my body. The pain came but seemed somewhat lesser. It felt like it was duller, not the sharp jolt I was used to, but more like a dull ache. Elias moved behind me and pulled me into him again.

"I can feel what you are doing, you know," he whispered into my ear, sending shivers down my spine. I froze, not knowing if he meant the actual act, or if he felt me pulling away. I shuffled and tried to untangle myself from his arms, but he held on tighter.
"No, not yet," he murmured. "You smell so nice. I bet you taste nice, too." I felt his lips against my neck. It lit a fire in me, and I couldn't help the sigh that slipped from my lips as I tilted my head to give him more access. His hands reached under the t-shirt I was wearing, and he caressed my stomach before moving lower to play with the edge of my panties. I twisted my body to reach my mouth to his. His lips met mine in a gentle touch before pressing them more firmly against mine. He pulled me, so I was fully on my back and climbed between my legs without breaking contact with the increasingly passionate kiss. I reached up to pull him down, and his hard member grinded against me. We both moaned at the touch as the fire that had lit now felt like a roaring inferno. Everything inside me was screaming to let him in, let him claim me, and then claim him in return. I reached down towards the boxers that he was wearing and-

He broke away from me with a growl.

"Fuck's sake Marcus, not now," he growled, and then there was a knock at the door before it flew open.

"I hope no one is naked in here," Marcus called as he walked in with his hands over his eyes. I couldn't help but giggle as he bumped straight into a chair and went flying over it.

"Ouch!" he exclaimed from his new place on the floor as he rubbed his arm.

"Serves you right," Elias called over before kissing me on the nose and pulling himself out of bed. "Shouldn't burst in when not invited."

"Well, I didn't think you would want to miss the meeting this morning, boss." Marcus picked himself up from the floor and dusted himself off. Elias leaned over to the table and picked up his watch before hissing.

"Fuck!" he exclaimed and turned to me. "Sorry, baby. I need to be at this meeting." He then headed into the bathroom, and I heard the shower turn on. I looked up to see Marcus grinning at me and scowled at him.

"You make him happy, you know that," he said, and I shrugged.

"I'm sure it's just the bond. It messes with your head," I said and sighed before getting out of bed.

"You don't know because you don't know him all too well," Marcus said. "But I have known him for over fifteen years. That man has never been happier than he is when he is looking at you." I stopped in my tracks towards the door and turned and looked at Marcus.

"And I might not have known you for fifteen years, lady, but I can see you are happy too," he said, and I squirmed under his gaze.

I didn't want to admit it, but he was right. Elias took me to a place where I felt safe and protected and, yes, happy. I didn't know what to do with that. Especially seeing as the only reason I was here was because the man I was too quickly falling in love with was suspected to be a player in a major underground criminal ring. I mean, what did I do with that? Sorry Nathaniel, but I can't get you the evidence you need against the man I love, and now I'm going to go play happy mates with him as he builds his criminal empire. Or sorry, Elias, I might love you, but you are under arrest in the name of the Council for crimes too awful to talk about. Either way, I was hitting a losing situation.

"It's complicated," I said, and Marcus rolled his eyes. Hell, even I knew that sounded lame.

"What do you mean, Stokes?" he asked. "Say the word, and the scroate is in an unmarked grave, never to be seen again, but rumours have heard of him living it up in Las Vegas or somewhere else, so people don't go looking." I quirked my eyebrow at him in amusement.

"Not thought about this at all, have we?" I said with a chuckle, and he grinned.

"Every goddess day," he said. "I dislike that guy immensely, the slimy little weasel." I smiled at the look of disgust on his face. "I'll be happy when we don't need him anymore." That piqued my interest.

"Whatever could you need him for?" I tried to maintain a casual tone. "Why him when the others were so quickly taken care of?" Marcus narrowed his eyes at me, the humour dropping from his face.

"You don't need to worry about that," he said, and I was almost shocked at the turnabout tone of the menacing command that came out. I smiled nervously and looked away submissively, which I hated.

"Oh, I'm sorry," I said quickly. I wanted him to think that not only I had noticed his sudden change of tone, but that it had scared me because I was the weak, innocent werewolf, and he outranked me while mentally rolling my eyes.

"Hey," he said, touching my arm. I looked back, and the menacing look had gone, replaced with a concerned look. "Don't worry about any of this stuff. The Boss knows what he's doing, I promise." I smiled shyly at him.

Just then, the bathroom door opened, and a billow of steam came out, followed by Elias with a towel wrapped around his waist and his hair wet from the shower. He searched the room until his eyes rested on me, and he smiled. He then glowered at Marcus, whose arm was still on mine.

"What's going on?" he asked carefully, and Marcus backed away instantly.

"Nothing, boss," he said, and Elias walked over to me and smiled. He took my hand and pulled me into him, wrapping his arm around my waist. There were beads of water on his chest, and he smelt fresh of his sea salt and mint. It was almost intoxicating, and I had to stop myself from leaning in and burrowing my nose into his neck. He chuckled, lifted my head up with his finger under my chin, and gently leaned in to kiss me.

"I have to work, but how about we retry the date tonight and just watch a movie here with some snacks?" I smiled and nodded my head, my mouth suddenly dry.

"That would be nice," I said and then internally cringed at my own sweet tone. He smiled again and kissed my nose before releasing my waist. I stepped back, away from the warmth of his body, and reached for the door behind me. I turned the handle, and with one last smile to Elias, I slipped out of the room, closing the door.

I stood by the door for a minute and listened.

"What was that all about?" I heard Elias say, his tone harsh.

"Nothing, boss," Marcus responded. "She just asked a question that she shouldn't have. I don't think it was intended. I was just making sure she was okay."

"I told you to protect her, not fondle her," Elias spat. "I see your hands on her again where they are not needed, and I'll break your fingers."

"Yes, Boss," Marcus responded, his tone serious. I stepped away from the door quietly before making my way back to my room. There were a couple of things that I had learned from that little encounter. First, Marcus had a mean side to him I hadn't witnessed before. I would definitely need to watch out for that. And two, that despite his size and his mean scary side, Marcus was most definitely scared of Elias. I remembered Nathaniel in his review of Marcus before I had arrived. He had said he was one of the best warriors that came out of the training there. So how bad did you have to be to scare a scary, mean, elite-trained warrior? I knew I needed to be on my guard with Elias and keep my head in the game, not the love cloud.

I slipped into my room quietly and noticed a white folded piece of paper on the floor. I already knew who it would be from before I opened it. I sighed and unfolded the paper.

"I don't know what you were playing at with that display last night. But you better meet me in the woods by the great swing at noon, or I'm telling lover boy everything.
All my love,
Colton x."

I stared at the note in disbelief. All my love? I wanted to throw up just seeing that. I glanced at the clock on the side table and saw that it was already eleven am. I would need to be quick if I was to get a shower and still meet at the swing on time. It was about a twenty-minute walk to the old tree that the swing hung from. I knew the route well and had spent many a time with friends up there in past summers. I sighed and crumpled up the paper before throwing it into the bin and headed quickly for a shower before going to meet the slimy wolf himself.

CHAPTER 53

Colton

Ten years ago

"Hey!" I felt a sharp pain in my arm and glared around at Damien.

"What the fuck, man?" I exclaimed, rubbing my arm where he had just punched me.

"You just got us killed, you idiot!" he said, and pointed to the large screen in front of us. I blinked and saw the words GAME OVER splashed across the screen in red writing that was meant to look like blood splatter. "Seriously, man, those twerps annihilated us because you were too busy mentally wanking off in your head," Damien snapped. Geez, it was just a computer game, but he had been restless lately, so I let him off.

"Shit, sorry, man," I said. "I guess I was just thinking about-"

"Harper," Damien rolled his eyes, "Yeah, I know."

"It's just that she seemed different today," I said, thinking back to the morning I had spent with my angel.

"She seemed like she was coming around to things." Which I was happy about since tomorrow night we would complete the mate bond, and she would finally be mine, mind, body, and soul.

"Good!" Damien said. "Because I am dying to get my hands on that tight little ass of hers." My hand automatically tightened on my controller, and I felt like punching him. I didn't understand it. We knew the score. In this family, we shared, and it was good for Harper, too. The woman was amazing. It was the least I could do to show her all the love she deserved. I knew right now to Damien, that Harper was just a chance to get regular sex. But I knew that he would soon fall for her, just like I did! Just like Alex did. After lying to me about where Harper was yesterday meant that Alex would have to earn his place back in the inner circle.

It didn't matter, though. They might be able to fall for her and show her their love, but Harper would still be mine, and only mine. Plus, when things changed, and my dad's plan came to fruition, then I would be the Alpha, not Damien. Harper was a part of this. As my mate, bonded in the eyes of the moon goddess herself, The Order couldn't deny my rightful place with them. And my dad said that this was instrumental to our overthrowing Daniel Chambers and taking the pack as our own. Dad said that Daniel's father had used our own connections and my parents' own mate bond, and my grandfather's declining mental health to take the Alpha title from Samuel Kirby in the first place. Of course, his own father's disappearance had prompted Darren Kirby to turn his back on The Order in the first place. But all this had happened before I had even been born. I didn't care much about it unless it got me my Alpha title and my Strawberries her Luna title. Clearly, we were just righting the wrongs from that generation and bringing the Kirbys back into leadership. Under my own rule, of course.

"Seriously, man, again?" I looked up at Damien, who had obviously been talking to me, and was now glaring at me. "Why don't you just go fuck her and get it out of your system now," he scowled. I had a feeling he was still bitter about everything. He had rejected his fated mate when he found out she was an Omega, and now he was being forced to mate with Louise, not that she knew anything about it. The plan was to get Harper to help convince her once she was won over.

And I felt it was close after this morning. I had rushed things the other night at the gazebo. But once I had put her in her place last night, she had seemed more willing this morning. I swear she was even happy to see me. I just knew that once we had completed the bond, she would understand how important I was to her.

"I can't go see her," I said to my scowling best friend. "She and Louise are having a girly night." I scowled at that myself. I was suspicious when Louise had suggested the pamper evening. I knew she had also lied about Harper's whereabouts yesterday and knew that she had a thing with Tommy. I didn't trust her not to poison Harper's thoughts against me. If it weren't for the Alpha's plans for her and Damien, I would have already arranged for her to have had an accident by now. But my father had agreed and said that it would help put Harper at ease after my mess up.

Still, I felt uneasy, even with Alex at the door. I'm sure he would stand loyal. He was already in enough trouble with me after the other night. He had let Harper get away on purpose, and then when I found out that he had gone back for her and taken her to Tommy's, I was furious. Him being on guard duty was his penance for his disloyalty. I mind linked him to put my mind at ease.

"How is everything going there?" I asked. His uneasiness came over the link straight away.

"Erm, all good, man," he responded, but something didn't feel right. I closed the link and stood up. Damien grinned at me.

"Changed your mind, did you?" he sneered. I shook my head.

"Something isn't right," I said, and his smile dropped, and he stood to attention straight away. For a future Alpha, he was a good little lap dog.

"What is it?"

"I dunno, but I'm going to check on my mate." I stormed out of the entertainment room and ran up the stairs to the third floor. I headed down the hall to Harper's room and saw Alex's face turn to worry as soon as he saw me.

"Hey, what's up?" he asked, and I nodded to the door.

"Open it," I said, and he hesitated.

"Do you really wanna see that?" he laughed nervously. "I heard something about face masks. I'm not sure even the mate bond can survive green goo on the face."

"Open it now, Alex," I commanded, and he winced and turned to the door.

I already knew that no one would be in the room before the door had opened fully. I growled at the empty room and turned and slammed Alex into the wall.

"Where is she?" I growled at him, baring my teeth. I knew it was him that had let them go and wanted to rip his throat out right now. My wolf Canyon started howling in my head. He knew his mate was missing. I pulled away from Alex and growled at Damien, who still had his hand on me. He backed off with fear in his eyes.

"Kill him later," he blurted. "Find your girl now." I glared at Alex, who, despite everything, was glaring back at me.

"I hope she gets away from you," he growled. "You don't deserve her." Then I saw his eyes glaze over and knew instantly he was warning them that I knew she was gone. I punched him in the face, knocking him out cold.

"I'll deal with you later," I said as I delivered a kick to his unconscious form.

"Leave him," Damien said. "I called the guard to search the territory. We'll find her."

I ran down the hall, down the stairs, and out into the night. Canyon was howling to get out to search for her, but I knew I had to stay in control. I headed into the woods after her scent. It was strongest in one direction, so I went that way. I could see guards all over the woods. But I knew she was heading for the border and linked out orders to head to the borders straight away.

I was halfway towards the border closest to me when I felt the first snap. It felt like I had been winded, not painful, but uncomfortable, like something had changed in the energy of the pack. I wasn't Alpha, but I knew Harper had cut her connection to the pack even before Alpha Daniel confirmed it. She had renounced her claim as a member of the pack. Canyon howled again as I ran quickly through the woods. I had an awful feeling about what her next action was. But she wasn't strong enough, and I knew it would kill her wolf, if not her, too. Surely she wouldn't do it. Being my mate wasn't that bad that she was willing to risk her wolf. I heard the words in my head a second before the pain slammed into me.

"I, Harper Kirby, acknowledge the rejection of Beta Colton Stokes and accept it now, breaking our bond in the eyes of the moon goddess," her sweet voice floated through my brain, followed by Canyon's howl and the searing pain. I half screamed, and half howled as I stumbled and fell to the floor. It felt like my body was on fire but also covered in ice. I couldn't breathe as I tried to pull myself to my knees, but the pain was unbearable. It wasn't the pain I had craved all this time. Feeling the breaking of the bond felt like my soul was being ripped out slowly and left with a gaping hole of emptiness in its place. I felt like I was being ripped in half, and everything that was good in me was taken away. I howled again because I couldn't do anything else. I could feel myself falling into the black of unconsciousness and tried to cling to anything to keep me awake, knowing that it would be too late if I blacked out. I would not just lose the love of my life, but my own heart as well. But I knew I couldn't fight it as I slipped into the dark black hole of my own despair and pain.

Present Day

I shook myself from the memory of that awful night as I looked at my watch again. 12:05pm. As I had said, I was impatiently waiting by the swing, and still no Harper.

What the hell was she playing at? I was still trying to figure out what happened last night. The last time I had seen her looking that vulnerable was when I had picked her up from school after that whore Donna had attacked her. I still remember her clinging to me as I carried her into her room and took care of her. Because that's what mates do. They take care of their mates. I remembered cleaning her back, laying a gentle kiss on each wound as I cleaned it, and how she reacted to my touch as I got further down her back. Her sweet moans were just for me, and her scent intensified as she became more and more aroused. I lowered my hand to my hardening cock as I saw the memory that was still etched in my brain as I found how much she wanted me. She practically begged me to pleasure her, taking her sweetness in my mouth and drinking in her juices as she screamed in pleasure just for me.

Just for me! She was just for me. Harper was mine. I allowed her to have her fun these last ten years. But it was time for her to come home, not to that bastard Owens, but to me. He had no claim, and I would refuse to let him think he would have my Harper. If he thought he could take her from me after everything we had been through, well, he could think again.

My mind drifted back to that night, the night she had left me. I had tried so hard not to remember that night. Or what had followed? The anger, the rage! I searched for her and would have probably killed her if I had found her. It had been a year of hell before I had found out that she was at the Council. I wanted to go in and demand my mate back, but my father had convinced me to hold off until the time was right. He said that he would get reports on her and would find a way to get her back to the pack in time. The last ten years had been hard, but now she was back, and stronger than ever, she would help me take my place, not only in The Order but also as the rightful Alpha of this town. And her place would be by my side as my devoted angel and bonded mate.

I got the scent of strawberries before she came into view and smiled as she walked up the path towards me. She rolled her eyes, which only made me smile more. The defiance in her was cute, and I knew it was also the mark of an amazing Luna too.

"What do you want, Colton?" she asked as she got close enough, although she still stood out of arm's reach. Something seemed different about her. Like she had a little more light in her or something. I didn't even know what that meant, but it was the only way I could describe what I saw.

I smiled again. Yes, it was only a matter of time before I could call this woman mine again. Truly mine. Mind, body, and soul.

CHAPTER 54

Harper

I walked up the path and saw Colton smiling at me. I couldn't help but roll my eyes. The idiot really did still think he had some sort of chance with me. His smile widened, and I shook my head.

"What do you want, Colton?" I asked, making sure I kept away from him. I might have warrior training, but he still had brute strength on me, and he had caught me off guard more than once. He gave me a confused look and then scowled.

"What was last night all about?" he shot at me. I didn't know what he was talking about for a second, but then I remembered briefly seeing faces at the pack house when Elias carried me in. I couldn't have said whose faces they were. I guessed one was Colton.

"It was personal," I said and shrugged.

"I don't like the way he thinks he has a claim on you," he said, and I rolled my eyes again.

"Did you just pull me out here to criticise my love life?" I said and smirked as his face turned red as he struggled to hold back his fury.

"Well, from what I heard, you haven't really been into anything love-related for quite some time," he snapped. "I heard you were more than willing to spread your legs over at the council. What makes you think I am going to believe that this thing with Owens is anything other than that?" I laughed at him, and his face turned a deeper shade of red.

"And yet, despite all that, I still won't open my legs for you," I said. "Clearly, even I'm not that desperate." I wasn't about to tell him that he was the reason I refused to let almost anyone get close. Other than Aaron and Nathaniel and a few of the female warriors, I didn't trust anyone with anything as important as my heart.

"Maybe I should have come to the Council sooner. I was told to wait, but If I had been there, I could have shown you how amazing we could be before you allowed those disgusting mutts to take pleasure in your body." He really did have some deluded, warped sense of belief. I could imagine him chasing me around the Council grounds with this type of rambling crap. I laughed at the thought of it, or mostly at Sydney, one of the warriors I spent the most time with, who would have suggested finding him a cactus to deep throat, just to shut him up.

"Do you mean rather than you allowing Damien and Alex, and probably who else you thought of, to use my body instead?" I shot back, and he cringed.

"That was different," he said, and I shook my head.

"Yeah, sure it was," I spat, and then it occurred to me what he had just said. "Wait, who told you to wait? And where the hell were you getting the information about what I was doing at the Council?" He just smirked in response.

"Oh, Strawberries, you wouldn't believe where I have eyes working for me," he said, stepping closer to me. "I have known every single thing you have done since you left me." I stepped back away from him and glared at him. I didn't like the idea of being spied on at all.

"Anyway," he said, his mood suddenly shifting and an easy smile on his face. "That doesn't matter now. You came home to me, and I am willing to forgive your past. Just as soon as we get rid of the nuisance in the town, and I get my rightful place."

"I came back to town, not to you," I snapped. "I'm never coming back to you, Colton. When will you learn that?"

"We'll see about that," he said, and I growled at him. I was starting to get annoyed.

"There is a safe," he said, and I stared at him, confused.

"What?"

"A safe in Owens' office," Colton clarified. Oh, so we were talking about business now. Geez, this guy was giving me whiplash with his moods.

"What about it?" I shrugged.

"That is where you will get the evidence the Council needs to take down Owens and his men." I flinched internally at what he said. Taking down Elias meant taking down his people, including Marcus. It was beginning to get hard to think of Elias as the bad guy in all of this. The thought that Marcus was wrapped up in this as well made me feel sick.

"What's wrong?" Colton asked. "You look sad." He stepped closer again, and I glared at him.

"Step back," I warned, and he actually had the balls to look hurt.

"Fine, the safe," I said. "What's the combination?" He looked at me like I was stupid.

"If I knew that, I would have opened it already," he scowled at me. "I'm sure you can get it out of him, though." I rolled my eyes again.

"What, by opening my legs again?" I said sarcastically, and he glared at me.

"Fine. I'm sorry I said that."

"I don't really care," I said. "I'll get the combination and the stuff in the safe. And then I can get my ass out of here."

"Back to your boyfriend?" he spat, and I looked at him, confused. "I saw him drop you off." Oh, he meant Aaron. I didn't need to tell him that he wasn't actually my boyfriend.

"I guess you don't get all the details from your spies then," I mused, more to myself.

"Well, since Owens turned up, I've been watched. Harder to get information."

"Hmmm, good point. Where is that weasel of a non Alpha buddy of yours?" I asked, and he just smirked.

"I'll tell you for a kiss," he said, and I stared at him.

"Yeah, not that important. But if I see him, I will kill him for what he did to Louise," I then stepped forward and glared at him.

"And don't think I won't pay you back for what you did to her, and Katie, too." He looked shocked and then looked at the floor.

"You don't understand," he said. "I was hurting, you left me, and then Canyon left me when you accepted the rejection. I felt alone and angry and had no way to let it out."

"What?" I didn't know that his wolf had gone too. "You lost your wolf?" he shook his head.

"No, he abandoned me," he whispered. "Told me I had caused it all and that I didn't deserve to be a werewolf, much less a Beta or Alpha. He shut me out for three months."

"Three months!" I exclaimed, and he looked up with tears in his eyes. I didn't care. I was furious.

"Three months. I hadn't heard from Maya in ten years." I shouted at him. "Because of what you did to me, I haven't been able to shift since before I turned eighteen!" He looked at me with sadness in his eyes.

"Harper, I am so sorry," he said, and I scoffed. "You don't have to accept my apology, but I would go back and change everything if I could. I would have claimed you that night instead of rejecting you. I would have worshipped the ground you walk upon."

"Well, you can't," I spat. "And I don't accept your apology." I turned to storm off.

"You said hadn't," he called after me, and I turned and looked at him again.

"What?" I asked.

"You said you hadn't heard from your wolf, not haven't. Have you heard from her now?"

"Yeah," I said.

"When?" he asked. Although, from the pained expression on his face, I could tell that he already knew the answer.

"When I met Elias," I said, and he nodded sadly. I turned to go again.

"What about the other one?" he called again, and I sighed.

"What?" I snapped

"The other part, the an-"

"Harper!" I looked towards the new voice in the woods and saw Marcus rushing over

"Did he hurt you?" he asked, putting himself between Colton and me, and I smiled.

"No, Marcus, we were just talking." Marcus glared at Colton and then looked at me.

"Out here in the woods?" he asked, and then glared at Colton again. "Did you follow her after I told you to stay away from her after the Alpha told you to stay away?" he growled at Colton, and I sighed.

"Marcus, one he didn't follow me. I followed him." Marcus looked at me again. "I wanted to warn him that I would be kicking his ass about Louise and Katie." Which was technically true.

"And two, I can look after myself. I told you!"

Marcus huffed. "And I told you that I'm Gamma, so I protect the Luna." Colton growled at the mention of Luna, and I rolled my eyes as both werewolves glared at each other.

"I've had enough of this," I said and walked off. It wasn't long before I heard footsteps coming and Marcus appeared next to me with a big grin on his face. I rolled my eyes again, and we walked the rest of the way back to the pack house in silence.

It was early afternoon by the time we got back. I found a note under my door telling me that Elias expected me in his room for dinner at 5pm and to dress comfy. Let's hope he didn't have any more demolition plans for me this time.

CHAPTER 55

Harper

I looked at myself in the mirror and scowled. Dress comfy! That's what the note said. I mean, what the fuck did that mean? Dress comfy meant pyjamas or joggers, but a date required more. What did date comfy mean? I had changed between my skinny black jeans and my black joggers twice now. I huffed in the mirror, pulled my messy bun down, and let my hair fall down my back. It was already 5pm, and I was getting annoyed at myself for being such a girl. I sighed. Screw it! Black joggers and a purple sleeveless top. With my hair down and a touch of lip gloss and mascara, I was giving in.

I grabbed my mobile phone and headed out the door, and bumped straight into a wall of muscle. I looked from the black t-shirt pulled tight around the chest to Elias's smiling face. I got a full-on smell of his sea salt and mint scent, and I forgot what I was doing as I felt a stirring inside of me. Elias' smile widened, and he brushed my hair back over my shoulder. I saw his nostrils flare as he took in my scent, too.

"Geez! Get a room, you two." I heard Marcus' voice float down the hall, and it snapped me out of the brain fog I was in, and I rolled my eyes. Elias scowled behind me before looking back down at me.

"Dick!" I called back to Marcus, and he laughed.

"I thought you were going out," Elias said, and I looked around to see Marcus in a black shirt and slacks.

"Got a hot date?" I asked, and he grinned.

"Nah, but gotta look good for the ladies." He winked. "Have fun, you two. Don't do anything I wouldn't do," he said, turning towards the stairs. Elias scoffed.

"That doesn't rule out much, does it?" Marcus waved his hand, laughing as he disappeared down the stairs.

I smiled and turned around to face Elias. He smiled down at me, leaned in, and brushed his lips against mine. I took a breath, leaned in, and felt his arms wrap around my back as he deepened the kiss. I pulled away slightly and smiled.

"Maybe we should take Marcus' advice and get a room," I said, and Elias chuckled. He took my hand, and we walked down to his room. I walked in and gasped. The living area of the room was set up with candles, and the coffee table had bowls of snack food on it. It looked so cosy and nice. Definitely different from last night's activities.

"I thought we could watch a movie," Elias said, and shuffled his feet on the floor and looked up at me nervously.

"I would love to." I smiled. I thought it was cute. I had never really gone on dates so much, but then I avoided a connection, and most of the time, the warriors I picked were happy to just have mindless sex. Elias smiled and guided me to the sofa. I sat down, and his eyes glazed over for a few seconds. I waited expectantly until he had finished mind linking with whoever.

"I ordered some pizza from the kitchen," he said, sitting down. "They should be up in about ten minutes." I nodded. Elias handed me the remote, and I flicked through the choices on the streaming service and found a cheesy action movie. And after assuring Elias that I really did enjoy them and wasn't just trying to appease him, we settled down to watch the movie.

By the end of the movie, most of the food had been eaten, and I was snuggled into Elias while his arm was over my shoulder. I was starting to nod off when I felt him kiss the top of my head. I tried to lean over to the remote, and his arm tightened.

"Don't please," he whispered. "Just stay like this for a bit longer." I snuggled back into him and felt him relax.

"It's strange," he said after a few minutes. "I always admired my parents and how much they loved each other. I would see them sitting like this and think it was the whole point of a relationship." He had never really spoken to me about his family or his past, and I wanted to know more.

"Were your parents fated?" I asked and felt him nod against my head.

"Yeah, my dad was Alpha of the Crescent Dawn pack, and my mum was a rogue." I sat up and looked at him in shock. I was trying to search my mind for the Crescent Dawn pack, but couldn't place them. He pulled me back into his side, and I let him with no resistance.

"My mum had fallen in with a Rogue Alpha that was trying to get territory or something and had even agreed to be his chosen mate. They attacked my dad's pack, and my parents met while fighting with each other. It was my mum turning sides that won the fight. She is an amazing warrior. You would love her."

"Is? Your parents are still alive?" I asked. I always thought of Elias as a more lone leader.

"Yeah, they live in a tiny village on the east coast," he said.

"But they don't have the pack now?" I felt Elias stiffen slightly before relaxing again.

"No, it doesn't exist anymore," he said. It wasn't uncommon for the smaller packs to disband or merge with bigger packs, either through territory fights or alliances, but I felt there was something more to this story. I didn't want to push him, though, so we lapsed into silence for a few minutes.

"I was fifteen when it happened," Elias said finally. "It was planned that I would take over the pack when I was eighteen, which annoyed my sister Lily to no end."

"You have a sister?" I asked, and he stiffened again.

"Had," he said sadly. "She was beautiful and smart. She was in university to be a solicitor." He went quiet again, and I let him. I leaned against him as he ran his fingers up and down my arm. It wasn't too long before he spoke again.

"Lily was twenty-two and was annoyed that dad insisted that I took over the pack because it was a male thing. She would argue that women could be Alphas, but my dad had always been old-fashioned or, as my mum says, pig-headed." I smiled at the sentiment in his voice.

"My dad took me out of regular school and sent me to the Council for warrior training." That did shock me.

"Wait, you trained at the Council?" I asked, sitting up again, and he nodded.

"It was where I met Marcus, although I didn't get on with all the rules." He grinned a boyish grin, and I could see the sparkle in his eye. I could definitely see a young Elias pushing it at the Council and getting into a world of trouble.

"I decided that I wasn't going to stay and was feeling the urge to go home. I guess I was homesick, so I skipped out and headed home." He stared off into the distance, the sparkle now gone.

"I was about a mile out from the border when I saw them. This wasn't a rogue attack. This was organised and planned. There were hundreds of them. I managed to get home to sound the alarm minutes before they descended on us. They came at us from all sides, and we fought the best we could, but we were nowhere near prepared. We managed to push them back, and my father ripped out the throat of the leader's second. That seemed to deter others, and the battle stopped." He went silent again, and I saw a single tear slip down his cheek. I took his hand, and he looked at me in shock, like he had forgotten I was even here.

"We thought we had got off easier than we could. Of course, we suffered a few warrior losses, but it could have been worse. Or so we thought. It wasn't until we had got to the safe house that we really saw the damage. The warriors on guard were dead, ripped apart, and there were bodies all over the safe house. We could tell that the women and the men that weren't warriors had put up a fight, but they had been no match." I squeezed his hand. I had seen my fair share of packs and towns massacred in my time as an officer. It was an awful sight when you had no connection. But for it to be your own people, it must have been devastating. Elias sighed sadly.

"Twelve women and children had been taken, and my sister was one of them." I could feel his sadness through the bond, and I wanted so much to take it away from him. It was like I could feel his heart breaking.

"We went in search, of course. My dad pulled in every favour, every alliance, every resource he could get his hands on. And we found almost everyone. They were locked in a container at a port, ready to be shipped off to goddess knows where. Everyone was so relieved. Apart from that, my sister wasn't among them. My dad and I continued to search, but resources dried up, and he abandoned his Alpha title. My mother blamed herself. She was adamant that it was her fault somehow, and she got depressed and spent her days a shadow of her former self. It was six months later when we found my sister's body. She had been violated and mutilated, and I don't know what else." I had tears running down my face as he continued his story. I didn't know what to say.

"My mum took it really hard, and she tried to end her own life. She said that she didn't deserve to live while my sister paid the price for her sins." He shook his head. "I never understood what she was talking about, and my dad just put it off as being grief. I really thought we were going to lose her to it." Elias looked at me again and leaned over and wiped my cheeks, and smiled.

"But you know what?" he said. "We didn't. It took a while, but my dad helped my mum through the grief, through the pain. He used the bond the goddess had given them to pull my mum back from the brink of hell and show her the light again." He leaned over and kissed my still wet cheeks.

"Don't you see? This is what I am trying to do with you, to help you heal." I looked away and shook my head, and he cupped my chin and turned my head, so I was looking at him again.

"My parents are happy. Yes, they grieve for my sister, as do I." He smiled. "But they are able to live each day because of the bond they have. And that is how powerful the fated mate bond is and why I am so determined to help you do the same, Harper." He got down on his knees in front of the sofa and held my hands.

"Harper, I have been in love with you since the moment my wolf recognised your wolf since I got your scent. And I knew that I was here to make you whole again." I shook my head again. "Baby, I know that bastard perverted the bond, but please believe me that it really truly is an amazing gift. My parents are both alive because of it, and I know you can truly be happy again, too."

"Elias, I..." I didn't know what to say. I felt overwhelmed by what he was saying, and everything in me wanted to turn tail and run. I knew my feelings were growing for him at an alarming rate, but love? He said he loved me. Did I love him?

"Of course we do, you silly goose," Maia's voice came through loud and clear, loud enough that I actually jumped. "Don't you feel him? He is our completion."

"Elias, I," I said again, knowing that tears were streaming down my face again. Elias smiled and sat back on the sofa and pulled me, so I was sitting in his lap. I instinctively curled into his body, and his arms went around me. I didn't understand what was happening, but I couldn't deny that I felt safe in his arms once again. I felt him kiss my head again and murmur words I couldn't quite hear.

We stayed like that in comfortable silence for I don't know how long. I didn't realise that I had drifted off until I woke up still curled into him, only we were both now laid on the sofa, and I saw Elias was asleep. I watched his steady breathing for a while before I started drifting off again. I knew without a doubt that I did love him. But that left me with a bad feeling in my stomach. I was sent here to investigate and find evidence against Elias. He was suspected of being a part of one of the world's biggest and most dangerous crime rings. Maybe he had done it, joined the Circle to find the people who took his sister for revenge. But did that make him a good man in a bad situation, or was he really still a bad guy? And if so, could I really help convict the man I loved? I fell asleep, internally cursing the moon goddess and also thanking her for the fated bond between Elias and me.

CHAPTER 56

Harper

I woke up the next morning, still wrapped in Elias' arms. I opened my eyes as Maia hummed, content in my head. She seemed louder than ever and happy.

"Maia?" I asked in my head and felt her shift around.

"Not yet," she said, knowing what I was asking. I mean, after all, she was me. "Not yet, but soon. I can feel it." Then she curled up and went back to humming. I was suddenly feeling restless, like I did when I was fifteen, before my first shift. It felt like something was trying to break through. Then it was Maia, but that wasn't it this time, because Maia was already here.

I felt Elias move behind me, and he snuggled into me, nuzzling his nose into my neck.

"Goddess, I love that smell," he whispered, and I couldn't help but giggle as his stubble tickled my shoulder.

"Good morning, beautiful," he whispered and ran his nose up my neck, and I shivered at the feel. I twisted around on the sofa to face him and smile.

"Morning," I said, and he leaned down and gently ran his lips against mine. I wrapped my arms around his neck and pulled him in tighter, opening my mouth to deepen the kiss. Elias complied and ran his tongue along my lips before finding my own. In the heat of the kiss, I found myself lying on the sofa with Elias above me, and I wrapped my legs around his torso. I felt his excitement as he pushed against me, and I tightened my grip to pull him in closer. Elias broke the kiss and began kissing down my neck, pausing briefly on my marking spot before running his mouth along my collarbone. We were both breathing heavily when I felt a buzzing against my leg, and I looked down, shocked, and Elias groaned and buried his head into my neck again. The buzzing happened again, and I realised what was happening.

"Is that a bee in your pocket, or are you just happy to see me?" I said with a chuckle, and Elias groaned again.

"It's Marcus," he said as he lifted his head and kissed my nose.

"Marcus is using the phone?" I asked, and he winced.

"I've been ignoring his mind links for about five minutes," he said as he pulled himself up from the sofa. "And I told him that if he busted into my room again after yesterday that he would find himself in a considerable amount of pain."

"You know violence isn't always the answer," I said flippantly, and Elias grinned at me.

"This coming from the girl who has kicked the ass of my Beta at least twice now," he said, and I shrugged.

"Special circumstances, he's a dick," I said, and he laughed.

"Can't argue with you there, darling," he said, and I chuckled. I stood up and stretched. Sleeping on the sofa wasn't the most comfortable position, and I felt a stiffness in my muscles.

Elias looked at his phone and groaned. His eyes glazed over for a few seconds, and I waited patiently for him to finish his link conversation. He looked at me and smiled.

"I will be busy all day with it being the Midsummer ball tonight," he said, and I realised it was Saturday, so of course the ball was tonight. "I would love it if you did me the honour of accompanying me this evening." I felt a weight in my stomach. I had no plans of going to the ball. I mean, I wasn't a pack member, and well, the last time I went to one pretty much ruined my life.

"Erm, well," I said, looking down at the floor, and Elias took my chin in his hand and lifted my head, so I was facing him.

"I promise that you will be safe," he said, and I laughed nervously. "Please," he said, his eyes full of pleading. I looked at him and smiled slightly. What was the worst that could happen?

"Okay," I said. "Yes, I will go to the ball with you." His face lit up into a massive smile that I couldn't help but return. He pulled me into a kiss just as there was a knock at the door, and I pulled away, laughing as he groaned again.

"I'll see you later," I said, and he smiled.

"I'll pick you up at seven," he said, and I nodded.

I headed to the door as Elias walked into the bathroom whistling. I opened the door to see Marcus standing on the other side.

"Whoa, princess," he said with a big grin. "Walk of shame two days in a row, eh?"

I rolled my eyes. "And I wonder if you slept in your own bed last night," I said, and his grin grew.

"Caught me there," he said, and I laughed.

I didn't have to guess that most of the girls in town would be fighting over Marcus' attention. I knew that the former Alpha was particular as to who was allowed in the territory, so the takeover by Elias brought a series of fresh choices for the singles. And Marcus wasn't exactly hard on the eyes. His stocky but muscled build was pretty standard for a werewolf warrior, but add the golden tan skin tone, the rich brown hair and chocolate brown eyes that always seemed to have hints of gold, and his chiselled jawline, I could imagine he would have his pick of the bunch.

I made way for Marcus to enter the room and pointed to the bathroom door.

"He's just gone in," I said, and Marcus nodded.

"Thanks, princess," he said and threw himself on the sofa. "By the way, I am gonna be busy with the Alpha today, so I would prefer it if you didn't go for walks in the woods or anywhere for that matter," he said, and I scowled at him.

"Marcus, I don't need a guard. I told you I could look after myself," I huffed, and he rolled his eyes.

"Just let me do my job, princess, please."

I huffed again. "I can't promise anything," I snapped. "If I get bored, I won't be sitting around twiddling my thumbs." I stormed out of the room before he could respond. I was getting annoyed at the constant watching. Not only did it make it ten times harder to do my job, knowing that he was watching me, but I felt like some prissy girl who needed saving. Which I clearly did not.

I was getting a headache. Again, it felt like something was trying to come through, like some sort of pressure at the back of my mind. I decided to take a nap since my quality of sleep wasn't so great last night and crawled into my bed, and it wasn't long before I drifted off to sleep. However, I was rudely awoken by a knock on my door. It felt like I had maybe been asleep for five minutes, but looking at the clock, I saw it was almost midday. I groaned and pulled myself out of bed, feeling worse than ever. Maybe I was coming down with something. Werewolves didn't get standard colds and such, but there was a small variant of supernatural viruses that could knock a wolf down for a day, rare but could happen. I stumbled to the door and opened it, ready to shout at whoever was interrupting my sleep. It was Louise, standing on the other side. She grinned at me and barged into the room, pushing past me and heading towards my suitcase.

"You know, it really would be easier if you unpacked," she muttered as she started rooting through.

"Erm, hi?" I said, confused, and she looked me up and down.

"Go get a shower and be quick about it. Our first appointment is in thirty minutes," she said and pulled out some black jeans. "Geez, Harper, do you wear anything other than black jeans?" She scoffed.

"No, I don't, and what appointment?" I asked, and she grinned again.

"Well, we have dress shopping first, and then lunch with the Luna." She glanced quickly at me. "I mean former Luna, and then we have hair and make-up ready for tonight."

I shook my head, still confused. "What, wait, how?" I asked, and she winked.

"Marcus arranged it for us once he found out that you said you would go to the ball with Elias."

The son of a bitch! I growled to myself. I had said that I wouldn't sit around doing nothing, so he filled my day with stuff and got my best friend involved in it, too.

"Why lunch with the Luna?" I asked, and Louise rolled her eyes. "Harper, you are going to the ball with the Alpha, who everyone knows is your fated mate," she said. "Whether you like it or not, they will see you as the Luna, and that comes with certain responsibilities." I scowled at her again.

"I would never have thought I would have heard that coming from you," I said, and she laughed.

"Trust me. I am as shocked as you are. But this pack is divided right now, and seeing someone who is one of them, even if you have been away, trusting their new Alpha might be enough to sway the balance away from Colton's dickery." I chuckled at that last part. But I admitted that what she was saying was indeed true. I sighed in defeat and headed to the shower while Louise laid out some clothes for me. I would play the role of Luna for now and hope that it would help me get what I wanted to get out of here and back home.

CHAPTER 57

Harper

I looked in the mirror at my reflection and smiled. The full-length black dress had a sheer back with diamonds sewn in that looked like they floated on my bare skin, and one leg could be seen through the thigh-high split. My hair was styled in a curled updo with a few curls trailing down against my shoulders and sparkled with diamond-style hair clips. I had my makeup simple with barely a silver sheen across my eyes and cheeks and pale, almost skin tone lip gloss. The only jewellery I wore was the ring that I couldn't remove. I looked at Louise in the mirror, who looked stunning in her silver satin full-length dress, and I was reminded of ten years ago when we were in my room getting ready for the ball.

So much had changed in that time. I was sad that Katie wasn't here with us, but it had become apparent that the distance between Katie and Louise was more than just time. I had tried to ask Louise about it, but she had just said that they weren't meant to be friends and changed the subject. I could never get any more out of her. And I hadn't seen Katie much since I had got into town.

We had spent the day getting ready for the various appointments that Marcus had arranged, but from what I had heard, Elias had bankrolled. Throughout the day, I would think of what Elias had told me last night. His past and about the mate bond. Could I really believe that all it took was him and the mate bond to help heal the crap I had dealt with? Goddess only knew that sleeping around and avoiding any sort of emotional attachment hadn't been a winning combination. And even if I didn't want to admit it, I knew Elias had made such a difference to the hole in my heart, even in these short days. I sighed and looked at myself in the mirror again. I was playing a dangerous game; I was falling for Elias, but what did that mean once I found the evidence I needed?

"Hey," Louise said, touching my shoulder and pulling me from my thoughts. "You look sad."

I smiled. "I don't know, Louise," I said, and she smiled, sympathy all over her face.

"Tommy said that he's a good guy," she said. Louise knew everything about why I was here. I had already told her about my mission. She had acted very differently when I first told her.

"But you said that he was dangerous," I pointed out. "You said you heard him with other prisoners. You said I had to be careful with him." Louise shrugged.

"I dunno. Maybe I was wrong," she said. "Like I said, Tommy is pretty happy with him." I gave her a look, and she shrugged again.

Just then, there was a knock at the door, and we both looked over. I suddenly felt really nervous as Louise headed to the door with a smile. She opened the door to both Tommy and Elias. They were both wearing tuxedos, but whilst Tommy's was the standard black and white with a silver bow tie, Elias seemed to be that little fancier. I could see the silver waistcoat underneath his black jacket, and even someone as useless in fashion as me could tell that it was no off-the-rack deal. He was smiling when the door opened, but the smile vanished, and his jaw dropped when his eyes fell on me. I smiled at the reaction as a little red flushed into my cheeks. He stepped forward into the room, his eyes never leaving mine, and the butterflies in my stomach got stronger as he got closer.

"You look beautiful," he said as he regained his composure. He bowed before taking my hand and laying a gentle kiss on it. Maia was yapping in my head, suddenly very excited, and for a second, I thought I saw something shift behind Elias' eyes.

"The moon goddess herself marvels at your beauty." I rolled my eyes as I heard Tommy chuckle behind him.

"Dude," he said, "Cheesy line alert." Elias half-glanced back, slightly annoyed, before smiling again. He half-turned to Tommy and Louise, who were already both in the hallway.

"Have a good night, you two," he said, clearly dismissing them. I could tell Tommy wanted to say something else, but Louise shushed him and smiled.

"And you, Alpha," she said and then winked at me. She then tugged on Tommy's arm, and the pair headed off down the hallway while I could clearly hear her chastise Tommy about being so informal with the Alpha. I couldn't help smiling. Seeing two of my favourite people together like this, despite everything they had been through, really did make me see a nicer side of the bond.

I turned to Elias, smiled, and saw that he was back watching me. He smiled in response as he pulled out a box. It was black velvet with a silver clasp. I looked at the box with suspicion before looking back up at Elias.

"It would do me the greatest honour if you would wear this," he said and opened the box. Inside, laid on a bed of black velvet, was a pendant. It was a hollow circle with the shape of a crescent moon inside, with some pretty pattern swirls. On one tip of the moon was a white stone, and on the other tip, a black stone. I couldn't help but look closer at the piece of jewellery. It looked to be silver, which I knew wasn't possible. I looked up at Elias again, and he smiled.

"The metal is platinum, and the two stones are moonstone and obsidian," he said. "This was my sister's and the official crest of the Crescent Dawn pack, the pack I grew up in." I looked up at him in concern. This wasn't just a pretty piece of jewellery. This was a major significant piece.

"It's beautiful," I said, "But I couldn't wear it. It's so important to you."

He smiled. "Not as important as you," he said and took the pendant attached to a delicate chain from the box and held it open to place around my neck.

"Don't worry, this isn't me making my claim," he said, and I narrowed my eyes at him. He laughed nervously.

"Okay, well, it sort of is, but only so that certain people understand to leave you alone." I knew that the certain people he was referring to were just that one person. I nodded and lifted my hair so he could put the necklace on me.

"The two stones represent the duality of life," Elias said as he did up the clasp. "The dark and light, the sweet and sour, the pain and pleasure." I could feel his fingers on my neck, and I shivered as his touch sent electricity down my spine.

"Each must live in balance with each other to truly experience the full extent of what this world has to offer. One side gets overbalanced, and it can desensitise and lessen the experience."

I looked at Elias as he spoke. "Huh?" I asked, suddenly feeling dumb. It felt like he was saying something important, but my mind couldn't seem to grasp his words. Again, the feeling of overwhelm crawled over me, and I could feel the pressure of something trying to push through. I felt my panic rising and quickly found the spot on my hand that I knew would ease the panicky feelings. I rubbed the spot, felt the pressure recede, and started to feel like I was a little more clear-headed.

I looked up to see Elias watch me with curiosity as I regained myself and smiled. He smiled back at me before holding out his arm to me. I nodded and linked mine through his, and his smile grew.

"Let's get this party started then," he said, and we headed out the door and down the hall. I could hear noise, like a general din of conversation, music, and other sounds that indicated a crowd as we headed down the stairs. And as soon as we hit the last flight of the stairs to the ground floor, I could see that half the town was already here and enjoying the festivities. Marcus was standing at the bottom of the stairs with the redhead that worked the reception for Elias on his arm.

"Alpha," he said, looking at Elias, and bowed slightly. He looked at me and smiled. "Lun-, erm, I mean Miss Harper," he said quickly as I scowled at the initial name. "Please, may I introduce my date Kylie?" he asked, and I smiled at the woman. I was sure I recognised her from somewhere but couldn't quite picture her.

"Oh, Harper and I go way back." She giggled in a high-pitched, sickly sweet voice that I could tell was completely fake. I could also see the nasty look in her eyes as she smiled. "We even used to go to school together." I looked at her in shock and focused on her face, and tried to go through high school memories. Then it hit me, of course. She had been one of Donna Tobbins' girl gang of vicious vipers. I returned the smile with a slight smirk.

"Of course," I said, "How could I forget?" I then turned to Elias. "Kylie was one of the popular girls, me not so much." And then I looked back at Kylie. "I remembered as you followed Donna around everywhere. That's a point. That is one person I haven't seen since my return. Where is Donna?" Kylie looked uneasy, and I noticed Elias and Marcus exchange a look that I couldn't quite decipher.

"Donna Tobbins?" Elias asked, and I nodded my head, and he shrugged. "She and her family are no longer in town," he said nonchalantly. But despite his attempt at downplaying the subject, I could tell that there was more to this story. I went to push further when we were interrupted by a cough. I looked to where the cough came from and felt Elias' arm on mine tense up.

I looked over and saw Colton standing to one side. He was also dressed in a tuxedo, although it was just black and white.

"Alpha, the stage is ready when you are," Colton said, although his eyes never left mine. Elias growled next to me, and I glanced over before moving closer to him. I saw a flash of gold in Colton's eyes. I shook my head at both of them and went to pull my arm out from Elias's, but he stopped me.

"I have my speech right now," he said, like it explained something.

"Okay, I can go find a drink," I said and went to pull my arm back again.

"Please, Harper, it's important to me that we walk in together," he said, glancing at Colton again. I finally got it. It was important to show the pack that he was to be trusted and to show Colton that I didn't belong to him. I smiled at Elias, feeling the headache returning. This being between an Alpha and a Beta was starting to wear thin on my patience.

"Well, let's do it because I am really starting to need a drink," I said and stepped down the last few steps, pulling Elias with me. I heard Marcus chuckle and mumble something like being a handful. I shot him a glare as we passed, which just made him laugh harder.

Elias and I walked into the room, and despite there being no announcement or indication that it was happening, I still felt the eyes of every person in that room looking at us. Most had their heads bowed in respect for the Alpha, but some stared at us straight on. I made a mental note of who these people were. I suspected that Colton's supporters were very evident in the room.

As we walked to the stage, there was the occasional greeting to which I smiled, and at one point, I saw my sister waving her arm and grinning like a madwoman. We made it to the stage steps, and Elias made a show of turning to me and kissing my hand before letting go and heading up the stairs. I looked around for a waiter and snagged a glass of something sparkling as one passed by.

I contented myself with standing to one side while Elias began his speech. He started with the usual stuff about the time of year that Alpha Daniel would do each year and then moved on to some important announcements. I tried to listen to what he was saying, but the headache and the pressure were starting to make me feel a little dizzy. Finally, Elias finished, and I welcomed his cold hands on my arm when he came over. I looked up at him to see the concern in his eyes and smiled.

"Are you feeling ok? You feel warm?" he asked, and I smiled and nodded,

"I'm ok. I've just had a headache today," I said, and he continued to look concerned.

"Maybe we should get you back upstairs," he said, and I shook my head.

"I'm fine," I said. "Why don't we dance?" I pulled him onto the dance floor. He resisted a little, but not for long, and soon we were dancing to a slow song. I moved slowly, feeling Elias' hands on my back and my arms looped around his neck, and felt his nose running against my neck, sending shivers down my spine. I wasn't sure how many songs we danced to or even what they were. I just knew that I had never felt so safe and comfortable as I did right there.

Then Elias took my left hand in his and whispered in my ear. "Do you trust me?"

I smiled, and without even thinking, I did. I trusted him! I didn't understand how I knew it, but I knew he wasn't the man I had been sent to look for and that I could trust him. I felt him tug gently on my hand and looked up to see why, when suddenly a hot flash went through me, my legs buckled out from under me. I felt Elias' arms around me as he scooped me up. My head was suddenly spinning, and I couldn't see straight. Elias moved us to the side of the room. He sat me in a chair and kneeled in front of me. He looked at me with concern as I tried to regain focus. I could tell that I was sweating, and the pressure in my head was almost unbearable.

"What's going on?" I stuttered as someone rushed over, and I felt cold water against my lips. I focused on Elias in front of me and saw Tommy kneeling next to him. He had a smile on his face.

"Harper," he said. "Kid, think back to the last time you felt like this," he said, and both Louise and Elias looked at him funny. And then it hit me. The last time I felt like this was just before my 15th birthday. I had spent a week with a fever and headaches, only for it to finally end in...

I looked up at Tommy and realised tears were streaming down my face. He grinned at me before whispering something to Elias, whose eyes widened.

"Let's get you outside," he said, composing himself quickly and scoping me up, and heading for the door. He made a straight line for the woods, and I could feel someone undoing my dress as we went. Elias placed me in a clearing that was just off from the pack house but still hidden by the trees. I looked up to see Tommy and Louise watching me. I was suddenly very scared.

Tommy tugged on Louise's hand and smiled. "Come on, she's in good hands." He smiled at me again before they headed back out through the woods. I cried out as pain shot through my body and felt Elias' cool hands on me again.

"It's okay, baby," he said soothingly. "Breathe through it." I screamed as another pain shot through my body, and I started to shift into my wolf for the first time in over ten years.

CHAPTER 58

Harper

My shifting for the first shift wasn't fun. It was long; it was hard, and it was painful as hell. I remembered back a couple of weeks before my fifteenth birthday; I had started to get a fever. I had been so unwell and couldn't understand why my parents seemed so excited about it. Around a week later, I had started to feel the aches around my body adjusting. I had been confused because I had watched my sister's first shift, and it had seemed like a disappointing event. My parents got excited, of course. Shifting for a wolf is one of our most treasured abilities and is always celebrated. But after my sister had shifted, something had changed in the family dynamic. Before her shift, my parents would dote upon her every word, and she could do no wrong. I had always felt a little out of place, the second child that no one really wanted but had got, anyway. I wasn't mistreated or anything, but it was obvious who the favourite was. That changed with my sister's shift.

So when I realised I was about to shift for the first time, I got upset. Despite the wedge it had put between Susie and me, I had really enjoyed being seen for a while. And so, when I was told I was going to shift, I had started to cry. It was earlier than most, too, as first shifts normally happened closer to the sixteenth birthday, and I felt cheated out of my spotlight time. And then I was confused because my sister's shift had been easier. One day, she was a pre-shifted wolf. The next, after a painful few hours, she was a full-fledged werewolf. I vaguely remembered my uncle Tommy's being similar, although his had happened a few years before.

The night it happened, I had been dizzy and in pain. I couldn't keep anything down and had awful headaches. Tommy had basically slept in my room for the entire week. He had argued with my father about it, something about responsibility and honour. I had asked about it, but no one would give me an answer. On the night in question, six days before my fifteenth birthday, I started to feel so much worse. My uncle had taken me to the woods behind our house and had sat with me for the six hours it took to finally shift. My parents and sister had been there too but sat on the sidelines just watching. It had been the worst night of my life.

It wasn't like in some movies, where shifting was instantaneous and fluid. It would be eventually, but the first time you shift, your body has to get used to the massive physical transformation that is going to occur, and it can be enough to send you into shock. I had screamed and cried and declared I didn't want to be a werewolf and to take it away for the first five hours and then laid there drenched in sweat, exhausted for the sixth hour. I had cried to Tommy that something was wrong, because this didn't happen to Susie. All he had done was tell me that I was special and it would be worth it and would get easier. When it finally happened, the actual change took a little over ten minutes. It was ten minutes of pure agony. I felt like my throat would be raw from screaming so much. But it happened, and I finally rose on shaky legs—a brand new werewolf. And to my surprise, I was grey. My whole family had chocolate brown fur, but mine was grey. My parents were so happy. Later, Tommy had said that after my eighteenth birthday, my fur would actually turn white. He told me that every few generations, our family line produced a white wolf. I had asked why, but his only response was that I would find out soon enough.

The more I shifted, the easier it got, and I was pretty proud of the fact that I could shift with ease, in seconds with no pain. Of course, now that I hadn't shifted in over ten years, I wasn't surprised that I was here on my hands and knees, almost naked and in a substantial amount of pain. I looked up at Elias, who was sitting next to me, stroking my back as another wave of pain eased off.

"What's taking so long?" I snapped, and he chuckled.

"It's only been about ten minutes," he said, which earned him a glare and a growl.

"Only ten minutes. You try going through this and tell me ONLY ten minutes," I snapped again, and he chuckled again.

"You got this, baby, I know you do," he said as he continued to stroke my back.

I could feel another wave coming on and braced myself for the pain seconds before it hit. It didn't do anything, though, and I screamed out as my fingers dug into the ground beneath me. I felt my nails lengthen into claws before retracting again, and the pain disappeared.

"Trust the process," Elias whispered. "Trust me to protect you and let go of the control."

"You trust the process, dickhead," I snapped, and he just smiled. Of course, I knew he was right, but I didn't have to admit it. I sighed and closed my eyes. I could feel Elias' hand up and down my back and the gentle breeze caressing my skin. I could hear the wind in the trees and the distant sound of the party still going on at the pack house. I could taste the blood in my mouth when I bit my tongue a few pain waves ago. And I could smell the night and Elias. His sea salt and mint scent caressed my skin even more than the wind. It wrapped me in a warm, safe cocoon, and I focused on that. I allowed myself to absorb his touch, scent, and bond into me, to let it take over me, and I submitted control to my inner beast, knowing that Elias was there to catch me if I fell.

I felt the shift almost before it happened. The next wave hit me with a powerful force, and I screamed as my bones broke and reformed and my skin tore and healed. I felt as fur sprouted across my skin, and my hearing and sight improved. I lay panting for a few minutes as I became accustomed to my wolf body again and called out to Maia, who had been quiet through the experience.

"Maia?" I called in my head.

"I'm here," she said, her voice louder than ever before. I nodded my head, knowing she was there. I was still in control of our body, so I tried slowly to get to my feet. I was shaky, and I stumbled a little, but as soon as I did, I felt arms around me and turned my head to see Elias still sitting next to me. He helped me stand on my feet and slowly let go while staring at me. I turned and nudged him with my snout, and he stroked my fur.

"I don't know why I would be surprised, but you are beautiful," he said, and I yipped in response. I tried to walk a little, and Elias jumped up and followed close behind as I circled the perimeter of the clearing, getting used to the feel of my new body. I got to one side just as the moon came out behind a cloud. I dashed into the moonlight and heard a gasp behind me.

I turned to see Elias staring at me. I opened my mouth and tried to frown at him. What the hell was wrong with him?

"My goddess!" he exclaimed, and I padded my paws at him and huffed, and he laughed.

"Okay, baby, I get it. Baby, look at yourself. You're not just white. You are glistening!" he exclaimed. Glistening? I looked down at my paws, and just as he said. My fur was white as snow, but in the moonlight, it sparkled and glistened. Not obviously, but enough that there was almost a sheen across my fur. I looked back up at Elias and huffed again, and he came closer and ran his hand through my fur.

"Absolutely beautiful," he said.

"Maia?" I said in my head, "Why am I glittery?" I heard her giggle and then, to my shock, heard something else. It sounded like another laugh. I jumped around, expecting to find someone behind me, but there wasn't anyone there.

"Maia?" I asked again

"It's not time yet," she said. "We aren't at full strength yet, but soon." I wanted to ask more, but Maia had a question of her own.

"Harper?" she suddenly asked quietly again, and I nodded in response. "Can I play with Jax?"

"Jax?" I asked. "Who's Jax?" And then I saw Elias' head lift, and he looked our way. He looked like he had his own conversation. I realised then who she was talking about. Oh, Jax must be Elias' wolf. I huffed at Elias, and he looked over at me, slightly confused. I was starting to get annoyed at not being able to communicate, so I circled him a few times and bit at his ankles, and then yipped. He cocked his head to the side and then laughed.

"Oh!" he said. "Are you sure, baby?" I bounded into the woods and then back to him, and he laughed again.

"Ok, give me a moment." He headed into the woods on the other side, and a minute later, a big black wolf came bounding out of the trees. I knew instantly it was Elias and Jax, and he bounded over to me and nuzzled against my fur. I marvelled at his size and the deep black colour that looked almost blue. Maia was already yipping in my head, and I grinned, the best I could as a wolf, at Elias before handing full control over to Maia. I saw the shift in Elias as his golden eyes shifted through. And he had also given control to Jax. The two wolves bounded together and chased each other around the clearing for a few minutes before Maia yipped at Jax and nipped at his legs. Jax playfully growled at Maia, and she bounded off through the forest. We could tell without looking that Jax was on her trail. I knew I could stay here, present in the moment, and enjoy the feel of the wind and experience the wolf. Still, since I had had control of our body for so long, and this was Maia's first run for so long, I decided to retreat into the dark and allow her to experience this herself. She felt what I was doing straight away.

"Thank you, Harper," she said in our head, so grateful.

"Just no mating for now, please," I said, and she laughed.

"I know the rules." It was an unwritten rule that a werewolf mated and completed the bond in human form before wolf form. Werewolves in wolf form are lifetime partners, and it was the ultimate almost unbreakable bond. I smiled and allowed myself to slip into the dark so Maia could have her fun with Jax.

I wasn't sure how long it was before I was pulled back into my body again. But as soon as I did, I felt exhausted. My whole body ached, and I barely felt myself shifting back to human form before falling asleep again.

CHAPTER 59

Harper

I woke up in Elias' arms as he carried me into the pack house. I was wrapped up in his tuxedo jacket as he snuck in through the back door, through the now darkened kitchen, and up the backstairs. The ball was still going strong by the sounds of it, although I had no clue what time it was. We made it to Elias' room without being spotted, and he smiled at me as he gently put me down on the sofa and kissed the top of my head. I watched as he headed to his large chest of drawers and pulled out a clean t-shirt. He came back over and slipped the jacket off me, and helped me with putting the t-shirt on. My whole body ached and felt heavy; even lifting my arms was a concentrated effort.

Once the t-shirt was in place, Elias settled on the sofa next to me and pulled me onto his lap. I curled into him, suddenly feeling exhausted again.

"How long did we run for?" I asked as he stroked my hair.

"About an hour, not that long," he said. I huffed. An hour and I felt like crap. He chuckled against my head.

"Remember, baby. It takes a lot out of you when you first shift. The fact that you lasted an hour is impressive," he said. "And bloody hell you ain't half-fast. Jax and I could barely keep up half the time." I smiled at that, at least.

"I suspect that Maia was long overdue," I said and snuggled further into him. "But it wasn't my first shift, just my first in a long time. I don't like that it was that hard."

"Well, it was a really long time," Elias said. "Don't be so hard on yourself."

"I should have realised, I have been getting headaches for the last couple of days. It just didn't even occur to me," I mused. "I just wonder what triggered it after all this time." I felt Elias fidget and glanced up at him when he didn't say anything. The look on his face told me he wanted to say something, but he looked uneasy about it.

"What?" I asked suspiciously, and he grimaced. "Elias!" I narrowed my eyes at him, and he sighed. Elias lifted me from his lap and put me on the sofa, before standing up.

"Elias, what is it?" I asked, suddenly worried.

"I might have something to do with you shifting," he said and put his hand in his pocket. "It actually makes complete sense, especially with your headaches."

"What are you talking about?" I asked.

Elias turned around and looked at me, uncertainty on his face.

"Remember at the dance I asked if you trusted me?" he asked, and I nodded. "Well, I might have done something that could only have been done if you were ready, but I suspected that if you knew, you would resist." I suddenly resisted the urge to check my neck for bite marks, but surely, if he had marked me or completed the bond, I would have felt it. Plus, we hadn't even slept together, and you needed that to complete the bond. My hand must have twitched or something because Elias looked at me a little insulted.

"Harper, I would never mark you without your permission. Please don't even think that," he said, a slight edge to his voice.

"Well, what then?" I exclaimed. "Because you are starting to worry me now," I demanded, and Elias sighed. He pulled his hand out of his pocket and held it open in front of me. I looked at his hand and gasped in shock. I looked up at him with tears in my eyes. And then down to my left hand. No, it wasn't possible. I looked back at him and then to the single item in his hand. The engagement ring that had been on my finger for over ten years. It had been forced there, compelled by Colton. The one thing that had caused me so much pain was now sitting harmlessly in Elias' hand.

"I don't...." I said. "How?" I asked, with tears streaming down my face. I looked down at my hand again, at my finger where the ring had been for so long. There was a slight indentation mark, but otherwise, it was simply like it had never been there. I couldn't take my eyes off my hand, and my vision was beginning to blur from my tears. I felt Elias kneel in front of me and his hand encased mine. I looked up at him, and he wiped the tears from my eyes.

"I don't get it," I said. "How did you...." I couldn't form words fast enough to match my racing thoughts. Elias smiled and stroked my cheek.

"I knew that the mate bond, our bond, could help heal the trauma you were dealing with," he said. "Remember, I had seen my dad do it for my mum." I nodded, and he carried on.

"Well, I knew that damn ring had something to do with this," he glanced back at the table where the ring was sitting. "I mean, Stokes's compulsion should have lost its power, if not when you accepted his rejection, then sometime in the last ten years," he scoffed. "He doesn't have that much pull. The guy is barely a Beta. Goddess only knows how he thinks he will take the Alpha title from me."

My eyes widened. "You knew about that!" I exclaimed, and he smiled.

"Yeah, I've known for a while, and I knew that he was trying to recruit you in on it too."

I shrunk back a bit, suddenly concerned, and he chuckled.

"Marcus has been following you for a while. He told me that Stokes had been bothering you and trying to use his former bond with you as some sort of blackmail."

"You had Marcus follow me," I said suddenly, annoyed that he would do that, and he chuckled again.

"Well, technically no, but yes, I would have done anyway since you are my mate," he said. "But Marcus comes from a very proud line of warrior

Gammas. His lineage takes their responsibilities seriously, and as soon as Marcus knew you were my mate, he was itching to take the official protection role that runs in his blood." I couldn't help but smile at that. Marcus had told me on multiple occasions that he took protecting me seriously.

"But anyway," Elias said, stroking my finger where the ring was. "I knew that the ring must be some sort of key. And after the other night when we had our first, erm... well, I guess it wasn't a date," he said, and I smiled.

"Yeah, property destruction is a new one for date activities," I said, and he chuckled again.

"Well, I noticed that you seemed different. Like there was a new light about you." I tilted my head at that. I was sure Colton had said something similar, if not the same.

"I also noticed that your response when I felt you tug the ring seemed different. And then again, last night when we talked about my family, you felt different, more open somehow." I thought back to last night and how, even without thinking about it, I did feel different. Although, the headaches had probably masked it at the time.

"I spent all of today looking up what information I could find on the mate bond and its use as a healing property. I sent Marcus near crazy, making him help me, which is why he planned all those appointments and things for you and got Louise involved. He hates leaving you unprotected, he said, and I am quoting him here, that it's like a divine calling for him." He used air quotes as he spoke.

"But when I saw you this evening, you looked stunning," Elias said, "Like, of course, you looked amazing in your dress, but I mean, it was like there was something new in you. And then when I put the necklace on you, I swear I saw a shimmer in your skin."

I gasped suddenly, my hand shooting to my neck. "The necklace!" I exclaimed in horror, "I've lost it. It must have snapped when I shifted." Elias smiled, reached into his other pocket, and pulled out the necklace. The chain was snapped, but it all looked to be still there.

"Don't worry, I saw it come off and picked it up," he said, and I breathed a sigh of relief.

"So, did the ring come off at the same time?" I asked, and he shook his head.

"No, I took the ring off," Elias said. "When we were dancing, I asked if you trusted me, and when you said yes, I slipped the ring off." I couldn't believe what I was hearing.

"I don't understand," I shook my head. "How does trusting you mean that Colton's compulsion doesn't work anymore?"

"Baby, because it wasn't Colton's compulsion keeping the ring on your finger," he said, lifting my chin so we were face to face, "It was you that kept the ring there. It was your attachment to the trauma that you had suffered. The only power that damn ring had was the one you gave it." I shook my head again. Was that even possible? Was it me all this time?

"I could have taken the ring off all this time?" I asked, and he nodded.

"Potentially, but I think you needed to process what had happened and then let go of the power it had on you." I couldn't help the tears that started streaming again. "Baby, you need to know that you had to do this. You had to heal from this. I could only help because I had seen the bond help before." He stroked my hair again as I tried to process what he said. I looked back down at my finger again and then up at Elias. His eyes were shiny with tears, but there was pride there, too. Deep down, I knew trusting him was one of the final pieces, one of the final snaps of the chain on me. And once the ring was removed, like a bind on my soul, Maia was finally able to come out. But it wasn't the final piece.

This was a lot, and I felt so exhausted after my shift, but I knew without a doubt that I had allowed myself to not just trust Elias, but to love him. And I was completely in love with Elias, mind, body, and soul.

CHAPTER 60

Harper

I looked at Elias and smiled. He smiled back and stroked my cheek.

"Harper, I-" he started to say, but I leaned forward and kissed him. Just barely a touch at first, but then as he kissed me back, I deepened it. I felt his tongue against my lips and opened my mouth for him. Elias pulled me down onto his knee, and I straddled him as he pulled my body tight against his bare chest. I wrapped my arms around his neck and followed his tongue with my own. I was naked apart from the t-shirt, and the feel of his increasing hardness beneath his slacks caused heat to stir in me as I rubbed against him. I pulled away from the kiss and began kissing along his neck, nibbling here and there as I went. I moved against his pants, knowing that I was getting aroused.

Elias rubbed his nose against my neck, and I shivered as the scent of my excitement reached him.

"Goddess," he muttered and grabbed my hair in his hand and pulled me enough so I could see his face. The desire in his eyes was enough to make me tighten, and we both panted.

"Are you sure?" Elias panted, and I nodded. "I mean it. After this, you're mine. I could never let you go, Harper. Do you understand?" I nodded again, the desire, the need taking over my ability to speak. I just knew that I needed Elias right now. I didn't care what it meant, but he already had me, mind, body, and soul. There was nothing else he could take.

"We can't complete the bond tonight. You're too weak," Elias said as I tried to get to his mouth again. "But soon."

"Geez, Elias, shut up!" I exclaimed, and he chuckled. How was it that he was so level-headed? And yet, I was almost foaming at the mouth to feel him on me and in me. He stood up with me still clinging to him, and I wrapped my legs around his body as he moved to the bed. He tried to lay me down, but I refused to let him go and pulled him down on top of me and between my legs. Elias managed to disentangle from me and lifted me enough to slide the t-shirt off over my head. He began kissing down my body until he reached my breasts. I felt his breath tickle against one of my nipples before feeling his tongue flicking at them. I gasped at the feel, and a warm current rushed through my body. I arched my back as his mouth covered my nipple and his tongue swirled around it.

Elias ran a hand down my torso, hooked it under my leg, and lifted it to his shoulder before his hand continued to between my legs and his fingers ran against the outside of my already wet folds. I gasped again as his fingers found my clit and began rubbing slowly in circles. Each rotation increasing pressure. I grabbed at his hair as the heat intensified in my body. The sparks from his touch were already bringing me close to my first orgasm. I cried out as it hit and tried to push myself more into his hand.

"Elias, please," I cried. "I need you." I cried out again as he bit down on my nipple. "Goddess, please," I pleaded, and he rolled his eyes to look up at me, and I almost lost it again. Elias let go of my nipple and watched me as he slowly pushed a finger inside me. I saw the desire in his eyes increase to full-on lust as he felt how excited he was making me. He groaned at the feeling as I tried to hold on. But I could feel another wave about to hit as he pulled his finger out and pushed in two the next time. I cried out and gripped his arm as he began a slow, steady rhythm. I wanted to both feel him speed up and also take his time so I could savour each sweet stroke of his fingers as he watched me writhe under his control. I could feel the heat beginning to rise again. Elias looked down at me, a glint of something in his eye, and I felt as he curled his fingers inside me and smashed them against me inside. I screamed as pleasure washed over me and it felt like fireworks went off in my head. Elias didn't stop the action, and I came again before I had recovered from the last one. He pulled out his fingers, and I lay in a shaking mess as I basked in the haze of the post-orgasm.

Elias moved off the bed, and I followed him with my eyes as I saw him unbutton his pants. I sat up quickly and grabbed his hands before he could finish. Kneeling in front of him on the bed, I kissed down his chest slowly as I played my hands over the waistband of his pants. I mimicked his own movement when I reached his nipple and took it into my mouth and sucked, applying gentle pressure with my teeth. I heard Elias hiss and looked up to see him looking down at me, his eyes almost a full shade of gold. I unhooked the last button of his slacks and pushed them down past his hips. Elias stepped back away from me and pulled the slacks off. He had clearly forgotten underwear after the shift, and he was now standing naked in front of me. I looked up and down his toned torso, and my eyes rested on his large and very ready member. I bit my lip as he moved closer, and he cupped my chin so that I was looking up at him. He leaned down and kissed me again, and I wrapped my arms around his neck again as we deepened the kiss once more. Elias pushed back onto the bed so that I was laid back down, and he was positioned between my legs. I felt his tip rub against my entrance and moaned from desire. Elias broke the kiss and looked down at me.

"Harper Kirby, in the name of the goddess, I love you with everything I have and everything I am." He rubbed his nose against mine. "Whatever is mine belongs to you, from now until forever. Do you understand?" I nodded again. I didn't know what to say. I could feel the weight of his words, and I felt them, too. I was his. Everything about me was only his. It always had been. He didn't need to claim me in the bond. I was already his. But I didn't know how to say what I felt. I tried to convey my feelings, but I choked up and could feel tears in my eyes.

The head of his member grazed my entrance again. I moaned again and looked up into his eyes, which were full of adoration. His eyes were very much filled with the gold of his rank again and raw, and I could feel the need burning through his body. I nodded and in one quick forceful motion; he thrust himself deep into me. I arched my back and cried out once more. He stayed still within me, his eyes closed as he controlled his breathing and himself. He opened his eyes again and smiled down at me.

"Harper, I love you," he said again before moving back out again, not getting all the way before thrusting back into me again. His pace became more fluid and quicker, and he found my neck with his mouth nipping and biting along my collarbone.

I honestly thought I was completely done from the foreplay, but was surprised to feel the build-up of tension inside me again. Only this was different. There was something more carnal, more feral about it this time, and I could feel something surging through my body, getting stronger and stronger with each powerful thrust. I felt like I was too big for my own skin and desperately wanted to be set free from what was binding me to this prison. The feeling got stronger and stronger, and just as I felt like I was going to pass out, I erupted. I saw explosions of colour as I screamed his name. I felt like I couldn't possibly be contained in this shell anymore as wave after wave of orgasm ripped through me over and over.

I dug my nails into Elias' back, riding the ecstasy, and he pounded into me over and over again. I heard him moan my name before, with a final thrust and a roar, he climaxed inside of me. He collapsed onto me, panting, his member still inside me, twitching and sending smaller aftershocks through my body.

We stayed there connected in the body for I don't know how long, as we both took time to come back down to our bodies. At some point, he lifted his head and looked at me with glazed eyes before kissing me on the nose. I smiled up at him, feeling so complete and so loved at this moment. He moved and pulled himself out, and I felt empty suddenly.

Elias collapsed beside me on the bed, and I pushed my aching body to curl up against him. I felt his arm loop under me, and he pulled me closer. Somehow he managed to pull the covers over our naked, trembling bodies, and I slipped into the post-shift and post orgasm hazed sleep. I felt Elias tight his arm around me further, so I was almost completely laid on his chest, and I felt him kiss my head as his hand played up and down my back. I fell asleep cocooned in the warmth of his body and knowing and feeling loved.

CHAPTER 61

Harper

I woke up still in Elias' arms. I felt warm and comfortable and smiled as I snuggled further into him and closed my eyes to go back to sleep. I ran my thumb down the ring finger of my left hand by instinct, and my heart jolted when I didn't feel the ring there. Somewhere in the back of me, Maia shifted around. It was common for our wolf's side to disappear for a few hours after the first shift, so I wasn't worried that I hadn't heard from her. I could still feel her and knew she was happy. And so was I. I had never felt more content, more complete than I did at this point. It was like Elias filled up an empty space in me I really didn't even know existed. I couldn't understand it. It was never like this with Colton. Urg! Just the thought of that weasel was enough to put a bad taste in my mouth. I was so happy that Elias knew about his plans to attempt to take over. And even happier that Elias wasn't in the least bit concerned. In fact, he had seemed more amused that Colton thought he had a chance.

But that didn't stop the issue that Elias didn't know I was Council and why I was really here. I got a terrible feeling in my stomach at the thought of him finding out. Or at least finding out the wrong way, that way being that Colton was about to tell him. That meant that I still had to work with Colton, or at least make him think I was working with him. I didn't know what I was going to do. I knew Nathaniel wouldn't just take my word, that Elias wasn't connected to the Circle. I needed something more concrete. Once I could prove that Elias wasn't a threat, then maybe I could get Colton off my back and explain the truth of who I was to Elias.

Colton seemed to think that the answers were in the safe in Elias' office, and I had a feeling that he was right. If I could get into the safe, I could show that there wasn't anything there. After our talk the other evening, I had sent some requests back to the Council for some information about the Crescent Dawn pack. I had a feeling that the combination to the safe was in that information.

I sighed. Now that my brain was racing, I knew there was no way I was getting any more sleep. I pulled myself slowly from Elias' grip and out of bed. Thankfully Elias remained asleep, so I found the t-shirt from last night, pulled it on quickly, and headed out of the room. I made my way to my room and let myself in. A glance at the clock on the bedside table told me that it was a little after 4am. So, it was still early for anyone to be up, and from its sound, the party had also wound down downstairs. I rushed over to my bedside table and picked up my mobile phone. There were several messages on there. Two from Louise telling me she saw Elias and me coming in and had retrieved my dress from the clearing, and the second that she was excited for me with lots of hearts. I smiled at the messages for a minute before looking at the others. There was a message from Aaron about the information I wanted. He may have been one of the Council's best researchers, although he focused on the supernatural lore normally. But he came through with the details of the Crescent Dawn pack, including the dates of the first battle that Elias had told me about and the date of the second one where his sister had been taken. He also said that something didn't sit right with him, and he would do more research and be careful.

The final message was from Nathaniel. He wanted to know how far I had got and said Drake had been sniffing around again. A cold feeling went down my spine at the thought that Drake was still watching out. I knew he was keen to get me in his claws again and that Nathaniel had done a lot of work to ensure that I didn't end up back under his control. I didn't remember too much from the time at Drake's mansion, but I was sure that I didn't want to go back. I could tell from Nathaniel's message that he was getting impatient, which I understood. I wanted to get this finished myself.

I quickly pulled on some clothes and pulled my hair into a ponytail. Tucking my phone and some other things into the pocket of my jeans, I headed down to the first floor, where the offices were. It was dark along the corridor as I headed towards Elias' office. I got to the door and pulled out my lock picking kit, and worked on the lock to open the door. It was a simple enough task, and I soon gained entry into the dark office. I put the torch on my phone on low so that I had a little light but not enough to alert someone through the windows that there was someone here. I found the safe tucked into the corner of the office and quickly assessed the make and model. My initial thoughts were right. There was no way I was going to crack the safe. I was good at what I did, but this was built to withstand even werewolf hearing and strength. The only way I was getting this open was with the code. I sighed, opened my notes app, and looked at the numbers I had written. I had four sets of numbers. Elias struck me as a sentimental type, even though he hid it from most. The first date I tried was the date of the first battle or the date his parents met. That didn't work. I then tried his sister's birthday and the date his sister was taken, again, no luck. The last date was the date that his sister's body was found, and when the red light flashed to say it was the wrong combination, I huffed in frustration.

I sat back on my heels and glared at the safe as if I could open it with the power of my mind. I was sure that one of those numbers would have worked. But now, I was back to square one. Of course, I could just ask him to open the safe, maybe. If I told him why I had been sent and that, I just wanted to show that he wasn't who they said he was. But something inside me told me I didn't want to do that. I sighed and glanced at the safe again. For some reason, I couldn't see the combination being something random. Everything inside me told me it was of some significance to him. But what else was important to Elias? His family, and maybe…

I stared at the safe, an idea forming, but quickly pushed it aside. No, that wasn't going to be it. There was no way that Elias would have done that. I looked at the safe again, and with shaking hands, typed in another set of numbers. I was shaking my head. There was no way this would work. I hit the last number, the green light hit, and the safe unlocked. I shook my head in disbelief. I couldn't believe that worked. I felt both happy and scared that the combination was recently changed to the day after I came to town. The day we had first met just a few days ago.

I shook myself. I couldn't get caught up in the warm fuzzy feelings I was getting right now. I needed to get the evidence to clear his name and get this closed down once and for all. I pulled the door open and saw that the safe was full of papers. There were the usual things there. A passport and some other official documents. Then a file marked pack businesses, a file with my name on it that I was very tempted to look in, and then finally, at the bottom, a thick file marked "The Circle." I pulled the file out, my hand shaking. Suddenly I felt sick. Why would Elias have a file on The Circle if he wasn't a part of the Circle? I was hoping to find something which explained the other packs, but it was here plain as day. The information in this file covered the Circle. I opened the file to see a top layer marked with yesterday's date that detailed the shipping route of some containers set to travel through town during the ball. It was all here, details of the shipment, what was in it, and even the details of the next three routes. I flicked through the papers quickly until I landed on a picture of a familiar face. She was older, but I could still recognise the face of Donna Tobbins looking up from the picture. There was a note scribbled on top of the paper saying NEUTRALISED. I continued to look through, and there were maybe thirty or so smaller files with people's names and pictures, including Donna's parents, and even Greg Henderson was in there. All were saying that same word in them. NEUTRALISED. I recognised so many of the people. It was now occurring to me that I hadn't seen any one of the people in this file in town since I had returned. I thought back to what Louise had said. How she had heard people being tortured in the cells next to her, and my body began to shake with the realisation of what I was seeing. Right in front of me was the evidence I was looking for. Not the evidence to clear Elias, but the evidence that showed as clear as day that Elias was very much a member of the Circle.

I had tears streaming down my face as I recalled him saying he had pulled his resources to find his sister's killers. Was the Circle one of his resources? Had he joined them to be able to get revenge? I quickly snapped pictures of the files and sent them in a message to Nathaniel. I couldn't believe that I had misjudged and allowed myself to fall in love with someone so awful. I had tears streaming down my face when my phone lit up as a message came through.

"Good girl," the message from Nathaniel said. "This is everything we need. Be ready. We are moving in immediately." I should have been happy. I had completed my mission. Just like that, I had found a member of the Circle, and this was great news. So why did I feel like half of my soul had been ripped out? I glanced through the papers again and saw another set of papers, this time with faces I had seen in town. There was one with Katie's picture and one with Alex on too. Alex's file had POTENTIAL ASSET written over the top.

I was about to open the file and look deeper when the room flooded with light suddenly. I grabbed my dagger from my boot as I turned to face the door. Standing in the doorway was a very angry-looking Elias. There was no love in his eyes, no trace at all. It was all monster. The Elias I thought I knew was nowhere to be seen, and what was left made me involuntarily shrink in fear.

"What the hell are you doing?" he spat, and I tried to think of an explanation as to why I was here. I only needed six or so hours, and the Council would be here. Hell, I just needed to get out of this room, and I could hide for that amount of time.

"Elias, I-" I started, but his growl cut me off. He rushed at me quicker than I anticipated and knocked the dagger from my hand. I tried to duck out of the way as he swung at me, but he grabbed hold of my ponytail, and I felt myself flying face-first into the wall. I looked up as the world turned to black, as I lost consciousness. The last thing I saw was the furious eyes of my mate.

CHAPTER 62

Harper

I woke up to the sound of voices arguing. I kept my eyes closed and tried to assess the situation without alerting anyone to the fact that I was awake. I could tell that I had been put in a chair, and both my hands and legs were tied to it. I tried flexing slightly, but the ropes holding me down gave me no movement. Fuck, I really didn't know how I was going to get out of this one. I had a feeling that my usual charm wasn't going to go very far.

I could tell the voices were Elias and Marcus, although they were whispers and even with my hearing barely audible.

"Just don't go crazy," I heard Marcus. "It could all be a misunderstanding. Give her a chance to explain her side of the story."

"I think it's pretty clear whose side she is on, don't you?" Elias whispered back. "I knew there was something odd about her story. I should have listened."

"Boss, please, she's your mate," Marcus pleaded.

"And that makes it so much worse. The fact that she can betray her mate so easily makes me sick." The venom in Elias' voice was clear, and it took all my control not to flinch at it.

"Boss-" Marcus started, but Elias made a shushing sound, and the room went quiet.

"I know you are awake." I heard louder and closer, making me jump slightly. "I can feel your fear." I opened my eyes to see that Elias was sitting in a chair in front of me. His back was straight, and his face was impassive, but his eyes were fuelled by pure cold hatred.

"You have every right to be scared," he said, and the corners of his mouth turned into a half-smile. I could tell by his posture, voice, and how he looked at me. He meant it, and he meant to hurt me. I resisted the urge to gulp or to struggle in the chair. I wasn't going to give this evil bastard the pleasure of that.

"Now," he said in an almost flat tone. "I am going to ask you some questions, and if you answer them quickly and correctly, then this will go a lot easier for you."

"Boss," Marcus said, and I looked up at him standing behind Elias. He looked very uncomfortable and wouldn't quite meet my eyes.

"If you don't answer the questions, well then...." Elias's voice trailed off, but a sideways glance at a rolled-up canvas pouch finished the sentence for him. I recognised the type. I had one myself. I didn't like torture, but that wasn't to say I hadn't done it when it was needed.

"Boss, please," Marcus said again, and Elias sighed.

"Marcus, if you can't be here, then fine, but mind yourself, or I might start to wonder who your loyalty belongs to." Marcus visibly flinched at that, and he finally made eye contact with me. The look in his eyes scared me the most. He was worried, worried for me. Things really didn't look good.

"I'm not going anywhere," he hissed at Elias, and Elias nodded his head.

"Good," he said. "Then let's begin, shall we?"

He looked directly at me, and I met his glare with unwavering confidence. I was sure I had been in worse situations than this and had got out of them. I think I was sure, anyway.

"Who do you work for?" Elias asked. Straight to the point, I see.

"Go to hell," I spat at him, and he smiled a little.

"Oh, I have no doubt about that, my dear," he said. "Maybe you can save me a seat." He leaned over and sniffed the surrounding air. Just his closeness was enough to confuse my senses. How could I love someone so evil, first Colton and now Elias? The moon goddess really had a thing for bad guys and me, didn't she? But maybe I could use that. He hadn't moved away, and I could tell that he needed my scent as much as I needed his.

"Elias please," I pleaded. "I'm sorry. I was just curious." I tried to put on a vulnerable act. Men loved that, saving the damsel in distress, even from themselves. I felt Elias shift closer to me and felt his breath on my neck.

"I would do anything to believe you," he whispered, and I felt his nose graze my neck. I closed my eyes and tried to pull myself against him. "I want to believe that you were just in the wrong place, that you never meant anything other than curiosity." I felt his hand in my hair a second before he yanked my head back. I yelped in pain, and I found myself face to face with him again.

"But I know that you are lying to me," he spat. "I know that you have betrayed me, your own mate." He let go of my hair and stood up and walked to the other side of the room.

"I should have known," he said, not looking at me. "You betrayed your mate before. Of course, you could do it again." He turned and looked at me.

"Or maybe you didn't. Maybe it was all a lie." He stalked towards me with fury on his face. "Was this all a ploy? Did you and Stokes have a good laugh after I told you my deepest, painful moments?" He glared at me, and I could see the hurt in his eyes, and despite everything he was doing to me, I felt somewhere inside me like all I wanted to do was soothe his pain.

"Please, Elias," I pleaded, tears running down my face. "Please, I didn't want to hurt you." He growled in response.

"You are a liar," he growled and turned and punched a wall before turning on me again. I flinched at the hate in his eyes as he was about to say something else, but then something happened. Something I didn't understand. It was like his body jerked and his eyes went black. I looked on in fear at what was looking down at me. I didn't know what it was, but it wasn't Elias. Even in his fury, whatever this was, was cold, evil, and soulless. I felt frozen in fear and even heard Maia whimper in the back of my head.

"Oh my goddess," I whispered. "What are you?"

Marcus seemed to jump to attention all of a sudden and jumped in between whatever it was and me.

"No, you leave her alone," he said, and the creature just laughed.

"Like you could stop me, you pitiful little wolf," the voice that came out of Elias' throat was deep and guttural, again, nothing like Elias.

"But you protect her from me," the thing said, and Marcus stiffened as if ready to fight, and the thing in Elias' body nodded.

"Good, now protect her from him, or I will do it for him." The thing looked at me and smiled, but I felt a chill run down my spine from it. He then looked back at Marcus. "He won't like it if I have to do it myself." He looked back at me with a smile, and then the black bled out, and the familiarity of Elias's eyes was back. He looked confused for a moment as he looked between Marcus and me.

"What the!" he exclaimed, and Marcus stiffened again.

"He said not to hurt her," Marcus said, and stood taller. Elias looked at me, the confusion still on his face, but then it cleared, and his face fell into a blank look again.

"I won't have to if she answers my questions," he said and walked to the table where the black pouch was.

He stood in front of it for a couple of minutes before turning around and looking at me. He then untied the pouch and unrolled it. I could see glints of silver as it unrolled, and a new fear crept in. I could tell that Elias meant business. He turned and looked at me again and then pulled something out. I tried to see what instrument he planned on torturing me with, but he quickly pocketed it before coming and sitting back in the seat in front of me.

"Now, let's start again," he said, and a shiver ran down my spine.

"Did you come here to spy on me?" he asked, his eyes capturing mine. I knew there was no way that I was going to be able to sweet talk myself out of this. I looked him square in the face and sighed.

"Yes!" I said clearly, and heard Marcus gasp. I glanced up at him quickly and saw that he looked at me, hurt on his face.

"Good. The truth, finally," Elias said. He picked up my phone and looked at it. "And what was the reason for your mission? What did you hope to gain from spying on me?" he asked, and I glared at him.

"To take you down, you son of a bitch," I snarled. "To stop you from what you were doing." How could he even ask that? Why else would he be so protective of his operations if it wasn't to get away with the evil things that his Circle does?

"So you mean to stop my plans?" he asked, and I nodded.

"Damn straight, I do. I don't know how you think you have the audacity to be even shocked by it, you evil bastard," I spat again. "Do what you want to me. I've already sent evidence to my superior. We will take you down," I screamed at him.

It wasn't just shouting at an evil man like the one in the club the other week. This wasn't just another mission to me anymore. This man had broken down my barriers and got me to trust that he was even remotely good, and I felt every bit the fool I was for doing so. I put all my anger into that, all the pain that I was feeling right then. Elias just sat there, unmoving, unflinching. Like this didn't even bother him one bit. He looked down, pulled something out of his pocket, and then looked at me. If I hadn't been staring at him, I would only have seen the cold hardness, but I saw the flash of something else again for just a moment. It was that hurt that angered me the most. How dare he be hurt?

"Last question," he said. "I already know the answer, but I want you to admit it to my face," he said. "Who do you work for?"

"And I said go to hell, you son of a bitch," I spat back at him. Elias sighed and looked down at the sharp tool in his hand.

"Fine, we'll do it the hard way," he said.

Just then, there was shouting from outside, and part of me hoped The Council had got here just in time. The door burst open, and Tommy came flying in.

"Elias, stop!" he shouted. "She's not The Circle!"

Both Elias and I glanced at each other in confusion, and then at the same time, we both looked at Tommy and exclaimed.

"What!"

CHAPTER 63

Elias

"Fine, we'll do it the hard way," I said as I handled the rough handle of the scalpel. This was no ordinary scalpel, though. The blade was coated in silver and soaked in wolfsbane to maximise pain. It was one of the most effective tools I owned and required the least effort. I wanted so desperately to get this over with. The last thing I wanted to do was torture the love of my life. But she betrayed me. Not only had she managed to open my safe, thanks to my stupid sentimentality. But a quick hack into her phone saw that she had sent images of the contents, contents that I didn't want anyone seeing, to some contact of hers called Nathaniel. I had no idea why, but that name sounded so familiar.

It hurt so much that she had betrayed me, but I just needed her to admit that she was The Circle. Then I would finish this once and for all and-

"What?" the guttural growl inside my head asked. "You will kill her? You couldn't do it. I would make your pitiful life a misery if you did." I sighed silently and looked at my mate tied to the chair in front of me. Why did it have to be her? Why did she have to be the one working for that damn poisonous organisation? It didn't matter. I couldn't let them stop me. I had to take them down.

I moved towards my beautiful mate, barely an inch, when there was a commotion outside, and then Tommy Kirby burst into the room and shouted at me.

"Elias, Stop! She's not the Circle." My eyes widened as I looked at Harper and saw the shock on her face too, before I turned to Tommy.

"What!" I exclaimed, and was shocked again that Harper echoed my sentiment.

"Tommy!" I exclaimed. "What are you talking about?"

"Circle!" I heard Harper exclaim at the same time, "Damn right, I'm not the bloody Circle. He is, the evil bastard." I turned and looked at Harper again.

"What?" I asked in confusion, and then Marcus started to laugh. I looked over at him as his full-on belly laugh filled the room, like he had just heard the funniest joke in the world. He was bent over with tears streaming down his face, and I glared at him while wondering if he had gone mad.

"Marcus, what the hell?" I shouted, and he looked up at me and laughed again.

"Seriously, we are all idiots," he said while he calmed down from his temporary insanity. "Don't you see?" I looked from Tommy to him and then to Harper. We were all as confused as each other.

Marcus moved in between Harper and me. He bent down on his knees in front of her.

"Darling, just do us a favour and tell us in whose authority you are working?" he said, and Harper glared at him but stayed silent.

"She's with the Council," another voice sounded, and I looked around to see a very worried Louise standing behind Tommy. Tommy glanced back at her before nodding to me.

"Louise!" Harper exclaimed, and I looked around at her in horror. I was about to torture and potentially kill my own mate for no reason.

"Darling, who do you think we are working for?" Marcus asked Harper, who was still glaring at Tommy. She looked at Marcus with disgust on her face.

"I know who you work for," she said. "I wanted to be wrong, but if you are The Circle, then you deserve to burn in hell." I couldn't contain my shock.

"Harper, darling, we aren't working for The Circle," Marcus said, and her eyes widened a bit as he said it.

"But I found the evidence in the safe. It's all the Circle information, shipping times, and people you have killed!" I sighed as she spoke. I couldn't believe how messed up this had got.

I moved towards the chair to undo the ropes holding her there, and she flinched and looked up at me, the fear clear in her eyes. I stopped, slightly taken aback at her reaction. I felt the hurt slice through my heart. The hurt that my own mate was somehow terrified of me. I shook my head.

"Marcus, untie her and let's move this upstairs. I think there is some serious explaining to do here." I walked out of my office and nodded to Tommy to follow me.

We got to the third floor before I said anything.

"Did you know she was Council before she came back?" I asked.

"Yes," he said. "She never left there. She trained as an Elite warrior." I nodded as he spoke, suddenly making so much sense. Her fighting abilities, her keen sense of awareness, hell, even back a few days ago when she was trying to break into the cells. I should have known that there was more to her.

"Why didn't you tell me?" I asked.

"Would you have granted her entry?" he retorted, and I nodded. He and I both knew I wouldn't. I was paranoid enough about the people in the town. Having a trained Council warrior would have been too much.

"Did you know why she was coming?"

"No," Tommy answered. "Aaron phoned me last week, saying that they needed a man on the inside and that it was to do with the Circle. I just assumed..." he trailed off, and I nodded again.

"Aaron?" I asked, "The boyfriend?" and Tommy nodded,

"Yeah, Aaron Jacen, although he technically isn't her boyfriend," he said. "Or not anymore." I couldn't help but stiffen at that comment. Of course not. She's mine, I thought to myself.

We headed into my room, and I sat down on the sofa and looked up at Tommy.

"Last question," I asked. "How the hell did you know to come down and stop me? I mean, how did you know what we were even doing?" I asked. Tommy looked towards the door and then lowered his voice.

"Because of who she is," he said, and I was back to being confused.

"I don't understand."

"Harper doesn't know, and personally, I'd rather she didn't know. It's bad enough that she had that bloody vampire Drake chasing her around," he said and then looked at me. "Harper is the Order."

"How could she not know that she works for the Order?" I asked, and then it hit me. "Wait!" I exclaimed. "Are you saying my mate is..." Tommy nodded.

"Are you sure?" I asked, and he laughed.

"I have been sure since the day she was born," he said. "Plus, it was her fear I felt, and then I found out from Louise what her mission was, and I put it all together."

"So my mate is The Order," I said in disbelief. This was a lot to handle all at once. "Why doesn't she know?"

"Why doesn't she know what?" I looked towards the door and saw Harper, Louise, and Marcus all standing there. Harper was still looking at me with an uneasy look in her eyes.

"Why doesn't she know the full story," Tommy said and smiled at his niece. "Come in, let's get this cleared up," he said, and the three moved into the room. I stood to give space on the sofa, and Harper stepped back, her eyes on me. I had really screwed up. I had hit her in anger and threatened to torture and kill her, but there was something else that was causing this reaction. I could feel it. I just didn't know what. I stepped away from the sofa and gestured to it, and she moved and sat down, her eyes never leaving mine.

"Okay," Tommy said. "Let's start with the most obvious thing right now. No one in this room works for The Circle," he said, and Harper looked down at her hands and then back up at her uncle.

"But the evidence in the safe, it's all Circle paperwork," she said.

"You're right," I said, and she looked at me. "The shipping information, the cargo stuff, all of it. It's the Circle. But I have it to take them down, not as a part of them." Harper continued to watch me as I spoke.

"I have been systematically taking down units of the Circle for the last six or so years."

"We have been," Marcus said, pride showing clearly on his face. Harper looked at him and smiled before looking back at me.

"The attack on my pack, the one that took my sister," I said, and Harper nodded. "That was The Circle, and I have been hellbent on taking them down ever since. It just took me a while to build my army."

"So that is why you have been taking over the packs?" Harper asked, and I nodded.

"My information led me to the fact that the Circle was using isolated packs to move their shipments, hiding in the packs. I was invading and taking over, clearing out the corrupt element and rebuilding the packs myself, something I couldn't do for my own pack," I said, looking down. I hated that my father had let go of our pack. I understood it, but still hated that we couldn't rebuild it.

"I always kept one of the corrupted ones so I could get as much information about the Circle before deciding what to do with them," I said. I could see that Harper was thinking through everything that I was saying. She looked up at me, uncertainty on her face.

"But this pack, do you mean to say that the Circle operated here?" she asked, the upset clear on her face.

"Harps, this pack has been one of the central points for the Circle ever since Alfred Chambers stole the Alpha title from my father." Harper looked at Tommy in shock.

"Grandad Samual was the Alpha?" she asked, and Tommy nodded.

"Yeah, that's partly why Daniel brought your dad on as pack financial advisor," he said, and Harper shook her head.

"No," she said defiantly. "You are not saying that my dad was working for the Circle."

Tommy went over and kneeled down in front of her. "Sorry, Kid," he said. "I hated it, but he was angry after our dad left. He said he abandoned his family." Harper shook her head again, and I could see tears on the brim of her eyes. Tommy pulled her into a hug, and she muttered something that I didn't quite hear. I was so desperate to go over and comfort her, but kept my distance. She pulled away from her uncle and looked at me.

"So Colton?" she asked, and I nodded. "Yeah, he's the Circle, or the last ranked member, well, him and the scared little shit Damien."

Harper nodded. "So if this pack is such a major pack for the Circle, why did you only just come now?"

"Because I only just called them in," Tommy said, "After Darren was killed-"

"Wait, what!" Harper exclaimed, "My dad was killed?" and Tommy nodded.

"Yeah, there was some altercation, and Darren said that he wouldn't do what Daniel wanted, and Daniel killed him for it." Harper watched her uncle in horror, and I couldn't stand any more of the pain she was feeling, I could feel it through the bond.

"Okay, that's enough for tonight." I looked down at my watch. "Or today rather, as it's almost 6am. We can talk more later when we have all rested." I looked around the room at everyone and saw nods from almost everyone. Everyone but Harper. She was simply staring into space. I moved towards her, and she jumped up from the sofa and moved away.

"Okay, well then, I guess I should go to my room," she said and headed for the door.

"I don't want you alone right now," I said, and she stopped but didn't turn around.

"I need to be away from you right now," she said quietly. But it still hit me like a train. It was me she was avoiding.

"It's okay," Louise said with a nervous smile. "I'll stay with Harper." Harper nodded.

"And I'll set up guard outside her room," Marcus said. Harper sighed in response.

"Fine, whatever," she huffed, and headed out the door without looking back. Louise followed quickly, and Marcus shrugged and followed them. I glanced at Tommy, and he shook his head.

"It's a lot for her," he said. "Give her time." He then followed the others out the door. But I knew this wasn't anything to do with all the revelations. This was something else. There was a reason why my mate was scared of me, and I needed to find out.

CHAPTER 64

Harper

I couldn't sleep. My head was so full of questions and scenarios. I couldn't help going over all that I had heard over and over. I sat on the window seat in my room and just stared out of the window, not really seeing anything other than the thoughts in my head.

And those eyes! No matter how much the other things pushed forward in my mind. Those eyes, the deep black vacuum that I saw in them, just kept coming back to me. I had seen a lot as an Elite Warrior, but I don't think I had ever seen anything like that.

"Hey, Harps?" I heard a voice and jumped slightly. I had been so lost in my thoughts that I had forgotten that Louise was still here. I looked around to see her sitting up in my bed, her hair ruffled and her eyes still full of sleep. "Did you sleep at all?" she asked.

"No, she didn't," a muted voice from the other side of the door answered. Marcus sounded disapproving as he spoke. "She wouldn't eat either."

I smiled. He had come in about an hour ago, offering to get breakfast for me. I had politely declined his offer, and he had grumbled something about me being difficult and stubborn. I smiled as we heard him mumble something similar now. Louise watched the door and laughed.

"Get used to it," she said and looked at me, smiling. "I think stubborn is our Harp's middle name." I stuck my tongue out at her, and she laughed again. Then her face fell into her no-nonsense Louise look.

"Seriously though, Harps," she said. "You need to sleep, even if just for a few hours." I looked at the clock beside my bed. It had only been a couple of hours since we had left Elias' room. I sighed.

"I can't sleep," I said. "To be honest, I think I'm getting a headache, but I can't stop all these thoughts racing." I rubbed my temples and stood up from the window seat and stretched. "I'm going for a shower," I said. "See if I can clear my head."

I headed for the bathroom. I took my time in the shower, letting the almost scalding water flow down my body in hopes of washing away the turmoil that was going on in my head. After about half an hour and when my skin was very red, I gave up and got out. I wrapped a towel around myself and delayed leaving the bathroom a bit longer by brushing my teeth and hair and whatever else I could think of. Sighing, I finally opened the door, feeling the rush of cool air from the bedroom prickling my skin.

I walked into the room, and the first thing I saw was Elias sitting on the sofa. He stood up as soon as I laid eyes on him, and I fought the urge to step back. My mind was so conflicted. Everything in me wanted to run to him, to seek comfort in him, but then those eyes, the ones I saw earlier. The thing that had taken over Elias' body. That stopped me, and my blood ran cold at the thought of it.

"What are you doing here?" I snapped without thinking and then closed my eyes and took a breath. I opened my eyes again to see him just watching me. I looked over to see Louise sitting on the bed, looking rather uncomfortable. She mouthed an apology, and I shook my head and smiled at her, so she knew that I wasn't annoyed at her.

"Can we talk?" Elias asked, drawing my attention back to him. "Please, Harper, I need to explain." He stepped towards me, and I stepped back involuntarily and shook my head.

"Sorry, I-" I stopped talking because I didn't know what to say. Did I want to say that I was afraid of him? Was I afraid of him? No, I wasn't, but there was something in him I was afraid of. And I didn't like that. I had no idea what it was.

"Okay," I said quietly and saw Elias visibly relax at my agreement.

I looked at Louise and smiled, and she nodded.

"I'll just go see what my mate is doing," she said and headed towards the door. She opened it and looked at Marcus, who was leaning against the wall, looking sullen. I could see a bruise forming on his left eye. I raised my eyebrows to Elias, and he just shrugged. "I'll take this one to get some food too," Louise said, and Marcus shook his head.

"Nope," he said, glancing at Elias and then at me. "I'm staying right here."

"Marcus, she is safe," Elias growled, and I couldn't help the amused grin appear on my face.

"It's okay, Marcus," I said. "If he gets out of hand, I'll throw him out of the window." I winked, and Marcus grinned.

"Bloody deserves it too," he grumbled, but nodded. He glared at Elias one last time and then nodded again. He then let Louise pull him down the hallway. I walked over and closed the door, and turned to face Elias, suddenly nervous that we were both alone in the room.

I gestured for him to sit down again, and he sat down at the far end of the sofa. I smiled, knowing he did it to give me the illusion of safety. But I sat at the other end, anyway. We sat in awkward silence for a good few minutes before I felt like I was going to burst if someone didn't say something.

"So," I said, maybe a little too loud, and Elias looked at me expectantly. "Marcus is pretty pissed off at you right now," I said, and Elias chuckled.

"Yeah, just a bit," he said, rubbing his face. "His type takes their job seriously. He is from a strong Gamma Warrior bloodline, so the second he knew you were my mate, you became his number one priority."

"Wow," I said. I knew he was persistent, but not to this degree. "Even against you?" I asked, and he nodded.

"Yeah, he was pretty conflicted earlier in the office," he said. "I know he is loyal to me, but everything in his blood was telling him he had to protect you." I nodded. I remembered the worried look on Marcus' face and how he had tried to stop Elias.

"About earlier," Elias said, suddenly looking nervous as he looked down at his fingers. He looked up at me, and I could instantly see the sadness in his eyes. "I can't apologise enough. I shouldn't have reacted the way I did. I feel sick that I hit you and what I was willing to do. I should have listened to you." I held my hand up to stop him from talking.

"Don't," I said. "I get it. You were protecting your pack. I'm a warrior, Elias. I know the dangers." I chuckled and shook my head. "Hell, I'm more annoyed at myself than you." He looked at me in surprise.

"Why? I mean, I'm the one that acted rashly without thinking," he asked.

"Yeah, but I'm an Elite warrior, trained by one of the best organisations in the world. I am meant to be one of the best warriors, and yet I let you get the drop on me," I said. "I was trained way better than that." Elias looked at me like I had gained an extra head or something.

"I hit you, knock you out, and threaten to torture you, and you are annoyed at yourself?" he asked, and I shrugged. He let out a laugh that was laced with relief, and I smiled. Sure, I could have been angry at him, but let's face it, I was a threat in his eyes, and I would have probably done the same if the situation had been reversed. Elias looked at me and smiled.

"So I'm forgiven?" he asked tentatively, and I laughed.

"Oh hell no, prepare to have your ass kicked sometime soon. A woman needs to defend her honour," and he laughed again.

"Okay, I can deal with that. I am curious as to how I would fare against one of the top Council warriors. And maybe a little proud that person also happens to be my mate."

He leaned toward me, and I couldn't help but flinch and move away. Elias looked shocked again and hurt. I sighed and rubbed my temples. The headache that had been forming seemed to have dissipated a little, but I was sure it was just on the other side of something waiting to get through again. I stood up from the sofa, headed to my suitcase, and pulled out some panties and a pair of jeans. I shimmered into the panties before letting the towel drop and pulled the jeans on. I could feel Elias's eyes on me the whole time and even felt them when he moved from the sofa to stand behind me.

I was frozen in place with a bra in my hand when I felt the tips of his fingers run down my back. Part of me wanted to move away, but the strongest part, the one that felt the current from the mate bond, wanted to lean into him so badly.

"What is it?" his voice was barely a whisper in my ear. "Why do I scare you then?" he asked, and I shook my head.

"You don't," I whispered, and I felt his hand firmer on my arm.

"You're lying, Harper," he said. "I can tell that there is something else, and it has you terrified."

I turned around to look at him. I looked into his beautiful blue eyes and marvelled at the clear blue in the centre that was circled by the dark inky blue around the edge. They were something I could get lost in, unlike... I shivered at the thought of those empty black eyes again.

"There," he said, his fingers under my chin while his other hand traced my arm, which was now covered in goosebumps. "That fear? What is causing it?"

"I don't understand it," I said. "But while you were interrogating me, it was like something took over your body," I said, and his eyes widened.

"He showed himself to you?" he asked. "Did he hurt you?" I shook my head and stepped back.

"He?" I asked. "You know what I am talking about?" He nodded.

"Yes and no, I know what you're talking about, but I don't know what he is. He appeared around the time my wolf did, around the attack on my pack. Just before actually." He looked over my body again and stepped forward. "He's a destructive force, but other than that, it's like there is someone else living in my body."

"Like another wolf?" I asked, "Is that even possible?"

"For a single body to have three dominant entities..." He shook his head. "It shouldn't be. Goddess only knows I have done enough research on it. But I'm coming up empty. I just try to do my best to control him." He rubbed his face again. "I was hoping that The Order would be able to help me figure it out. That's why I have been helping them with the Circle. Well, that, and getting my revenge on the man that took my sister."

"The Order," I asked. That sounded familiar, but I wasn't sure why. "Who's that?" and Elias suddenly shifted uncomfortably in his spot.

"Erm, that's who told me of the Circle's presence in the pack," he said, his tone dismissive. "But are you certain that he didn't hurt you?" he asked, clearly changing the subject. I narrowed my eyes at him. I was going to have to find out more about this Order business. I sighed and shook my head.

"No, actually, he told Marcus to protect me from you, or he would," I said, and Elias' eyes looked like they would pop out of his head.

"What!" he exclaimed, and I shrugged. He reached out and pulled me into his arms. I resisted for about half a second before allowing myself to melt into him.

"Well, I just can't understand it, but goddess, I am so glad that neither of us did something that I would regret." I felt him sniff my hair and moved my head so I could look up at him. My whole body was tingling with the bond, which felt stronger than ever. I leaned up towards him, and he reciprocated, and I felt his lips graze mine.

I pushed against him and deepened the kiss when the door to the room suddenly burst open. I jumped back in shock and covered my bare top half as the room suddenly filled with Council Warriors. Elias was pulled forward and slammed against a wall by two of them.

"Elias Owens, you are under arrest for the act of treason and murder, by order of The Council."

CHAPTER 65

Harper

"Wait!" I exclaimed as one of the warriors held Elias with difficulty while another tried to put on silver-coated and spellbound handcuffs. I pulled a top on quickly as I tried to get their attention.

"There's been a mistake," I called, but no one seemed to be listening. I saw one of the warriors that I recognised standing to one side.

"Paul," I urged. "Please, we got it wrong," I said, grabbing his arm and pulling him to face me. He just grinned at me.

"Hey, Kirby," he said. "I knew you remembered my name. Good job, by the way. Nathaniel is seriously impressed. He was singing your praises the whole way here."

"Nathaniel!" I exclaimed, and I saw Elias stiffen. "He's here? Where?" I knew Nathaniel would listen to me. He would understand the mistake and that we had the wrong person.

"He's downstairs, coordinating the warriors to pick up the traitors." I shook my head and glanced at Elias, who was now cuffed, although still fighting. I had to sort this out. This was my fault.

I ran out into the hallway and bumped into Louise and Tommy.

"What the hell is happening?" Tommy asked as I pushed past him to get to the stairs.

"The Council arrived," I called back. "They've arrested Elias." I made it to the stairs and ran down them.

"Harper!" Tommy called after me. "Stop a minute."

"No, I need to get to Nathaniel. He will sort this out," I called back. I glanced back as I reached the next set of stairs and saw both Tommy and Louise were on my heels as I ran down the stairs.

I reached the top of the main stairs and saw a swarm of Council warriors. I searched the room for Nathaniel, but I couldn't see him.

"Harps, why are they here?" Tommy asked, as I continued to search.

"When I found the stuff in Elias' safe, I sent pictures to the Council," I explained, not taking my eyes off the ground floor. I could see Marcus struggling under three warriors as they held him down and winced. I turned to Tommy. "I didn't know. I just reacted," I said. That was the real reason I couldn't be angry at Elias for what he did. I did exactly the same. Tommy grimaced, but then forced a smile.

"Don't worry, kid, we'll get it all cleared up, and then you and-" Tommy stopped mid-sentence, his eyes widening.

"What the fuck!" he exclaimed, and I followed his sight.

I didn't know what Tommy had seen because just then, I spotted Aaron and Nathaniel at the entrance of the house.

"Nathaniel!" I called as I headed down the stairs. He looked up and smiled. I could see the pride on his face and internally winced at how quickly that was going to change.

"Harper, my dear," he called. "Good work, girl. You have really come through here."

"Nathaniel you don't understand," I said as I reached him and Aaron.

"Harper..." Aaron looked concerned. "What's wrong?"

"Nathaniel, I got it wrong. Elias isn't in the Circle. Colton is!"

"What?" Aaron exclaimed. He looked over at Nathaniel, who just smiled at me.

"Harper, sweetheart, it's okay. I got the evidence we needed," Nathaniel said. "We have enough to put Owens and his men away for good. You don't have to be scared of him."

"I'm not scared. Elias was sent to stop the Circle. He's not a part of it." Why wasn't he listening?

"Harper, calm down. It's okay, I already know," Nathaniel said, and I breathed a sigh of relief.

"What, you know?" Aaron looked confused, and I looked between them, my own confusion growing.

"Don't worry. I will explain everything. You'll both understand." Then he glanced behind me, and a grin appeared on his face.

"Thomas Kirby," Nathaniel said, and I looked around to see Tommy glaring at Nathaniel. "What a pleasure."

"What the fuck are you doing here?" Tommy spat, his face twisted in anger. I glanced at Louise, and she shook her head.

"Now, Thomas, let's not be so rash," Nathaniel said, and Tommy growled.

"You were exiled!" Tommy growled. "You are not allowed on the territory by order of death."

"What?" I looked between them. "Nathaniel? Tommy, what are you talking about?"

"I see you have your father's spirit," Nathaniel said. "How is Samual? Did he ever come out of hiding?" I was getting more confused by the minute.

Then Tommy growled again, and I felt myself being pulled to the side as he lunged at Nathaniel. I looked around to see Aaron had grabbed me, so I wasn't in the path of the raging werewolf. I glanced back in time to see Tommy flying across the room and Nathaniel stalking toward him.

"You may be older, boy, but you still have nothing on me!" he snarled, and then I screamed as he backhanded Tommy. He glanced up at some warriors.

"Detain him. He's with the traitors," he ordered, and two warriors were on a dazed Tommy. I tried to struggle out of Aaron's grip, but his hands circled my arms like a vice.

"Nathaniel, what the hell?" I shouted, and he turned to speak when another voice came from the doorway.

"Uncle Nate, I think we've managed to locate almost all of Owens' men." I stared in shock as Colton walked up to Nathaniel, who grinned at him.

"Good work, my boy," Nathaniel said and clapped him on the back.

"No!" I exclaimed and tried to struggle out of Aaron's grip again. "Dammit, Aaron, get off me!" I snarled.

"Yes, unhand my mate," Colton said with a growl, and I growled in return as I felt Aaron's grip tighten.

"Actually," Nathaniel said, looking at me. "It might be best that you keep a hold, just for now." He walked slowly towards me. "Harper, sweetheart. Why don't we go and get a cup of calming tea, and I can explain everything to you?"

"But Colton!" I exclaimed. I glared at Colton, who was grinning at me. "He's the Circle." Why was he not listening to me? Nathaniel glanced around as he walked closer to me.

"Harper, you need to calm down," he said, holding his arms out in front of him. He then leaned right into me and whispered in my ear.

"I already know," I pulled back as my eyes widened. He just smiled again.

"Don't worry, sweetheart. I will explain everything as soon as I can." Then he turned to Colton. "Now, where is your mother? It has been a long time since I have seen my sister." I felt frozen in shock.

I was still trying to process what was going on when I heard a growl from the first floor. I looked up to see Elias being dragged down the stairs by three warriors. Even with the spellbound handcuffs, they were still having a problem controlling him. I saw his eyes were fixated on Nathaniel as he growled again.

"YOU!" he snarled and lunged down the stairs, pulling the warriors with him. He was on Nathaniel in a heartbeat, and even with his hands cuffed behind his back, he was still reaching for Nathaniel's throat with his teeth. Nathaniel roared and pushed him off with surprising ease. Elias slammed into the wall and was up on his feet in seconds.

"I've been waiting to kill you for years," he snarled, and lunged at Nathaniel again. "I want you to suffer the way my sister suffered." Nathaniel just laughed as he slammed Elias back against the wall. I saw Elias' eyes shift to that awful black as whatever the beast was took control of him.

"What the fuck!" Aaron exclaimed. "No, it's not possible."

"I see I took the wrong sibling," Nathaniel sneered as he stood over Elias' body. And everything clicked into place as I realised what he said. Nathaniel was the Alpha that had led the attack on Elias' pack. The one where his sister had been taken and then killed. An attack that was ordered by the Circle, which meant that Nathaniel was the Circle!

"But you're not an Alpha," I exclaimed. "You're a Beta." I looked over at Colton, watching me intently as all the pieces began to fall into place. Colton was Circle, and Nathaniel was Colton's uncle. Nathaniel turned and glanced at me quickly before looking back down at Elias. Or at the beast that currently controlled his body. Even though the glance was quick, it was enough time to see something that sent me reeling even further. Nathaniel's eyes were as black and soulless as Elias'. He growled down at Elias.

"Control your human, dammit," he growled, and the beast growled back.

"Stay away from her." His deep, guttural voice felt like death itself, and Nathaniel turned back and looked at me again, a sneer appearing on his face.

"Interesting, how very interesting," he said, as I felt frozen under his gaze. The beast in Elias snarled again, and Nathaniel sighed.

"I'll deal with you later." He lifted his foot and stamped it down on Elias' head, knocking him unconscious. I screamed and tried to pull myself out of Aaron's grip again.

"I'll kill you!" I screamed, but Nathaniel shook his head, his eyes switching back to blue.

"Oh, Harper dear, maybe you need a little time out, just until you calm down a little, my dear." He started walking towards me again, and I shrunk back.

"Just a little break in the cells until you start to see sense." He motioned towards a couple of warriors who headed towards me.

"It's okay," Aaron said from behind me as I started to struggle again. He twisted my arm up to my back, and I felt the sting of silver as he cuffed one of my wrists. I tried to turn and snarl at him, but he had my other arm behind my back and cuffed in seconds. "I'll take her myself."

"Good, man," Nathaniel said and clapped him on the back. I felt a push as I growled at Nathaniel again.

Aaron began pushing me out the door. I tried to struggle, but the silver was already doing its job, but I refused to give in, not while I still had strength in myself.

"Dammit, Harper," Aaron exclaimed as I swung my head back into his face. I heard him growl, and then I was lifted off my feet, and he flung me over his shoulder.

"Let me go, you bastard," I shouted and tried kicking him. He just grunted and grabbed my legs, pinning them to his body. He stopped suddenly and growled again.

"Get out of my way," he said, and I tried to look around.

"I'll take her," I heard Colton say. I felt hands on me, and then Aaron pulled back. "She's my mate," Colton growled.

"Like hell I am," I snarled back, and heard Aaron grunt a laugh.

"I got her," he growled.

"Colton, just let him take her to the cells. You can have her back when she calms down," Nathaniel called, and I glared at him.

"But Uncle Nate-"

"Dammit boy, if you are going to be the Alpha, you better start bloody acting like it," Nathaniel snapped. I guessed Colton must have moved because Aaron started moving towards the door again. I tried to struggle as he walked out into the courtyard, but the silver had taken effect, and I was pretty much as weak as a human. I settled for promises instead.

"I swear to the goddess Aaron, I will rip out your heart and feed it to you, you lying bastard," I snarled as he headed to one side of the house.

"Sure you will, darling," he chuckled, and I tried to slam my legs into him again, but he had me held secure.

"Hey dickwad, you're going the wrong way," I snarled as he headed in the opposite direction to where the cells were.

"Notice that, did you?" he chuckled again. We rounded the corner of the house, and as soon as we were out of sight, Aaron swung me off his shoulder and dumped me on the floor.

"Ow!" I exclaimed, and he grinned. He leaned down, pulled the handcuffs off me, and then crouched down beside me while I rubbed my wrists.

"Are you ok?" he asked. I replied by slapping him in the face.

"What the hell, Aaron?" I hissed, and he chuckled.

"Good thing you aren't at full strength. You meant that," he said, rubbing his cheek.

"Damn fucking straight I did," I hissed again.

"Listen, you can bitch at me all you want, but right now, we need to get somewhere safe," he said, and I shook my head.

"I don't know where. It's like no one is what they seem," I said. Just then, I saw headlights, and a car pulled up beside us. Aaron went into a fight stance, but I grabbed his arm. The window rolled down, and Louise looked out.

"Get in already. We need to get out of here. I know where to go." Aaron looked at me, and I nodded. He picked me up since I was still struggling with the after-effects of the silver. He opened the back door, put me in before running around to the front of the car, and jumped in the front.

"Where are we going?" he asked, and Louise laughed.

"I need a drink, don't you?" she said and then started the car again and drove around the corner and down the driveway of the pack house.

CHAPTER 66

Harper

I had my eyes closed and concentrated on building my strength back up from the silver while Louise drove. I had a feeling about where Louise was heading, and when the car stopped, I opened my eyes to confirm I was right. The sign for Howlers was off, and the carpark was empty, which was actually unusual for 11am. The car door opened, and Alex poked his head in.

"Hello, beautiful," he said cheerfully. "Need a hand?"

I could have refused his outstretched hand, but to be honest, I was still feeling a little weak, and despite being a stubborn bitch sometimes, I also knew that I had to accept help sometimes, too. I smiled at him and held out my hand, and he grabbed it and gently pulled me out of the car and to my feet. I wobbled a bit and sent a glare to Aaron before Alex picked me up and carried me into the bar.

It was dark inside and empty. Or almost empty. I looked around as Alex put me down in one of the booths and headed over to the bar. Sitting in the booth next to me were the two goons that I had seen at the bar a few days ago. I knew they were Elias' men but didn't know their names. Sitting next to one of the goons was an older man. He was almost completely bald with grey hair cut short. He was short but stocky and a familiar sight in the town. Harry was the owner of Howlers and also the oldest werewolf I knew. Werewolves had a reasonably long lifespan, and it wasn't unusual for us to reach well over a hundred in years, but rumours had it that Harry was at least double that. He saw me looking and flashed me a big toothy grin that I couldn't help but return despite everything going to shit.

Louise had slid into the seat beside me and was mind linking with someone, although I had no clue who. Whoever it was, she didn't seem happy. Aaron stood awkwardly looking around the bar while Alex busied himself behind the bar, making drinks. He walked over, passing Aaron a bottle of beer as he passed him and planted a glass of, from the smell, rum and coke in front of me and white wine in front of Louise. He slid into the other side of the booth and took a drink from his own bottle of beer.

"Bit early for this, isn't it?" I asked with raised eyebrows. And he laughed, although I could tell there was a hint of tension in it.

"Ha!" he said. "Not if I heard right, it isn't. We could drink this place dry, and it still wouldn't be enough."

"You bloody won't," Harry piped up. "Not unless you are gonna pay for it. And don't think I'm not watching what you are already pouring, Bennet. That'll come outta your wage." Alex rolled his eyes and grinned.

"Calm it, old man. I'm not screwing you out of your profits," he said and winked at me.

"Old man, eh?" Harry retorted. "Don't old man me, I could still put you on your ass." I smiled at the banter.

Then I remembered what was happening and shook my head.

"What do you know, Alex?" I asked, and he grimaced.

"Only what I heard in the last half hour or so," he said. "Council are in town and pulling people out of their houses, declaring them traitors for siding with Owens."

"Dammit!" Louise exclaimed and slammed her hand on the table, almost knocking her glass of wine over. "I can't get hold of Tommy," she said, and took a big gulp from the wine.

"It'll be the cuffs," I said and glanced at Aaron. "Silver-coated and spellbound, right?" and he nodded. I then looked at Louise.

"They block your wolf completely, no shifting, no linking, nothing. You are practically human." I glanced at Aaron again.

"You better come sit down. You got some talking to do," I said, and he sighed before reluctantly walking over. He slid in next to Alex, who grinned at him and then at me.

"Well, you clearly know each other. Poor man looks terrified," he said and clapped Aaron on the back. Aaron glanced at him and then at me and smiled weakly.

"Did you know?" I asked him. "Did you know that Nathaniel was setting me up or setting Elias up?" and he shook his head.

"Harps, I wasn't even supposed to be here," he said. "Nathaniel picked the task force, and I was pissed off that I was left off. So I went storming into his office, where he was arguing with Drake. It was Drake who insisted that I come along."

"Drake!" I exclaimed, and he nodded.

"Yeah, he said to keep him informed." He laughed and rubbed his chin. "I pretty much told him to fuck off. But he clearly knew something we didn't."

"Maybe get in contact then," I suggested, and he nodded.

"So you didn't know that Nathaniel was Circle?" I asked, and he shook his head.

"Hell no." He laughed. "Hell no, that's bloody apt, isn't it?" He laughed again. We all looked at him in confusion.

"What are you talking about?" I asked, and Aaron sobered up from his giggling fit.

"I heard rumours, obviously, but I thought it was bullshit," he said, and I glanced at Alex, who just shook his head and shrugged.

"Aaron," I snapped, "Sense, make some, please." He grimaced.

"I have never seen one up close, and honestly didn't think it was possible, and to think I had been working with one for so long."

"AARON!" I exclaimed loudly, and he looked at me, shocked. "For goddess sake, will you tell me what you are talking about?"

"Nathaniel's eyes," he said as if it explained everything, and then I remembered that they had gone black like Elias' had.

"Wait, do you know what that is?" I asked, and Aaron grimaced again and took a long drink before nodding.

"Yeah, I just don't quite believe it," he said. "Even in all my years of researching the paranormal, there were still things that I thought were myths." He looked at me and then back down at the table.

"Aaron darling," Louise said. "You seem sweet, and I have heard good things about you, and you are definitely easy on the eyes, but if you don't start making sense soon, I'm gonna beat down on you." She then smiled sweetly at him. I wasn't sure if Aaron was more scared of her or whatever he was talking about at this point. Alex was trying to contain his laughter, and I just smiled. Aaron looked up at me, and the look in his eyes told me this was more serious than I thought.

"Demon," he said, and Alex stopped laughing and stared at Aaron and then turned and looked at Harry, who was also staring at Aaron.

"What?" I exclaimed, "Like from hell, demon?" He nodded.

"Wait, this Nathaniel character?" Alex asked. "What's his last name?" and I glanced at Louise and back at Alex.

"What the hell does that matter?" I snapped, and he blew out a breath and glanced back at Harry.

"Right now, very much. I'd like to know on a scale of one to ten how fucked we really are."

"Bethrinton," Aaron said, and Alex paled. He looked back at Harry again, who just stood up and walked behind the bar and pulled out an expensive-looking bottle of whisky. He opened it and took a long drink. He then looked over at us all.

"Drinks are on me, kids," he said and then walked in through the room behind the bar. I looked back at Alex, who looked like he was going to vomit.

"So I guess this is a ten?" I asked, and Alex shook his head, "More like ten million," he said.

"Tommy said he was exiled," Louise said, and Alex laughed.

"Oh yeah, he was exiled, alright? The man is crazy," he said.

"He's Colton's Uncle, right?" I asked, and Alex nodded.

"Yeah, you know how Caroline Stokes isn't quite fully with us?" he asked, and both Louise and I nodded. "Well, that's hereditary. Caroline is harmless. She fights it, but Nathaniel, her brother. He was ruthless. He embraced the crazy. Neither of you were born when he was exiled. It was just before Chambers challenged Kirby for the Alpha title. I was only young, so I don't remember too much myself." Alex said, "I just remember mum being really upset and trying to get dad to leave town."

"Well, I remember everything." Harry walked out from behind the bar, holding a dusty box. "It was carnage. That son of a bitch went all-out crazy. He went up against poor Samual, telling him to stand down. Told him that The Order had lost, and he needed to hand over the town."

"The Order!" I exclaimed. "I've heard of that. Elias and Tommy mentioned something about it. Elias said that he was helping The Order."

"Can we go back to the demon thing?" Louise asked, "Are you saying that this bastard is possessed or something?" She looked at Aaron and he shook his head.

"Not exactly. Demon possession exists, obviously, but when it does, the demon is too much for the human vessel that it burns through the body in a matter of days. This is different. There are some demons born into a vessel, where one or both parents have that demon bloodline." He rubbed his face. "Like I said, it was just a myth, but basically, a demon and human can't possess one vessel at once for a significant time. The demon either sends the human part crazy or burns humanity right out of existence. They are meant to be soldiers in the wars between good and evil or something."

I stared at him while he was talking about all this, trying to wrap my head around it.

"Like the apocalypse?" Louise asked, and Aaron shrugged. She sighed. "Yup, I'm gonna need another drink."

"There are four seals, one each in a place of power. When each of the seals has been broken, then the gates of hell will open, and fire will reign on Earth."

We all looked over at Harry, who was reading from an old-looking book.

"What's that?" Aaron asked, standing up, and Harry passed him the book. Aaron looked at the front, and his eyes bulged out, and then he shook his head.

"Well, at least it's a saving grace that part of the myth is real, too." He walked over and put the book down on the table. It was made of leather and had a gold inlay on the front. I recognised the symbol straight away as the pendant that Elias had me wear the night of the ball. The one that belonged to his sister. The title of the book stood out to me, and just seeing it felt like it unlocked something in me. I wasn't aware whether I felt excited or scared.

"The Divine Order of the Angels," Alex read, and I looked up at Aaron.

"The Order?" I asked, and he nodded. Angels, demons. My head was swimming with a million questions, so many that I couldn't form any answers. And worse of all, I could feel my headache coming back on. Harry walked over and rubbed his hand on the crescent moon on the front.

"The Divine Order is four bloodlines sent to appease the demons," he said. "One for each of the seals. It is each bloodline's undertaking to protect their seal and set forth the divine warrior to counter the demon army."

Aaron opened the book and flicked through.

"Ah yes," he said and then began reading from the book. "The four seals are governed by each of the major supernatural races. This is so that one race does not hold power over another. Balance is important in this and every area."

"Four races?" I asked, "Shifter, Magic Worker, Fae, and Immortal?" Aaron nodded his head.

"That's right," Harry said. "See the crescent on the front?" He turned back to the cover, and I nodded. "That is the mark of the shifter bloodline of The Divine Order. It is worn by allies of The Order or the shifter ones." He pulled the arm of his shirt up and showed a faded tattooed version of the Crescent.

"And that is why Nathaniel Bethrinton cannot get control of this pack or this town," Harry said. I looked at Aaron again, and he shook his head.

"Why's that old man? Other than the obvious crazy demon, of course," Alex asked, and Harry grumbled about being called an old man before turning the pages in the book again. He revealed a hand-drawn map which I recognised as a much less developed version of the town, and right where the pack house was, was the crescent symbol in gold again.

"Because Midnight Moon is the location of the shifters seal," he said, and then he looked at me.

"And you Kirby girl, your family is the bloodline of the Order!"

CHAPTER 67

Harper

"I'm sorry. What now?" I stared at Harry, dumbfounded. He flicked through some more pages of the book and then turned it to face me. I apprehensively looked down at the book. The page was titled "Bloodline," and there was a picture of a wicked-looking blade down one side. The writing was a little faded and handwritten, but despite all that, it felt so familiar. I could read it like it was something I had read a thousand times before.

"The Divine Order is made up of four bloodlines. One each governs one of the four base elements: earth, air, fire, and water. Each bloodline is made up of guardians, one in each generation. The duty of the guardian is to protect the seal from demon interference, in addition to preparing and training the Divine Warrior." I looked up at Aaron. I was starting to feel a headache coming on again. This, on top of everything, was too much. He smiled and turned the book around, scanning the page.

"The Divine Warrior will lead an army to counter the demon's influence on earth. She will be recognised for her advanced and accelerated abilities in combat and keen alternative reasoning skills." Aaron glanced up at me and then back at the page. "While the number of guardians can be many, only one Divine Warrior from each bloodline can inhabit the earth at any one time. It is due to her containment of the spirit of angelic presence at her core."

"So, this Divine Warrior dude," Alex said, looking over Aaron's shoulder. "He is part-angel? Like the demon in Nathaniel?"

Aaron shrugged. "She," he corrected. "And it looks like it. I know some about the lore, but until today, I thought the Divine Order was little more than a myth. Something to make the people feel safe and protected against evil. I need my books to be able to know more."

"So, if Harper's family is this bloodline, does that make her a guardian?" Louise asked, and I scowled at her.

"Erm, nope," I said, shaking my head. "This is the first I'm hearing about this. Don't you think if I were some guardian thing, I would have known by now?"

I stood up, suddenly feeling restless. My head was pounding, and I felt like I could rip my skin off. Maybe I needed a shift. I felt inside for Maia, but the effects of the silver must still have been wearing off because I got no response.

"This is great and all," I said. "But we have a more pressing matter at hand right now." I looked at the blank faces and could feel the irritation setting in.

"You know the apparent demon wolf and his crazy nephew currently in charge in the pack house," I snapped. "Oh, and half of our people are in the cells. Shouldn't we try to break them out and find a way to take them down?" I was starting to feel sick. The headache made it hard to think, and my eyesight was beginning to blur.

"Harper, are you okay?" Louise came towards me, but her voice felt tinny. "You've gone really pale. Maybe you should sit down." I shook my head and instantly regretted it. I bent over and threw up everywhere.

"Oh, crap." I heard someone exclaim, but I couldn't make out who it was as I felt cool hands on me, pulling me somewhere. I didn't have the strength to fight them as I was lifted off my feet.

"She's burning up," someone said, and I was laid down on something soft and cool. I could feel myself slipping. I realised I was feeling the familiar signs of a panic attack and tried to move my arm to hit the pressure spot on my hand to control it, but I was already too far gone, and everything was heavy. I quickly slipped into a heavy unconsciousness, unable to stop the freefall into the black.

I woke up to the sound of raised voices. I was laid in one of the booths and could feel someone stroking my hair.

"I don't care what the book says," Aaron shouted. "I'm not having her in danger."

"It's her choice," Alex shouted back.

"It's not a choice. If she is, then she is," Harry said, his voice ringing calmly compared to the other two. "She will need to learn to contain and control it, it's not pretty, but it can be done."

"No, I want to know how to stop it! And I refuse to let her put herself in harm's way." Aaron slammed his hands down on something, and I groaned.

"Seriously, guys," I called. "Can you keep the bickering down over there?" Everyone went silent. "Thank you," I said, feeling strangely amused by the instant compliance. I heard Louise chuckle and opened my eyes to see her smiling down at me.

"She might be half-conscious, but she still commands with ease," she said, and I shrugged while attempting to sit up. I was hit by nausea and froze in place until it passed before, with Louise's help, making it all the way up to a sitting position. Yea me.

"How are you feeling?" Harry said as he handed me a glass of water.

"Like a herd of elephants has run over me," I said, taking a sip. "Twice!"

"You've cooled down for now," Harry said, feeling my head. "I don't know for how long, but you are going to have to stop fighting it."

"Fighting what?" I asked. "It was just a panic attack."

Harry grunted. "Get those panic attacks a lot, do you?" he asked, clearly amused at something.

"Most of my life," I shrugged. "But I can control them easily enough with pressure points."

"Sure," he said. "Pressure points and panic attacks." He walked away muttering something to himself, and I looked at Louise, confused. She smiled weakly, but I could tell that something was wrong.

"What?" I asked. "What is it?" I looked between her and Aaron, who had slid in on the opposite side of the booth.

"Harper, there's something you should know," he said, and Alex slid in next to him.

"Harper, do you remember me telling you about Nathaniel and how he burnt out his humanity?" Alex asked, and I nodded.

"Well, the reason for that is that both the demon and the human fight for the control of the vessel, or the body. But both are dominant, and the vessel can't take the pressure of the two dominant forms. So either one form burns out or the vessel, the person, starts to see signs of mental health decline."

"Oh, like Caroline Stokes? That makes sense." I thought back to my last conversation with Elias. "Or in a werewolf's case, three dominant forms?" I asked, and Alex looked confused.

"Harper, our wolves aren't dominant," Aaron said. "They can sometimes take over, but in essence, it is the human form that controls if and when they come out."

"Oh," I mused, "So Elias was wrong then."

"What do you mean?" Aaron asked.

"Elias," I said, suddenly realising that not everyone knew, although, by the sudden fidgeting from the next booth where the two warriors had been silent, some knew. "Elias had the same eyes that Nathaniel had, and he said that the other thing was destructive. He's got this demon thing as well, then?"

Aaron shrugged. "I did hear Nathaniel say something to Owens before rendering him unconscious," he said. "It would make sense, given the new information." He looked at Alex, and I could see the worry in his eyes.

"Aaron," I said, and he looked at me.

"Harper, Nathaniel has been in contact with me," he rubbed his temple. "Actually, he's being rather persistent."

"Mind link?" I asked, and he nodded.

"I'm trying to block it, but he isn't letting up." He sighed. "Harper, he is demanding that you return to the pack house."

"Ha!" I exclaimed. "Let the bastard demand." But I had the feeling that it wasn't so simple. "What?" I asked, feeling a sense of dread.

"Harps, the panic attacks," Aaron said, and I nodded. "We don't think they are panic attacks."

"Well then, what else would they be?" I scoffed. I had been having panic attacks since I was around fourteen years old. They were infrequent at first, but got worse. It wasn't until I learned about the pressure points that I could manage them.

"Harper, are you being intentionally dumb?" Louise scoffed, and I glared at her. I looked around at everyone, who was looking at me expectantly.

"The Divine Warrior will be recognised by her advanced and accelerated abilities in combat and keen alternative reasoning skills," Harry called over, and I looked up, the penny suddenly dropping.

"Whoa!" I exclaimed, "You aren't thinking I'm this Divine Warrior dude, are you?"

"Kind of fits," Alex said, and I shook my head.

"No, nope, not happening," I said. "I'm just a werewolf. Nothing special about me."

"Apart from the fact that you are from the bloodline," Alex said.

"And was one of the quickest rising Elite warriors in the history of the Council," Aaron added.

"No!" I exclaimed, "I don't agree. Don't you think I would have seen some angel sign by now?"

"Because of the danger to the human, the angel only activates itself in the presence of demons," Harry called from the bar.

"But Nathaniel is a demon," I said, and he nodded.

"Exactly, so now you are feeling the effects of the angel trying to come through."

"But I have been around Nathaniel pretty much constantly for the last eight years. He was my mentor," and Harry stopped what he was doing.

"Plus, this pack has had the demon bloodline in the pack house for years," Alex said. "Both Colton and Caroline are from the same bloodline as Nathaniel."

"Huh," Harry mused. "Show me that pressure point thing," he said, coming around the bar and to the table. I shrugged, but complied. I lifted my hand, pressed my thumb on the point just below my other thumb, and rubbed in a circular motion. Harry barked a short laugh.

"And who showed you how to do this?" he asked. I thought back to when I started using the pressure points to stop panic attacks.

"Well, Colton was the first to use it on me, but then it was Nathaniel that explained in detail about the different points."

"Sneaky bastards," Harry laughed again. "They've been suppressing your angel side on purpose."

"What?" I exclaimed.

"That works by reducing the circulation of your energies," he said. "You can use it to suppress the energy that is used to shift, too."

"So Nathaniel knows about Harper?" Aaron asked.

"Oh, my goddess!" Louise exclaimed, and we all looked around at her. "That's the reason why Colton went back on the rejection. He knew." Alex's eyes widened, and he let out a breath.

"Geez, I knew it was funny that Eric Stokes was so annoyed at Colton for rejecting you." He looked sheepish. "I mean, I was annoyed because he had warned me away from you a couple of years before and then rejected you, but I didn't understand why it mattered so much to the Beta and the Alpha. They must have known who you are."

I leaned back in my seat and tried to process everything. I could see the logic behind what they were saying, but didn't want to even consider that I was this special half-angel thing.

"Wait, so if I am part angel, then why did the goddess see fit to pair me with not one but two wolves with demon bloodlines?" It seemed like a cruel joke to me.

"I don't know," Aaron said. "But Nathaniel is pretty insistent that it's for your own good that you go back. He even said before you burn up."

"Well, screw that dude," I said. The thought of Nathaniel made me feel sick. He had been my mentor for eight years and had betrayed me and lied to me. I didn't want to see him again.

"But..." Louise trailed off as Alex shot her a glare.

"What?" I asked and looked around at all the silent faces. "But what?" Louise looked down at the table and Alex and Aaron but avoided my eyes too.

"Aaron!" I exclaimed, and he cursed under his breath.

"Nathaniel said that if you and Louise don't return to the pack house," he whispered. "That he will have Elias and Tommy and all the other traitors executed."

CHAPTER 68

Harper

"No! Absolutely not. It's not happening, Harper." I stood glaring at Aaron as he blocked my way out of the bar.

"Aaron, move now before I set you on your ass," I snapped. I had been trying to get away for the last half an hour, but Aaron was adamant.

"Seriously, Harper, it's stupid," he hissed. "Like actually one of the most stupid things you can do. Let me get in touch with Drake first."

"Ha!" I exclaimed. "I'm not entrusting anything to that vampire."

"Harper, please," Alex pleaded from behind me. "Why don't we get a plan together first, okay?"

"Oh sure," Louise muttered. "And at the same time, they can be killing my mate." I looked over at Louise, and she shrugged.

"They won't kill Tommy," Harry said as he took a drink. "They can't. He's currently the only guardian. They need him to get to the seal." Everyone stared at Harry, and he looked up. "What?" he asked, clearly confused.

"How do you know so much, old man?" Alex asked.

"Exactly that, you mutt," Harry shot back, "I'm an old man. I've been in this pack and this town longer than any of you. I was here when the last Divine Warrior was."

"I'm not the Divine Warrior," I snapped, and he looked at me, amused. He walked over to me with the book in hand and pointed out a passage. Fuck!

"Oh, and what colour is your fur, angel?" he asked and winked when I put my head down.

"What?" Aaron asked and took the book reading the passage. "The Divine Warrior can be identified by the mark of luminescence in their secondary form." He looked up at me. "I don't get it, secondary form? They mean wolf form, right?" I nodded. "Well, you haven't been able to shift in over ten years, and I'm sure you said you were a grey wolf. I mean, it's rare for sure, but not exactly shiny."

"I shifted," I whispered, and his eyes widened.

"What, when?" he asked.

"Last night, after...." I trailed off, realising that there was so much that Aaron didn't know.

"After what?" he asked impatiently. I held up my hand for him to see, and his eyes widened further.

"The ring, it's gone," Aaron exclaimed, and I nodded.

"Elias took it off. He said it was me keeping it on, not the compulsion." I shrugged.

"So what colour is your fur then, not grey anymore, I take it?" he asked, and I shook my head.

"White, but in the moonlight, it shimmers," I said and heard gasps from Louise and Alex.

"Like a luminescence," Aaron said, and I sighed, "Sorry darling, looks like you can't fight this."

"Great," I said and sat down in a booth. I didn't want to be this special wolf or whatever. Why couldn't I just be Harper, an amazing, badass warrior?

"Well, now that we have deduced that our Harps really is from heaven," Alex said with a wink, and I grinned. "It's obvious that we need to figure something out because it is way too dangerous for you to let yourself get into the hands of that demon."

"Agreed," Aaron said, and I scowled.

"I'm old enough and skilled enough to look after myself," I snapped. I just needed some sort of distraction, something long enough to be able to slip out of the bar.

"I don't care, Harper. You are clearly important, so we need to-" Alex started to rant until he was interrupted.

"What's that smell?" Aaron said suddenly. His eyes unfocused as he sniffed the air. But I couldn't smell anything, and neither could anyone else by the look on their faces. Just then, I heard a noise from the back, and a voice floated through.

"Harry, I wasn't sure whether to come in today, what with the town being on lockdown, but thought I better-" Katie walked in from the back of the bar and stopped dead. She stared at Aaron like he was the most surprising thing she had ever seen, and one glance at Aaron confirmed he was doing the same thing. I looked up at Louise, and she grinned. We both knew what was going to happen next. In a blur of movement, Aaron shot across the room and grabbed hold of Katie. He buried his head in her neck and took a deep breath. Katie all but gasped as she clung to him.

"Mate," Aaron muttered, but it was loud enough for us all to hear. Alex and Harry jumped up to congratulate the couple while Aaron and Katie introduced themselves to each other. I was smiling. At least one good thing would come out of this. Then I realised that my wish had been answered. Everyone was distracted and not looking at me. I took the opportunity and slowly headed towards the main entrance.

I slipped out into the evening and headed for Louise's car. It wouldn't take me long to break in and hot wire her car. I was sure she wouldn't be too angry, maybe. I headed across the empty car park when two large shadows appeared in front of me. I sighed as I looked up at the two slabs of meat who had clearly followed me out of the bar. I guess they weren't as distracted as everyone else.

"Are we going to have a problem, boys?" I asked, and they both just stood there, not answering.

"Listen, boys," I said, "If I'm gonna save your boss from the firing squad, then I will have to get on the inside. This is the best plan." I tried to reason with them as they stood there silently.

"I mean, do you guys even talk?" I asked, and they just glanced at each other. I sighed and narrowed my eyes.

"I don't want to hurt your egos here, but I will move you if you don't get out of my way." I was beginning to lose my patience. One of them rolled his eyes, and the other smirked. He looked like he really wanted me to prove that I could move them. Then the one with the smirk moved to one side and inclined his head. The other one looked at him like he was crazy, but then shrugged and moved aside too.

"Thank you," I said and walked past them.

"You know Marcus is gonna kill us, right?" I heard one mutter to the other,

"Did you see the look on her face, man?" the other one said. "If she really is an angel, what if she can smite us?" The first one laughed at him. I couldn't help but crack a smile myself.

I headed to the car and picked up a rock on the way. I would have to pay Louise back later for the broken window.

"You know keys are quieter," a voice from behind me startled me a little, and I turned to see Louise standing there, her keys hanging from her hand.

"Nah, ah." I shook my head, and she rolled her eyes

"What, you can be stupid, but I can't," she scoffed. "It's my mate there as well, you know."

"Yeah, but you heard Harry, they can't kill him," I said, and she rolled her eyes again.

"You think that means he's safe?" she had me there. "Plus, the demon guy said I had to go, too."

"Please don't call him demon guy," I said, and she laughed. She unlocked the car, and I pulled the driver's side open.

"I'm driving," I said, and she threw me the keys. I felt awful for bringing her into my bad decision, but I knew she was right. We jumped into the car, and I started the engine just as I heard a shout from the bar. Both Aaron and Alex were heading our way at speed.

"Whoops, we've been found out," I said. "Buckle up." I set the car off in a wide circle around the furious boys and out of the car park towards the other end of town. We were soon heading towards the pack house, and probably the stupidest thing I had ever done.

We reached the pack house way too soon, and I saw warriors headed our way before I had even turned off the engine. I looked at Louise.

"Last chance," I said. "You can still get out of this."

She shrugged. "Nope," she said, and I smiled. She might not have been trained to be a warrior, and she was probably terrified, but the woman still had nerves of steel and didn't let her fear show. I turned off the engine, the car doors were pulled open, and we were instructed to get out. I jumped out and recognised one of the warriors from training.

"Geez, Warner," I said. "I didn't think you for the evil type."

He just shrugged. "More like the winning team, love," he said, and I rolled my eyes. I was going to respond with some comment about him being an idiot, but then stopped as the doors to the pack house opened and Nathaniel walked out, followed by Colton.

"Harper," he called like we were long-lost friends. "My dear, thank you for coming."

I watched him carefully as he came near. "Okay, we are here, Nathaniel," I said. "Now, let our people go."

Nathaniel laughed. "Not quite how it works, my dear," he said, and glanced at Colton. "I'll consider letting them go when my nephew is the official Alpha of this pack and has his mate by his side."

My eyes widened as I realised what he meant. I shook my head and backed up straight into the two warriors. Their hands encircled my arms, and I felt something snap onto my wrist. I didn't need to look down to see that whatever it was, was silver. I felt the effects almost straight away. I tried to struggle, but one silvered wolf against two full-strength ones had no chance. I shouted at Louise to run, but she had already been circled by warriors and put in cuffs.

Nathaniel stood patiently to one side while I shouted obscenities at the warriors and tired myself out. Even in my logical mind, I knew it was what they wanted. I couldn't help but try to fight the warriors. I half noticed Louise being dragged off into the direction of the cells and screamed for them to stop. Finally, I lost my strength and could barely even keep my feet under me as I slumped in the warrior's arms. I shot Nathaniel a look, half thinking that this smiting skill would come in handy right now. Nathaniel responded with a grin and then nodded at Colton. Colton stepped toward me, and I tried to pull away as the silver sickness began to cloud my vision. Colton lifted my hand, and I felt something cool slide onto my finger. I didn't have to look down to know what it was. Colton lifted my hand to his lips.

"I will kill you slowly and painfully the first chance I get," I snarled at him, and he smiled and kissed my hand.

"I don't doubt you, my Angel," he said. "But for now, you're all mine, Strawberries. Again."

CHAPTER 69

Harper

I woke up in the dark. I vaguely remembered being carried into the pack house, and then I must have blacked out from the silver sickness. I could tell I was in a bed and wasn't alone. I tried sitting up, only for a wave of nausea to hit me like a truck.

"Fuck!" I muttered and then heard a chuckle.

"Go back to sleep," Colton croaked, his voice full of sleep. I felt him reach out to me, and I shrunk back. He grabbed hold of my wrists, and I jerked away hard enough that I fell off the bed.

"Ow! Damn it!" I exclaimed, and I heard Colton sigh. The bed rustled, and I held my arm out to try to stop him from coming near me, but I couldn't see a damn thing. Suddenly, the room was flooded with light, and when my eyes adjusted, I saw Colton standing by the door, watching me.

"If I come and help you up, will you try to hit me?" he asked, his tone strangely calm, like he was talking to a child who was being stubborn.

"Yes!" I said, and he sighed again.

"Goddess sakes Harper," he said, the frustration clear in his voice. "Just let me help you back on the bed, will you?"

"Go to hell," I snapped, and he grinned.

"Yeah, probably," he said, walking over to me. "But I'm used to it." He leaned down towards me and I growled at him. He wasn't fazed in the slightest. Even when I tried to kick out at him, he just dodged my legs and scooped me up off the floor, and dropped me onto the bed.

"See," he said while I glared at him. "That wasn't so bad, was it?" He pulled the covers back and put them over me. I wanted to fight, but I felt exhausted. I looked down at my wrist and saw the silver cuff sitting there. I lifted my arm in the air and looked at Colton.

"Take this off me," I demanded, and he just chuckled.

"Not yet," he said, walking to the door again. "We need to talk first, and then we can take it off." He reached for the light switch, and the room was back in darkness. I heard Colton as he walked across the room and felt the bed move as he climbed back in. I was losing my fight against sleep again and was frustrated with myself for being so exhausted. I felt Colton's hand on my arm and flinched.

"Touch me, and I will feed you your dick," I snarled, and he just chuckled again, but moved his hand away.

"Go to sleep, Strawberries. We'll talk in the morning," he said, and I felt the bed move as he turned away. I could feel the compulsion in his voice pulling me under into sleep again, and I fell asleep, mentally cursing myself for being too weak to fight it.

"Hey, Strawberries," I was softly shaken awake, and I opened my eyes to Colton sitting on the bed. He was fully dressed, and his hair was damp, I was guessing from the shower. The room was bright from the sunlight pouring in through the big windows. I looked around the room. It was decorated in greys and blacks and had a masculine tone, so my guess was that I was in Colton's room.

"It's time for breakfast, Harper," he said, and pulled back my covers. He reached down to lift me, and I glared at him.

"Get off me," I snapped, and he held his hands up in mock defence. I swung my legs off the bed and set my feet firmly on the floor. I thought I was doing well until I tried to stand up, and my legs gave out. I would have crashed to the floor, but Colton reached out and caught me. He lifted me into his arms, and I had no other choice than to hold on to him, and he carried me out of the room.

Colton headed down the hallway, and once we got to the stairs, I saw we were on the third floor. Colton headed up the stairs to the top floor and towards the dining room hallway. I could tell that the room was pretty full as Colton opened the door, although the room went suddenly silent as he walked in confidently. Colton headed to the Alpha's seat at the table. The seat that was only recently sat in by Elias. Colton put me down in the seat next to his seat, the one meant for the Luna, before sitting down himself.

I looked around the table at the faces watching me. Lisa and Lily Chambers both looked uncomfortable and bordering on scared, while Jamie Bennet looked like he wanted to punch Colton. Nathaniel was sitting directly opposite me. He looked like he wasn't paying attention, but I knew that look on his face and how his eyes occasionally darted around. He was watching every movement in the room.

"Harper," Caroline Stokes called excitedly. "How are you, my dear?" she asked, and I glanced at Colton.

"Terrible," I said to Caroline. "This damn cuff is making me feel like shit, but they won't take it off." I held up my wrist for her to see, and her eyes widened.

"Colton, take that off your mate, young man," Caroline scolded him, and Colton glared at me. I grinned at his discomfort. I saw amusement cross Nathaniel's face too.

"It's for her own good little sister," he said to Caroline. "It's stopping her from burning up." Caroline looked at Nathaniel in confusion, and then she looked at me in sympathy before looking down at her food.

"Burn up?" I asked, and Nathaniel looked at me.

"In good time," he said and gestured towards a plate being put in front of me by one of the omega servers. "Eat something, and then we'll talk." I wanted to protest and refuse to follow his orders, but the smell of the food made me feel hungry all of a sudden. I looked down at the food, picked up a fork, and dug in. I glanced up to see Nathaniel watching me. He nodded and then turned back to the paper he was pretending to read.

Once I had eaten enough to satisfy myself, I realised someone was missing. I looked over at the twins and smiled. "Where is your mother?" I asked, and they both glanced at each other before looking at Nathaniel.

"She is in the cells with the rest of the traitors," Nathaniel said, without looking away from his paper.

"What the fuck!" I exclaimed, and Jamie muttered something before standing up so quickly that his chair went flying backwards. With barely a glance, he stormed out of the room, slamming the door behind him. I raised my eyebrows, and Colton turned to Nathaniel.

"I think we need to watch him," he said, and Nathaniel nodded.

"Put some men on him, see what he is up to," Nathaniel said, and Colton's eyes glazed over as he began mind linking orders. Nathaniel put down his paper and smiled at me.

"Why don't we have that talk now," he said. "And then we can see about getting that little accessory off you." I glared at him, but then nodded. If I could get the cuff off, I could get my strength back. Colton was on his feet and lifting me out of my chair before I had a chance to even protest.

"I can walk, you know," I said, and he grinned.

"Sure you can, Strawberries," he said.

He and Nathaniel headed out of the dining room and into a room I hadn't been to before. It was all set up like the living room on the next floor. Colton put me down on one of the sofas and then sat next to me. Nathaniel walked to a bookcase and picked out a large book before taking a seat on the sofa opposite. He put the big book down on the table, and I immediately recognised the symbol on the front of the book straight away as the same one on the book, back as the bar. I glanced at the book and then back to Nathaniel. He was watching me with interest.

"I see you recognise this," he said, and I stared at him, keeping my expression blank. I held out my arm, the one with the cuff on, and looked at him expectantly.

"Let's have a little talk first," he said, and I shook my head.

"First rule you told me was to work from a place of power. This," I pointed to the cuff, "Is not from a place of power. I think I need my wits about me talking to you right now, and this is stopping me from doing that." I held out my arm again. "Take it off if you want me to talk."

Nathaniel smiled like he was proud and nodded to Colton. I heard Colton muttering to himself about it being a bad mistake, but he took my arm and unlocked the cuff. As soon as it was off my skin, I felt a rush of energy and felt ten times better.

I pulled my arm away from Colton and sat back in the seat.

"Also, I want Louise back with me, and..." I glanced at Colton. "I want my own room back." Colton opened his mouth to argue, but Nathaniel nodded.

"Done. I will have you and Mrs Chambers put in the suite on the third floor for now."

I nodded. The short conversation Louise and I had on the way to the pack house after she had received a mind link from Alex shouting at her was that staying together kept us in contact with Alex and, through him, Aaron. That was important. I told Louise that I hadn't jumped in half-cocked to run back into the viper's nest-like an idiot they undoubtedly thought I was. I had a plan, and the plan always worked better from the inside.

"Wait, but-" Colton exclaimed, and Nathaniel glared at him, shutting him down with a single look. I smirked at the gesture and turned to Colton.

"Looks like you're not the one in charge right now, sweetie," I said, and his face started to turn red with anger. "I guess the Alpha title is just an empty placeholder, eh?" Colton glared at me, and then it happened, just as I half expected it would. His eyes shifted to the soulless black that I had seen in both Elias and Nathaniel. I could tell it wasn't the same, though, like there was a struggle between Colton and his demon. I had wondered how he had kept it hidden, but now I realised it was less hidden and more powerless.

"Yep," I said with a smile. "Just like your little friend in there, an empty placeholder." Colton growled in response, and Nathaniel sighed.

"Harper, stop trying to bait him," he said, and I glanced his way with a grin.

"Trying?" I asked. "That was hardly trying."

Colton growled again, and Nathaniel turned his stare on Colton. His eyes shifted to black, and I immediately felt the power in his demon. Even though he wasn't looking at me, I could feel the pull of the black abyss.

"Colton, control yourself," he scolded, and then, by the time he glanced back at me, his eyes had switched back to the blue I knew.

"Now that you have had your fun, and I have agreed to your demands," he said, leaning back. "Let's talk about you."

"What about me?" I asked innocently.

"Don't play coy with me, child. I had known who you were since before I laid eyes on you at the Council," Nathaniel said. "I haven't been turning you into one of the fiercest warriors for nothing. You and I both know how special you are, Harper. And that is why it is my number one priority to keep you alive."

"Great, so no killing the half-angel girl," I said flippantly. "I can get behind that plan."

"I have no plans to kill you. Quite the opposite," he said with a chuckle. "You are already feeling the burn ups, the headaches, yes?" he asked and nodded at my surprise.

"All this is a result of your angel side trying to come forward. Unfortunately, that can have a very damaging effect on a body, including one built for such use." I mulled what he was saying over in my head and knew he was telling the truth. The headaches and pressure had got worse in the last few days. I thought it was the return of my wolf form, but now I could feel the presence of something else in the background.

"So the number one priority is that you and Colton complete the mate bond as soon as possible." I felt Colton move beside me and glanced at him to see him watching me with an intense need.

"Whoa!" I exclaimed. "What does tying me to this psycho for life have to do with my angel coming forward?" Nathaniel leaned forward and smiled.

"Because that is the only way to save your life, my dear."

CHAPTER 70

Harper

"What the Hell are you talking about?" I scowled at Nathaniel, and he raised an eyebrow, which I knew was his subtle way of showing disapproval. I rolled my eyes, and he shook his head.

"Balance, my dear," Nathaniel answered, and I waited for more.

"Okay, you are going to have to give me more than that," I snapped. I was getting a headache again and could feel Colton's eyes constantly on me, and I was this close to punching the creepy bastard in the face.

"How much did the old man tell you?" Nathaniel asked, and I was confused for a moment as to who he was talking about. Of course, Harry.

"I don't think he likes being called an old man," I said, and he scoffed.

"He was an old man when I was young. Even then, I knew he was the one who watched things in the town, and I've seen the ink. I know which side he is on."

I sighed and rubbed my temple, and Nathaniel leaned forward, a look of concern on his face.

"A headache, already?" he asked, and I rolled my eyes at him. Where did he get off pretending to be worried about me?

"The cuff has only just come off. You should have had more time." I shook my head and immediately regretted it.

"Okay, so why is this suddenly happening now?" I asked, and Nathaniel sat back, still watching me.

"I'm not sure about that," he said. "It could be the proximity to the seal or the increase in the number of demon blood around. The angel in you could be trying to come through to fulfil her role. Other than coming back to town, has anything changed?" I thought about what he asked. A fair amount had changed. I had met Elias, my second chance mate, who was also a demon. With Elias' help, I had healed a lot of traumas. I looked down at the ring that Colton had put on my finger again. I had been scared to try to remove it, worried that the damn thing had cursed me to be broken again. I pulled on it slightly and felt nothing. With a sigh of relief, I slipped the ring off. It was just a ring, nothing more. I put the ring on the table as Colton growled. I glanced at him and rolled my eyes in response.

Then I thought of something else that had changed, something big. I glanced at the ring again and then back at Nathaniel. I wasn't sure that I wanted him to know that piece of information.

"She shifted," Colton said, and I glared at him. Well fuck, I guess I wasn't keeping it quiet. Nathaniel sat up straight and looked between the two of us, his eyes alight with interest.

"Shifted?" he asked. "As in into your wolf?" he looked at me, and I sighed and nodded.

"Well, of course, then that makes sense," he said, nodding his head, and I could almost see the thoughts whizzing through his head at lightning speed.

"Wanna share with the audience," I snapped after a couple of minutes of silence from him, and Nathaniel looked at me like he had forgotten I was even there.

"Of course, my apologies," he said and picked up the cuff. "This is designed to suppress your wolf side," he said, and I nodded. I knew that already. "You lose access to all the elements that make you a wolf, the speed, the strength, the link to your pack, and, of course, the ability to shift."

"Yeah, I get it. It's a real drag," I snapped. "Get to the point." Nathaniel stopped and glared at me. I held his stare for a bit but could never last too long under that particular look.

"The shifters that are born into the demon bloodline suffer the most," he said. "For the other supernatural types, they don't have another form most of the time. Sometimes, the fae might have, but the immortals and the magic users, their supernatural side is an essence. But as wolves, we have two distinct personalities in us. Two souls sharing one vessel. Are you with me so far?" He looked at me, and I thought about what he said. It made sense. Maia was her own wolf with her own wants. I nodded, and Nathaniel carried on.

"So when the demon bloodline is introduced, we are then faced with not two, but three separate personalities, three separate entities inside one vessel. This is too much for the vessel, so the burnout rate for a shifter with the demon bloodline is much more accelerated than the others." He stood up and began pacing the room. Oh good, I knew this was his teaching move. It looked like we were in class.

"The wolf side, or whatever animal the shifter is, naturally takes a back step to the human side. It is inherently stronger, but our natural form is human, and the wolf respects that. That is why we don't shift until our teens. The wolf is always there but not dominant, so waits for permission to come forward. This protects the vessel from being overwhelmed by two different souls. But the demon part, the third part, isn't quite so placated," he said. "The demon wants to hold the controls. It is the struggle for dominance between the demon and the human soul that causes the stress on the body and mind." He glanced at Colton briefly. "The human soul is neutral, and the demon, of course, lands on the dark side, so the scales will often slide into the darkness. There is no anchor for the human to stay in the light. This is why the human almost always take the back step."

"Okay, I get that demons are shitty and everything, but you are showing the human side right now, right?" I asked, and Nathaniel smiled.

"My dear, I wear my human as a mask of convenience, but it is the demon that is running the show in here." He pointed to his heart. "I made that decision to prevent myself from burning up and from destroying my own vessel. With my wolf and my human in the back, the demon holds dominance, and I am not subjected to the misery and madness that my sister and nephew both deal with because they won't accept the truth." I looked at Colton in shock. Was he still fighting?

"Why?" I asked, and he glanced at Nathaniel before looking back at me.

"Love," he said, and I felt like the breath had been knocked out of me. "The demon isn't capable of love, and if he reigns dominant, then neither is the human." He leaned towards the table and picked up the ring and looked at it.

"The truth is, I fell in love with you even before you knew we were fated. It was like an anchor for me and meant that I was able to fight for longer. Even my demon is calm when you are around. My soul allows me to feel the joys of life, the love for my mother, and, of course, for you." He looked back at me. "I would rather go insane than give that up." The sincerity in his voice caught me off guard, and I could feel the prickles of tears in the back of my eyes.

"Which you will," Nathaniel said abruptly, and Colton glared at him. "Unless you complete the bond." I narrowed my eyes at that part.

"Okay, so what does all that have to do with the bond and saving my life, then?" I asked, and Nathaniel smiled.

"Because, my dear," he said. "Just as with the demon, your own vessel can not contain three separate entities, and your burning up is a clear sign that your angel is fighting to come forward. Too much light is just as destructive as too much dark," he said. "And I know you very well. You are not about to take a backseat in your own life."

"Damn straight, I'm not," I said. "But how does mating with him stop my angel?"

"It doesn't," Nathaniel replied. "It placates her, creates a balance in you, an anchor as it were," and he gestured towards Colton. "When you complete the bond, you carry a piece of each other inside you, connecting you, a little dark in the light and vice versa."

"So balance?" I asked, and Nathaniel nodded. "So you are saying that as long as I complete the bond with someone with demon blood, I'm good, right?" Nathaniel nodded again.

"Okay, well, if you just wanna run along and get my mate from your cells, I can jump on that, so to speak." I winked at him. Colton growled beside me, and I rolled my eyes.

"No!" he exclaimed. "You're mine."

"No, Colton, I'm not," I shot back. "You rejected me, remember? You treated me like absolute crap and tried to share me with your friends." I stood up from the sofa and turned and faced him. "You have no right to me at all." I was pissed off and tired, and I felt like throwing up.

"Harper, sit down now," Nathaniel said quietly.

"No!" I shouted, "Why should I? You have my friends locked up in the cells and are trying to mate me off to this jerk." I pointed at Colton, who also stood up and glared at me. "All you have done for the last eight years is manipulate and use me. Why the hell should I do anything you say?" My eyesight was starting to blur, and I could already feel myself beginning to burn up, but I was so angry, and I couldn't think straight.

"Harper!" I heard Nathaniel and saw him heading towards me, but I backed away from him.

"Harper, please calm down. All getting angry does is make it worse." He followed as I rushed to the door. I needed to get out of there.

I had my hand on the handle when I felt an arm wrap around my waist, and I was pulled back into something solid. I tried to struggle, but the arm held me tight, and I felt something in my hand. My legs gave way, and I collapsed, but something held me, so I didn't hit the floor, and I felt a familiar circular rub on my hand. I looked up to see that I was in Colton's arms. He had me wrapped tight against him and was rubbing the spot on my hand. He was whispering something against my head and his face set in concern. I then felt something cool on my other wrist and looked up to see Nathaniel clipping the cuff into place.

"No!" I exclaimed, and he looked at me sadly.

"I would rather you be weak than dead, my dear," he said. "I treated you like a daughter I never had, and if making you uncomfortable saves your life, I will do what it takes. I promised your father that. And contrary to what young Colton here thinks, demons can and do love. You only need to see your caged mate see that."

CHAPTER 71

Harper

I once again woke up in darkness, only this time, it wasn't completely dark. I felt a hand stroking my head and lifted my hand to bat it away. I heard an indignant huff and smiled as Louise moved off the bed. She fumbled with something beside the bed, and the room lit up. I winced against the light.

"Crap, sorry," she said. "Is it too much?"

"No, it's okay, I just need to adjust." I shook my head and immediately regretted it, as the world seemed to roll around, and I felt like I was going to throw up. I lifted my arm and scowled at the cuff on my wrist.

"Damn thing," I muttered as I pushed myself slowly up to a sitting position. I looked around at the unfamiliar room. I didn't recognise where I was, but I did recognise my suitcase next to the drawers. The room had an arch that separated the living area from the bedroom area, and I vaguely remembered Nathaniel saying Louise and I could have a suite.

"We are in one of the guest suites," Louise said as she watched me looking around.

"On the second floor?" I asked excitedly, and she grinned and shook her head.

"Yes, but don't get too excited," she said. "I was told to tell you that there are warriors at the door and all the windows. And to remind you that you are practically human, so it would be unwise to attempt to jump." She rolled her eyes as she said it.

"Damn it!" I exclaimed, and she chuckled.

"I guess this Nathaniel knows you well." It wasn't a question, but I knew she wanted to know more.

"Yeah," I nodded. "He was my mentor at the Council for the last eight years." I looked up at Louise. "I was a mess when I met him. Aaron was getting regular reports of Colton tearing apart packs, and my nerves were shot. Then Nathaniel showed up, and he took me under his wing. Taught me how to deal with my fear, how to take my anger and channel it into strength." I felt the sting of tears against my eyes. "He was right. He treated me like a daughter, and he was like a father to me." I shook my head again and wiped at the tears. Now wasn't the time to mourn over the loss of an illusion. I needed answers.

I got out of bed and headed over to my suitcase. I didn't need to check that my blade roll had already been taken out of the top lining. It was really annoying when the enemy was the one who taught you pretty much everything you knew. I pulled out a pair of jeans and a black top, as well as fresh underwear, and headed to the bathroom. I quickly showered and got ready in the bathroom before walking back into the bedroom.

"What are you doing?" Louise asked, as I searched in my suitcase for a hairbrush.

"Get ready. I need to see my mother," I said, and she shook her head.

"Your mother?" she exclaimed, and I nodded.

"Nathaniel said he promised my father he would save my life or something." I looked at her as she stared at me like I had gone crazy. "I need answers, Louise. I feel like every answer I get creates two more questions." She nodded her head and headed into the bathroom. I had finished putting my hair up in a high ponytail just as she came back out. She was still dressed in the same clothes, but looked like she had splashed water on her face and such. I handed her my hairbrush, and she neatened up her hair.

"I need to get some of my stuff," she commented. "I didn't know what was happening when I was pulled out of the cells and brought here."

"Louise?" I asked, and she stopped and looked at me. "How is everyone?" Louise looked down at the floor.

"Tommy is annoyed. Marcus is trying to joke his way out of his anger. Most of the others in there are angry or scared." I knew she was leaving him out on purpose. I could tell that there was something wrong.

"And Elias?" I asked. She looked up at me, something in her eyes that I couldn't figure out.

"He's not there," she said quietly.

"What?" I exclaimed. "What do you mean, he's not there?"

"I mean, Elias was in a separate cell, away from the rest of us. But close enough to hear."

She looked at me again, and I figured the look this time. It was fear.

"There's something in that cell, but it's not Elias." She shuddered. "I guess it would have been worse if I didn't know. Tommy said that he had been like that since he was taken in. But the raw screams of anger and the threats of violence." She looked back down at the floor. I knew what she was saying. Elias' demon side had taken over and was out of control," I was worried. I wasn't sure how he had contained him for so long, but I needed to find out so that I could get him contained again. I closed my eyes and nodded.

But before then, I needed answers. I opened my eyes again and offered Louise a weak smile.

"Are we ready?" I asked, and she shrugged with a dubious look on her face.

"Sure," she said. "But I don't know how you plan to actually get out of here," I grinned at her.

"I'm going to ask very nicely," I said, and I banged on the outer room door. I heard the door unlock and watched as it was opened. I inwardly groaned as I saw Paul on the other side.

"Hey Harper," he said with a smile, and I smiled back.

"Hey Paul, I'm really sorry." His face barely had a chance to register surprise as I jammed my hand into his nose. I jumped and grabbed hold of around his neck and used the moment to smash his head into the wall. He dropped to the floor in a crumpled heap, and I checked quickly to confirm he was still breathing, but unconscious. I turned towards Louise, who was staring at me in shock.

"How, what?" she exclaimed, and I shrugged.

"I used his strength against him," I said, and she shook her head and pointed to my wrist. I looked down at the cuff and shrugged. Huh? I had forgotten about that. I wasn't feeling my own strength, but I wasn't feeling as weak as I had been.

"I dunno. Maybe I'm building a tolerance?" I asked, and Louise shook her head and laughed. It had a slight edge to it, like the stress was getting to her. I shot her a sympathetic look. She wasn't used to this kind of stress, that I knew for sure.

"Come on," I said. "In a house full of werewolves, I am surprised that no one has come running already."

We headed down the hallway and passed the games room. I moved quickly, checking that Louise was still behind me. I knew that there was no way that no one had heard that, but nonetheless, the place seemed deserted. I looked down the stairs and frowned.

"I don't like this," I announced. "Where is everyone?"

"Maybe they are at lunch," Louise shrugged, and I chuckled. We made it down both flights of stairs onto the ground floor without seeing a single person. I looked into the main entrance. There should have been at least two warriors on guard at the entrance by default, but again, it was empty. I sent a worried glance to Louise, who shrugged again.

"Staff meeting?" she asked, and a giggle escaped my mouth before I could stop it. Maybe I wasn't holding up so well, either. I grabbed Louise's hand and ran across the entrance towards the main entrance. I kept a lookout in case of ambush, but again, nothing. Finally, I grabbed the handle to the main door and pulled it open. Light flooded in, blinding me until my eyes adjusted. I looked down the steps into the courtyard and groaned. Right in front of me, leaning against a black sports car, was Colton. His arms were crossed, and he had a smug look on his face. I narrowed my eyes and glared at him, and his smug grin just widened.

"What? Did you think that I wouldn't know you were going to try to make an escape?" he asked, and Louise stiffened behind me. "Harper, I know you better than you think, just like I know where you are planning on going."

"So, are you planning on trying to stop me?" I asked, getting into a fight stance, ready for combat.

"Nope," he said. "I'm giving you a lift. Get in." Then he opened the driver's side door and climbed into the car. "Come on, if we are going to see your mother before Nathaniel finds out," he called from the car. I turned to look at Louise, and she shook her head. I glanced back at the car and to a waiting Colton and then back to Louise. Louise sighed, and I smiled, and we both headed to the car and got in. I was sitting in the front next to Colton, and he turned and grinned at me and then set off down the drive.

"How did you know?" I asked, and Colton glanced at me before returning his eyes to the road.

"I told you, I know you better than you think," he said.

"Colton!" I demanded, and he grinned.

"I saw the look on your face when Nate mentioned your father." He glanced at me again. "I knew you would need answers." I sighed as he drove. Of course, he was right, and I didn't like that he knew me as well as he did. We drove in silence the rest of the way, and it wasn't long before we pulled up outside my childhood home. I got out of the car and knocked on the door. I saw that both Louise and Colton had followed, too.

It was Susie that opened the door, and she looked shocked to see me standing there.

"Oh my goddess, Harper," she exclaimed. "Mum and I have been worried sick about you, what with the Council being here. Come in." I walked into the living room and saw two of the three kids playing. I saw my mum through the arch into the kitchen and headed in.

"Look, mum," Susie said. "Harper is here." My mum turned around to look with a smile on her face, but I saw her glance down at my cuff, and her smile froze in place.

"Oh my goddess," she cried as she broke down in floods of tears. "No, please, no. Not my baby, please."

CHAPTER 72

Harper

It took us a solid hour to calm my mum down. She cried hysterically almost the whole time, and it took both Colton and me on her pressure points before we got her down to gulps.

"He said he wanted nothing to do with it. Why did they not listen?" My mum sobbed quietly into a tissue.

"Mum," I said, and she looked up at me. "Please, I need to know what you know." Louise handed my mum a glass of water, and she took a big drink before putting it on the kitchen table where we were sitting.

"That band you are wearing used to belong to your great-great-aunt Angela," she said, pointing to the cuff. I looked down at it and then back up to Colton.

"Where did you get this from?" I asked, and he shrugged.

"Nathaniel brought it with him."

"Nathaniel!" my mum exclaimed. "Nathaniel is here?"

"Yeah, mum, do you know him?" I asked, and she nodded her head and smiled.

"Nathaniel and your father were best friends growing up."

I couldn't keep the shock off my face.

"Your father was very upset when your grandfather exiled him. It's why your father helped Alfred Chambers to take the Alpha title and then to run your grandfather out of town."

"What?" I exclaimed. "Dad gave up the chance of being Alpha?"

"Well, yes," my mum replied. "He did it to protect you."

"But I wasn't even born when all this happened," I said, and my mum nodded.

"No, but I had just found out I was pregnant with you." She looked up at Susie, who was standing at one side quietly.

"Listen, Harper, I love you so much," my mum said. "You are my baby girl, and no matter how stubborn you get or how long you stay away, you will always be my baby. But we didn't want a second child. We were too scared of what it would mean." Well, that stung. I sat back in my seat and shook my head. I always felt like I was a hassle to my parents. I looked up at Susie again, and she avoided my eye contact.

"Ok, so why were you scared to have another child?" I asked.

"We thought we had got lucky with your sister," my mum said, and looked up at Susie. "We thought that turning our backs on the Order and joining the Circle would be enough to stop all things happening again."

"All what, mum?" I asked, and she shrugged and pointed to the cuff.

"I never wanted to see that thing again, especially not on my child."

"Mum!" I exclaimed. "Seriously, you need to start making sense." I was getting annoyed, and my head was beginning to hurt again. I rubbed my temples and felt a presence beside me. I looked up as Colton took my hand and began rubbing the circular motion below my thumb. I went to pull away, but he tightened his grip.

"Don't be so stubborn," he growled, and I gave up resisting, mostly because I felt the strength falling out of my way too quickly to really fight it. I was trying to make sense of all this. My father had helped Chambers take the pack. And my parents were Circle.

"So, how did dad betraying his bloodline protect me?" I asked when the headache had subsided a little.

"Your grandfather wanted to remove Nathaniel and his family from the pack and the town," my mum said. "He had been planning it for years. He blamed Angela's demise on their presence. He said it was too much for her. But he didn't know how the Bethrinton's were actually helping." She looked up at Colton and smiled. "That was why we were so happy when you were fate bonded with Colton. It had become obvious that you were to suffer the same fate as Angela did."

"So Angela was a Divine Warrior?" Louise asked, and my mum nodded.

"For all intents and purposes, yes," she said. "But she never pursued it, she didn't train, and she kept the Angel Blade under lock and key."

"Angel Blade?" I asked. I looked up at Colton and he shrugged.

"Yes, I don't know too much, mind you," my mum said. "Because we actively tried to keep away from all this. And when Samual was run out of town, we were sure he took the blade with him. But it was seen as being an activator to the angel inside you." My mum stood up and moved around to the seat next to me.

"Harper, darling, the angel inside you is just like the demon in Nathaniel or this boy." She nodded to Colton. "It will burn you up so that you don't even exist anymore. I saw the change in Nathaniel when he finally accepted the demon as dominant. He changed from the kind, gentle boy I had grown up with into the monster he is now. I don't want that to happen to you or what happened to Angela."

"What happened to Angela?" I asked.

"She burnt up, cooked from the inside out. And because she didn't want to be consumed by the angel, she refused to take the angel blade. That was how she died!" She shook her head, and a tear fell down her cheek.

"Your father and I had just completed the mate bond. I was so excited to be mated to the future Alpha of the pack. It was unusual, especially for an omega such as myself." I could tell by the way that Susie's eyes widened she was as shocked at that one as I was. "Angela had started talking about her time being passed by, and she needed to make way for the next generation. I remember Samual being upset at her taking off the cuff. We knew, of course, but I was new to the family, and I didn't know the whole lore. Very few do in this town. Of course, the headaches and the dizziness started, and it wasn't long before her temperature began spiking. Samual begged her to take the blade, but she refused. She said that she knew the next generation was more important, and she had to make way for that."

My mum looked up at me. "I still remember the day Angela died, screaming in pain. Your father was devastated. He knew the lore, of course. He was training as a guardian, just like your grandad did. But then, when we fell pregnant with your sister, we knew there was a chance that she would be the next Divine Warrior, so your father hit the old books." She looked up at Susie and smiled and then looked back at me. "We still weren't sure when Susie was born. The mark of a Divine Warrior was the luminescence on the skin at birth, and she didn't have it. And your uncle Tommy had been born the year before and showed the mark of the guardian, just like your father." She sighed.

"It was then that your father found the passages about the balancing of blood." She looked at Colton and smiled. "When one with angel blood and one with demon blood connect, they balance each other out. Your father was furious. Angela could have been saved. Her angel could have been neutralised if she had bonded with one of the demon blood families in the area."

"There are more?" I asked, and mum shook her head.

"Not now. Your grandfather had them all slaughtered. He said they were filthy, and his bloodline would not be tainted with demon blood. That's what caused Nathaniel to accept his demon in full. Your grandfather and his men attacked him and his family, killed his parents, and tried to kill him and his sister." She glanced at Colton again, whose lips were pinched. He shook his head and walked to the other side of the room. "If Nathaniel hadn't done what he did, they would have all been killed." She nodded to Colton. "Including Caroline's little one."

"Son of a bitch!" Colton exclaimed. "I need air," he said and stormed out of the room. I glanced up at Louise as we heard the front door slam. That had to be hard to hear, finding out the one responsible for taking out most of your family.

"When Nathaniel accepted his demon, Samual exiled him, and your father turned his back on the Order. He said he wanted no part of it. Samual was potentially putting our child's life in danger." She looked up at Susie. "That is why your father helped Alfred Chambers so that the demon bloodline could stay in Midnight Moon."

I took a deep breath. This was a lot to take in. I looked down at the cuff and then back up at my mum.

"So this cuff, it's keeping the angel from coming out?" I asked, and she nodded. "And the only way to permanently do that is to complete the mate bond with someone with demon bloodline?" She nodded again.

"So, this is why you agreed to the engagement and actively encouraged Colton, despite how awful he was?" My mum looked down at the table, and I shook my head. "Geez, mum," I scoffed.

"Hold on there, princess," Susie spat, and I looked up in disbelief. "Do you think this was easy for mum and dad? Dad worked for them. He knew what the Circle was, how evil they were, but he did that for you so that you would be safe." She looked angry. "Everything was all for you. If you had just done what you were supposed to do and completed the bond with Colton, we would have got the Alpha title back, and dad wouldn't have died trying to stop Eric Stokes from coming to collect you from wherever you ran off to."

"What?" I exclaimed.

"Susie!" my mum exclaimed at the same time. "Do not talk to your sister like that!"

"Really, mum?" Susie exclaimed. "All she had to do was be with her mate, and then we would all have been happy."

"Everyone except Harper, that is." Louise shot back, her face turning red,

"What do you care? You struck lucky in all this, Mrs Chambers," Susie spat at Louise.

"Do you even know what went on at that place?" Louise shouted. "Do you know what Harper was put through, what I have been put through?" She advanced on Susie, and I jumped up and got between the two of them.

"Louise, leave it," I said.

"No, Harper, she thinks you ran away for kicks. Maybe people should know about the shit you went through." Louise was furious, and tears started to stream down her face.

"What the hell are you talking about?" Susie spat.

"I'm talking about being abused and manipulated and shared between friends. I'm talking about my own father siding with the people who ripped me away from my own fated mate's arms and the ones who left your sister in the middle of the woods in pain because she wouldn't sleep with his mates."

"Louise, please," I begged, and she stopped and looked at me.

"I'm sick of hiding it, Harps. I'm sick of being the bad guy in all this."
"Harper?"

I turned to face my mum and saw there were tears in her eyes.
"Is all that true?" I nodded my head. She started crying again.
"But mum, I'm fine now," I said. "Elias has helped me so much."
"But your father knew," she cried. "That's why he contacted Nathaniel, isn't it?" She looked up at me. "He knew you were at the Council. He wanted Nathaniel to look after you. He told me that he was making sure you were safe." She looked at Susie, and I glanced over. Susie looked white and was staring between Louise and me.
"Oh Harper dear," my mum said. "We never knew, but I think your father did. The night he died, he said something about it not being safe for you here." My mum was back to crying hysterically, and I pulled her into a hug. I looked at Louise, who shrugged.

The door opened again, and Colton popped his head in.
"Nathaniel knows where we are. I have to get you back," he said, and my mum stiffened at his voice. I heard her growling before she looked up at him.
"Get out of my house," she growled, and he looked shocked. "Stay away from my baby," she clung to me like he would swipe me away at any minute.
"I, er-" Colton looked confused, and my sister stepped forward.
"You heard my mother. Get out!" she growled. I nodded at Colton to go. Despite my family standing up to him, I knew I couldn't bring Nathaniel down here. I needed to go back. Plus, I had a feeling that the old books were still in the pack house. It was why I let myself get caught by them in the first place. And now I need to know about this blade.
"Mum," I said. "I have to go."
She shook her head. "Not with him," she cried. "Harper, listen to me. You can't take off the band." She fingered the cuff on my wrist. "Not until you complete the mate bond," she said and then cried again. "But I don't want to see you with that monster."
I smiled at her. "It's okay, mum," I said. "Luckily, I know more than one monster." I saw Louise smile again. I hugged my mum and my sister.

"Look up the Angel Blade," my sister whispered. "It might be another way, I dunno." I nodded. It was a moot point if my grandfather had it, but it was worth knowing, anyway.

Louise and I turned to leave when my sister turned to Louise.

"By the way, congratulations on the baby." We both stopped and stared at her.

"The what now?" Louise asked, her eyes wide.

"Yeah, I guess you don't know yet, but I recognise the glow you have. It was the same as when I was pregnant with James." She shrugged. "Looks like we are both mothers to future guardians."

CHAPTER 73

Harper

I watched Louise in the rear-view mirror as Colton drove us back to the pack house. She was staring out of the window, and her hand was absent-mindedly resting protectively on her stomach. I could tell by the dazed look that she wasn't actually seeing anything outside the car.

"Did I hear right?" Colton asked, and I shifted my view to him. He glanced over at me a couple of times, but mostly kept his eyes on the road. I glanced in the mirror again and then back at Colton and nodded.

"You can't tell Nathaniel," I begged him quietly. "Please, Colton, if there is anything right you do, please don't let Nathaniel know this."

"If there is anything right?" he shook his head, the bitter tone clear in his voice. "Harper, everything I have done, I have thought, was the right thing." I laughed at his statement, and he glanced at me and let out an exasperated breath. "Okay, well, maybe I was wrong, but I swear I never meant to hurt you, not really."

"Colton, you are way more deluded than I gave you credit for," I spat, and he growled low in his throat. We sat in silence as Colton turned into the driveway of the pack house. I tried to think of ways that I could get Louise out of harm's way.

The door to the pack house opened, and I saw Nathaniel on the steps. He had that look on his face that said I was about to get into a world of trouble. Great, just what I needed.

"I won't say anything," Colton said, drawing my attention to him as he stopped the car. "I promise." He looked at me with something close to sincerity, or maybe regret, in his eyes. I nodded in response, and he held my sight for another few seconds before nodding and then getting out of the car. I turned around and looked at Louise, who was still staring out of the window.

"Hey," I said, leaning back and touching her knee. She looked down at my hand and then up at me. Her eyes shimmered with tears not fallen.

"Fuck, Harper," she exclaimed. "What am I gonna do?"

I smiled at her. "We'll figure it out," I said, and she returned my smile, although I could tell she wasn't convinced. I looked over to the pack house and saw Nathaniel and Colton arguing. I sighed and looked back at Louise.

"Come on, let's try to avoid that shit show," I said, and she nodded. We got out of the car and walked towards the pack house steps together. I was massively aware that my headache was back, and I was feeling really drained again. What I needed was to lie down, but by the look on Nathaniel's face and the way he and Colton went silent, I suspected that what I was going to get was a mouthful.

"Not now, Nathaniel," I said as I tried to walk past him. But he grabbed my arm tightly, and I winced at the pain that shot through my arm. Colton caught the wince and growled at Nathaniel. Nathaniel rolled his eyes without even glancing his way.

"Quiet down, boy," he said. "Don't think you are man enough or demon enough to go up against me." I looked at Colton, who glanced at me before lowering his head in submission. Yeah, Elias was right. He was no Alpha.

"And you young lady," Nathaniel glared at me, "What do you think you were doing, sneaking out of here without permission?"

I screwed my face up at Nathaniel. "Young lady? Sneaking out? Permission?" I spat. "Who do you think you are? My father?" I pulled my arm away from him, and I swore for a brief second I saw hurt. "I don't owe you anything, Nathaniel. You are lucky I even came back in the first place," I exclaimed. I grabbed Louise's hand and pulled her past him. I headed towards the stairs, knowing that he was following me.

"You will start showing some respect," he called after me, and I laughed dryly and spun around to face him.

"Respect? Respect?" I spat. "You lost any respect I had for you the moment I found out that you had been lying, using, and manipulating me for the past eight years." I could already feel the tears. I was exhausted, and I held back the pain of betrayal from one of the people I had trusted for way too long.

"You don't think I haven't figured out that you have had me working for the one organisation, the scum bottom-feeding bastards I thought I was actively against?" I glared at him. "You have nothing I will ever respect, Nathaniel." I spun around again, grabbed Louise's hand, and headed up the stairs without looking back.

We made our way to the suite that had been assigned to us, and I pushed the door open as soon as we were both in. I slammed the door shut and leaned against it. The tears hit hard as I gave up trying to hold back the sobs. I really didn't want Nathaniel to know how much he had hurt me. He really was like a father to me. So, finding out that he had been using me in such a horrible way, for what I didn't know. And that he had been instructed by my actual father to protect me. Paired with the tiredness and everything else was just too much. I felt broken as I slid down to the floor in tears. I felt Louise's arms around me and ended up crying into her shoulder. A good hour later, I finally felt like I had got it out of my system. The headache was raging, though, and I could feel pressure all over my body. I didn't even need to check my skin to tell that it was hot, and I could tell by the worried look on Louise's face that I probably looked as bad as I felt.

I tried to stand, but needed Louise to help me up and to the bed. I hated feeling so weak and helpless, and it made me moody.

"I'm gonna get you some water," Louise said. She headed to the mini-fridge in the corner of the room after I had snapped at her a couple of times.

"I'm sorry, Louise," I said. "I should be looking after you." She smiled at me with a water bottle in her hand.

"Nah, I think being consumed by an angel is way worse than finding out you are pregnant with some sort of magical baby. Well, other than a werewolf, that is." I chuckled. She handed me the bottle as she glanced over at the door.

"Oh, Alex is linking with me," she said, and her eyes glazed over. I sat impatiently, waiting. I hadn't been able to mind link with anyone for years and found it frustrating how everyone else could, but I was always on the outside looking in.

"Alex said that Aaron finally got in contact with the Council," Louise said, her eyes still glazed. "Someone called Drake is mobilising a team and should be at the territory line in around six hours." I breathed a sigh of relief. I didn't really trust Drake, but at this point, I was willing to give him a chance if it meant us getting out of this shit.

"Oh!" I exclaimed. "Ask Alex to ask Aaron about the Angel Blade," I said, and Louise nodded. I was back to waiting.

"Alex said that Aaron has heard of it but doesn't know anything concrete. He's going to ask this Drake character now," she said.

"Yeah, I'm not sure I'm comfortable with that," I said, and Louise held her hand out.

"Okay," Louise said about thirty seconds later. "Apparently, this dude knows something. He said he would need to find something, but it's gonna delay rescue until tomorrow evening." Louise inclined her head, and a concerned look appeared on her face.

"Aaron is asking if you are wearing the band again." I looked down at the cuff and shrugged.

"I guess this is what they mean, so yeah," I said, and she nodded.

"Okay, he said good. Do not take it off until they can get to us."

"But it makes me weak," I scoffed, and Louise chuckled.

"Aaron said to just do as you are asked, for once." She chuckled. "Wow! He knows you well then." I rolled my eyes, even though I knew she couldn't see it.

"Fine." I sulked and leaned back on the bed. I knew Aaron was right, but I didn't have to like it. I was annoyed that we were nowhere closer to getting Elias and everyone out of the cells, and I could feel this pressure inside me getting stronger as I got weaker by the hour. Part of me wondered if I should just complete the bond with Colton to keep the angel at bay and then figure something out afterwards. Another part of me called me an idiot for even thinking that.

Louise finally finished her conversation with Alex and looked at me with sympathy.

"I guess you didn't tell him he would be an uncle," I said, and she screwed her face up.

"Nope," she said. "He doesn't need to know that right now. This time tomorrow, we will be out of all this, and then I can find out for real and give everyone the happy news," she said, and I grimaced.

"Louise," I said, and she scowled at me. "You know it's not going to be just as simple as getting rescued, right?" I asked, and she sighed. "The place is crawling with warriors Nathaniel brought with him. They won't go down easily."

"Yeah, Harps, I know," she said. "But I choose to live on the positive side of life."

I laughed. "Yeah, okay, Katie," I said, and she screwed up her face in disgust.

"No, thank you, I have way more taste than that trollop," she sneered, and I looked at her, my eyes wide.

"Whoa!" I exclaimed. "I mean, I knew you guys hadn't talked and all, but seriously, what happened?" I asked. Louise huffed and sat next to me on the bed.

"She's a gold-digging whore. That's what happened," Louise said. "I mean, she saw what he did to you, and I'm being locked away, but the little blond bimbo couldn't wait to try to get her hooks into a rank title." She laughed. "Shame for her that she failed and just ended up being their little toy instead." My mouth was open in shock as Louise went on. "I mean, last I heard, she was wearing a wig and taking money for sleeping with Colton. I mean, how low can you really be?"

"Louise," I exclaimed again, and she looked at me. "Who told you all this?" I asked, and she shrugged.

"It was all over town," Louise said.

"Oh no, Louise," I said, upset. "That's not what happened at all."

"What?" she asked with a confused look on her face.

"Katie was forced into it by Eric Stokes. Basically threatened her and her family if she didn't do what Colton wanted. Even the wig and shit was all him." Louise looked at me in despair.

"What!" she exclaimed, the look of horror on her face, and I nodded. "I thought, I was told...." She dropped her head in her hands. "Oh my goddess, and I just turned my back on her," she said as she began to cry. "I'm so awful. She was going through the same thing I was, and I believed what I heard. Oh, goddess, I need to speak to her," and I watched as her eyes glazed over. Quickly, frustration crossed her face.

"Dammit, she is blocking me, but I don't understand how." His eyes cleared again. "She's an omega. I should easily be able to get through."

"Unless," I grinned. I couldn't help contain my excitement. "Wow, they didn't mess around," I said and giggled.

"Harper," Louise huffed, and I grinned at her.

"Katie and Aaron are fated," I said, and Louise nodded. "Well, I am guessing they have already completed the bond because Aaron is an Alpha rank. This means that Katie has had quite the up rank." Louise's eyes widened.

"Oh," she said, and her eyes glazed again. I watched as her face lit up and then dropped, and then tears began to fall again. Finally, after around ten minutes, where I had started to nod off, Louise bounced on the bed, a smile on her face. I huffed as she bounced next to me.

"I got Alex to get her to talk to me, and I explained everything and apologised until I was blue, and we said that we would talk later, but she said that she didn't hate me. I mean, that's good, right?" Louise asked, and I smiled.

"Yeah, that's good," I said as I laid my head on the pillow. "It would be nice to spend time with my two best friends once all this is over."

Louise smiled. "Yeah, I agree."

We had just decided to settle down for the night when there was a knock at the door.

"Oh, goddess!" I exclaimed. "What now?" Louise got off the bed and headed to the door. She opened the door and scowled.

"What do you want?" she asked whoever and then looked over at me and rolled her eyes. She stepped back, and Colton stepped into the room with a look on his face that told me I wasn't going to like this.

"My uncle wants to see you as a matter of urgency," he said, and I sat up in bed.

"What for?" I asked, but he just shrugged.

"I'll carry you myself if I have to, Harper," he said, and I growled. "Or would you prefer to walk?" I shuffled off the bed and glared at Colton.

"Okay, whatever. It better be quick," I said. "I'm tired, and I'm cranky." Colton laughed at that.

"Yeah, I suspect cranky won't be the word by the time this conversation is finished with," he said and then waved his hand towards the door. I continued to glare at him for a couple of minutes, but then sighed in defeat. I thought, let's just get this over and done with and then I can rest and wait for the rescue.

I walked out the door with a quick glance at Louise as I walked past her. I could feel Colton on my heel as I headed down the hallway to the stairs and down to the first floor.

"Where am I going?" I asked, although I already knew.

"Alpha's office," Colton said, and I grinned. We headed towards the office, and I stood in front of the door. Colton stepped in front of me and opened the door. He walked in and held the door open for me. I looked in to see Nathaniel sitting at the Alpha's desk, and my grin widened.

"Once a beta, always a beta, eh?" I said as I passed Colton into the room. His responding growl just made me grin more.

"That's enough," Nathaniel said, looking up at me. I sat down in the seat opposite and glared at him.

"What do you want, Nathaniel? I'm tired," I said, and he smiled at me.

"Tomorrow night is the pack dinner," he said, and I shrugged.

"Great. What do you want me to do about it?" I retorted, and his eyes narrowed. I knew I was getting on his nerves. One good thing about having him as a mentor for the last eight years was that I knew how to press every single one of his buttons.

"What you will be doing is beginning the ritual for completing the mate bond with Colton here at the dinner," he said, and I glanced at Colton, whose face was surprisingly blank.

"The hell I will," I snapped. Nathaniel leaned forward and grinned. His eyes switched to black, and I felt an instant fear wash over me, although I tried to hide it.

"Oh, you will, Harper dear," he sneered. "Because if you don't do exactly as you are told, your friend Louise and her precious little unborn baby will die!"

CHAPTER 74

Harper

I turned to Colton, a look of disgust on my face.

"So this is what your promises mean then," I sneered. "Good to know." Colton shook his head, his eyes wide.

"No, Harper," he exclaimed. "I didn't, I swear." But I was so angry. I was angry at him, of course, but I was also angry at myself. I knew I should have got Louise out of here as soon as possible.

"Don't blame him, dear," Nathaniel said, his face full of amusement. "He held loyalty to you on this occasion, although I'm rather concerned that he held valuable information from me." He then sent his own cold look Colton's way. Colton shrunk back in fear. "But nonetheless, I have other sources for this particular little tidbit."

"Who?" I asked, narrowing my eyes, and Nathaniel laughed.

"Harper dear, I know you know that I wouldn't just give such a thing away now," Nathaniel said with a chuckle, and I growled in frustration.

I would find out who it was, and then I would rip out their tongue so they couldn't share any other tidbits. But I had to deal with the current matter at hand.

"So you expect us to just throw down and mate on the dinner table tomorrow night, then?" I asked with a sneer. "Not exactly a family-friendly activity there, Nathaniel." He chuckled again.

"Well, no, my dear, tomorrow night, you will both set your intention at dinner and then consummate and complete it after dinner in your own private quarters, of course," he said, and I relaxed a little. The Council was meant to be here by tomorrow evening. I could say a few words and then stall the actual mating ritual easily enough.

"Of course, the standard-issue setting of intentions won't be sufficient in this case," Nathaniel said, and I narrowed my eyes at him. Of course, it wouldn't be that easy.

"What do you mean?" I asked, suspicious..

"You will follow a much older, more stable tradition where the mating couple shares their bite in the intention," Nathaniel continued, and my heart sank. This didn't sound good at all.

"The bite will, for all intents and purposes, seal you both together, mixing your two separate bloodlines and connecting both the demon and angel lines permanently until you complete the bond later on."

I rubbed my temples, knowing that my headache was coming back. I was feeling like the pressure was getting worse by the day. I noticed Nathaniel incline his head and look at me with interest.

"This is for you too, you know," he said, and I shot him a blank stare. "I know the headaches and the tiredness are increasing significantly, are they not?" I didn't want to confirm what he was saying, but I could tell from the look in his eyes that he didn't need it.

"Your angel is trying desperately to come to the surface, and when it does, it will consume you into nothing. The completion of the mate bond will hold it at bay, allowing you to hold on to who you are."

"Why do you even care?" I asked. "I mean, I know this isn't all for my benefit. What do you get out of this? Why does it have to be Colton? Why not Elias?" Colton growled, and I rolled my eyes. I wasn't here to protect his bruised ego.

"Two reasons, my dear," Nathaniel said, holding his hand up to Colton. "First, I am highly aware that my nephew is losing his grip on his own sanity. He fights his own demon daily, and it is wearing thin. The bond will ensure that he doesn't end up like my own sister." I looked at Colton and he looked away, avoiding my eyes.

"The second is somewhat more of a matter of need," Nathaniel carried on. "To break the seal under our feet, it must be my bloodline that mixes with the angel bloodline."

"Your bloodline?" I asked, confused.

"As in everything else in this balance is key, dear Harper," Nathaniel said. "Just as there are four angelic bloodlines on earth, there are also four demonic bloodlines. It is of utmost importance to which bloodline breaks each seal as to which reins on earth when the gates do finally open."

My head was spinning with this information. There was too much for me to process.

"And Elias is of a different bloodline?" I asked, and Nathaniel nodded.

"Indeed," he said.

"So this is just a pissing contest then," I snapped, and Nathaniel chuckled again. The headache was becoming unbearable, and I needed to sleep so badly. I stood up and wobbled on my feet. Colton jumped up to steady me, but I held my hand out.

"I can't deal with all this now," I said, and Nathaniel nodded.

"Of course, there is plenty of time to educate you once you are bound to our line," he said, and waved to Colton. "But I need your answer before you leave." I glanced at him. "I have a man outside your room right now. Agree to my terms, or I will have dear sweet Louise dragged back to the cells so she can say goodbye to her lover." I clenched my fists as I glared at him.

"Well, I guess I don't have much of a choice now, do I?" I spat, and he smirked in response.

"No, dear, you don't," he said. I sighed and nodded my head in defeat. I only hoped that Drake could get here soon enough to stop this. Nathaniel nodded to Colton, obviously satisfied, and I felt Colton's hand on my arm. I went to move away, but his grip tightened.

"Don't be stubborn," he hissed. "Let me help you." I would have fought it, but my energy was bottoming out. I sighed and leaned into Colton as we headed out of the office and down the hallway.

It was late at night, so I didn't expect to see anyone other than warriors. So I was very surprised when we turned the corner for the stairs to see Susie talking to the redhead receptionist, Kylie, I think. Susie looked over and then quickly looked away. I stared at her as my confusion cleared, and it became clear exactly what she was doing here. I growled as anger took over, and I flew at her, slamming her against the wall.

"You!" I snarled as I felt the rage twist my face. "It was you who told him!" Susie's face paled and her eyes widened. Then a look of contempt crossed her face, and she pushed back against me.

"What do you expect, Harper?" she sneered. "All our family has done has been for you, and you can't even do this for us. We lost our Alpha rank to protect you. Dad died to protect you. I am sick of living less than we really are because of you and your precious ideals." She shoved me back, and I crashed into Colton.

"So yeah, I took matters into my own hands. My children will grow up with good rank and without being tied to this stupid town and that damn seal, just like Tommy has." She smoothed her clothes down. She looked at me. "Personally, I don't care if you do burn up and die, but I want more for my family and me, and if you are the way to go about it, then so be it!" I narrowed my eyes at her as I stalked back towards her. I got as close to her in her face as I could.

"You forget something, sister," I spat. "If I am going to be stuck being Luna of this damn place, then I will make damn sure that you will get nothing. In fact, I would run and hide now because the second I get my full strength back, I am going to hunt you down and rip you apart piece by piece." Susie laughed.

"Harper sweetie, you and I both know that the Luna is just a figurehead here. You won't hold any power at all. And I highly doubt that our new Alpha will be as inclined to punish the very person who got him what he wants." I wanted to smack her right in the face, but the last bout of anger had drained what energy I had left, and it took Susie barely a push for me to fall back again. I would have fallen on the floor, but Colton caught me and swept me up into his arms.

"Well, you doubt wrong," he said, and Susie looked at him, shocked. "When I become the Alpha of this town tomorrow night, you will have one day to gather your things and get out of my territory." Susie paled again, and I blinked in shock at Colton. "I don't want traitors in my pack. Consider yourself exiled from the Midnight Moon pack, Susie Kirby." And then he stalked past an open-mouthed Susie and Kylie towards the stairs to the second floor.

We were in the hallway, headed towards my room, when I finally broke the silence.

"She was right, you know," I said, and I felt him take a deep breath. "You are getting exactly what you want because of her."

"I know," he said.

"And you know that I don't love you," I said quietly.

"I know."

"In fact, I hate you." He stiffened slightly. "For what you did to me and what you did to Louise, how could I not hate you?"

"I know," he said again.

"So why, Colton?" I asked, and he sighed.

We had reached my room, and Colton nodded at the warrior standing outside the door. The warrior looked between the two of us before shrugging and heading down the hallway. Colton dropped me gently to my feet.

"Because of what I did," he said, looking down the hall. He then looked at me, and his eyes glistened. "I could pretend that I didn't hold blame, that I unknowingly let the demon in me control my actions with you and Louise. But it isn't true." He shrugged, "Hell, Harper, I didn't even know I had the demon in me. I never heard him talk like others do. I just knew that sometimes I blacked out, and then when I woke up there was destruction." He looked away again.

"But it's not an excuse. It was still me who did those things, and I know that no matter what I do, I will never make up for it." He looked back at me. "But I would rather you hate me than feel nothing at all for me because just like everything else in this fucked up situation, it's all about balance. And hate is a powerful emotion, as powerful as love."

"I won't ever love you," I said, and he nodded.

"I will spend the rest of my life trying to make up to you my atrocities. And if I could, I wouldn't make you do this bond," Colton said, and my eyes widened.

"Then don't," I whispered, and he smiled sadly.

"Unfortunately, it's not that simple," he said. "It's not my sanity that I care about. I would rather go mad than hurt you or let the demon take over. But despite what he says, Nathaniel has no love left in him. He is consumed by his demon and the greed for power he so desperately wants. He has my mother's life dangled in front of me and has made it clear that if I step out of line again, then he will put her out of her misery." Tears fell from his eyes as he spoke, "I have already lost you, Harper. Call me selfish. Still, I can't lose her too." He looked at me again. "And for that, I am sorry for what I have to do," Colton leaned forward, and I felt his lips on my cheek briefly before he pulled away again. He met my eyes one last time before turning and heading down the hallway.

CHAPTER 75

Harper

Left reeling in the wake of Colton's words, I headed into my room to find that Louise was already asleep in the bed. I didn't even have the energy to change my clothes, so I collapsed onto the bed and shuffled to pull the covers over me.

"Harps?" Louise asked sleepily, "What happened?"

"I'll tell you in the morning," I said. "Go back to sleep." She didn't need to know that her life was in danger just yet. Or ever, I had already made up my mind. I would stall as much as possible tomorrow night, but I would do whatever it took to protect my best friend and her baby if it came to it. I fell asleep, resolved in my decision.

I dreamed I was in a desolate wasteland. I looked around and saw shining lights up ahead. I headed towards the lights across the hardened ground and past destroyed buildings. The light seemed to be at the top of a ridge, so I climbed up slowly, feeling the stone ripping into my fingers and legs as I did. I reached the top to see a figure in white. The light seemed to come directly from her. I knew before she turned who it was that I would see, so I wasn't surprised when I found myself face to face with myself. She smiled at me, and I took a step back, almost falling off the ridge again. She reached out to steady me, and I flinched. I didn't know if this was just a dream or some mystical trick, but I did know that the woman standing before me with my face was my angel side. She was the pressure that I had been feeling. The one I was fighting not to consume me. I wasn't going to risk the chance that she could trick me into giving her the upper hand.

The angel frowned at my action and then sighed.

"You know you are only doing this to yourself," she said. "All of this is you resisting me." She waved her arm around, and I looked around. On the other side of the ridge was a crater. I could see thousands of moving bodies in the crater. There looked to be a battle going on, and it looked bloody. I felt the angel near me.

"If you do it, complete the bond like this, then you lose your power, we lose our power, and the seal will be broken." I looked at her in shock.

"You need to accept me, Harper, not fight me. It is important now, more than ever." I shook my head in despair.

"I don't want to lose myself," I said, and she smiled sadly and moved towards me again. I backed away and felt myself at the edge of the ridge. The angel reached out again.

"Do not fall in fear of who you truly are," she urged, and I stepped back again. But I ran out of the ground, and I felt myself falling back into the crater. I grabbed at a rock and managed to hold on enough to stop my fall. The angel leaned down and held out her hand.

"Please, Harper, let me help you. Help us." I shook my head again as my fingers began to lose grip. The rock slipped from my fingers, and I screamed as I fell.

I woke up drenched in sweat and breathing heavily. I laid where I was while my pounding heart settled back to a less, almost about to explode, level. Once I had calmed down, I took a breath and opened my eyes. And saw Louise staring at me. I could tell by her look that she was angry. It was written in the furrowed eyebrows and the tight lips. I sighed again.

"So you heard already?" I asked, sitting up, not waiting for an answer.

"Heard that you have agreed to complete the mate bond tonight?" The sarcasm dripped from her voice. "Oh, yes, Alex woke me up with that news around an hour ago. The town is buzzing with the details." I stood up and headed to my suitcase.

"It won't come to that," I said as I pulled out some grey joggers and a white top. "I just need to stall for time," I rooted for clean underwear, avoiding Louise as I felt her eyes boring into the back of my head.

"Why even agree to it, Harper?" she cried, and I cringed. She was clearly upset. I didn't want to add to it, but I knew she wouldn't let up. I turned and faced her.

"Because Nathaniel threatened to kill you and the baby if I didn't," I said, and her face dropped in fear.

"Colton told him?" she asked, and I shook my head.

"Susie," I said, the bitter betrayal from my own blood still stung.

"What?" Louise exclaimed. I then told her about the events of last night, about the talk with Nathaniel, the reasons he wanted me to mate with Colton, and the bloodlines. I told her about bumping into Susie and finding out that she was just a jealous title-grabbing bitch. And I told her about Colton and him exiling Susie and what he had said outside this room. And then I told her about the dream I had just had. We both ended up sitting on the floor beside my suitcase for the next hour as I relayed everything and then did my best to reassure Louise that I would protect her and the baby at all costs. Louise cried and demanded that I take back my agreement and that she couldn't have me do what I was going to do.

We were mid-way through discussing what the dream meant when there was a knock at the door. We both looked up and then back at each other. I shrugged my shoulders and got up to answer the door. Standing on the other side was Caroline Stokes, with a couple of Omega girls and what looked like a clothing rail. She smiled brightly at me and leaned in to give me a hug.
"Oh, Harper," she exclaimed. "I am so excited. I can't wait to finally call you my daughter." I winced at her happiness. I liked Caroline. She was such a nice person, and I didn't want to hurt her. She let go of me and then pushed me into the room and waved the girls in.
"Caroline?" I asked, "What is all this?" I waved at the clothing rack, which I could now see was full of evening dresses in various states of sparkle. There was also a chest of drawers on wheels that looked to be full of various shiny things when they were opened and closed.
"Why? I am here to get you ready for the ritual tonight," she said. "Colton said to leave you be, but Nathaniel said it would be lovely for us to spend some time together." I glanced over at Louise, and she shrugged.

The next several hours were filled with polite conversation and dresses, jewellery, and hair and make-up. It felt like it was a blur and that I was living outside my own body. All the time, my mind kept going back to my dream, and I could feel the familiar pressure of something trying to push through the whole time. My head was pounding, and I had a feeling of dread in my stomach. I knew that something important was about to happen. Whether the angel was feeling threatened by the impending demon dampener or whether I was just beginning to lose the battle for myself, despite all that, it was minutes before 7pm when I found myself staring in the mirror in my room. I was dressed in a knee-length black one-shoulder dress. My hair was in curls and seemed to shimmer in the light. Not that I remembered anything special being done to it. The cuff was the only piece of jewellery type thing and sat like a weight on the wrist of my bare arm. My make-up was simple and barely there. Again, despite all that, even I couldn't deny that I had a shimmer about me. Caroline came up beside me, lifted my hand, and looked at the cuff. She smiled sympathetically at me and brushed her thumb over the cuff.

"I'm an old lady now, you know," she said. "I have had a lifetime of this thing in my blood. Fighting it and losing everyone I hold dear because of it, because of their greed for the power that it represented." I looked at her, not knowing what to say.

"I know my dear Colton loves me, and I know he loves you. And I know what my bastard of a brother is doing to him." She stepped back and picked up something. I watched as she presented a matching cuff to the one on my wrist. It was silver and had an inlay of the crescent moon symbol from the books on the Order on the inside. I flinched as she fastened it to my upper arm.

"Don't worry, dear, it's not real silver, not that it will matter soon." I gave her a curious look at that. Then she looked around at the omega girls who were tidying up the leftover things and then at Louise, sitting on the bed in her floor-length dress. I could see her eyes were glazed and assumed she was talking with Alex, trying to get information on the incoming forces. Caroline then looked back at me and smiled. She reached up to the arm cuff and pushed slightly on the outside. I watched as she pushed it up, and a piece slid up. Attached to the piece was what looked like a wickedly sharp silver knife. My eyes widened at what she was showing me. The cuff was a weapon! She slid it back into place, and it looked seamless again. Caroline winked at me.

"There's still a little bad in this old woman yet, though," she said and then smiled before stepping away just as there was a knock at the open door.

CHAPTER 76

Harper

I looked over to see Colton standing there in a black suit and black tie. Despite everything that had happened between us, I couldn't deny that he looked good in the suit. He moved into the room and kissed his mother on the cheek before holding his hand out to me. I looked at the hand, not wanting to take it. Colton sighed and then nodded to two warriors dressed in all black. They both advanced on Louise, and she backed away.

"My uncle was clear. You are both to be escorted this evening," Colton said, his face blank. "It can be done the civil way or the not-so civil way," I saw one of the warriors handling what looked like a collar and lead.

"Fine," I snapped, and took Colton's hand. "But if he tries to put that on my friend, I will use it to strangle him with." The warrior stopped and looked at Colton, unsure of what to do. I narrowed my eyes at him and saw genuine fear cross his face. He was still a warrior from the Council and even working for the evil Circle. I knew he would have heard my reputation. Colton shook his head slightly, and the warrior relaxed. I saw Louise smile at the interaction, but quickly returned her blank expression as the other warrior took her arm.

Colton tugged on my arm, and we headed out of the room and down the hallway. I could already hear the buzz of the pack downstairs and felt sick at the thought of what was going to happen.

"You look beautiful, Strawberries," Colton whispered in my ear as we descended the steps,

"Bite me," I replied, and he chuckled.

"All in good time," he said, and I felt sick. The pressure in my head was almost unbearable. And my whole body felt hot enough that as we entered the main entrance and the warm summer breeze from the open door hit my skin, I actually shivered. We walked into the main hall, and the room fell almost silent as we made our way to the stage and the main table. I didn't want to look at the people around me but couldn't help but look up to see the room full of pack members. Some were smiling. Some looked sympathetic, and some looked scared. I saw my mum and sister sitting at the table opposite the main table. My sister sneered at me as I made eye contact, and my mum started crying. I couldn't see it, but by the wince of pain that crossed her face, I guessed my sister was stopping her from making any attempt to stop this.

We headed up the stairs, and Nathaniel stood there in a full tuxedo suit. He smiled at me like we were friends and took my hand as we reached him.

"Harper, my dear, you look simply delightful," he said loudly.

"Go to hell," I snapped, and he laughed. He turned to the crowd and spoke loudly so that everyone could hear. He talked about returned love and the gift that it brings. Every word seemed to get harder for me to hear as the headache hammered in my head. I felt like I was going to throw up, and my vision was blurring. I looked up to see Colton staring at me with concern. I glanced down off the stage to see Louise being held at the back of the room and then Caroline standing close. Her eyes shifted to my arm and then back to me. Colton leaned into me, and I flinched, thinking that we had got to the part where he would bite me. Had I already run out of time?

"My mother said you are running out of time, and they might not make it," he whispered in my ear. I pulled back and looked at him. My eyes widened in shock. Did he know? Was he aware of what was happening? Colton nodded again and looked at my arm.

I closed my eyes and took a deep breath. I fought through the almost unbearable pressure and found a place within myself that was quiet. It held a different type of pressure, like the eye of the storm. I looked up at Colton again and let go of his hand. I reached up to my arm and slid the knife from the cuff, barely aware that Nathaniel was still talking away, oblivious to what was happening between us. I gripped the knife and swiped outwards quickly. Nathaniel suddenly stopped talking as a thin band of blood appeared on his neck. The look of shock was clear on his face as he stared at me in confusion. I thought it was enough, but then the shock was replaced with anger as he sneered at the weapon in my hand. He looked down at Caroline, and I watched as she stared back at him in defiance. Colton stepped forward into his line of sight, and Nathaniel's face twisted in fury. I went for a second attack as I vaguely heard screaming and saw warriors fill the room as I swung the knife at Nathaniel's throat again. He grabbed my wrist before I could make contact and twisted it so that the knife fell out of my hand.

I saw his eyes shift to the empty black as he pulled me against him.
"I have had enough of your disobedience, Miss Kirby," he sneered in my ear. "I have learned that you are not as required as I once thought. And I will not tolerate it anymore." I tried to fight against his strength, but I couldn't as he dragged me down the stairs. I kicked out at him and tried to drop my weight.
"You think that the simple strategies you have been taught will be enough against me, you insolent child." He grabbed my hair and yanked my head back. "I was the one who taught you them." Nathaniel didn't let go of me as he kicked at my knees, causing them to buckle under me, and I fell painfully, feeling like half my hair was ripped out. He then picked me up by my neck and squeezed. I grabbed at his hand as I fought for breath, but I was no match for his obviously demonic strength. My vision began to blur as he dragged me out of the room and the pack house. I was vaguely aware of being dragged through the woods and only realised that we hit the entrance to the cells when I heard the clunk of the door. I could hear shouting and screaming, but everything seemed to narrow down to the returning pressure in my body. I felt like the lack of oxygen was causing me

to fade in and out of consciousness. The pressure inside me was about to burst out. I was jolted back to reality as my knees hit the cells' cold, hard concrete surface. I looked up to see that I was in front of a bank of open cells. I could see Tommy and Marcus on the other side of the bars. I saw they were shouting and pulling at the bars, but I couldn't hear anything against the roaring of the other cell. This one wasn't open. It had a big steel door and a small window. I saw the unmistakable eyes of Elias appearing and disappearing before the door shook against the weight of something heavy hitting it.

Tears streamed down my face as I saw Louise dragged into the room by two warriors, and Tommy began to frantically claw at the bars. I looked at Louise in horror. Had what I had just done signed her death sentence? Were we being brought here to see her being killed? I was dragged to my feet and felt Nathaniel's hand circle my throat again. I tried to struggle, but his grip only tightened.

"I have some good news," he sneered into my ear. "It turns out that sweet Louise's baby is more valuable than I originally thought, so she gets to live for now." I stared at Louise, who was screaming and struggling against the two warriors that held her.

"But with my new knowledge, I now do not need the risk you bring me. It may take another twenty years, but this time I will ensure I do it right. I will ensure that the child is raised in full obedience to me." I felt his hand on my wrist a second before I realised what he would do. I had no idea what he knew, but it was enough to know that it wasn't Louise that was in danger. I tried to grab his hand on my wrist, but he just batted it away like I was an annoying fly.

Nathaniel clicked at something, and I felt the cuff slide from my wrist and hit the floor. I heard it clank and saw it roll away. I looked up at the people in the cells and then at the eyes in the tiny window. I felt a calm wash over me as everything suddenly went deadly quiet. I stared at the eyes of the man I loved, committing them to memory. I felt tears flow down my skin as I felt the first lick of heat inside me. All the pressure that had been building up exploded through my skin, and I felt like I was being ripped apart from the inside out. I could feel the flames inside me reaching for my soul or whatever it was that made me who I was. I felt as it painfully burned through everything I was. I stared at the eyes in the window, wishing that for just one more time, I could see his face, feel his touch. I held on for as long as I could, clinging to the last seared edges of my humanity before the pain became too much, and I let out a piercing scream as the invisible flames consumed me. I dropped to my knees, the pain unbearable as I choked on my own blood. I wanted this torture to so desperately stop, for me to finally be put out of my misery. Finally, I collapsed fully to the ground, and the pain dissipated as I felt myself disappearing into the dark, empty blackness of death.

CHAPTER 77

Elias

Earlier in the Day

The last few days had been terrible. I had been in constant battle with whatever this thing was inside of me. The rage inside me at seeing the man responsible for my sister's death had been like a drug to the monster, and I had spent much of the time in the back of my own mind. All I was able to do was go over the events that had just happened. Finding out that Harper was a member of the Council was a shock. But then she mentioned that name, Nathaniel. There was no way that the man she thought could help me was the same man I had spent so many years hunting for. I stopped struggling against the warriors then. Either Harpers Nathaniel was going to help sort this epic misunderstanding out, or...

Seeing his face was enough to unleash the monster. The man I had been hunting had also been hunting me, apparently. But when his eyes shifted to the vast desolate black, I realised he had his own monster.

"Control your human," he had said to my monster. Did he know what this thing was? And was he just like me? No, I couldn't accept that I had anything remotely in common with that man. He had recognised me. I knew he did. He had even said that he had got the wrong sibling. I had too many questions and no way to get answers. Stuck in this cell. And stuck in the back of my own self, I only had my thoughts and questions going around and around.

It didn't matter where I was, though. I still saw and heard everything. Marcus had spent the first twenty-four hours raging against his bars, his need to protect his Luna practically burning through his veins. Tommy mostly sat in quiet thought until Louise had been dragged into the cells. She had explained that she and Harper had got away with the help of Harper's friend Aaron. They had gone to Howlers, the bar in town, and met with a few of the remaining allies we had that hadn't already been dragged down here.

Then things had got hazy for me because I thought I heard Louise talking about angels and demons. I had tried to pull myself to the surface, but the monster was strong enough to keep me down. It wasn't until I heard that Harper had turned herself into that bastard that I realised she was in danger. Marcus had gone on a descriptive rant about what he was going to do to Carlos and Demetri, the two warriors who had apparently allowed my mate to make such an idiotic move. It wasn't long before Stokes had turned up in all his snivelling cowardice and dragged Louise back out of the cells. Tommy had gone crazy, threatening many creative methods of torture towards Stokes as he disappeared down the hall.

Then the men and women in the other cells had settled into quiet confinement—all but me. My monster raged on, smashing my weakened body repeatedly against the steel door of my cell.
"Must get to mate," he snarled when I questioned his actions. I could feel a panic in him, one that seeped into my own self as I craved for my beautiful mate. We were on one of the monster's brief and sparing breaks of control when footsteps brought me from my thousand questions. I was lying on the small bed in my cell in pain from my monster's abuse of my body. Even as a werewolf, I wasn't completely indestructible.

I lifted myself up, wincing in pain, and made my way to the tiny window in the now battered and dented door. Standing in the centre of the main room was the bastard himself. I growled as he looked around at the different cells. I knew he heard me from the chuckle.

"Nathaniel," I snarled, and he turned to face me. He walked up to the door of my cell and looked in through the window so that all I saw were his eyes.

"Hello, boy," he said, and I growled again. "I see you are in control again. Good, I have some questions for you."

"I have nothing to say to you," I snarled, and he chuckled again.

"Well, if you want to see your mate again, you will answer my questions."

"You harm Harper, and I will hunt you down and kill you," I hissed. I could feel the rage boiling up again, and I tried to hold it in to keep control.

"How do you do it?" Nathaniel asked. "How do you both maintain dual dominance in the one vessel without it affecting your mind?"

"What?" I asked, confusion dampening the anger a little. Nathaniel sighed, and then I saw the corner of his eyes crinkle as they lit up with excitement.

"You don't know, do you, boy," he said. "You don't know of the power in you, do you? How can you go through life not knowing that you have demon blood in you?" I felt my eyes widen as I stepped back in shock. No! It wasn't true. He was wrong.

"He's telling the truth," the monster said from inside my head. "I am a product of the hell beneath our feet." I shook my head. This wasn't even possible. Suddenly, my mind went back to the words Louise was saying. Angels and demons. Was she talking about me? And if I was laced with the spawn of hell, then did that mean there were angels who walked the earth too?

Something that Tommy had said suddenly hit home. I knew he worked with the Order. He had been the one that had contacted me and asked for help against the Circle's influence in the pack. I didn't know much about the Order, but I did know that sometimes it was referred to as the Divine Order. Tommy had only recently also told me that Harper was the Order, not that she worked for them, but was them. Could it be that my own mate was one of these angels?

"Angel blood," my monster whispered, and I shook my head again. How could she be mated to something like me if she was of such a divine origin?

"She is our mate. We need her!" the monster said.

I heard a chuckle pulling me from my internal thoughts.

"I can almost see the revelations in your eyes, boy," he said. "Well, let me give you another one. Tonight my nephew and your dear mate will complete the mate bond, joining our bloodlines and giving me access to the first seal."

"What!" I heard Tommy exclaim. "No, you can't. She wouldn't!" Nathaniel moved away from the window and towards Tommy's cell.

"Oh, but she would, Guardian," he said, and I watched as Tommy growled. Nathaniel inclined his head, and I saw a smirk on his face.

"And our dear sweet Harper agreed to mate with my nephew?"

"No, she didn't," he said. But I was struggling to listen. The rage was growing inside me again. The thought that my Harper would allow Stokes even to touch her again.

"What do you have over her?" I asked because I knew she wouldn't agree unless she had to. Nathaniel inclined his head my way, but kept his eyes on Tommy.

"The life of her friend Louise," he chuckled and moved closer to the bars that Tommy was standing on the other side of and whispered something in Tommy's ear. Whatever it was must have been bad, because Tommy stiffened, and his eyes widened. I stood and watched through the little window as he reached through the bars at Nathaniel, who had already stepped back. Tommy's face set in a rage as he clawed at the air in front of Nathaniel.

"I will fucking kill you. Do you hear me? I will slaughter you if you harm one hair on my mate's head," he screamed. Nathaniel watched him for a few minutes before shaking his head and stepping back.

"Well, excuse me, everyone, I have dinner and a mating ritual to prepare for," he said and turned on his heel and walked down the hall without another word.

I looked over at Tommy, who was still raging in his cell.

"Tommy!" Marcus shouted. "Tommy, what is it?" Tommy stopped and collapsed to the floor, tears streaming down his face.

"Louise," he whispered. "She's pregnant."

Present Time

The room had fallen into silence over the last few hours as I tried to process my thoughts and the recent revelations about my monster's origin, or should I say, my demon. The demon in me seemed to have retreated wherever it was he went. Occasionally Tommy would get angry and rant, and his hands were bloody from his attempts at trying to pry open the bars that held him captive. But right now, we were all silent. Which is why we heard the screaming and shouting and stomps, even before we heard the doors of the cell building.

I jumped up to the window and made eye contact with Marcus in his own cell. I had a very bad feeling suddenly. From the look on Marcus' face, I could tell that he did too. The inner door opened, and suddenly the screaming was louder as I heard footsteps coming down the hall. Then I saw it. Nathaniel, his face set in rage, blood all down his front. And he dragged in his hands my screaming, struggling mate. The terrified look on her face was enough to set me off as the rage coursed through me. I had to get to my mate. I felt the demon in me, but instead of fighting me for the first time, we seemed to work together as I hurled myself at the door. It dented in the wake of my attack, but still didn't budge. I looked out the window again to see Tommy going crazy, as Louise was also dragged into the room by two guards. Stokes stood to one side, looking worried. But the one thing that drew my attention the most was my beautiful mate. She seemed to be almost glowing, without any actual glow. Her eyes met mine, and I couldn't pull away from the sight of those steel blue-grey as they seemed to lighten with her increased fear.

Then Nathaniel whispered something in her ear, and her eyes widened. She tore her eyes from mine, and I saw as she looked around the room. Something clattered to the floor, and Harper's eyes shot to mine again. I was stuck in their infinite beauty, as I saw something like serenity cross over them. She held me in her gaze as her skin seemed to begin to redden. I was pulled into the deep depths of her eyes and felt her need for me; her love for me. It felt like there were only the two of us at that moment.

And then Harper broke contact. She threw her head back and let out a piercing scream. Everything came back into focus as my mate fell to the floor in pain, screaming over and over as blood seemed to pour from her eyes, her nose, and her mouth. I couldn't move. I wanted to rage and break the door, and inside my head, the demon screamed.

"Give me control, give me control," he screamed, but I couldn't. The screams of my mate had me frozen in fear. I saw Tommy and Marcus ripping at their bars like they were in slow motion. I saw Nathaniel stepping back and Louise being dragged screaming from the room, and then I saw the room fill with warriors as they seemed to fight between them. But even though I saw all of that, I still saw as my mate collapsed to the floor and went still. I felt a sharp pain piercing me through my heart as I felt her connection to me being ripped away. Despite our bond not being complete, I felt the pain of it being severed in full as my beautiful Harper took her last painful breath.

That last final breath woke something back in me as the realisation hit. My face was wet with tears. I screamed and shouted as I fought with the solid metal barrier between my mate and me. I slammed myself repeatedly into it.

At some point, the door opened, and I flew into the room. I landed at the stilled body of my dead mate. Her face looked calm, like she was sleeping. But I knew her eyes would not open again. I pulled the empty husk of my mate into my arms, vaguely aware that it was hot to touch, and howled. I put all the pain of my grief into that howl. I mourned my mate right there. I clung to her empty remains as a mass of activity whirled around me. I looked up to see a man standing in front of me. I could tell by his scent that he was a vampire. He looked down at me with sympathy all over his face. He kneeled and reached for Harper. I growled at him and pulled her cooling body closer to me. I could feel the demon trying to rise to the surface. He, too, was protective of what was left of our mate.

"Mine," I growled again, and he frowned.

"I'm sorry, friend," he said. "I can't let you do that." He nodded behind me. I felt a sharp pinch on my neck, and then a strong sensation rushed over me as my body relaxed and I weakened. I tried to keep conscious as long as possible, but I was already being pulled under by whatever powerful drug was coursing through my veins.

I dropped to the floor, still holding onto my mate, but the last thing I felt as my eyes closed was her body being pried from my arms.

CHAPTER 78

Colton

I was dragged from the cells by two or three warriors, still hearing the painful screams of the woman I loved. I tried to fight, but I heard Nathaniel instruct them to drag me back to the pack house. I was thrown into the Alpha's office as Nathaniel strode in, instructing various warriors to surround the house and be on guard. Louise was in the corner crying, her makeup streaming down her face. I glanced over, and she looked up at me. Despite all the hatred, all that I had done to her, I knew that at this moment, we were both mourning someone we loved. I saw that acknowledgement in her eyes.

Nathaniel sat at the desk and began to speak, but he was interrupted by the sound of a mournful howl, one so powerful it could be heard all the way from the cells to where we were now. One so painful that it meant only one thing. Immediately, the sound made my heart break as I knew two things. One, that the woman I loved was dead. And two, that I didn't feel her die, which confirmed that our mate bond really had long since been dead. It didn't matter though because she was dead and the man in front of me was the one who killed her. I felt something inside me stir as the anger took over. I growled deep in my throat and flew over the desk at a surprised Nathaniel.

"You killed her," I snarled as I laid into him, punching him over and over in the face. "You killed her." I felt Nathaniel tense, and then I was thrown back across the room at speed and crashed into the wall opposite. I heard Louise scream in surprise as I slid down to the floor and lay in a crumpled mess.

"You killed her," I mumbled through the tears.

"Watch your place, boy," Nathaniel sneered at me as he watched me from across the room, "Don't be stupid now. You will still get the Alpha title." I looked up at him, not believing what I was hearing.

"I don't give a shit about the Alpha title," I spat as I sat up and glared at him. "I don't want to be Alpha. I want Harper!"

Nathaniel growled as he rounded the desk and was in front of me, and before I knew it, I was lifted and slammed against the wall by my shirt.

"Now listen here, boy," Nathaniel hissed. "Do not go soft on me now." He dragged me across the room and threw me back into the chair.

"Once we have exterminated the Council problem, you will become the Alpha of this pack, and you will produce an heir with my bloodline," he said, sitting back behind the desk.

"An heir?" I exclaimed. "What are you talking about?" Nathaniel looked over at Louise, who was still sitting on the floor in the corner.

"It turns out that our Mrs Chambers' little child is more special than your run-of-the-mill guardian." Louise's eyes widened, and her hands went protectively to her stomach.

"Oh, don't worry, my dear," Nathaniel said softly to Louise. "You and your baby are safe, for now at least. I have reason to believe that you could be carrying our next Divine Warrior right there, young lady." He smiled at her and Louise shook her head.

"No, it's not possible," she said. "Even if Harper is de-" she stopped before she could finish the word and closed her eyes as the emotional grief swept through her.

"Even if she is no longer here, she was still here when I conceived. You can't have two Divine Warriors. That was what we were told."

"That's not entirely true." I turned towards the voice at the door to see Susie standing there holding one of the old books from the library.

"You!" Louise hissed. "You traitorous bitch!" and Susie sneered at her.

"Oh, get off your high horse, you stuck up whore!" Susie spat. "I'm not the one who was all comfortable in the pack house as the future Luna and still went sleeping around."

"Sleeping around!" Louise shouted. "I was forced into a mating and taken away from my own mate. Your own family, if you remember. Oh, but of course, family means nothing to you now, does it," Louise was standing now, and the two women were inches away from each other.

"You're just jealous, now that you know that I was a higher rank than you all along," Susie spat.

"I don't give a flying fuck what your rank is, or was," Louise screamed. "I care about the fact that my best friend is dead, and now it appears you are the reason why. And here you are trying to gold-dig your way in without a single remorse that your own sister is dead. I bet your mother is really proud."

"Well, at least I know where my mother is," Susie screamed back. Louise slapped her across the face. I jumped up and grabbed Susie's arm as it began to rise.

"Whoa!" I said, and she turned and looked at me. Susie bowed her head and smiled sweetly.

"I'm sorry, Alpha," she said and then turned on her heel; and walked over to Nathaniel. I watched Louise, who looked to be on the verge of tears again, and she shook her head and moved back to the wall.

"You see this passage here?" Susie asked, and I turned to see both her and Nathaniel were pouring over a book. "It specifies that the number of Divine Warriors is proportional to the number of demons," Susie looked up at Louise and then at Nathaniel.

"I knew the glow on her was different from my son, so I'm sure that bringing your demons to Midnight Moon is giving us another Divine Warrior. And the fact that we now have two guardians, Tommy, and my son, that glow preempted my sister's demise."

"Pretty sure," Nathaniel growled. "Or certain?" he glowered at Susie, and she shrunk back.

"I'm certain, sir," she said and looked at me. "So it's just a matter of time. Once the child is born, you raise it in your influence, and then you can rip that seal right open."

"You are not raising my child," Louise spat, and I saw the black demon pass through Nathaniel's eyes as he looked over at Louise.

"You have no choice in the matter, my dear," he said. "I will wait until the child is born, and then I will take charge, and if you want to be even alive to be involved in the little angel's life, then you will cooperate. Do you understand?"

"Go to hell," Louise hissed, and Nathaniel laughed.

"Oh no, my dear, I plan on bringing hell here."

A few hours later, I slouched in my chair, the memory of Harper's screams running through my head while my uncle and Susie poured over various texts. There was a knock at the door, and I looked up to see my mum standing there.

"Mum!" I exclaimed and heard Nathaniel growl.

"What are you doing here, Caroline?" he said. "I thought I made it clear that I would deal with you later." My mum smiled first at Louise and then at me before turning to my uncle and frowning.

"I told you, I did what I did because it needed to be done." Nathaniel sighed.

"Since apparently, that was weaponising someone against me, then I think you should have thought about that course of action." He looked up at her over his glasses. "Make note, dear sister, it is with a heavy heart that once this is done, you will find yourself living out your days in a cell."

"What?" I exclaimed, sitting up. "You'll do no such thing." I stood up in front of my mum. The hell, I was going to let him hurt her. I felt my mum's hand on my arm.

"Don't worry, my misguided baby boy," she whispered in my ear. "I heard from the angels, and they forgive me for my sins." I look at her, but she is already looking at Nathaniel.

"You, however, you have been found guilty, and the light of the blade will punish you." Nathaniel looked up at my mum, and I moved to block his view. I didn't want one of my mum's crazy rants to anger Nathaniel right now.

"Shh!" my mum said. "Can you hear that? It's time for the reckoning."

"Caroline," Nathaniel snapped.

"Five," my mum sang.

"My patience..." Nathaniel growled.

"Four."

"Is wearing..." I could see Nathaniel getting more agitated.

"Three."

"Very thin..." his eyes switched to black, and I adjusted my stance, ready to protect my mum.

"Two."

"That's it!" he said and jumped over the desk. I felt him advance on us. Then there was a knock at the door, breaking the tension in the air. Nathaniel looked at the door, and I turned to see one of his warriors standing there looking nervous.

"Sir, there is a gathering outside the pack house. They have called to see you," the warrior squawked, and I rolled my eyes at his cowardice. I looked around at Nathaniel and saw the anger on his face as he growled.

"Fine, let's get this over with," he snapped. He looked at me. "Colton, my side now." I glared at him.

"My mother is not to be harmed."

He growled. "We will discuss it later," he said, but I knew he had no intention of discussing anything with me.

"Susie, watch our expectant mother," he said. "Ensure she doesn't go anywhere." Susie nodded. Nathaniel moved towards the door, and I made sure I stayed between him and my mother.

"Now, Colton," he called back without looking. I glanced at Louise, who looked terrified but tired. I pulled my mum into a hug.

"Get her out of here, get her back to her mate," I whispered, and my mum kissed my cheek. I let her go and nodded to Louise and then inclined my head to my mum, hoping she got the hint. I turned to walk out the door when I heard my mum's voice.

"One."

I headed after my uncle down the stairs and into the entrance filled with warriors. They parted as we walked up to the doorway. I followed closely behind and stepped out onto the steps. I looked out to see a line of warriors across the courtyard. At the centre, I saw Tommy and Elias, their faces set in blank determination. I knew at that moment my mum was right. The reckoning had arrived, and we were about to go to war.

CHAPTER 79

Elias

My head was pounding as I woke up to the buzz of activity. I sat up, looking around to see that I was laid in one of the booths at Howlers. The room was filled with Council warriors, as well as some of my own. I looked around for the centre of the activity and saw the vampire that had tried to take Harper from me.

Then it hit me again. Harper. My beautiful mate was dead. I felt like I couldn't breathe all over again as a single tear slipped down my cheek. The rage followed, and with it, the stirring of the demon inside me.

"Kill," it said. The guttural voice felt raw with hatred. I agreed with what he said. I had to find Nathaniel and rip him apart limb from limb. I would scatter his remains across the town, and the ground would be soaked with his blood. I would make him scream for her forgiveness before finally putting him out of his misery. I felt my mind slip into the hate-fuelled rage when I was pulled back out by a loud slam. I looked over to see Tommy growling at the vampire.

"I don't want to wait. You don't know what they are doing to her," he snarled.

"I told you they won't do anything to her, not yet," the vampire responded, unfazed by Tommy's threatening stance. "Now calm down and start thinking straight, young Thomas, or you will be useless to us all. Your mate included." I got out of the booth, walked over towards them, and saw Tommy looking up at me. The rage drained from his face and was replaced with a mix of sympathy and grief. I shook my head. The vampire was right. We needed to be clear-headed if we were to exact our revenge and take down the bastard responsible for killing my sister and my mate.

"Finally awake, I see," the vampire said as I got close. I knew that even though he never once turned around, it was me he was talking to.

"Well, if you hadn't dosed me with what the hell you used on me, I might have been awake sooner," I snapped, and his shoulders moved as I heard a chuckle.

"Ah yes, but then you would have also been useless in your grief," he said, finally turning around. He held out a hand towards me, and I eyed it cautiously.

"Drake Valcoin," he said. "High Council Elder."

"High Council, huh?" I scoffed. "So were you aware you had the Circle in your walls, or were you all idiots?"

"Elias!" I heard Marcus exclaim from behind me. "Don't be a dick." He came up beside me and placed his hand on my shoulder. "We are gonna need them right now, so hold off on the insults until we've run the filth out of town." Valcoin just smiled.

"No, you are quite right to question the integrity of the Council Alpha Owens," he said. "I am not happy to find we had high-ranking members of the Circle in such positions in the Council. They have poisoned the minds of several promising young warriors."

"And betrayed some of us in the process, too." I looked up to see Aaron walking up. He was holding hands with Katie, and I looked down, confused. Katie squirmed in my gaze for a moment until Aaron squeezed her hand, and then she looked up at him before meeting my eyes. For a brief second, I saw the flash of gold, and I realised. They were fated mates. I nodded and offered a brief smile her way,

"Congratulations to both of you," I said, and Aaron nodded in response.

The door opened, and people walked in, led by Alex. I immediately recognised some of my own men from other packs, including a few that had been relocated from this pack: Greg Henderson and Richard Tobbins among them. I had worked hard to pull the pack members who showed loyalty to me out of harm's way, but I could see that they were here willingly and ready to fight by the determined look on their faces. I nodded to the table in front of me and glanced up at Valcoin.

"What's the plan?" I asked.

"We have two objectives for this, rescue young Mrs Chambers-"

"Bennet," both Alex and Tommy said in unison, and Valcoin nodded.

"Apologies, Miss Bennet," he said, and Tommy nodded. "The second objective is to detain Nathaniel Bethrinton." I growled at the name.

"I plan on killing the bastard," I growled, and Valcoin rolled his eyes.

"I would rather you hold off from that, Alpha. I wish to extract any further possible Circle members in my Council," Valcoin said.

"No, get the information from someone else. Either he dies, or I do tonight," I said. I looked Valcoin squarely in the eye and waited for him to argue with me. He held my gaze for a moment and then sighed.

"Fine," he said. "Do what you must."

I nodded, and we launched into the plan of action for tonight's battle. It was already late, but Valcoin said he wanted to strike quickly. They had already captured many of Bethrinton's warriors on the way in, so he wanted to strike while their numbers were down. The more we talked about the plans for the battle, the more alive I felt. My body came awake at the thought that I would soon be on the battlefield, so to speak. And that I would be fighting against the people who had wronged me. It was like I was built for this, and the anticipation was a drug in my veins.

I was equipping myself when I felt the demon stirring inside me in excitement.

"Let me take control," he whispered. "I will ensure the blood of that bastard flows through our hands tonight."

"No," I said. "I want to kill him."

"Ha!" he scoffed. "You are too weak to go up against a demon of his status. I am equal to him, and I will end him for what he did to our mate." The sting of tears hit my eyes as I remembered the pain of losing her again. It came in flashes, and for a second, I would be right back there, cradling my mate's cooling body. I shook myself. I didn't have time to allow myself to be distracted. I could fall apart after he was dead.

"What's happening in your head?" I jumped slightly at the voice behind me. I had been so lost in thought and argument with the demon that I hadn't seen Marcus coming up.

"What do you mean?" I asked, and he scoffed.

"Elias, I have been with you for more years than I care to remember," he said. "Don't try to tell me that you aren't in deep conversation with your other self." I smiled weakly. I guess there were things that I couldn't hide from my best friend.

"He wants me to let him have control," I said. "He wants to take over for the battle. It's like he is caged, and all this talk of fighting is exciting him and me, more than I can handle."

"Are you going to let him out?" Marcus asked, and I shrugged.

"Honestly, I don't know," I said, and he nodded,

"Wanna hear my opinion?" Marcus asked, and I grinned.

"Do I have a choice?" I asked in return.

"I guess not," he chuckled. "I think that you only let him out if needed, but if you want closure, it has to be you who has to do this." I nodded in acknowledgement.

"Also," I said. "I can't help but think that Harper fought her angel to the end." I had to stop and breathe as the pain hit again. "How would she feel if I gave in and allowed the demon to consume me to exact her revenge?"

"It's not like that," the demon piped up.

"I don't think we know enough about all this to be able to accurately say for sure what would happen," Marcus said.

"I said it better," the demon said, and I let out a small laugh under my breath.

"What?" Marcus asked, confused.

"The demon thinks you talk too much," I said and shrugged.

"Well, he's a dick," he retorted, and I laughed again.

Marcus got serious suddenly.

"How are you doing, man?" he asked, and I shrugged again.

"Fits and bouts," I answered. "When it happened, I felt her being ripped away. There was a place inside me that was empty. But now I am searching for that place, and I can't find it. It's strange." I could tell that he was struggling, too.

"What about you?" I asked, and he laughed nervously.

"Honestly, I feel like I failed," he said. "My whole life, I was told that when I met my Luna, I should devote my life to protecting her at all costs, and here we are a week after meeting her, and she's no longer here." I nodded. Marcus came from a long line of Gamma warriors. Their particular line was one of the most dedicated I had ever seen.

I saw Valcoin walking towards us. He was dressed in all black like the rest of us, although he carried only one weapon. I overheard him saying that he didn't need anything other than that. Vampires thought so much of themselves but hit them in the right spot, and they could die as easily as the rest of us.

"We are setting out," he said, and I nodded. I picked up the last of my weapons and slid them into the loop in my vest. I could hear some of our people already shifting into their wolves. We had decided that we would fight in human form but have wolves in the woods ready to attack at the right time. I was itching to shift, but Jax was still in mourning at the loss of his mate and was strangely quiet. I nodded to Valcoin and set off for the door, with Marcus following close behind.

"Ah, Mr Farwell," Valcoin called, and we both turned. "Could I have a word please before we set out?" Marcus looked at me, and I shrugged.

"See you out there," I said, and he nodded. I headed over to Tommy and Aaron, and with barely an acknowledgement, we set off out of the bar and headed to the SUVs that were waiting for us. I got in the front seat and watched as the wolves disappeared into the woods as if they were never there. I had been in many showdown fights, but this felt strangely different, like electricity was in the air.

Valcoin joined us in the car, and I looked out for Marcus but couldn't see him. I inclined my head in question to Valcoin, but he just smiled. I shook my head as the car started moving. I had to get myself in the game here, so I spent the journey centring myself and ignoring the constant babble from my demon. It wasn't long before we made it to the drop point. We would be on foot from here. And we headed in silence up towards the pack house. Our sources told us that Bethrinton and Stokes were there, and that was where they held Louise as well. We formed a box around the pack house, taking out the few warriors we came across in the woods. I ensured I was standing on the front line alongside Tommy, Aaron, Alex, and Valcoin.

Alex called to one of the nervous-looking warriors.

"Get your boss out here. We have a message for him," he said, his face set in determination. In all this, he seemed level-headed to the point that I was very impressed, especially to say it was his sister in there. But now, I could see the hunger in his eyes and the thirst for blood as he stared at the entrance in anticipation. The door opened, and I saw Bethrinton stalk out, followed closely by Stokes. I had my war face on. No emotions. Just the fight. My body was wired with energy, and all I wanted to do was attack.

"Good evening Valcoin, Owens," Bethrinton called. "To what do we owe this pleasure?" I growled in response, and he chuckled.

"Curious Owens, do you feel it?" he asked. "The tension in the air? I can imagine that someone of your bloodline is thriving on the scent of war." My bloodline? What was he talking about?

"He's trying to disarm you," the demon said. "Don't fall for it." I nodded and centred my sight on Bethrinton. I didn't care about anyone else. All I wanted was him.

Bethrinton inclined his head to one of the warriors, and the warrior turned to face us, rage on his face.

"Attack!" he called. The battle cry was heard through the woods, and I glanced at Tommy, who nodded.

"Attack!" He called in return, and the fight began as the two sides rushed together in the courtyard of the pack house. I easily dispatched the occasional warrior who came across my path, barely even acknowledging their existence.

But my sights were on one figure that had moved towards the wood line, and it wasn't long before I found myself face to face with Bethrinton.

"So think you can take me, boy?" he asked as we circled each other. I growled and lunged at him, hitting him in the stomach and taking us both crashing into the woods. Bethrinton laughed as we rolled and quickly moved back to his feet. I jumped up, but he launched at me at lightning speed, and I grunted as he hit me. I flew back into a trunk and slid down, the breath knocked out of me.

"Do you really think you can defeat me without your demon boy?" Bethrinton called as he stalked after me. He picked me up like I weighed nothing and threw me into another tree. I felt bones crack and cried out in pain as the demon screamed to be let out. Bethrinton was on me again. And his hands closed around my throat. I tried to struggle, but all the energy had gone out of me. I looked into the soulless black eyes of the man that killed the woman I loved and realised why Jax had been quiet. He already knew what I was avoiding admitting. He had already accepted that I had no plans to survive this battle.

I wanted nothing more than to join my beautiful mate in death. I couldn't live in a world that she simply was not in. The demon howled in my head as the realisation hit, and he fought for control. But I was already beginning to suffocate at the hands of Bethrinton.

"You mean to die?" Bethrinton said as he looked into my eyes. "Interesting, maybe I don't know love, after all. Well, boy, I am more than happy to accommodate that desire." I had long since stopped struggling, and I closed my eyes, knowing that soon it would be over. The darkness clouded in as my body was starved of oxygen.

And then I saw a light, dim at first. But it grew brighter. Suddenly, the pressure on my neck disappeared, and my lungs burned as oxygen rushed in through my now unobstructed windpipe. I opened my eyes to see Bethrinton on the ground, looking up at a figure. She held something in her hand that glowed an incredible light. I could feel my body going into shock from the injuries, and I was fading fast into unconsciousness. The figure turned and looked at me, and I knew then that I must be in heaven because I was in the presence of an angel.

"Harper!" I exclaimed before the darkness took me and I passed out.

CHAPTER 80

Drake

I looked down at the werewolf in front of me in sympathy. I had heard many things about Elias Owens. I knew his family were allies of the order and also knew they had been ripped apart by the destructive Circle twenty or so years back. I even remembered Owen's brief time at the Council. He had disappeared one night, and then a couple of days later, I heard about the attack on his pack. I had no idea that he had a demon bloodline in him. He had hidden it well.

And now, here he was, cradling his dead lover. The sweet Harper. The beautiful woman who had risen in the ranks of the warriors with ease over the years. I was unsurprised by her progress as I watched her. I could tell at first sight who she was or what she was. Her ethereal glow was unmistakable and would be recognised by others of our kind. I was almost surprised that she didn't recognise me until I realised she had no idea of her origin. I had tried to enlighten her about her unique powers early on. I seduced her to my castle with the intent of showing her who she was. But it wasn't long before I received word from the Sovereign, the leader of our Council and the one who maintained balance, to leave her alone. He wanted her untouched, wanted her kept in the dark about her destiny. I didn't understand why, but I complied, and when young Mr Aaron turned up a few hours later, I allowed him to play the white knight with ease. But I kept watch. I watched the fledgling as she fell into mentorship with Nathaniel. I didn't like that he was so close to our little angel, especially with his bloodline. But again, I was instructed by the Sovereign to stand down and watch from afar. Something about keeping enemies close. I had no idea that Nathaniel was working with the Circle until Aaron contacted me the other night.

If I had known, I would have pulled Harper from his grasp a lot sooner. That was a conversation that the Sovereign and I were due to have. But for now, I had work to do. I reached for Harper's body, but the grief-stricken werewolf growled at me.

"Mine," he growled, and I hesitated before I spoke.

"I'm sorry, friend, I can't let you do that," I said. It was important that no harm came to the body he held. But I couldn't tell him that, not yet. I wasn't sure if I was on time, and I didn't want to be responsible for him losing a mate all over again if I was too late. I remembered that pain all too well. I wouldn't wish it on anyone. I nodded to Jacks, who was waiting behind Owens. He leaned forward and injected Owens with a sleeping concoction designed for werewolves. It would put him out for an hour. It worked almost immediately, and I was able to safely remove Harper from his arms as he crashed to the floor. I laid her gently down on the floor and called to Jacks.

"Take him to the base," I said, and Jacks nodded and picked Owens up and headed out of the cell. I looked around at the people. I saw Tommy standing to one side, watching me.

"I failed her," he said sadly. "What kind of guardian am I if I couldn't even get my niece ready?"

"Not yet, friend," I said, and nodded for a warrior to come forward.

"I need the room cleared," I said. The warrior nodded and ushered people out of the room, and although Tommy resisted a little, I knew he was also eager to get his own mate back.

"It's okay. I will take care of her," I said, and he nodded.

Once the room was cleared and quiet, I knelt beside the still form of Harper Kirby.

"Oh dear sweet girl," I said as I stroked the hair from her face. I used my shirt to wipe away the blood. I remember my own battle, and even for an immortal such as myself, the burn was enough to knock the breath out of me.

"I do hope I have got here in time." I reached into my jacket and pulled out the package that I had there. I unwrapped the cloth to reveal the angel blade. There was a slight hum to it that was promising as it recognised its rightful owner. Once Aaron called me and told me that her grandfather had taken Harper's angel blade, I knew I would have to detour to see the old crank. I knew he didn't want his granddaughter to suffer the fate of many before her, but he had to understand that fate was fate, and if the girl were to have any hope of survival, she would need to be released into her true image.

I held the blade over her stomach and plunged it in quickly. It slid in with ease, and I felt the energy spring out into the body. I took a deep breath and sent out a prayer before I removed the end of the cloth and grabbed the handle of the blade. I hissed as the burn hit me. Each blade was made in its own bloodline, and only that Divine Warrior could wield it. But this was the only way I could get the connection I needed. I closed my eyes and allowed myself to be transported in soul to the Neverplain.

I looked around at the desolate landscape surrounding me and sighed. The Neverplain was the plain of existence between heaven and hell and existed outside of earth. It had been called limbo, purgatory, and many other names over the years. But it didn't matter the name. It was still the place that souls went to before it was decided where they would go. Or most souls, at least. I searched the plain for Harper. I knew she was here, and that I had to get to her. I saw a light up ahead, and the blade in my hand seemed to pulse, so I followed that direction. I had gone maybe a hundred steps when I heard a voice calling out.

"No, no, no, leave me alone," the unmistakable voice of Harper called. I could tell she was frightened, so I quickened my step and rushed forward. The light grew brighter, and I rounded the corner to see the angelic form of Harper standing over a huddled figure. The angel turned to me and gestured to the figure frantically. She was silenced by Harper's death but still clung on to hope. I nodded to her and knelt by the terrified girl, who was hiding her head in her arms. I touched her arm gently, and she jumped.

"No, no, don't touch me," she screamed through sobs.

"Harper, sweetheart," I coaxed quietly, and she looked up, startled. Her face was dirty and tear-stained, and her eyes were wild with fear.

"Drake?" she exclaimed in surprise, and I nodded and smiled.

"Hello, sweetheart," I said, and she threw herself into my arms and began sobbing on my shoulder.

"Oh, Drake, what are you doing here? Why are you in hell?" she sobbed. I gently pulled her away from me so I could see her face.

"Harper, you aren't in hell," I said gently, and she gestured around her.

"How could I not be?" she asked. "I'm doomed to be chased by that for all eternity in this wasteland. How is this not hell?"

"Sweetheart, you are in the Neverplain," I said. "You have the power to change how it looks." She looked around and then back at me. "Just focus on yourself. Calm yourself. See, the world around you shift to what you want it to be." I watched as she closed her eyes. Her sobs became quieter, and her breathing evened.

As she calmed down, so did the world around us. The wind calmed, and the desolation gave way to lush green trees. Finally, Harper opened her eyes and looked around. She smiled and looked at me.

"I did it!" she exclaimed. "What else can I do?" I wiped the tears from her face and smiled.

"You can't stay here." I looked up at her angel self, who was standing patiently to one side. Harper followed my sight and frowned.

"No, why didn't that go too?" she cried in despair. "I told you to leave me alone. I don't want you stealing who I am?" I gave her a quizzical look.

"Harper, she is you. She can't go anywhere," I said, and she frowned at me.

"Drake, she killed me," she said. "Because I wouldn't let her consume me."

"Harper, sweetheart, your body couldn't contain you both being separate, but your angel self is a part of you. She isn't separate." I sighed. "I wish he had let me take you and teach you everything. Your transition would have been a lot easier."

"What?" She looked confused.

"Harper, you are the shifter bloodline Divine Warrior. I knew it from the first moment I set eyes on you," I said. "That's why I brought you to the Castle. I wanted to teach you and guide you."

"That wasn't how I remembered the Castle." Harper eyed me suspiciously, and I felt the sly smile creep across my face.

"Well, I may have gone about it the wrong way, but I have never experienced passions with another Divine Warrior before. I was curious," I said, and her eyes widened.

"Another one, do you mean…" she trailed off as I nodded. I stood up, and with my free hand, I reached into where I knew my own angel blade was and pulled him out. I twirled the hilt in my hand, and the blade flew through the air, leaving a trail of lights.

Harper watched with fascination until she noticed the other one in my hand.

"What's that one?" she asked, and I smiled and held it out to her. She looked up at the angel and shook her head.

"Doesn't matter now. I'm dead," she said and glared at the angel.

"Sweetheart, we have angel blood running through our veins. We are only dead if we want to be," I said, and the angel held her hand out. Harper flinched.

"I don't want to lose who I am. I don't want to be like Nathaniel," she said, and I smiled again.

"Oh, Harper, Nathaniel was a bastard before he accepted his demon," I said. "I remember him as a young boy at the academy. He had a self-entitled attitude even then. It is a curse of his bloodline." Harper looked at me, confused. Then she looked at the angel and shook her head.

"I'm tired, Drake. I've been fighting for too long. Can't I just stay dead?" she said. "It really hurts to be alive," and tears slipped down her face.

"Harper, there are some major things about to happen. I need you to be walking around to help us." I didn't want to say the next part. Still, she had to know. "Also, Nathaniel has your friend Louise and your other friends, and your lover seeks to go up against him. I am not sure that even with my help, they will be successful." Harper looked up at me with the force of determination that I knew to be at the core of her spirit.

"I will kill him," she said and then looked at the angel. "Promise, I will still be me?" she asked, and the angel side smiled and nodded, and I smiled too.

"I have to go, little angel, but I hope to see you on the battlefield. We will attack soon." I laid the blade at her feet, stood up again, bowed, and closed my eyes.

I opened my eyes in the dark empty room of the cells and looked down at the body. I had done everything I could. Even if she agreed to come back, it could be too late. The window was unpredictable after the death of the vessel.

"I really do hope we are in time, little angel."

CHAPTER 81

Harper

My eyes flew open as I woke up in the cells. I sat up and looked around, allowing my eyes to adjust to the low light after the brightness of the Neverplain. I looked down to see the angel blade still in my stomach. I inclined my head at it curiously. Was I meant to pull it out myself? Everything was beginning to blur for me. The Neverplain and my angel and the visit from Drake. Did Drake really visit? Or was that just my perverted imagination putting him there? And was he really also a Divine Warrior? A million questions were running through my mind, some repeated, some serious, some stupid. It was like my mind was in overdrive, and I couldn't focus on one thing.

I heard a chuckle to one side of me and looked towards the source.
"Hello darling," Marcus said from his perch on one of the desks at the back of the room. "Glad to see you have joined us back in the land of the living." I smiled back at him.

"Hello Marcus," I said, "What are you doing here?"

"Well, it appears that I have a bigger role to play in all of this," he said. "Valcoin told me to come here and wait for you. At first, I thought he was crazy. Still, then he explained that if his pep talk worked, the blade would be glowing." He pointed to the blade in my stomach. "So when I got here and saw the blade glowing, I sat and waited." He looked down at his watch. "Took your time, though. I was getting bored. You're lucky I couldn't find a pen. Otherwise, you might have woken up with a moustache." He shrugged and then winked at me.

"Dick," I shot back, and he laughed.

"That's the Harper I like to hear," he said. "What took you so long?"

"I was upset about dying painfully and all," I said, rolling my eyes.

"Yeah, that looked like it sucked," he said, and I glared at him. "Are you over it now?"

"Yeah," I said, looking down at the blade again. "I think I am."

"Good, because there is a battle going on, and I, for one, would like to get my hands bloody on some traitorous blood," he said, standing up. He walked over and held out his hand to me. I grabbed it, and he pulled me up to stand. The blade ripped on the dress, and I sighed. I reached down and grabbed the hilt, and it glowed as I touched it. I pulled it out with one swift movement and was hit by an awesome rush of power through my body. The aches that I was feeling eased, and the wound the blade had made healed, leaving perfect skin. I looked at the glowing blade and swirled it around like I saw Drake doing in the Neverplain. Just like with his blade, it made a light show in the air.

"Neat," I said, looked down at my tattered dress, and sighed. I didn't have time for a costume change, but I kicked off the broken heels. I looked up at Marcus expectantly.

"Lead the way," I said, and he grinned.

"Let's do this."

We headed out of the empty cells. Obviously, it was all hands on deck at the main fight. As soon as we made it out into the night, I heard the evidence of the fight going on at the pack house. We headed quickly in that direction. I could already see the effects of accepting my angel. My eyesight was clearer. Even in the dark night, I could see everything in such a sharp focus—so much clearer than my werewolf eyes. In fact, it was like all my senses were heightened, as well as my sense of presence.

I stopped mid-run and stood still. I scanned the surrounding woods, and Marcus turned back, confusion on his face. I signalled to be quiet as I sent out, well; I didn't know what it was, but it was like a radar feeler in my surrounding area. I recognised Marcus as I felt him and saw him react to this new touch. Then I felt something else, someone was following us. I turned towards the person and smiled.

"Come out now," I said, staring at the exact spot where I knew they were. I listened as the woods rustled, and finally, I saw a figure appear with its hands raised. Another step, and I recognised Paul, one of the warriors from the Council.

"Hi Paul," I said as I eyed the sword in his hand. "What are you doing there?" He let out a sarcastic laugh.

"So you really do remember my name then?" he asked, and I smiled.

"Oh, I remember everyone," I said and tilted my head. "Marcus, three behind you," I called, and heard a scuffle behind me. "Fuck!" I heard Marcus exclaim as he hit the floor.

"You just need to come quietly, Harper," Paul said. "And maybe we can catch up on that later you promised me back in the closet at the Council."

"I doubt it, cupcake," I said. "For one, I have no intentions of coming with you. I mean, let's face it, even when you tried, I had trouble cumming with you back in that closet." I heard a snigger behind me, and Paul growled at me. "And two, you'll all be dead in the next sixty seconds."

"Erm, darling," Marcus said as I felt him move up behind me, so his back was to me, and we had all four warriors in our sights. "I'm good, but I'm not sure I can do four in under a minute."

"Don't worry, Marcus, sweetie," I said, pulling the angel blade out from the one sleeve of my dress. It instantly glowed lightly in the woods. "You can sit this one out." I swirled the blade around and watched Paul's cocky attitude begin to melt in uncertainty.

"In fact, Marcus," I said.

"Yeah, darling?"

"Sit. Now!"

Marcus dropped to the floor, and at the same time, I swung the blade around and let go. I watched as it flew quickly towards the first of the three warriors behind me. I jumped over Marcus and rushed to the blade, meeting it as it entered the first warrior. The second my hand was on the hilt, it lit back up again, and the warrior screamed in pain as the blade burned right through him. He hadn't dropped to the floor yet when I pulled the blade out and used it to slice the throat of the second warrior. I saw as, in slow motion, the wound erupted in blue flames, killing the second warrior instantly. The third warrior had a chance to grab his weapon from his holster, and I sliced down at the wrist, taking his hand. He dropped to the floor screaming, and I plunged the blade into his chest, hitting his heart.

I swung around to see Paul heading towards me, his face in a state of rage. And Marcus' ass only just hitting the ground. I threw the blade again at Paul and met it again. I paused for a second to see Paul register. I was now back in front of him and smiled as I plunged the sword into his abdomen and up through his chest.

"You feel that burn?" I asked, as his eyes widened. "That is the burn of your demon blood coming in contact with the pure divine power of my angel blood." I twisted the blade, and he howled, "Sorry, Paul," I said. "You never stood a chance." I watched as the blade purified the demon's blood and burned what was left of his corrupted soul, and he dropped to the floor with his eyes wide.

I turned back to Marcus, who was staring at me, his jaw practically on the floor.

"Look at that," I grinned. "I have super speed now." I walked over to him and held out my hand. He hesitated before taking it, and I rolled my eyes as I pulled him up.

"Erm, what the fuck was that?" Marcus asked, and I grinned.

"Hell, if I know," I said and then realised what I said. I burst out laughing. "Hell if I know," I repeated, tears streaming down my face. It wasn't even funny, but with the day I was having, then I think my sanity was wearing a little thin. I finally stopped laughing and looked up at Marcus, who didn't look amused.

"Ouch!" I said, "tough room."

"Harper!" he exclaimed, "How did you know to do, well, this?" He waved his arm around at the four bodies on the floor. I shrugged.

"Honestly, I have no idea," I said. "It's like I have this knowledge that isn't mine or can't access it until I need it. Or like muscle memory, I just knew what to do." Marcus rubbed the back of his neck and blew out a breath.

"Damn girl," he said. "I don't know who's protecting who right now." I set off towards the pack house.

"Told you I could look after myself," I said, as I turned back to him and winked. Marcus laughed in response as he jogged to catch up with me.

"Oh, I'm convinced, darling, I always was. But damn, you impress me."

"Oh, I suspect we haven't seen anything yet," I said, and he chuckled.

We were close enough to the pack house by this point that I could see warriors fighting against one another. We headed towards it, and I was about to step out into the battlefield when I heard a frightened voice.

"Jax," Maia called from inside me, "Harper, he and Elias are dying."

"What, where?" I asked back in my head.

"The other side of the pack house," she cried. "They have given up." I turned to Marcus in fear.

"I have to get to Elias," I said. "He's being stupid. You try to find Louise." He nodded and rushed off towards the pack house. I headed around the fringe of the battle so that I didn't draw attention to myself. I could feel the pull of the bond with Elias and allowed it to guide me to where he was. I finally entered a clearing, realising it was the one I shifted in not so long ago. It was still bathed in the moonlight, but this time, I saw Nathaniel leaning over Elias, his hands around his throat. I pulled out the blade bathing the clearing in the light, and I rushed him, knocking him across the clearing. I stalked Nathaniel across the clearing and saw the exact moment he realised it was me.

"No!" he exclaimed. "You died. I saw you burn." I smiled down at him.

"Yeah, didn't take," I said. I heard a cough and looked over to see Elias looking up at me.

"Harper!" he exclaimed, and I ran to him just as his eyes closed again. I felt for a pulse and sighed when I felt relief sweep through me.

I felt Nathaniel advancing on me and swung around, swiping my leg, taking his out from under him. I jumped to my feet and stood over him.

"You can't beat me now, Nathaniel," I said. "You may have taught me everything I knew; however, it appears now I have a new, more divine mentor." His eyes widened as he eyed the blade in my hand.

"No," he cried. "You shouldn't have that. I made sure of it." I narrowed my eyes at him, ready to ask what he meant by that. But he took my confusion to his advantage and kicked out at me, hitting me in the chest with force. I flew back out of the clearing and into the main battleground.

"Son of a bitch," I exclaimed as I saw him rushing at me. I jumped up to my feet and sidestepped as he came close. He anticipated my move and adjusted, slamming his fist into my face. It knocked my head back and hurt like a bitch, but I recovered quickly and twisted and slammed my hand into his neck. He dropped to the floor, and I took the angel blade and slid it straight into his stomach. He cried out as his skin sizzled. The very strength of his demon blood was his own undoing, incapacitating him, attacking the angel blade, and his own body at the same time. I leaned into him, the blade still held in his stomach.

"Nathaniel Bethrinton, this is your reckoning," I said, and his eyes widened as if I had said something important to him. "You have been found guilty in the eyes of the Divine Order." I didn't need to know how I knew this, just that I knew it.

"Your punishment is served," and I pulled upward, slicing with ease through his body, bones, and muscle. I watched the light die from his eyes as the warmth of his blood-splattered and sizzled against my skin. He dropped to the floor an empty husk of himself. I looked down at the now dead body and laughed.

"Go to hell."

CHAPTER 82

Harper

The battle seemed to dissipate after I killed Nathaniel. I didn't know if seeing me slaughter their feared leader with the angel blade scared them or if it was just good timing, but there was no more fighting. I looked around to see the courtyard, a mess of dead and wounded.

"Harper?" I turned to see Tommy looking at me in disbelief.

"Hey," I said and shrugged. He grinned, tears down his face,

"Fucking hell, Harper," he pulled me into a hug, and I laughed. "Don't ever do that to me again."

"I'll do my best," I said. He pulled me to arm's length.

"You look different," he said, surveying me.

"Actually, I'm pretty much the same," I said, and he narrowed his eyes. "I'll explain later." I nodded to Drake as he walked up, smiling.

"Good to see you made the right decision," he said.

"Tommy!" a voice cried from the pack house. "Goddess dammit, put me down, you lug. I'm pregnant, not injured," I grinned as I saw Louise struggle out of Marcus' arms and run to Tommy, flinging herself in his arms. I looked behind Marcus and saw Colton walking while pushing my sister in front of him.

"You bastard!" Tommy shouted when he saw Colton and ran at him, but Louise stopped him.

"Tommy, don't. He protected me." I looked up at Colton and realised that he was staring at me, and so was Susie.

"Susie was trying to drag me somewhere, and it was Colton and his mum that stopped her." She then looked at me and smiled before hugging me.

"It was Susie who told Nathaniel that my baby was going to be a Divine Warrior." Both Tommy and I stared at her, and she shrugged. "I'll tell you later. I'm really glad you are alive, though," she said.

"You don't seem surprised, though," I said, and she smiled and nodded towards the house.

"No, she told me."

I looked up at the steps and saw Caroline Stokes smiling. She saw me looking and waved at me before walking back into the pack house. Tommy looked up at Colton, who was slowly walking towards me. He stood in front of me and then dropped to his knees.

"Thank the goddess," he said, and I smiled.

"Thank you for protecting my friend," I said, and he shook his head.

"It's not enough, nowhere near enough for what I caused," I smiled again.

"It's a start," Tommy said, and then nodded to a warrior coming up behind Colton. I watched as Colton was taken away. I saw another warrior place cuffs on Susie, and I walked over to her.

"Why?" I asked. "Why would you do that not just to me but to the baby, your own blood?"

Susie sneered at me. "All you had to do was complete the mate bond. Then we would have been free. But no, little miss angel had to be all difficult and selfish," she spat at me, and I heard Tommy growl. I held up my hand.

"Leave her. She can think about what she's done and if she will see her kids again in the Council prisons." Susie's face paled.

"No, my kids, please," she cried, and I nodded to the warrior who held her. He dragged her away as she wailed. I saw my mum stop the warrior at one side, and then she said something to Susie before slapping her in the face. Susie looked devastated after that and allowed herself to be dragged away.

"Mum," I said, and I rushed over and hugged her.

"My beautiful baby angel," she cooed. "I'm so sorry. I didn't know how we were hurting you." I smiled and hugged her again. I wanted to ask more questions, but then I heard a voice that hit me deep in my soul.

"Harper," I turned to see Elias running out of the clearing, his eyes wild, searching for me, "Harper, where is she? I know I saw her."

"Elias!" I called, and he stopped, frozen in place. Tears streamed down my face as he slowly turned towards me. I couldn't wait much longer, and I ran at him and threw myself into his arms.

"Oh my goddess!" he exclaimed. "I never thought that I would love the smell of strawberries so much in my life." I laughed through the tears, and he smiled at me, the love clear in his eyes. He leaned in, and I felt his lips against mine. I wanted to melt into the kiss, but instead, I pulled away and hit him hard on the head.

"Ow!" he exclaimed. "What was that for?"

"I swear to the goddess that if you ever do that again, if you ever give up and allow yourself to die again, I will be the one killing you. Do you understand Owens?" I scolded, and he smiled weakly.

"I just couldn't imagine living when you were not in the world," he said, and I hit him again.

"Not good enough," I said, the tears streaming. "I almost didn't get to you in time." He pulled me into a hug again. All the emotions over the last day hit me, and I sobbed onto his shoulder while he whispered it was alright and he loved me repeatedly in my ear.

I don't know how long I clung to him or when exactly we moved into the pack house. But it was breaking daylight when I finally peeled myself away from Elias to go for a shower. I scrubbed the blood and ash from me and then soaked in the heat and sensation of the water for a while. I knew there was still so much to do, but right now, I needed to just be still. I finally got out of the shower and wrapped myself in a towel. I stepped out of the bathroom and saw Elias was sitting on the bed. His hair looked wet, and he looked fresh out of the shower himself. He must have snuck into one of the other rooms while I was in this bathroom.

I watched him as he looked lost in his own thoughts, and they looked like sad ones. He finally looked up, and his eyes lit up. He smiled, but I could still sense the sadness. I walked over and stood in front of him and stroked his cheek. He leaned his head into my hand and then wrapped his arms around my torso and pulled me closer, burying his head into my stomach. I ran my fingers through his hair, and he groaned at my touch.

"Elias?" I whispered. "What is it?" He looked up at me and smiled.

"Nothing, baby," he said and pulled me down so that I was straddling him. I leaned in and brushed my lips against his. He groaned again and pushed against me, putting pressure on my lips and pushing his tongue into my mouth. I accepted willingly and deepened the kiss, pushing my whole body against his. I could feel that he was hard beneath my towel and his sweatpants, and I rubbed against him. He growled into my mouth and flipped us, so I was laid on my back on the bed, and he was on top of me, between my legs. I gasped for breath as his lips left mine and traveled down my neck and body. I shivered as his teeth grazed my marking spot and didn't even stop the moan that escaped my lips.

"Elias," I gasped as his hand found its way under the towel and between my legs. He found my clit and began rubbing slowly in circles. I arched my back and pushed against his hand, and he chuckled.

"Elias, please," I begged. I exposed my neck, and he kissed against my marking spot again. "Please, Elias, I want to." Elias slowed and pulled his hand away. He buried his head in my neck and took a deep breath.

Then he pulled himself away from me and sat up.

"Elias?" I sat up, unsure of what was happening. I moved to the end of the bed until I could see his face. There were tears in his eyes.

"What is it?" I asked, a feeling of dread in my stomach.

"Harper," he said as he turned to me and stroked my cheek. "I love you more than life itself, and I have every intention of making you mine completely."

"But?" I asked, and he smiled sadly and shook his head.

"But I'm not good enough for you."

"What?" I exclaimed.

"Harper, you are part-angel. We don't even know what that means, and me..." he said and lowered his head.

"And you what?" I asked. He looked back up at me, his eyes shining.

"I have a demon living inside me or something." He took my hand. "How could I possibly be good enough for you?" I pulled my hands from his and stood up. I felt like crying but pushed it into the anger that was brewing, too.

"Because I said you are," I shouted. "Elias, I don't care what you are. I love you for who you are. And the goddess saw fit to connect us with the mate bond." He shook his head and held out his hand. I stepped back and shook my head.

"No, I've been rejected and then played with already," I cried. "I won't allow this to happen again."

I looked down at him. "Elias, do you love me?" I asked, and he nodded.

"More than life itself," he said, and I nodded.

"And do you want to do this?"

"Yes, I want to so very much make you mine forever," Elias said.

"Then please, don't reject me," I cried, tears running down my face. "Please don't let me feel that pain again," he put his head down again, and I felt like I couldn't breathe. I shook my head and stepped back again.

"I'll give you some time," I said and headed towards the door. I needed to get out of here. I needed to control my emotions. I opened the door and went to step out when I felt a hand on my arm again. I was pulled back into the room and pushed against the door. I looked up to see the empty black eyes of Elias' demon.

"Elias," I called, and his eyes bled back to the dark inky blue that I loved. He nodded at me and smiled.

"I'm here," he said, and pulled the towel away from my body. "The thought of you leaving me was too much to bear. It took a demon to remind me of that." I searched his eyes and saw only lust.

"I'm probably going to hell for this," he said as he buried his head into my neck. I felt his teeth graze my neck and gasped as he lifted me. I wrapped my legs around his waist as he pushed his sweats down and lined up against my entrance.

"Then we will go together," I said, and he growled against me.

"Dear goddess, Harper Kirby, I love you so much," he moaned against me, and I gasped as I felt his tip push into me.

"I love you too, Elias Owens," I gasped and then screamed as he simultaneously pushed into me and bit down on my marking spot. I gripped him, panting and digging my nails into his back as he stilled there for a moment. Then he pulled back out of me before slamming into me again, and I cried out again. I could feel the pleasure rising already, coming fast as he worked his way in and out of me. He carried me to the bed still inside me, and we landed on the bed. He pushed harder into me, and my breathing quickened. I quickly exploded around him, the pleasure riding through my body. I pulled him towards me, found my way to his marking spot, and bit down. He growled against me, and I felt as he exploded inside me. I gasped as I felt the bond come alive inside me, connecting me to Elias. I felt the difference between Elias' energy and my own. It was like hot and cold and black and white, and all the opposites, but again the perfect balance between us. I felt the rush through me, and everything clicked into place. I let go of Elias, and we both collapsed to the bed, both panting. It was quick, and it was messy, but it was passionate and perfect.

Elias pulled me onto him, and I burrowed into him, and he sighed.

"You're mine now, forever," he growled in my ear. "Whatever the consequences," I smiled against his chest.

"Yep, you are stuck with me now," I said as I yawned. I suddenly felt very tired, the last few days finally catching up with me.

"Baby, go to sleep," Elias chuckled, and I smiled and snuggled into him and let my eyes droop.

"I love you," I murmured against his chest.

"I love you too, forever," Elias said. It was the last thing I heard before I fell asleep.

CHAPTER 83

Harper

The next few days seemed filled with so much activity. Elias and I announced we had completed the mate bond, and for the most part, people seemed happy. But I noticed both Drake and Tommy sharing a look that I tried to question later with Tommy. He continued to be evasive with me the whole time, but insisted that he was happy for us. Elias said that maybe I imagined it, but I was sure there was something that they weren't telling me.

The Council swept into town for debriefing everyone after the battle. Elias was cleared of any suspicion, and we heard the Sovereign had ordered a full sweep of every member of the Council to weed out any more Circle members. In private, Drake confirmed he was, in fact, the Divine Warrior for the Immortal line, and he, Harry, and Aaron spent many hours pouring over texts about the two bloodlines to see similarities. Drake showed us the seal for the Immortal line, which was a cross, like one on a compass, within a circle. Again, it had two smaller points where there would be stones. He said he had never seen a physical representation of the seal, so he wasn't aware of what the stones were, but he knew they represented the balance of dark and light. I felt like I understood this better after Elias' and mine mate bond. I had felt such a balance since we had bonded, and Elias even said he hadn't heard from his demon since either.

Drake informed me that the Council wished for me to continue working with them in hunting down and eliminating the Circle. After talking it over with Elias, we agreed we would accept the offer. We planned to do it anyway, and having the resources of the Council behind us would only help matters. We were given permission to choose our own team members for the missions, and it was an easy choice, really. Elias and Marcus would rejoin the Council, as Marcus made it clear that he would not leave my side, and despite seeing evidence that I could look after myself, he still felt the strong urge to act as my official Gamma guard. I didn't mind so much and loved Marcus and was happy he wanted to come along. I asked Aaron to join us, too; he was one of the best researchers and supernatural historians I knew, and I knew he would be an asset to our group. Plus, a small side of me wasn't quite ready to part ways, even temporarily, with the best friend I had in the last ten years. I wasn't sure if he would agree, as I knew he loved to teach, but he claimed that learning was his main passion and he could always teach when we had won. Katie automatically agreed to come with us, since she was Aaron's mate. She was terrified of leaving the town for the first time in her life, but was excited to be able to finally go on some of the adventures she had dreamed of. Finally, Alex asked if he could tag along. He said he had spent too much time in the pack and wanted to stretch his proverbial legs.

Louise got confirmation that she was, in fact, pregnant and was actually just over three months along. She has confessed that she was scared that the pup was Damien's, but with what Susie had seen, we could only see that as confirmation that Tommy was the father. Tommy and Louise would have to wait until the pup was born before they could break her bond with Damien and complete their own bond. The act and resulting pain of the breaking bond were too great of a risk for the pup, which no one wanted to take. Louise also told us about what Susie and Nathaniel had been talking about, and Drake found the passage they were referring to.

He seemed conflicted about the new information and announced that he would have to follow up with other members of the Order.

I had asked about the Order, and Drake said that it would be a good idea for me to come along to meet the other Divine Warrior, as well as the team of trusted individuals that made up the Order. He confirmed that there was one other Divine Warrior, an Unseelie faerie by the name of Brighid. He said she was a pleasant faerie but quite reserved in her manners and liked to keep to herself. I promised that I would visit the headquarters so I could meet the other people. Tommy had warned me they would probably not be so keen to be around Elias, but I shrugged it off and told Drake that where I went, so did Elias. Elias had tried to reason with me, knowing that I was still figuring out what being a Divine Warrior actually meant and what powers it came with.

Tommy explained that one of his duties as the guardian was to protect the seal from demon interference. This meant that he was tied to the town and could never spend any significant time away. Add in Louise's pregnancy, and the two of them were not going anywhere. So it made sense for Elias to announce Tommy as his successor and the new Alpha of the Midnight Moon pack. He had already given his life to protect them. Now he got the title with it, too.

Plus, Tommy reasoned that with a new Divine Warrior on the way and the confirmation that Susie's eldest son James was also a Guardian, he would have a lot of family training to do. He told me that he felt intimidated; he had never been formally trained himself after his father ran away when he was young, and my dad had turned his back on the Order. But my mum, who had moved into the pack house and taken custody of Susie's kids, said that she would help him figure it all out.

It was the morning of our intended departure from the pack, and the guys were making sure our things were packed into the cars. While they did that, Katie, Louise, and I were finally spending some much-needed quality time together.

"Do you know what's funny?" Katie said as she looked through Louise's closet in her bedroom. I looked up from my place laid on the bed, and Louise was sitting in the window seat staring out the window.

"What?" Louise asked

"We are all Alpha rank," Katie said, and I laughed.

"Yeah," I said. "I didn't realise that. Go figure."

"Not that it really matters anymore to me." Katie walked over to the sofa and dropped down onto it. "I wouldn't care what rank Aaron was. He's perfect the way he is." She smiled that sickly sweet, all-in-love smile, and I fake gagged. Katie threw a cushion at me, and Louise laughed.

"You know we haven't all been together like this since that night," Louise said. And I thought back to that night over ten years ago. I was so excited to meet my mate, unknowing what a chain reaction it would set off.

"Harper?" Louise asked as she moved to the sofa, pulling me from my thoughts. "Can I ask you something?" and I nodded.

"Sure, what's up?" I said. She seemed to hesitate as she looked down at her stomach and took a deep breath.

"How did you manage to control the angel in the end?" she asked. "I only ask because I may need to know for my own little angel." I smiled. I hadn't really talked about my time in the Neverplain to anyone, not even to Elias.

"I didn't," I said, and both girls looked shocked.

"What?" Katie asked, "So how did you, well, not stay dead?" Louise rolled her eyes at Katie's choice of words.

"It's all getting foggy, to be honest, but I remember hiding in the Neverplain screaming at my angel side. I was terrified of her. I mean, I had just died painfully because she had burned up my body. But it took Drake talking to me to explain that it wasn't her that had caused my death, but the fact that I was resisting her, or me," I explained. "Once I realised that she wasn't some outside destructive force trying to cancel me out but was actually a part of me that I was denying, I stopped fighting. That shift in mindset was enough for us to come together as one much stronger whole rather than two opposing weaker sides."

"But if she was always just a part of you, why did you burn up?" Louise asked.

"Imagine two magnets," I said, and was rewarded by two confused faces. "You hold a magnet in each hand. You hold them one way, and they actively push against each other. To get them together, you have to physically push them together. It takes effort to hold them there. That was what my body was going through, trying to push together two seemingly opposing forces.

It was no wonder that my body suffered when it was constantly having to work in such a way."

"Oh!" Louise said. "But flip one of the magnets, and they snap together with ease and hold themselves together." I nodded.

"And in fact, they become like one stronger magnet, their combined force making them that much more," I said. "I think it's the same with the demon bloodlines. Remember the book said that the angel was sent to appease the demon bloodlines, right?" Louise nodded.

"Well, Elias hasn't heard from his demon since we completed our mate bond," I said. "Part of me thinks that is what that sentence meant, that the angel in me and the demon in him actually compliment each other and appease each other."

"Like the yin yang thing," Katie said excitedly, and I nodded.

"And now that he accepted himself or our connection did, he no longer needs to hear that side because he is that side." I frowned. "I dunno. I'm still trying to figure out all this stuff." I shrugged and smiled.

There was a knock at the door at that point, and I looked up to see Alice Chambers and smiled. Tommy had asked the former Luna to stay at the pack house with her two daughters so that she could help Louise with her own Luna duties.

"Ladies, the young men asked me to let you know that they are ready to set off," she said.

"Thank you, Alice," Louise said, and we all got up and began heading down to the entrance of the pack house. We walked in silence the whole way, and it wasn't until we got to the main entrance that Louise grabbed my hand. I looked down to see she had Katie's hand, too.

"Goddess, I am going to miss you both so much," she said, tears falling down her cheeks, "I feel like I have just got you both back, and now I'm losing you all over again," I pulled her into a hug and Katie joined us.

"We will be back," I said. "I promise."

"Yeah, we have a beautiful little pup to celebrate real soon," Katie said, and Louise squeezed us both.

"You better do," she said, and we all just stood there in our group hug for a bit.

"Ladies, could you not squash my mate, please?" I heard Tommy say and pulled away, smiling. I wiped Louise's tears from her face and kissed her cheek.

"See you soon, I promise," I said. I then hugged Tommy while Katie and Louise said goodbye.

"Take care of my best friend. You," I said, and he smiled.

"With my life," he said. "Take care of yourself, kid." I rolled my eyes, causing him to laugh.

I headed outside to see Elias leaning against one of the cars, talking to Marcus.

"You do not need to ride with us. I think we can manage to drive safely," Elias was saying, but Marcus was arguing with him.

"No, it's safer if I stay with you guys," he said.

"It's okay, Elias," I said as I wrapped my arms around him and kissed his cheek, "Marcus can drive, and we can entertain ourselves in the back seat." I winked at Marcus. Marcus looked horrified and then turned away.

"Alex," he called. "I'm riding with you," he said, and I laughed.

"Harper played you, did she?" I heard Alex laugh, and Marcus uttered something under his breath. I laughed again and jumped into the passenger seat of the car. Elias headed around the car and jumped into the driver's seat. He smiled at me and held my hand for a minute before starting the car.

"Ready to take on the world, angel?" he asked as he began driving down the pack house driveway, followed by two cars. I smiled and nodded.

"I'm ready," I said. "And Heaven and Hell, and everything in between."

The Divine Order Series will continue in Book 2 – The Alpha's Tainted Blood

Aisling's Puzzle Pieces
READER COMMUNITY FOR FANS OF AISLING ELIZABETH

Get access to completed books, early access to new projects, free exclusive content and conversations with fellow readers and the author in this exclusive online membership.
Find out more at Aislingelizabeth.com/aislingspuzzlepieces

Or Join the free reader community on Facebook at www.facebook.com/groups/aislingelizabeth

About Aisling Elizabeth

Aisling (pronounced ASH-LING) Elizabeth is a bestselling author on episodic and serialised release apps, specialising in Paranormal Romance with a spicy twist. Her books have made it into Best Selling, Top Romance, Readers' Choice and many other categories in some of the top serialised platforms on the market. And all in her first year of publishing her work. In addition to this, Aisling also gained international number 1 bestseller status in a book collaboration and helped to raise money for much needed charity causes. Aisling released her first full length novel in April 2022.

When Aisling is not working on her latest books, she is a mum to two amazing children and two noisy superhero cats called Thor and Loki, and lives in Yorkshire, UK. She is a bit of a geek at heart and loves music, so she likes to visit fan conventions and music gigs.

Aisling can be found on most social media platforms as well at her website. Sign up to her email Newsletter on her website to be kept up to date, as well as get exclusive free content.

Website - www.aislingelizabeth.com

Facebook Reader Group – www.aislingelizabeth.com/puzzlepieces

Also by Aisling Elizabeth

The Divine Order Series
Beyond Beta's Rejection
The Alpha's Tainted Blood
The Gamma's Shattered Soul *(coming soon)*

The Dark Essence World
Alpha Hybrid Queen

Alpha Hybrid King
The Alpha's Human Seer
The Luna's Hidden Oracle *(coming soon)*

Printed in Great Britain
by Amazon